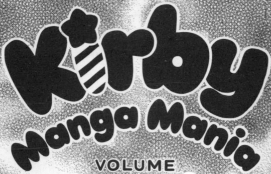

Kirby Manga Mania

VOLUME 1

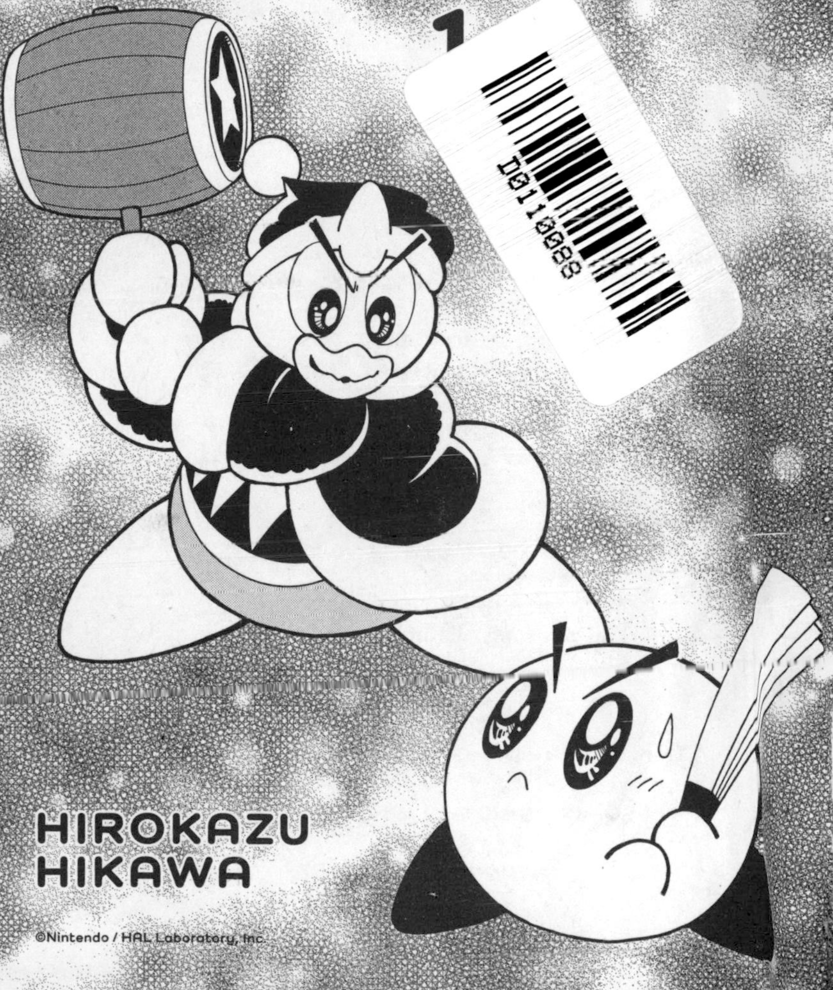

HIROKAZU HIKAWA

CONTENTS

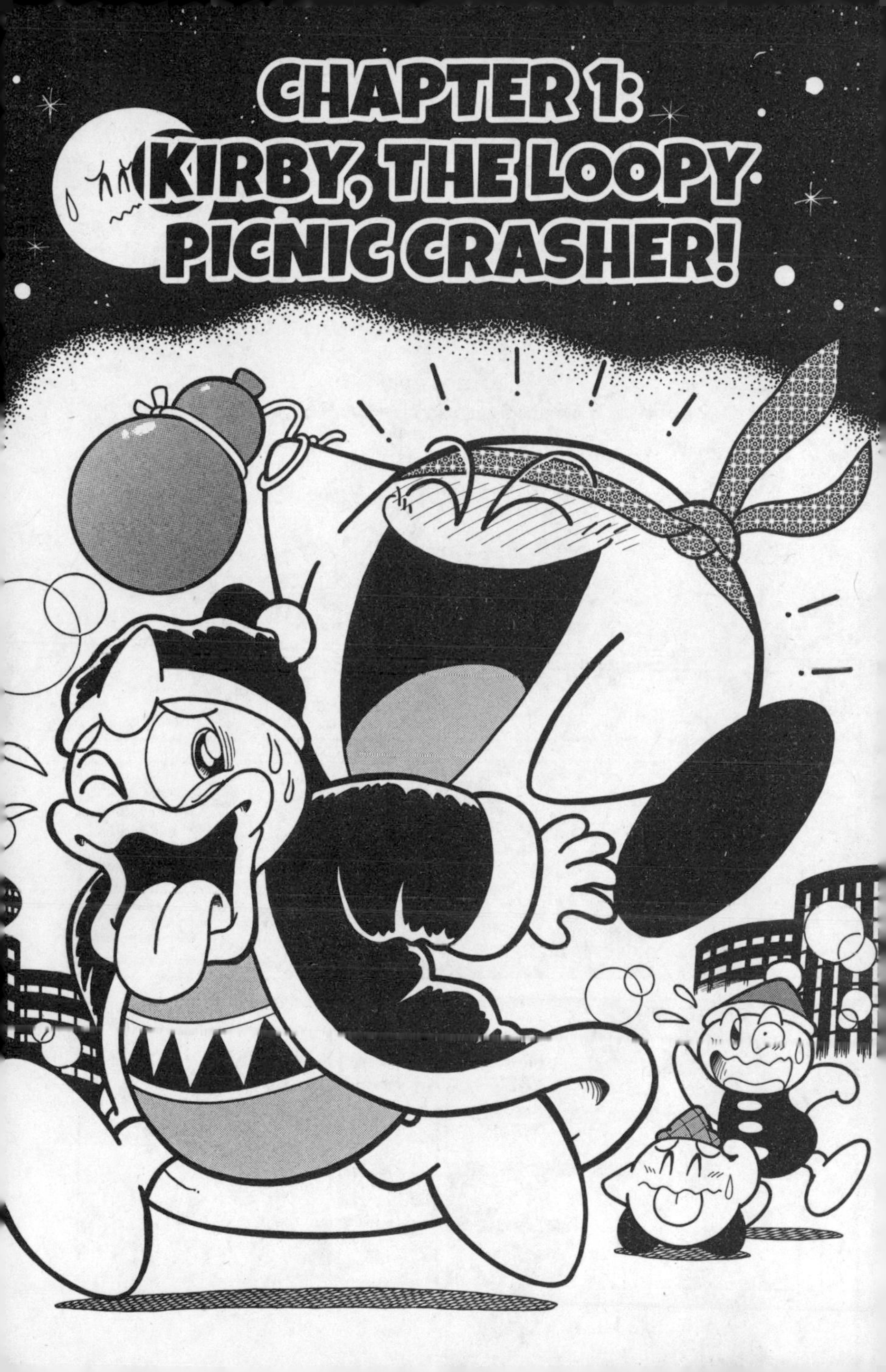
CHAPTER 1:
KIRBY, THE LOOPY PICNIC CRASHER!

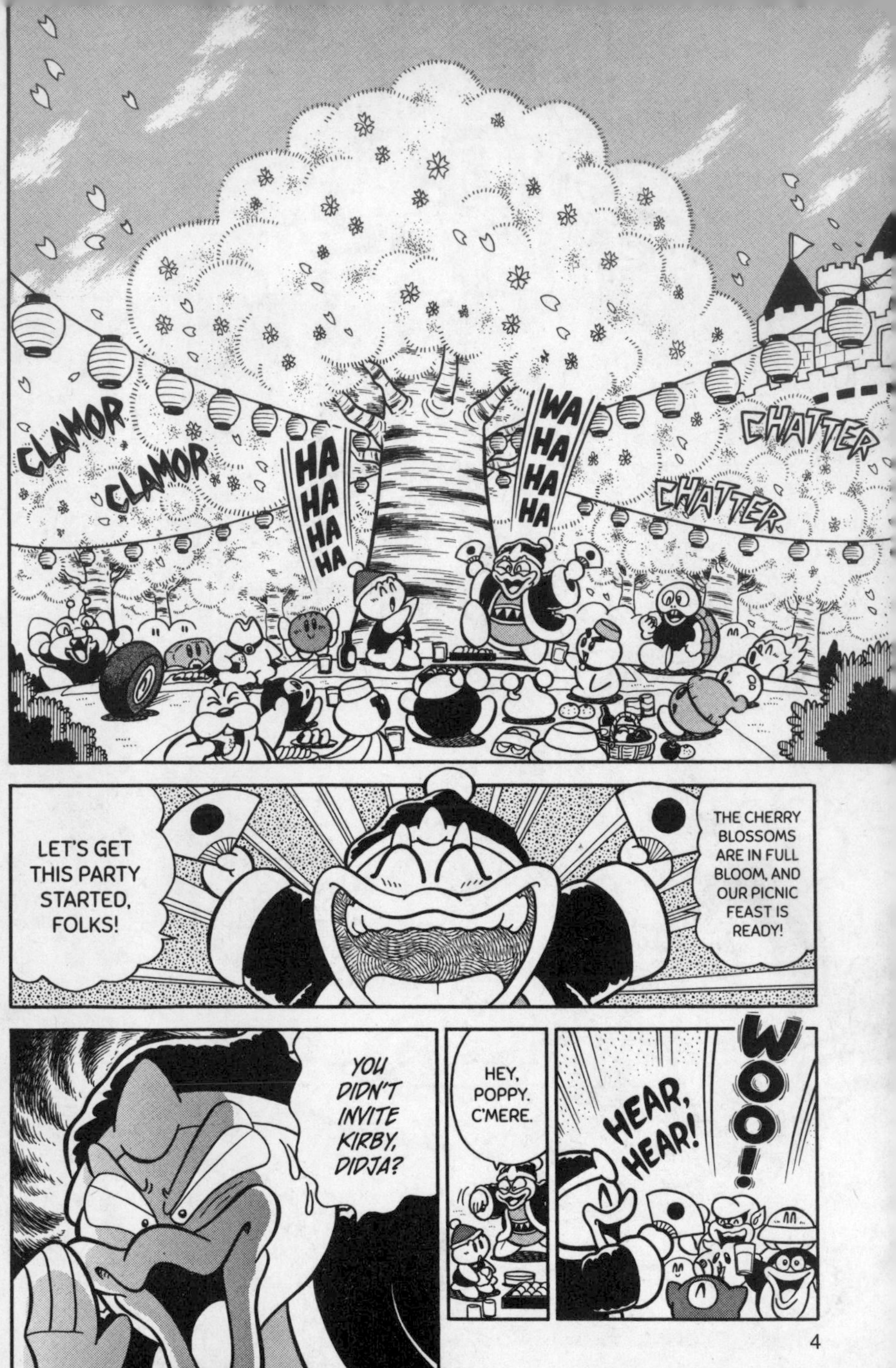
CHATTER
CHATTER
WAHAHAHAHA
HAHAHAHAHA
CLAMOR
CLAMOR
THE CHERRY BLOSSOMS ARE IN FULL BLOOM, AND OUR PICNIC FEAST IS READY!
LET'S GET THIS PARTY STARTED, FOLKS!
WOOO!
HEAR, HEAR!
HEY, POPPY. C'MERE.
YOU DIDN'T INVITE KIRBY, DIDJA?

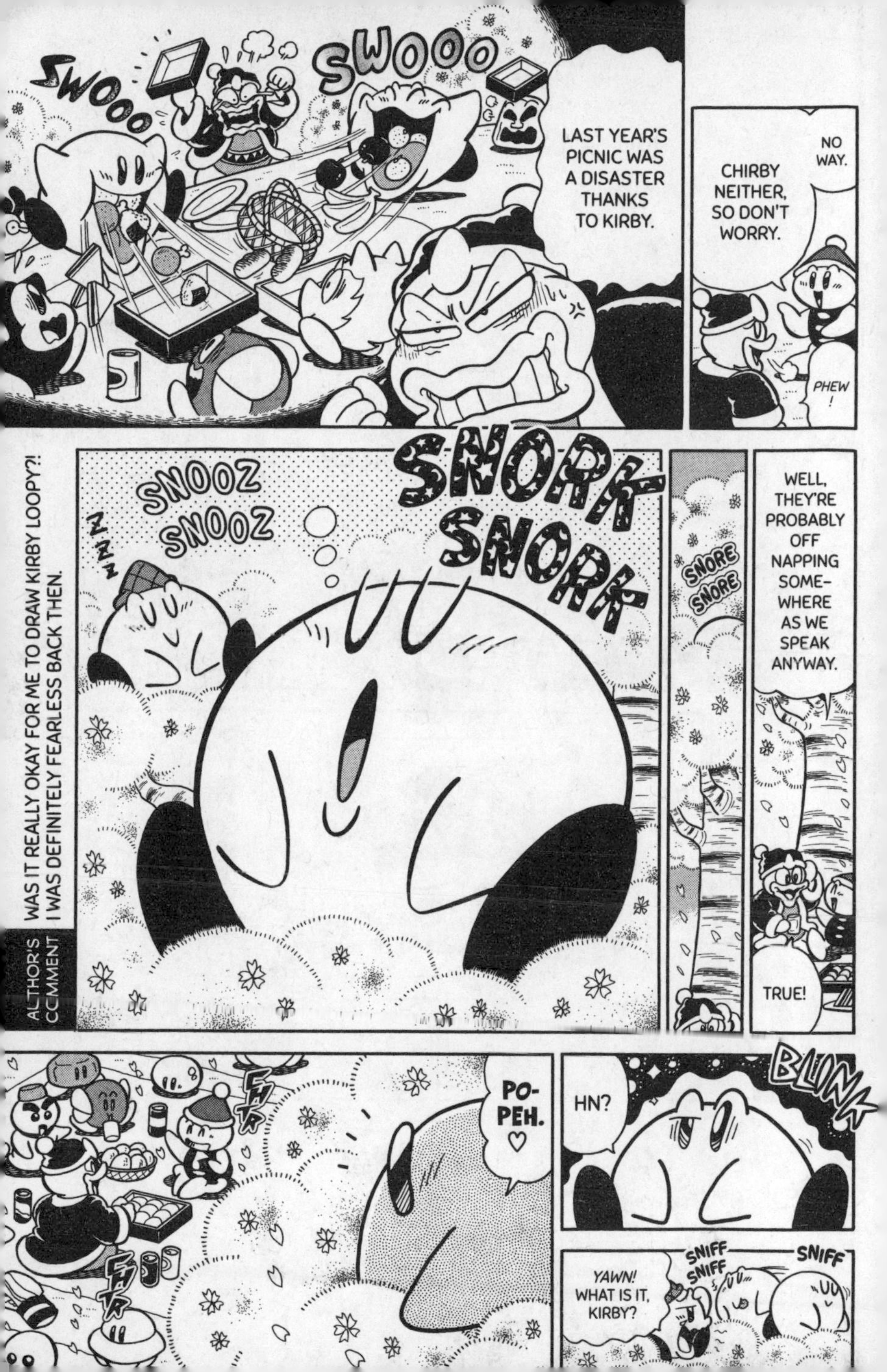
NO WAY.
CHIRBY NEITHER, SO DON'T WORRY.
PHEW!
LAST YEAR'S PICNIC WAS A DISASTER THANKS TO KIRBY.
SWOOO
SWOOO
WELL, THEY'RE PROBABLY OFF NAPPING SOME-WHERE AS WE SPEAK ANYWAY.
TRUE!
SNORE SNORE
SNORK SNORK
SNOOZ SNOOZ
Z Z Z
BLINK
HN?
SNIFF
SNIFF SNIFF
YAWN! WHAT IS IT, KIRBY?
PO-PEH. ♡
FHR
FHR

AUTHOR'S COMMENT
WAS IT REALLY OKAY FOR ME TO DRAW KIRBY LOOPY?! I WAS DEFINITELY FEARLESS BACK THEN.

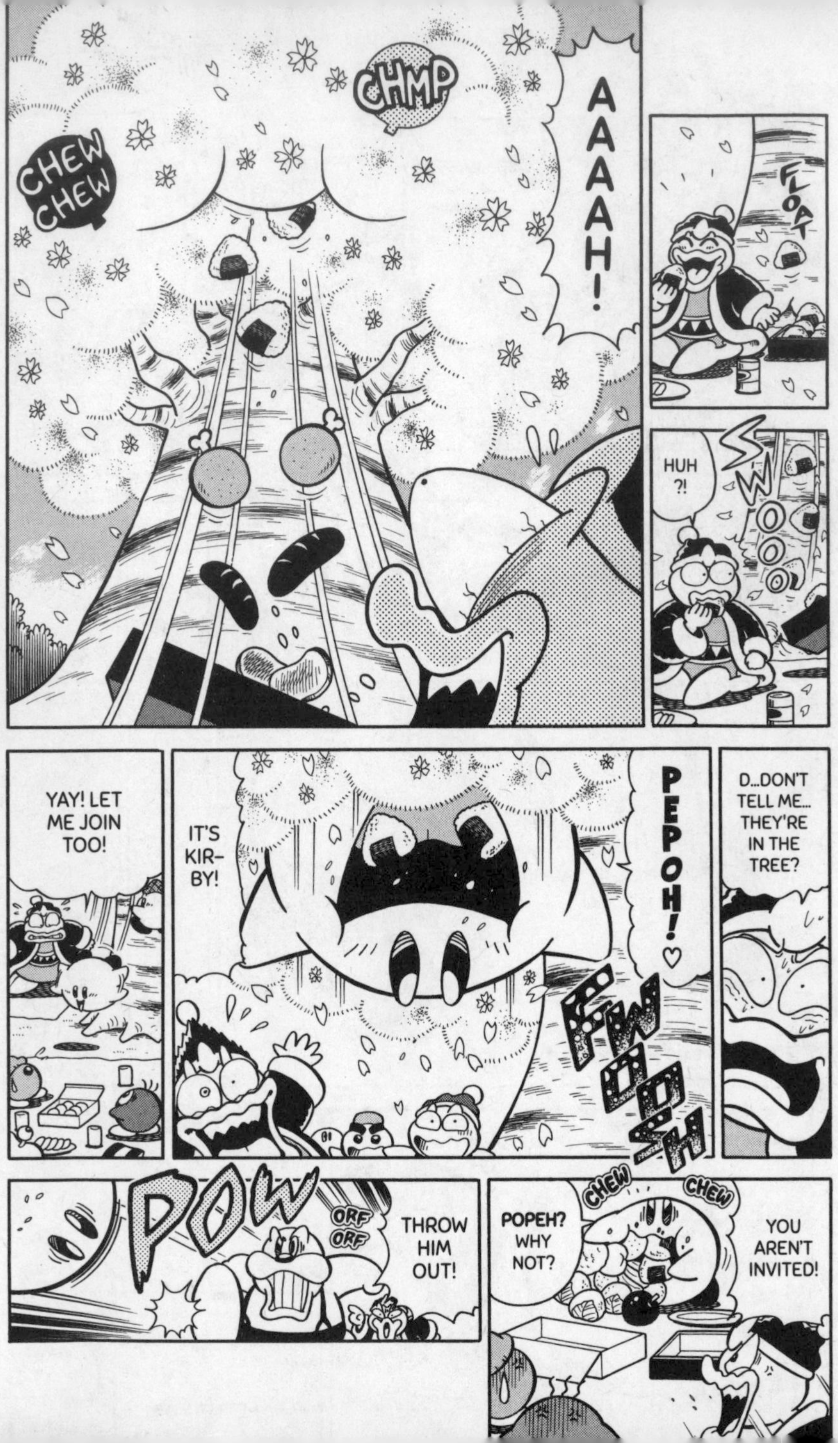

FLOAT
HUH ?!
SWOOOO
AAAAAH!
CHMP
CHEW CHEW
D...DON'T TELL ME... THEY'RE IN THE TREE?
PEPOH!♡
FWOOSH
IT'S KIR-BY!
YAY! LET ME JOIN TOO!
YOU AREN'T INVITED!
CHEW
CHEW
POPEH? WHY NOT?
THROW HIM OUT!
ORF ORF
POW

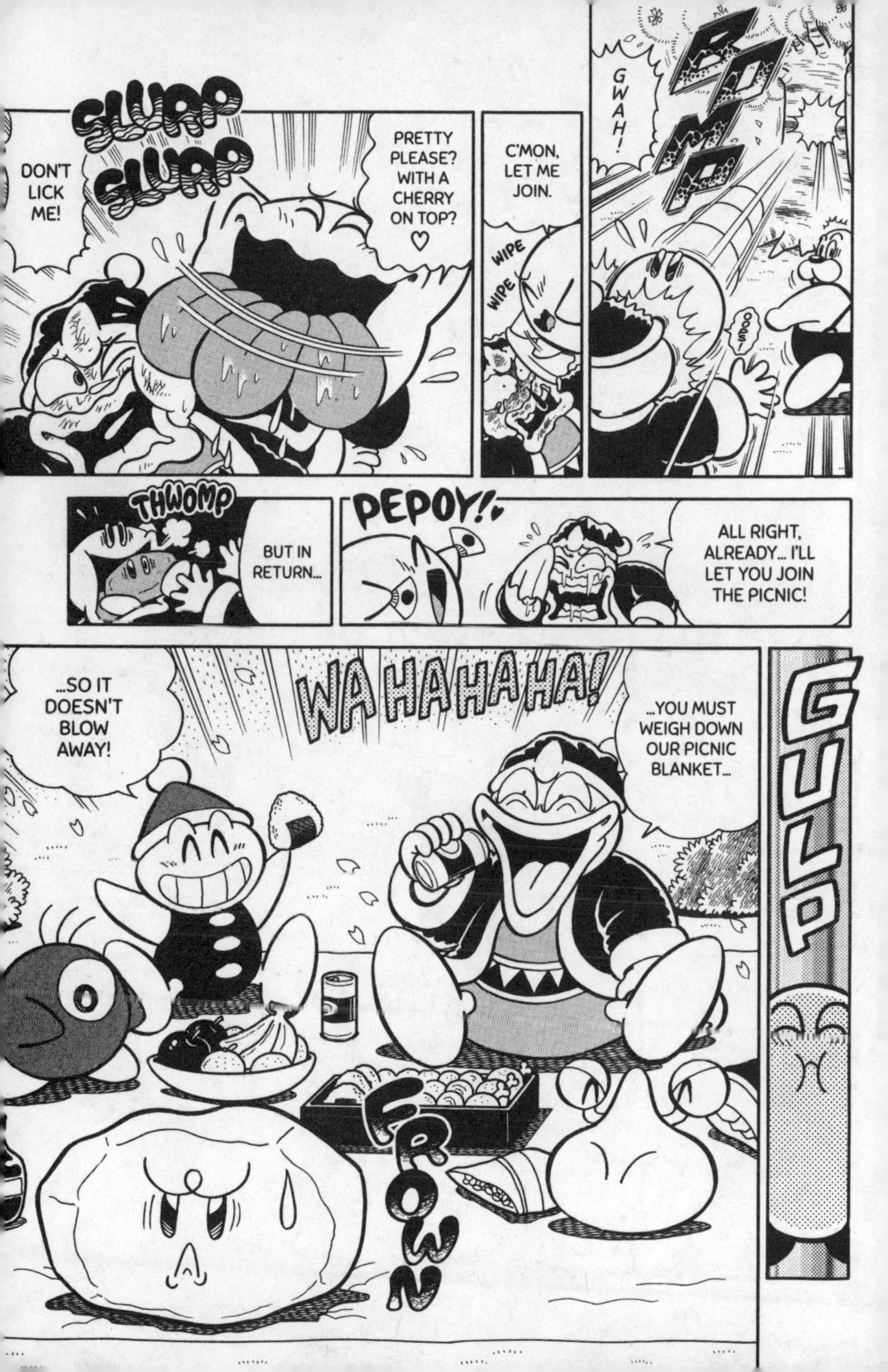
BOMP
GWAH!
OOPS!
C'MON, LET ME JOIN.
WIPE
WIPE
PRETTY PLEASE? WITH A CHERRY ON TOP? ♡
SLURP
SLURP
DON'T LICK ME!
ALL RIGHT, ALREADY... I'LL LET YOU JOIN THE PICNIC!
PEPOY!
BUT IN RETURN...
THWOMP
GULP
...YOU MUST WEIGH DOWN OUR PICNIC BLANKET...
WA HAHAHAHA!
...SO IT DOESN'T BLOW AWAY!
FROWN

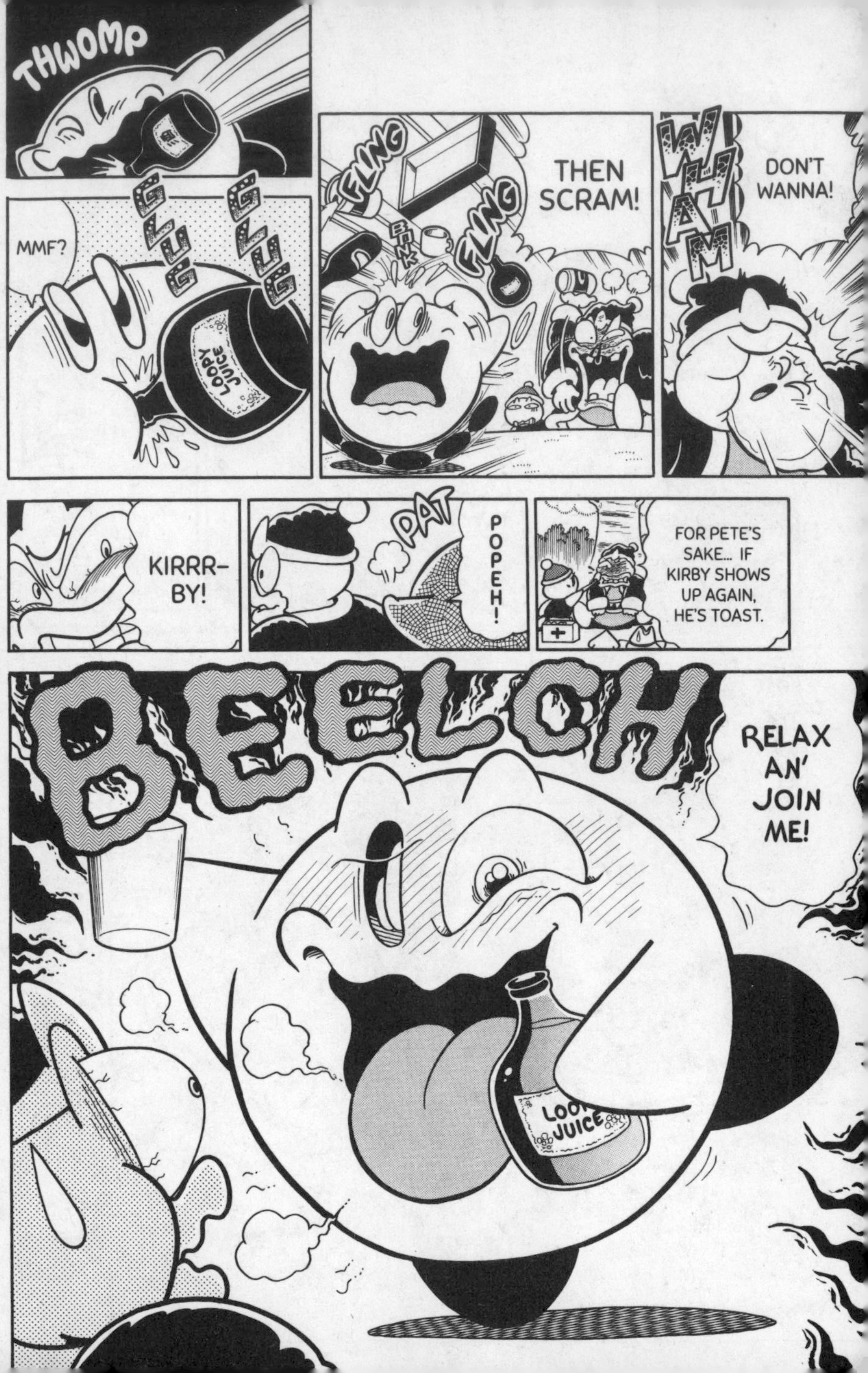
WHAM
DON'T WANNA!
FLING
FLING
BONK
THEN SCRAM!
THWOMP
GLUG GLUG
MMF?
LOOPY JUICE
FOR PETE'S SAKE... IF KIRBY SHOWS UP AGAIN, HE'S TOAST.
PAT
POPEH!
KIRRR-BY!
BELCH
RELAX AN' JOIN ME!
LOOPY JUICE

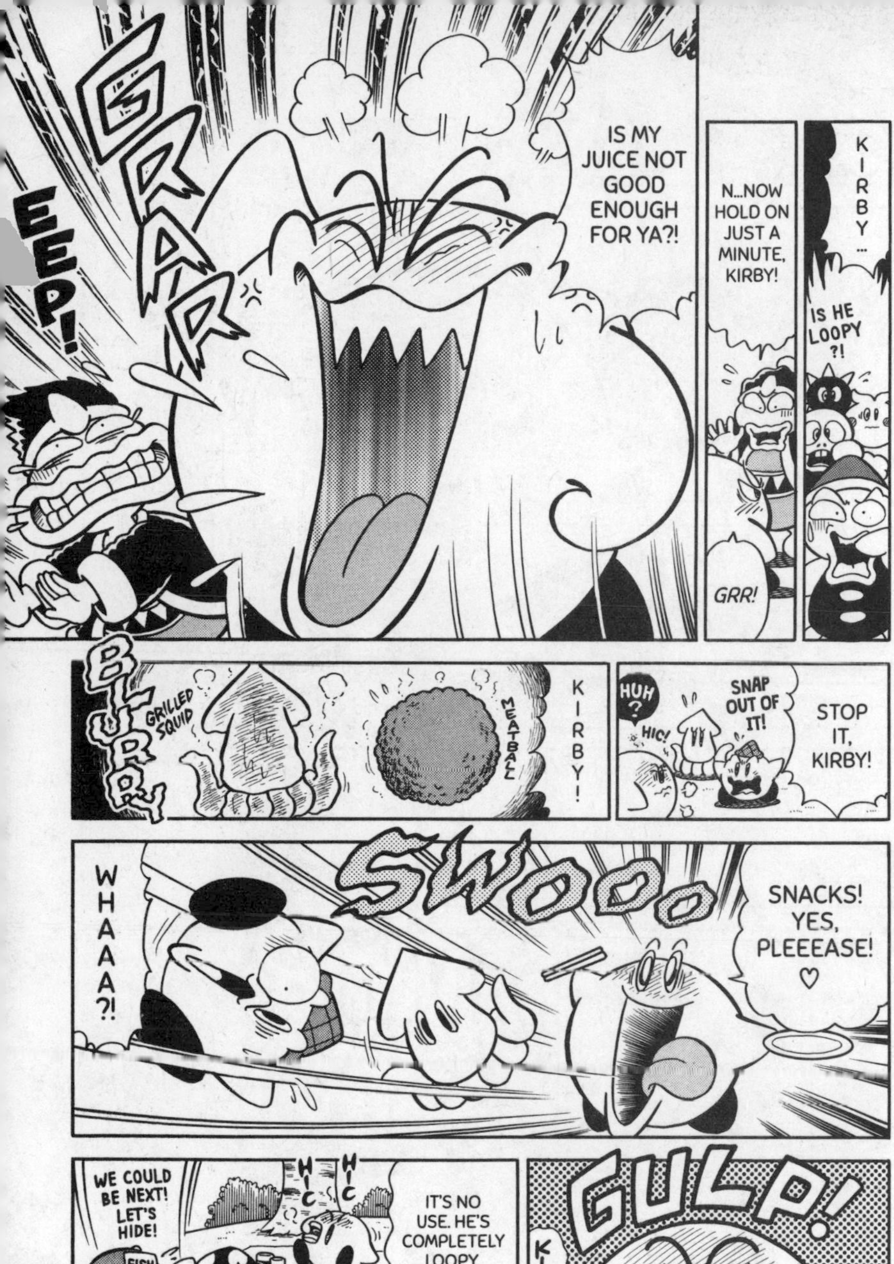
KIRBY...
IS HE LOOPY?!
N...NOW HOLD ON JUST A MINUTE, KIRBY!
GRR!
IS MY JUICE NOT GOOD ENOUGH FOR YA?!
GRAR
EEEP!
STOP IT, KIRBY!
SNAP OUT OF IT!
HUH?
HIC!
KIRBY!
MEATBALL
GRILLED SQUID
BLURRY
SNACKS! YES, PLEEEASE! ♡
SWOOO
WHAAAA?!
GULP!
KIRBYYY...
IT'S NO USE. HE'S COMPLETELY LOOPY.
HIC
HIC
WE COULD BE NEXT! LET'S HIDE!
FISH
MUSHROOM

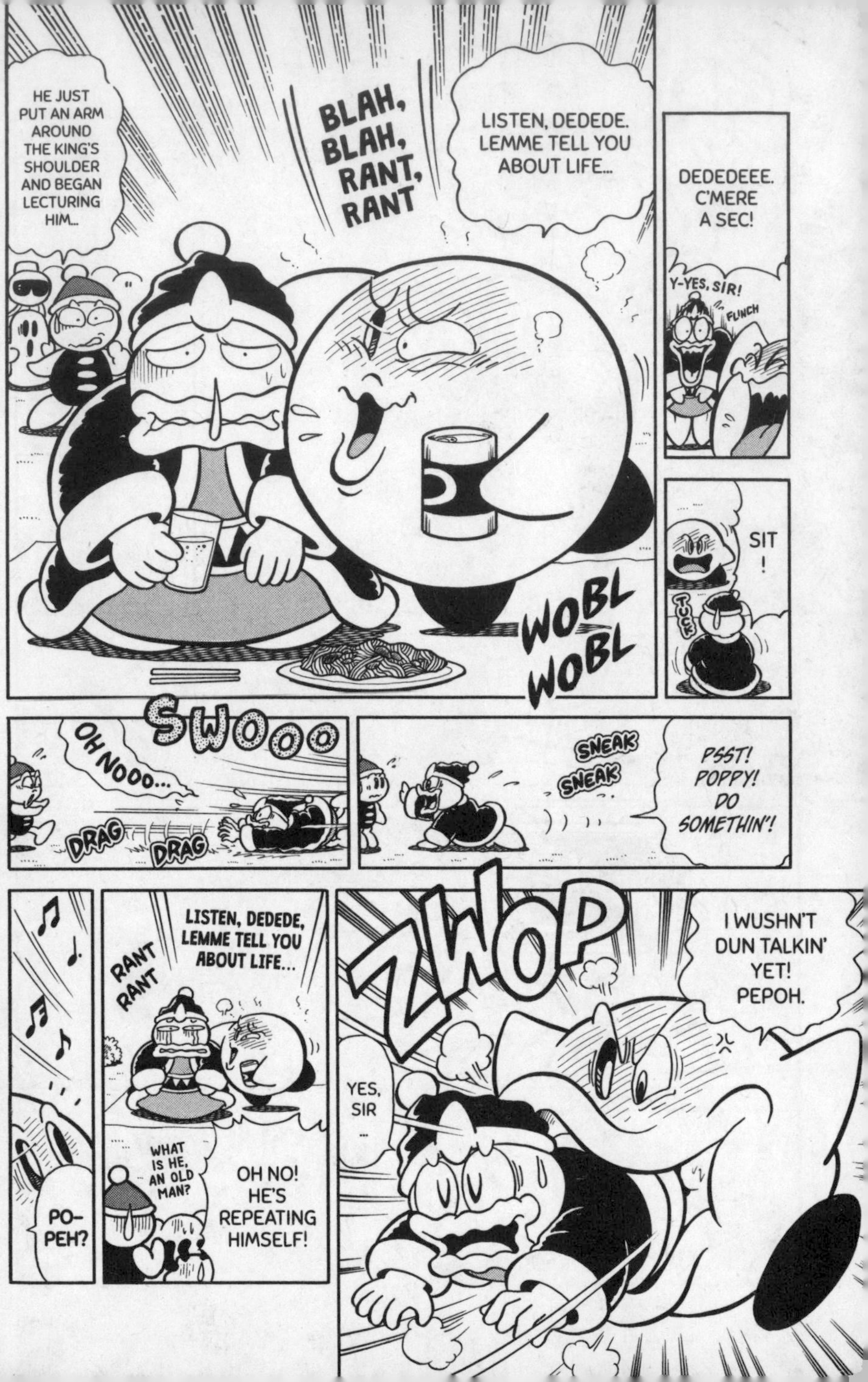
DEDEDEEE. C'MERE A SEC!
Y-YES, SIR!
FLINCH
SIT!
TUCK
LISTEN, DEDEDE. LEMME TELL YOU ABOUT LIFE...
BLAH, BLAH, RANT, RANT
HE JUST PUT AN ARM AROUND THE KING'S SHOULDER AND BEGAN LECTURING HIM...
WOBL WOBL
PSST! POPPY! DO SOMETHIN'!
SNEAK SNEAK
SWOOO
OH NOOO...
DRAG DRAG
ZWOP
I WUSHN'T DUN TALKIN' YET! PEPOH.
YES, SIR...
LISTEN, DEDEDE, LEMME TELL YOU ABOUT LIFE...
RANT RANT
OH NO! HE'S REPEATING HIMSELF!
WHAT IS HE, AN OLD MAN?
PO-PEH?

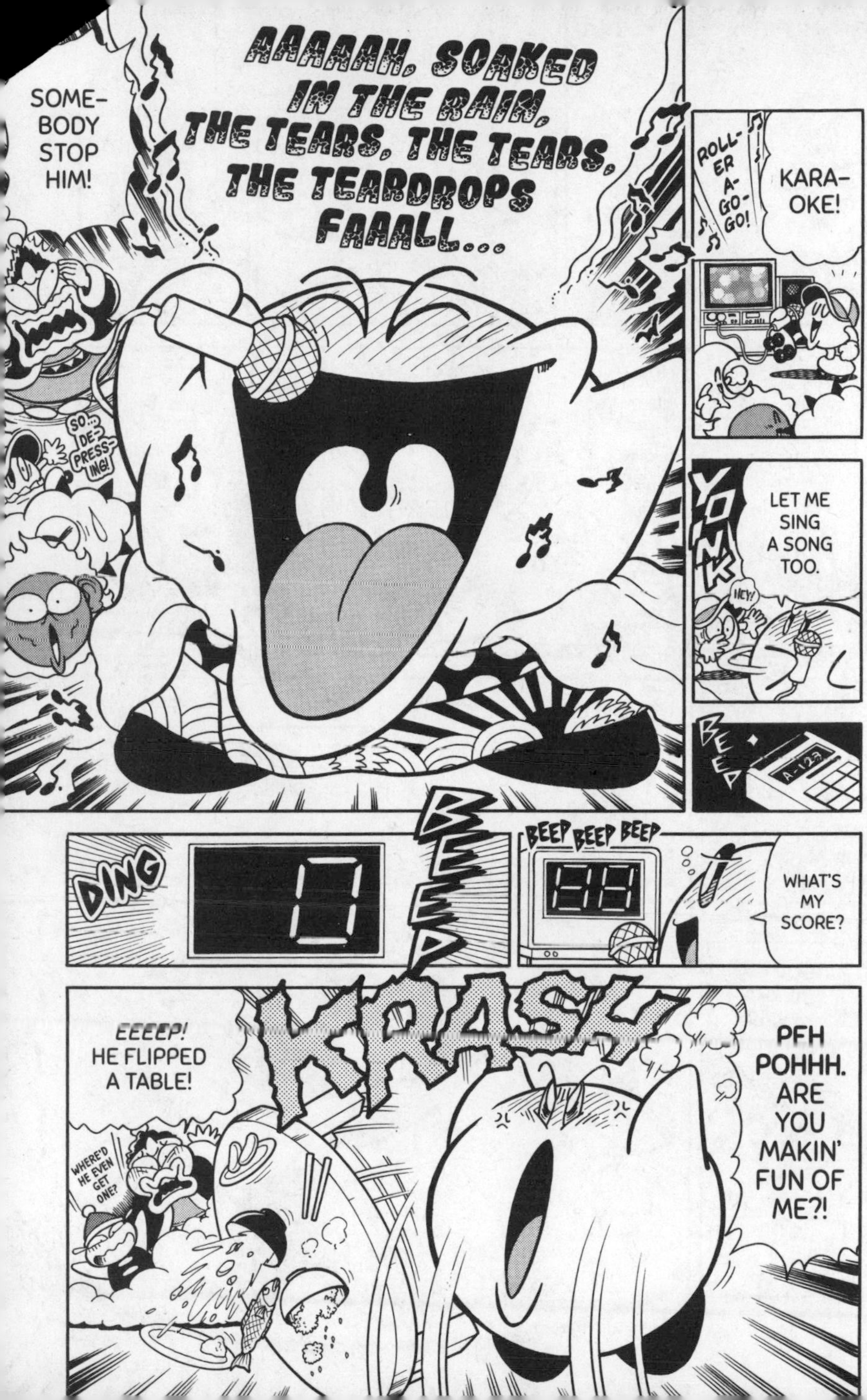
KARA-OKE!
ROLL-ER A-GO-GO!
YONK
LET ME SING A SONG TOO.
HCY!
BEEP
A-123
AAAAAH, SOAKED IN THE RAIN, THE TEARS, THE TEARS, THE TEARDROPS FAAALL...
SOME-BODY STOP HIM!
SO... DE-PRESS-ING!
BEEP
BEEP BEEP BEEP
WHAT'S MY SCORE?
DING
1
KRASH
PFH POHHH. ARE YOU MAKIN' FUN OF ME?!
EEEEP! HE FLIPPED A TABLE!
WHERE'D HE EVEN GET ONE?

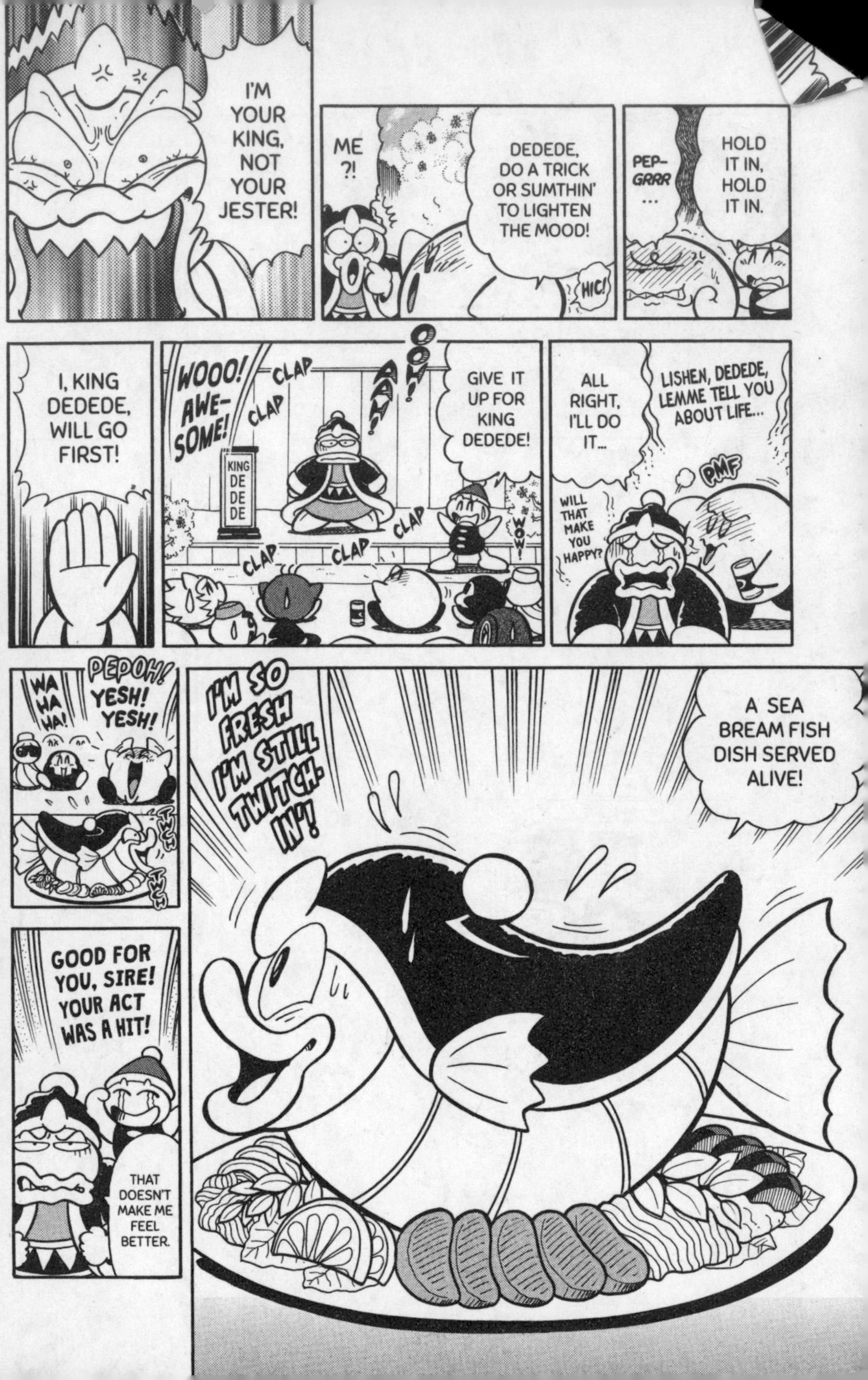
HOLD IT IN, HOLD IT IN.
PEP-GRRR...
DEDEDE, DO A TRICK OR SUMTHIN' TO LIGHTEN THE MOOD!
HIC!
ME ?!
I'M YOUR KING, NOT YOUR JESTER!
LISHEN, DEDEDE, LEMME TELL YOU ABOUT LIFE...
PMF
ALL RIGHT, I'LL DO IT...
WILL THAT MAKE YOU HAPPY?
GIVE IT UP FOR KING DEDEDE!
OOH!
AAH!
WOW!
CLAP
CLAP
KING DE DE DE
CLAP
CLAP
WOOO! AWE-SOME!
CLAP
CLAP
I, KING DEDEDE, WILL GO FIRST!
A SEA BREAM FISH DISH SERVED ALIVE!
I'M SO FRESH I'M STILL TWITCHIN'!
PEPOH! YESH! YESH!
WA HA HA!
TWCH
TWCH
GOOD FOR YOU, SIRE! YOUR ACT WAS A HIT!
THAT DOESN'T MAKE ME FEEL BETTER.

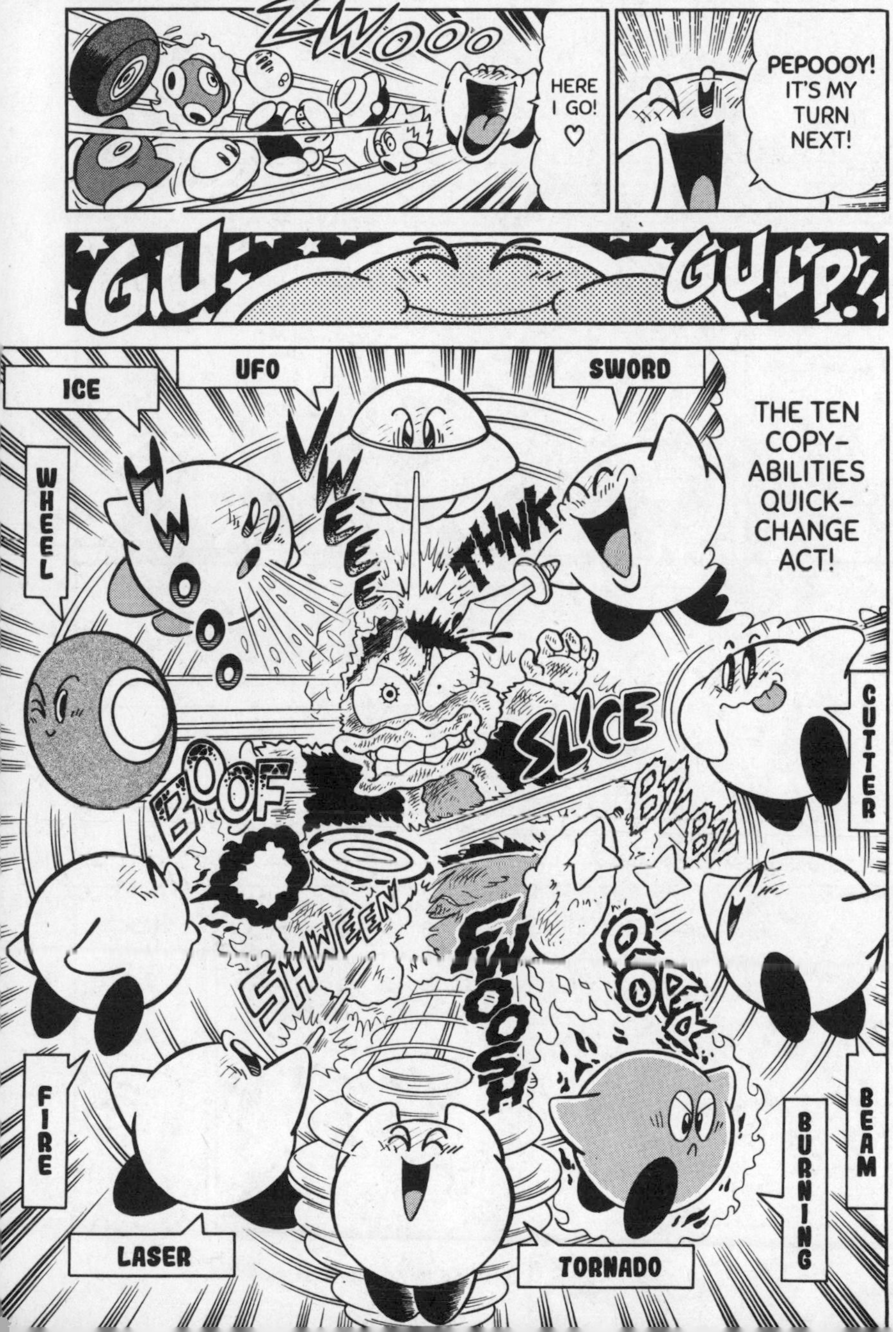
PEPOOOY! IT'S MY TURN NEXT!
HERE I GO! ♡
ZWOOOO
GU-
GULP!
THE TEN COPY-ABILITIES QUICK-CHANGE ACT!
SWORD
THNK
UFO
VWEEEE
ICE
WHEEL
CUTTER
SLICE
BZZ BZZ
BOOF
BEAM
BURNING
ROAR
FWOOSH
SHWEEN
TORNADO
FIRE
LASER

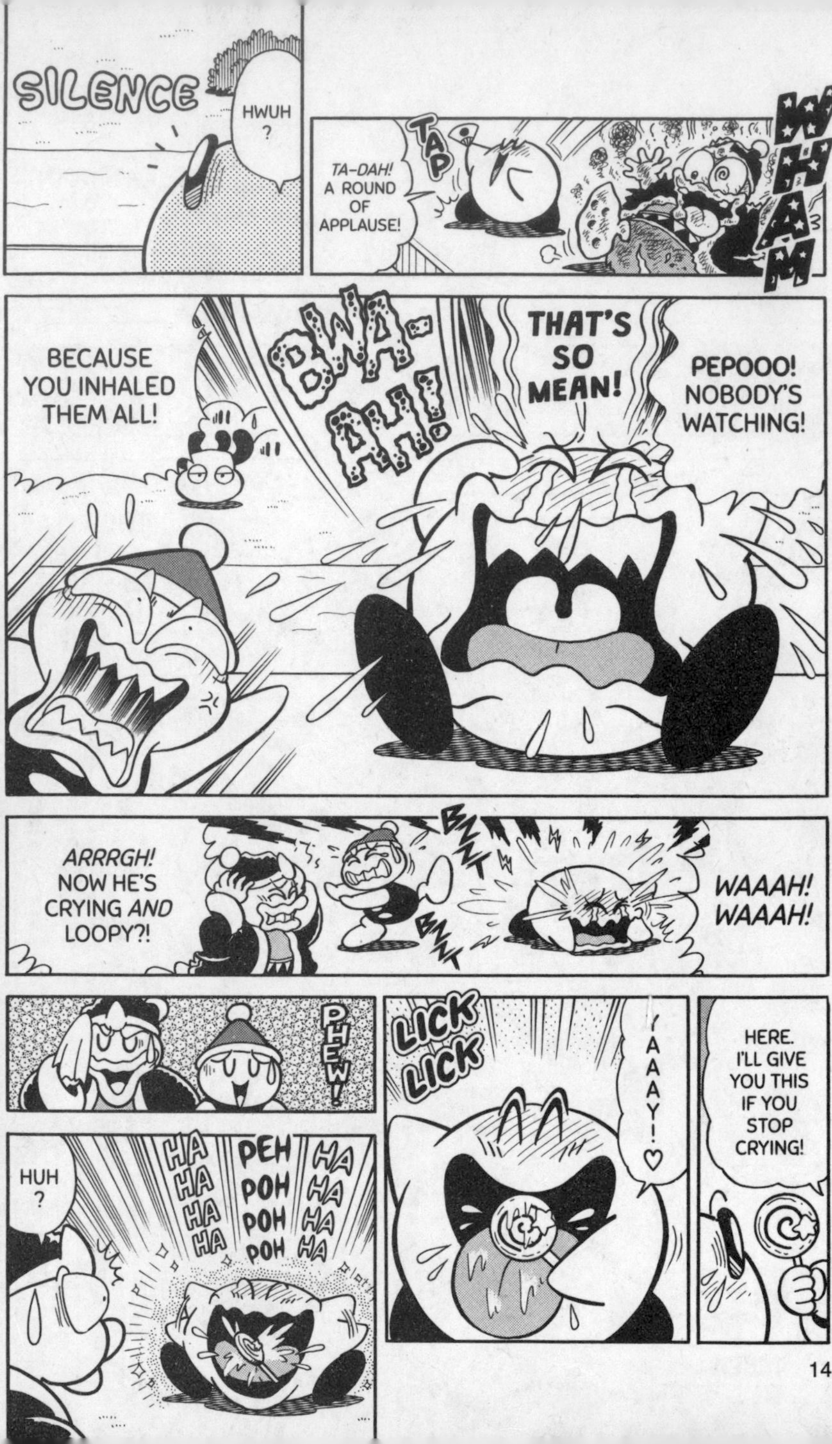
TA-DAH! A ROUND OF APPLAUSE!
TAP
WHAM
SILENCE
HWUH?
PEPOOO! NOBODY'S WATCHING!
THAT'S SO MEAN!
BWA-AH!
BECAUSE YOU INHALED THEM ALL!
WAAAH! WAAAH!
BZZT
BZZT
ARRRGH! NOW HE'S CRYING AND LOOPY?!
HERE. I'LL GIVE YOU THIS IF YOU STOP CRYING!
YAAAY!♡
LICK LICK
PHEW!
HA HA HA HA HA
PEH POH POH POH
HA HA HA HA HA
HUH?

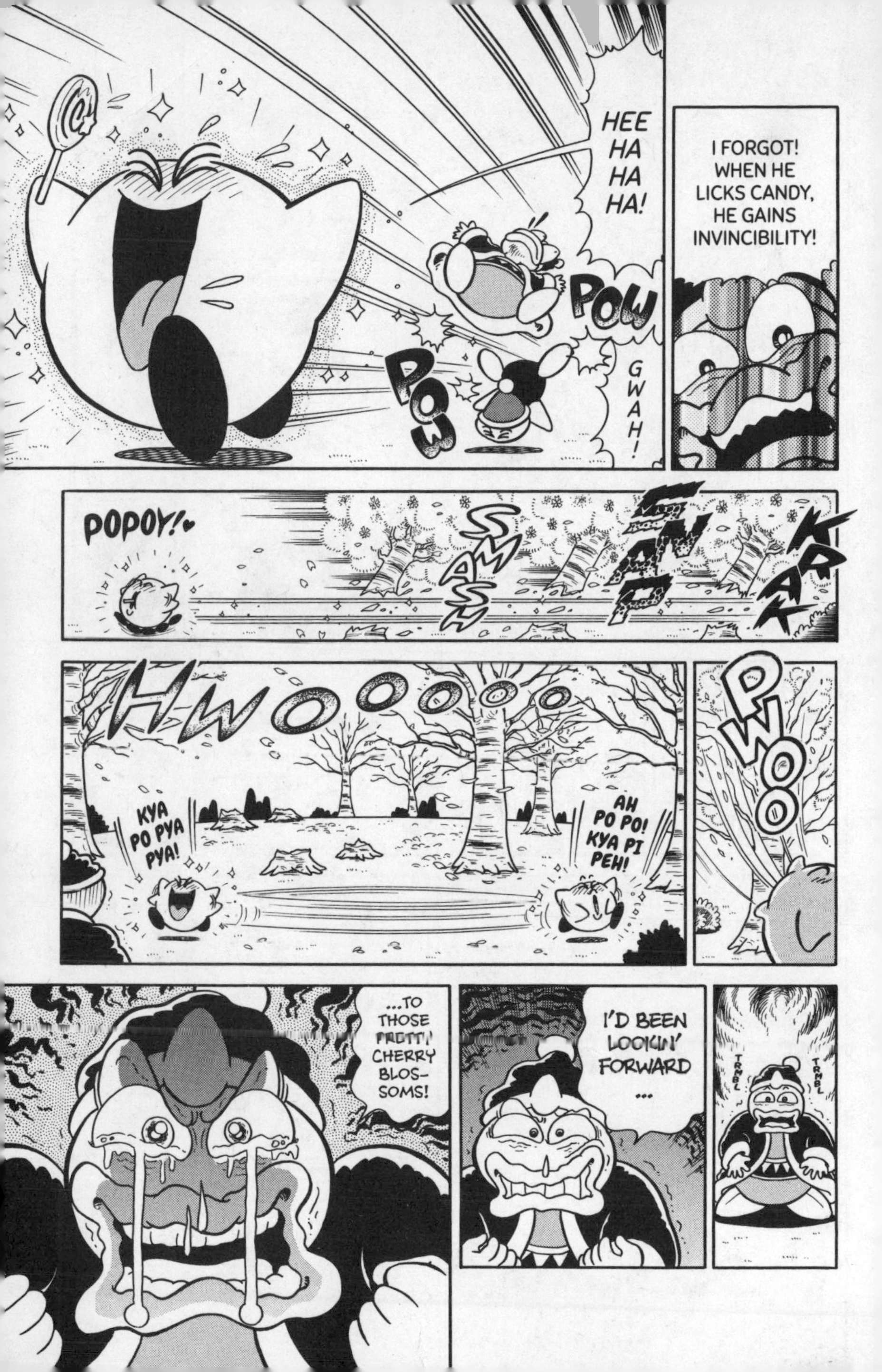
I FORGOT! WHEN HE LICKS CANDY, HE GAINS INVINCIBILITY!
HEE HA HA HA!
POW
GWAH!
POW
KRAK
SNAP
SMASH
POPOY!♥
PWOO
HWOOOOOO
AH PO PO! KYA PI PEH!
KYA PO PYA PYA!
TRMBL
TRMBL
I'D BEEN LOOKIN' FORWARD ...
...TO THOSE PRETTY CHERRY BLOSSOMS!

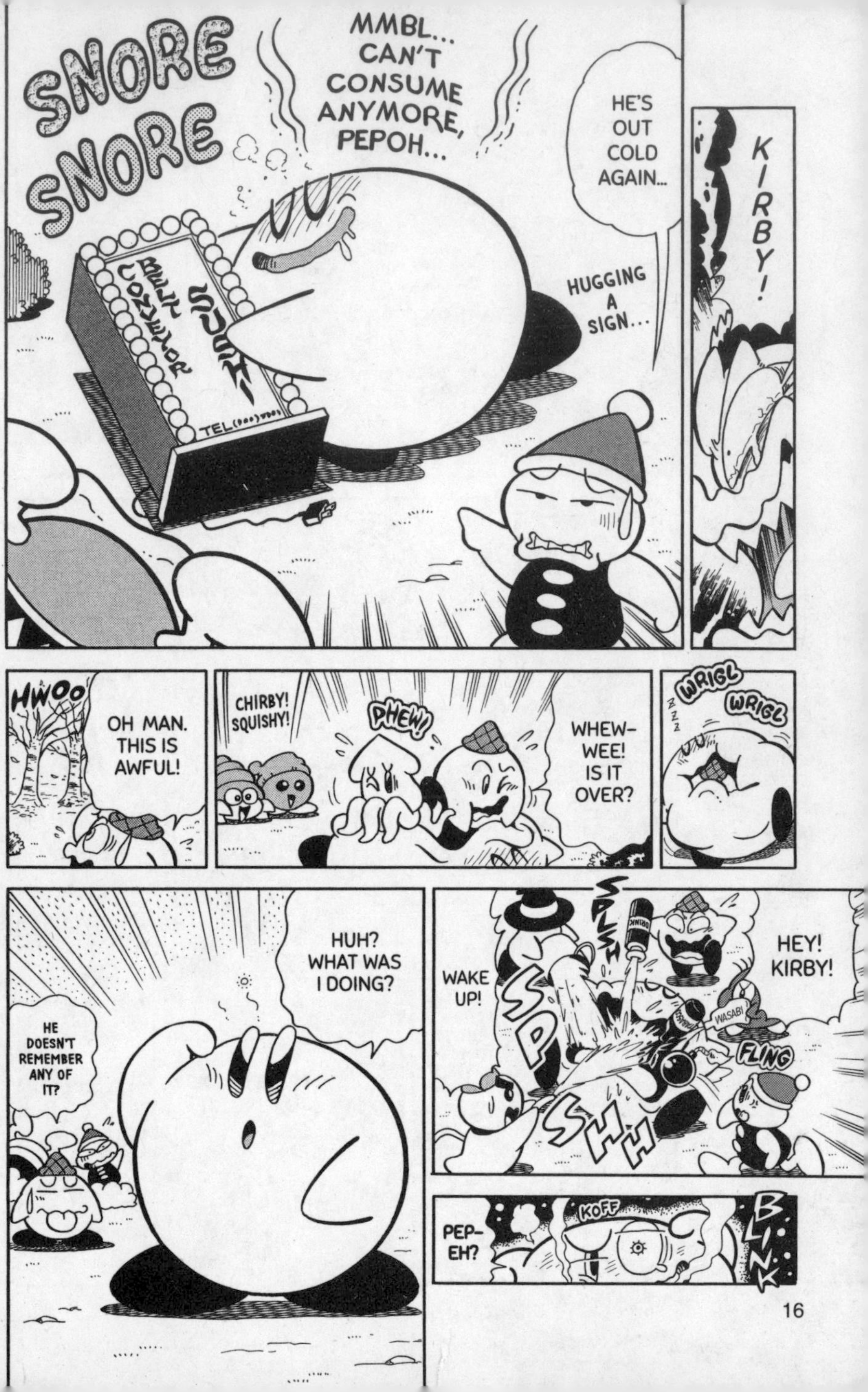
KIRBY!
HE'S OUT COLD AGAIN...
HUGGING A SIGN...
MMBL... CAN'T CONSUME ANYMORE, PEPOH...
SNORE SNORE
SUSHI
BELT CONVEYOR
WRIGL WRIGL
WHEW-WEE! IS IT OVER?
PHEW!
CHIRBY! SQUISHY!
OH MAN. THIS IS AWFUL!
HWOO
HEY! KIRBY!
SPLSH
DRINK
WAKE UP!
WASABI
FLING
SPSHH
BLINK
KOFF
PEP-EH?
HUH? WHAT WAS I DOING?
HE DOESN'T REMEMBER ANY OF IT?

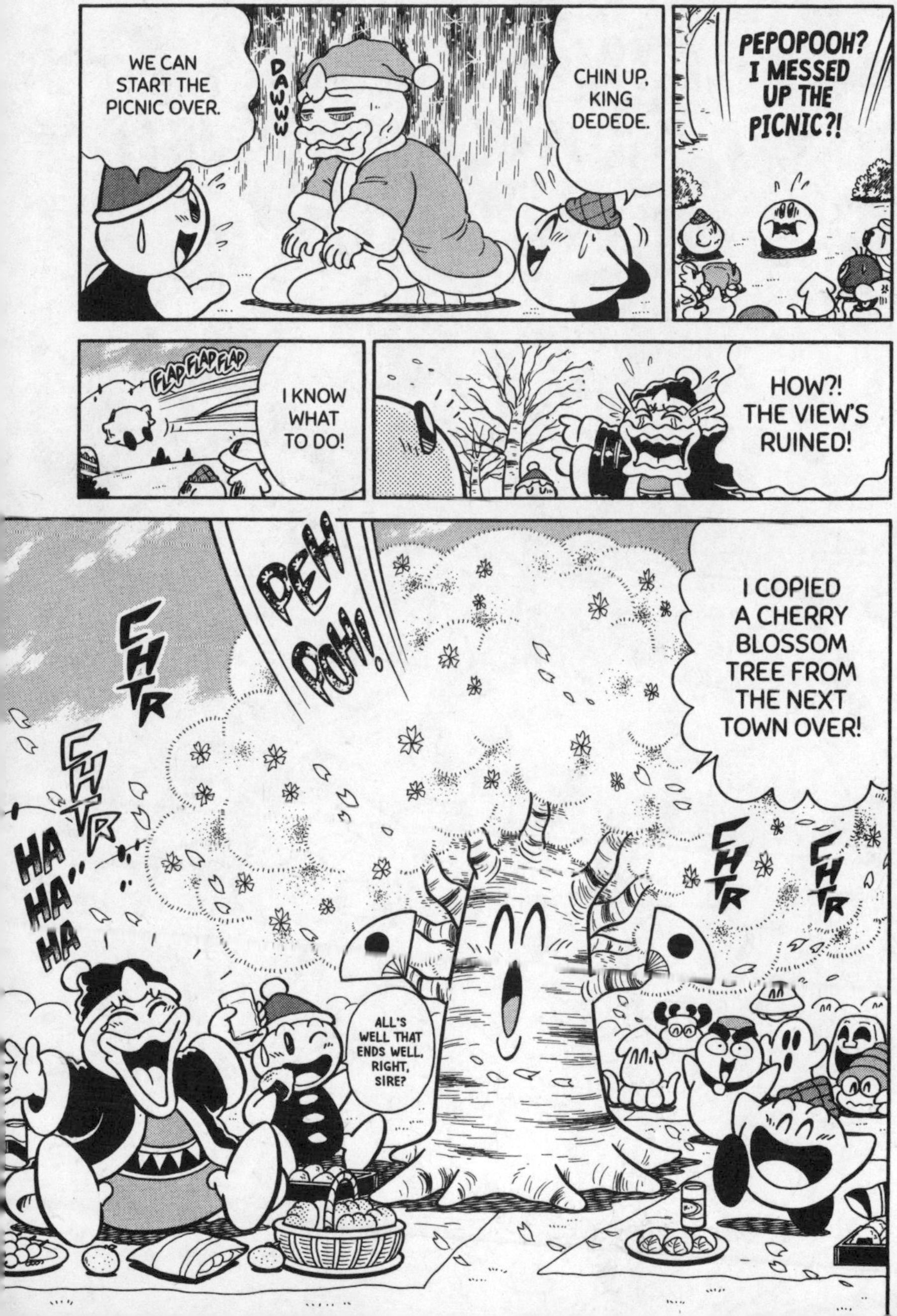
PEPOPOOH? I MESSED UP THE PICNIC?!
CHIN UP, KING DEDEDE.
DAWWW
WE CAN START THE PICNIC OVER.
HOW?! THE VIEW'S RUINED!
I KNOW WHAT TO DO!
FLAP FLAP FLAP
I COPIED A CHERRY BLOSSOM TREE FROM THE NEXT TOWN OVER!
CHTR
CHTR
DEH POH!
CHTR
CHTR
CHTR
HA HA HA...
ALL'S WELL THAT ENDS WELL, RIGHT, SIRE?

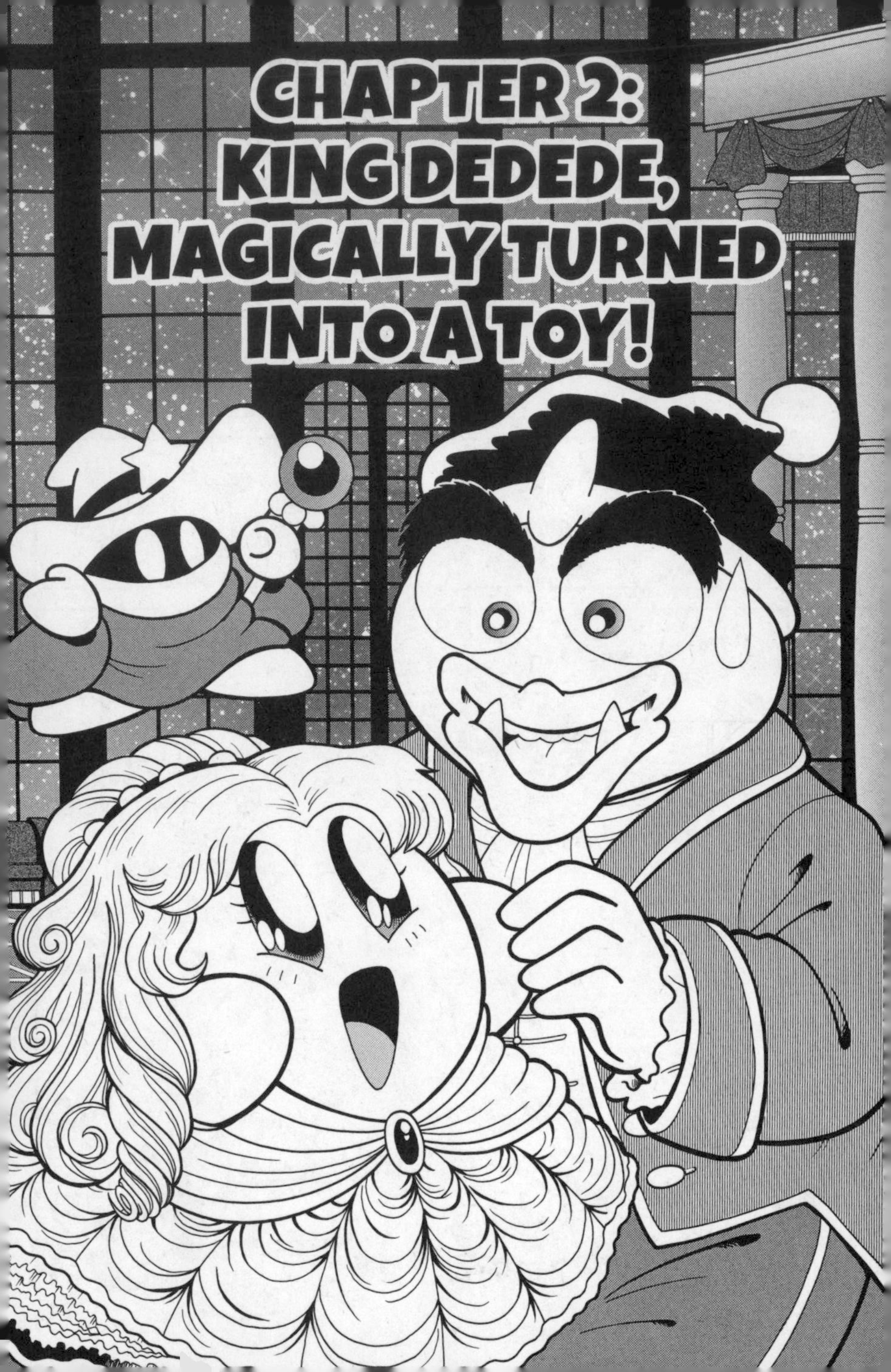
CHAPTER 2:
KING DEDEDE, MAGICALLY TURNED INTO A TOY!

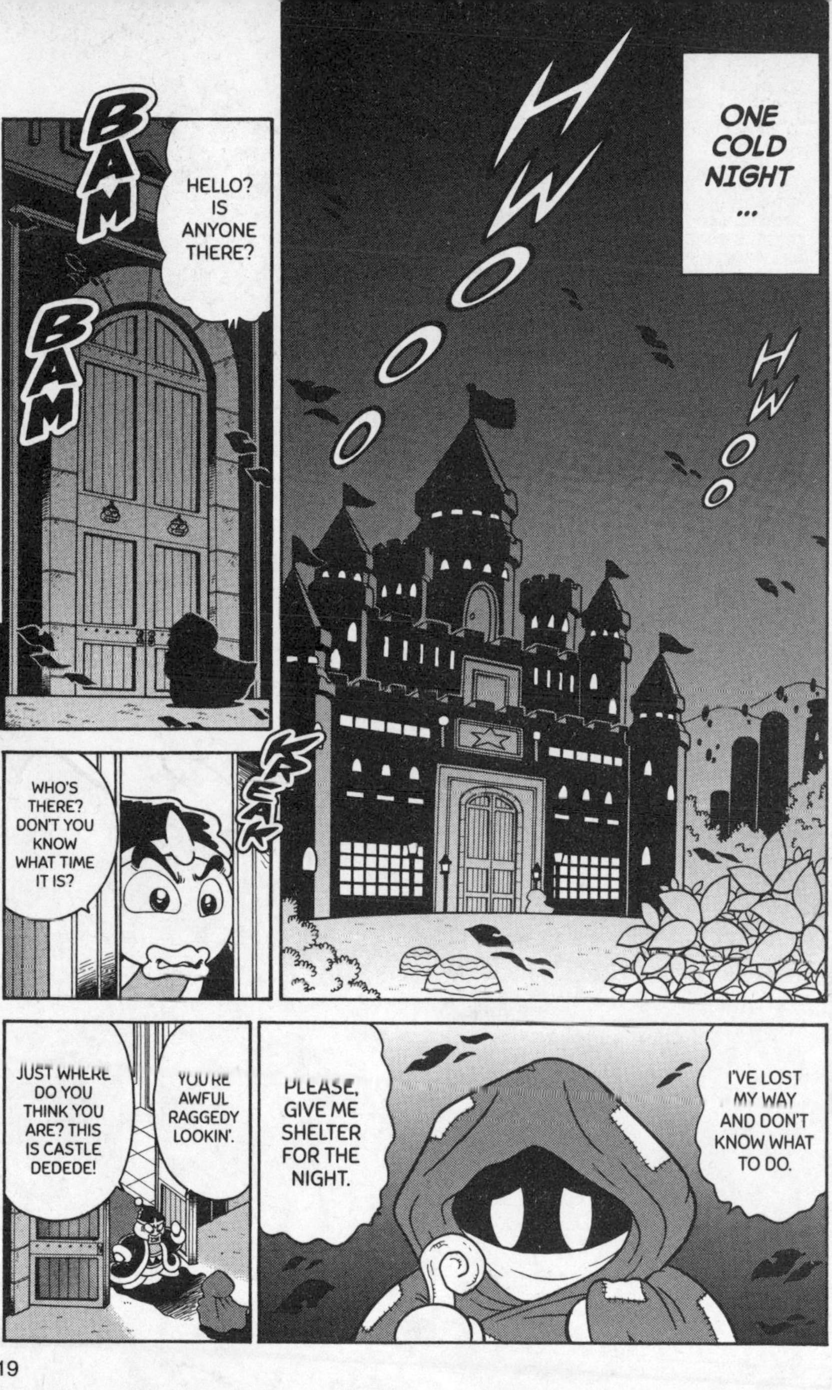
ONE COLD NIGHT ...
HWOOOOO
HWOO
BAM
BAM
HELLO? IS ANYONE THERE?
KREAK
WHO'S THERE? DON'T YOU KNOW WHAT TIME IT IS?
I'VE LOST MY WAY AND DON'T KNOW WHAT TO DO.
PLEASE, GIVE ME SHELTER FOR THE NIGHT.
YOU'RE AWFUL RAGGEDY LOOKIN'.
JUST WHERE DO YOU THINK YOU ARE? THIS IS CASTLE DEDEDE!

AUTHOR'S COMMENT

IT'S *BEAUTY AND THE BEAST*. I KNOW I DREW IT, BUT THIS IS A GOOD ONE. IT'S A FAVORITE OF MINE.

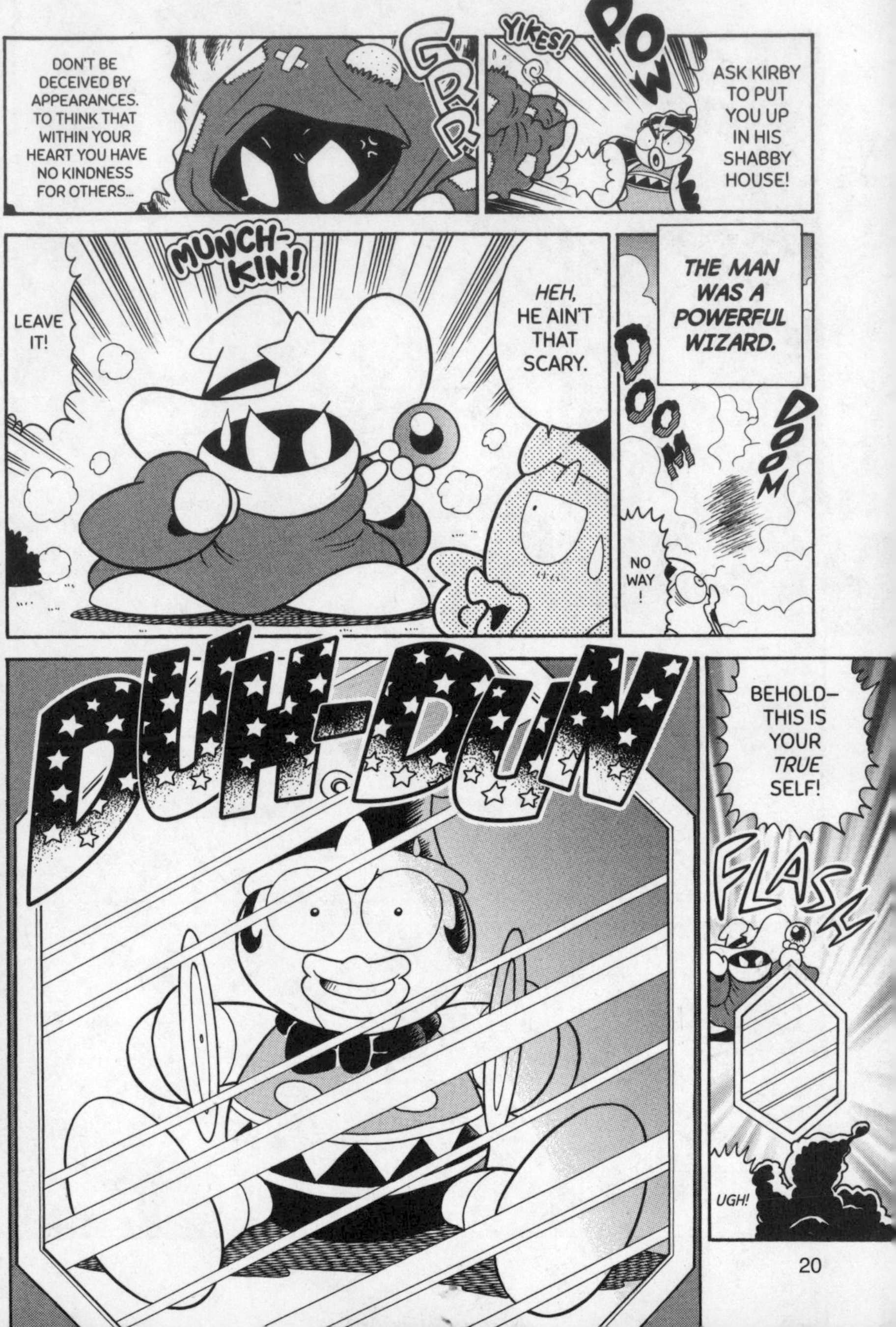
POW
YIKES!
ASK KIRBY TO PUT YOU UP IN HIS SHABBY HOUSE!
GRR
DON'T BE DECEIVED BY APPEARANCES. TO THINK THAT WITHIN YOUR HEART YOU HAVE NO KINDNESS FOR OTHERS...
THE MAN WAS A POWERFUL WIZARD.
DOOM
DOOM
NO WAY!
HEH, HE AIN'T THAT SCARY.
MUNCH-KIN!
LEAVE IT!
BEHOLD—THIS IS YOUR *TRUE* SELF!
FLASH
UGH!
DUH-DUN

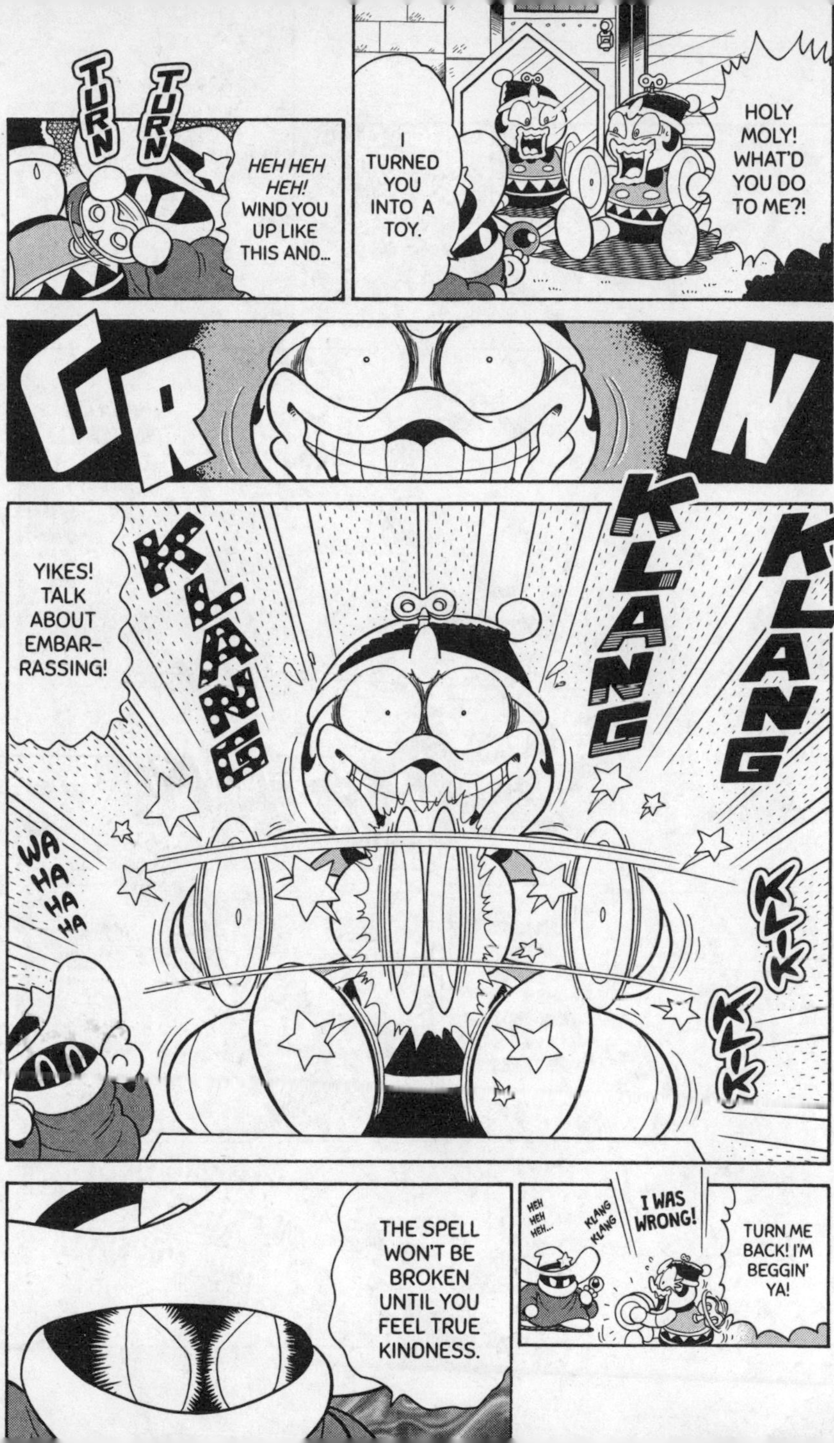
HOLY MOLY! WHAT'D YOU DO TO ME?!
I TURNED YOU INTO A TOY.
TURN TURN
HEH HEH HEH! WIND YOU UP LIKE THIS AND...
GRIN
KLANG KLANG
KLANG
YIKES! TALK ABOUT EMBAR-RASSING!
KLANG
KLIK KLIK
WA HA HA HA HA
I WAS WRONG!
TURN ME BACK! I'M BEGGIN' YA!
KLANG KLANG
HEH HEH HEH...
THE SPELL WON'T BE BROKEN UNTIL YOU FEEL TRUE KINDNESS.

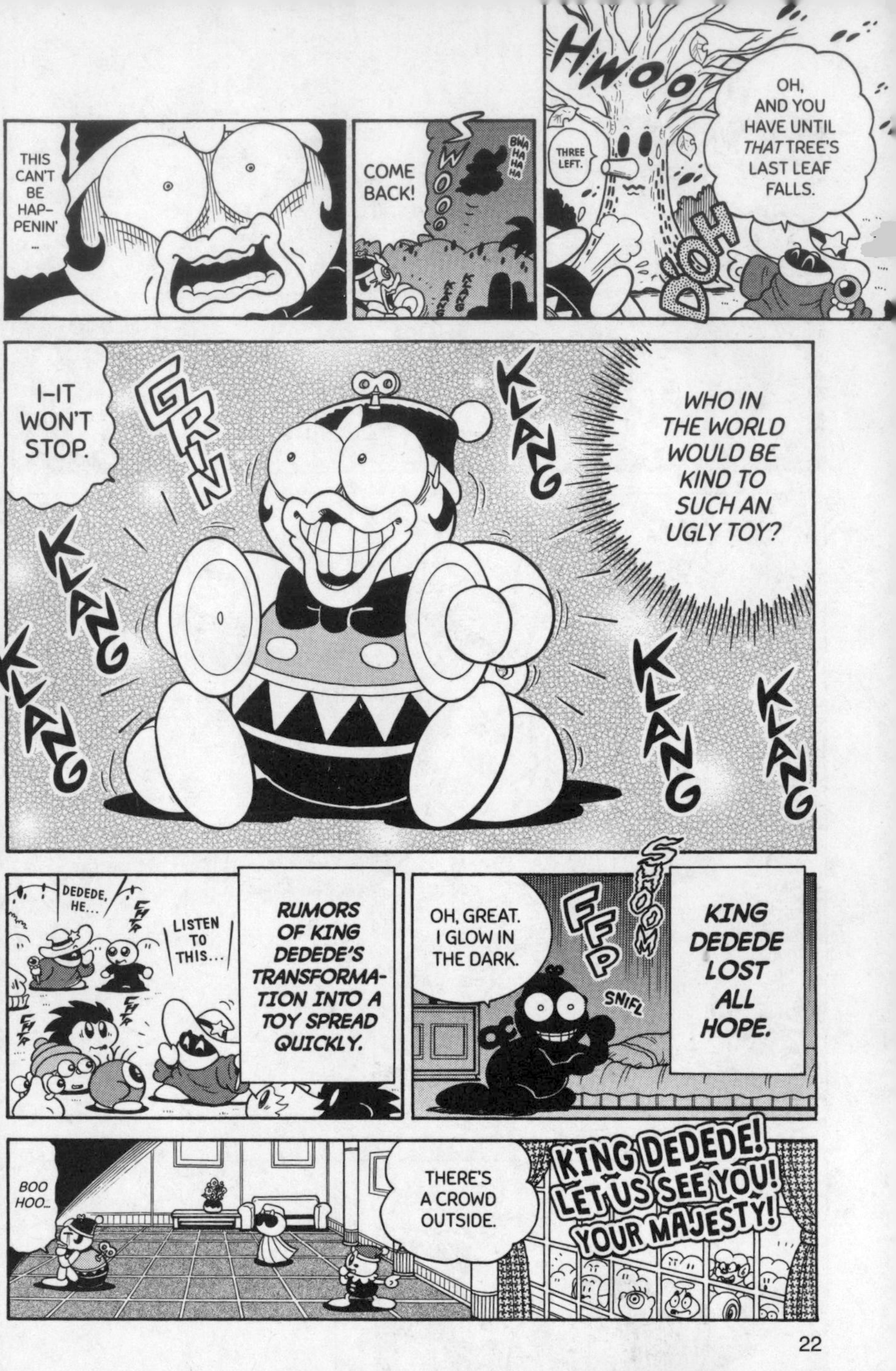
HWOOO
OH, AND YOU HAVE UNTIL *THAT* TREE'S LAST LEAF FALLS.
THREE LEFT.
D'OH
BWA HA HA HA
SWOOOO
COME BACK!
KLANG KLANG
THIS CAN'T BE HAP-PENIN' ...
WHO IN THE WORLD WOULD BE KIND TO SUCH AN UGLY TOY?
KLANG
KLANG
KLANG
GRIN
I-IT WON'T STOP.
KLANG
KLANG
KING DEDEDE LOST ALL HOPE.
SHOOOM
FFP
OH, GREAT. I GLOW IN THE DARK.
SNIFL
RUMORS OF KING DEDEDE'S TRANSFORMA-TION INTO A TOY SPREAD QUICKLY.
LISTEN TO THIS...
DEDEDE, HE...
KING DEDEDE! LET US SEE YOU! YOUR MAJESTY!
THERE'S A CROWD OUTSIDE.
BOO HOO...

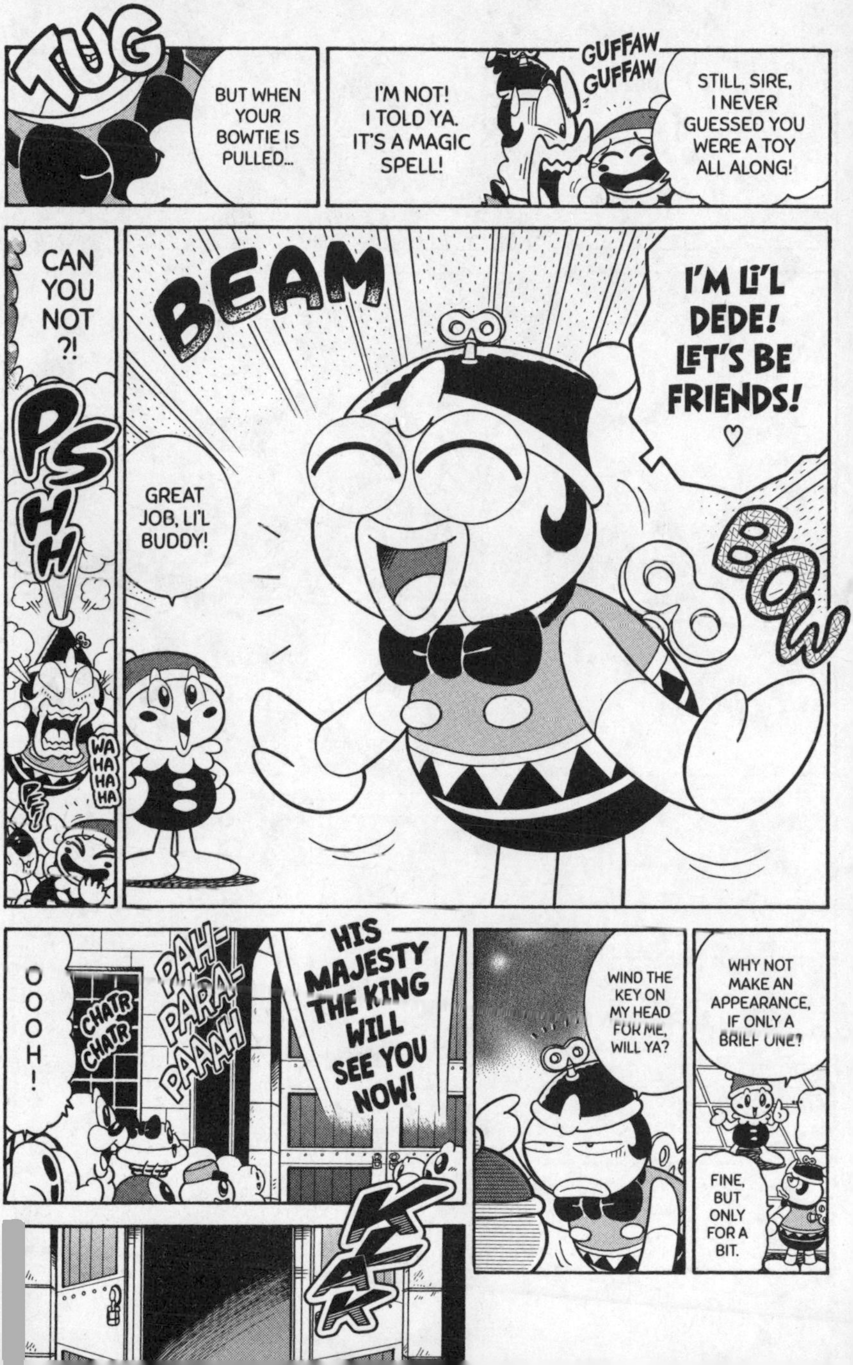
GUFFAW GUFFAW
STILL, SIRE, I NEVER GUESSED YOU WERE A TOY ALL ALONG!
I'M NOT! I TOLD YA. IT'S A MAGIC SPELL!
TUG
BUT WHEN YOUR BOWTIE IS PULLED...
I'M LI'L DEDE! LET'S BE FRIENDS! ♡
BEAM
BOW
GREAT JOB, LI'L BUDDY!
CAN YOU NOT ?!
PSHHH
WA HA HA HA HA
WHY NOT MAKE AN APPEARANCE, IF ONLY A BRIEF ONE?
FINE, BUT ONLY FOR A BIT.
WIND THE KEY ON MY HEAD FOR ME, WILL YA?
HIS MAJESTY THE KING WILL SEE YOU NOW!
PAH-PARA-PAAAH
CHATR CHATR
OOOOH!

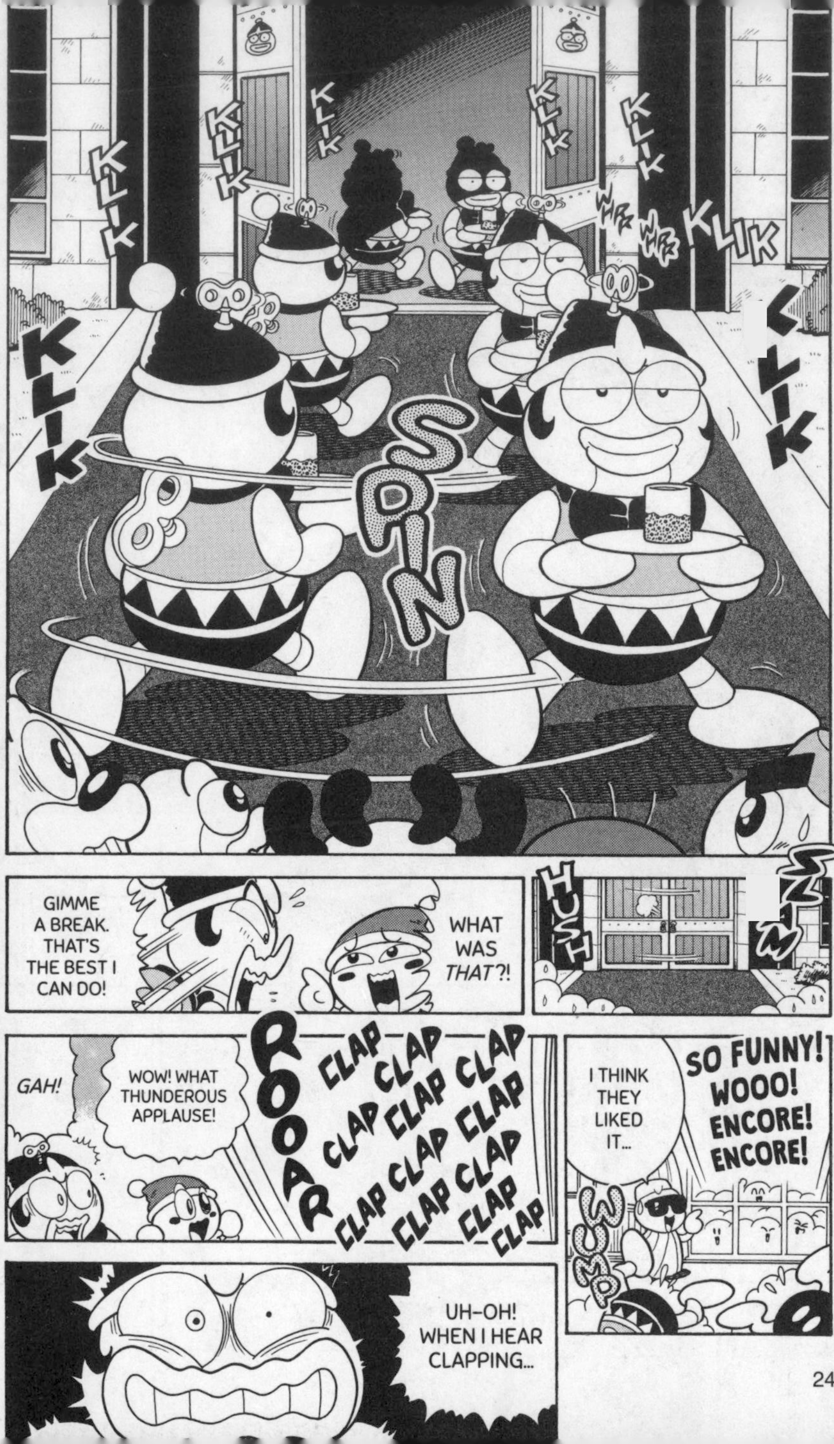
KLIK KLIK KLIK KLIK
KLIK KLIK KLIK KLIK
WHRR WHRR
SPIN
SLAM
HUSH
WHAT WAS *THAT*?!
GIMME A BREAK. THAT'S THE BEST I CAN DO!
SO FUNNY! WOOO! ENCORE! ENCORE!
I THINK THEY LIKED IT...
ROOAR
CLAP CLAP CLAP CLAP CLAP CLAP CLAP CLAP CLAP CLAP CLAP CLAP CLAP CLAP CLAP
WOW! WHAT THUNDEROUS APPLAUSE!
GAH!
UH-OH! WHEN I HEAR CLAPPING...

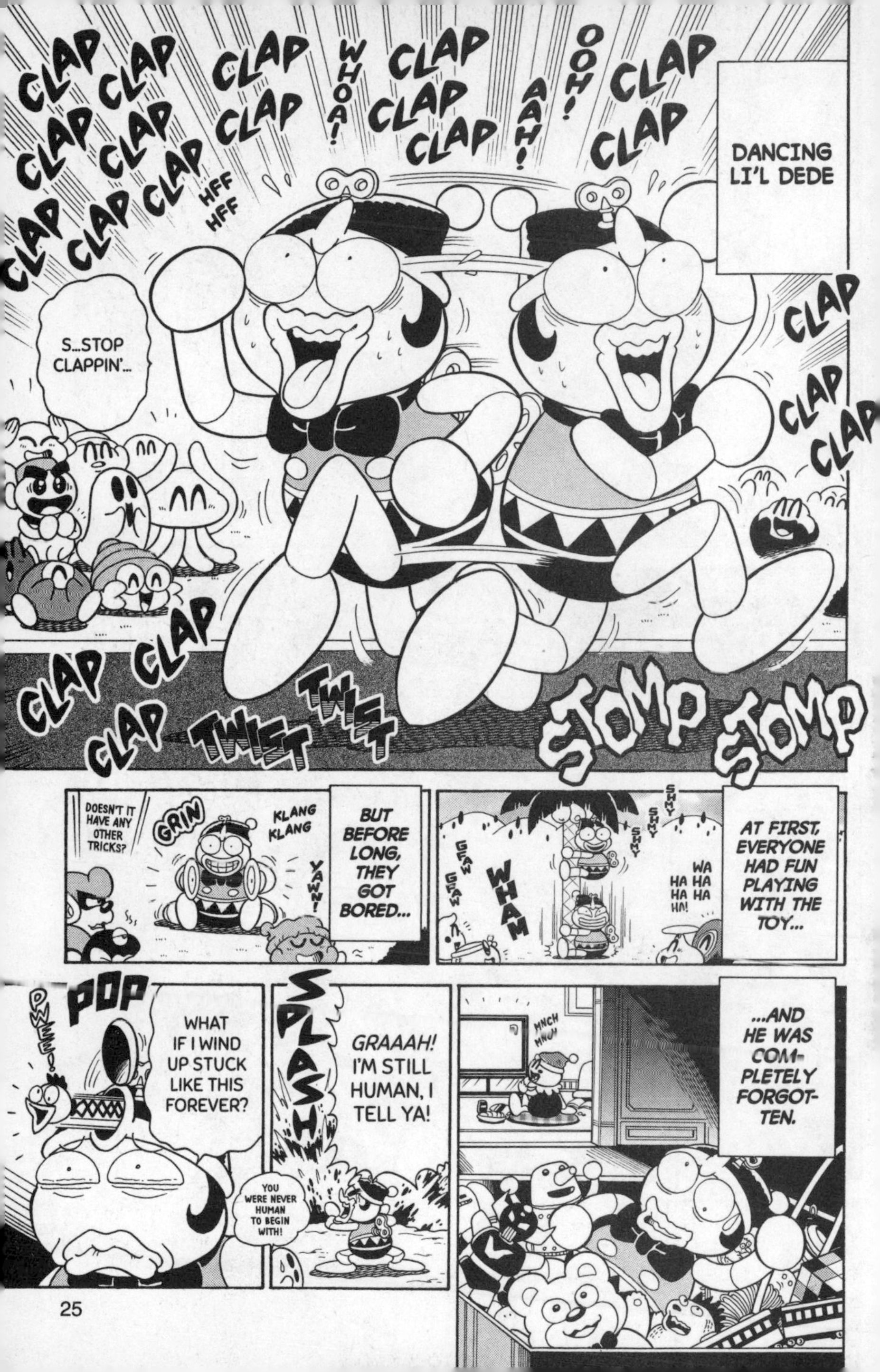
DANCING LI'L DEDE
CLAP CLAP
OOH!
AAH!
CLAP CLAP CLAP
WHOA!
CLAP CLAP CLAP CLAP
CLAP CLAP CLAP CLAP CLAP CLAP CLAP
HFF HFF
S...STOP CLAPPIN'...
CLAP CLAP CLAP
CLAP CLAP CLAP
TWIST TWIST
STOMP STOMP
AT FIRST, EVERYONE HAD FUN PLAYING WITH THE TOY...
SHMY SHMY SHMY
WA HA HA HA HA HA HA!
WHAM
GFAW GFAW
BUT BEFORE LONG, THEY GOT BORED...
KLANG KLANG
GRIN
YAWN!
DOESN'T IT HAVE ANY OTHER TRICKS?
...AND HE WAS COM-PLETELY FORGOT-TEN.
MNCH MNCH
SPLASH
GRAAAH! I'M STILL HUMAN, I TELL YA!
YOU WERE NEVER HUMAN TO BEGIN WITH!
POP
PWEEE!
WHAT IF I WIND UP STUCK LIKE THIS FOREVER?

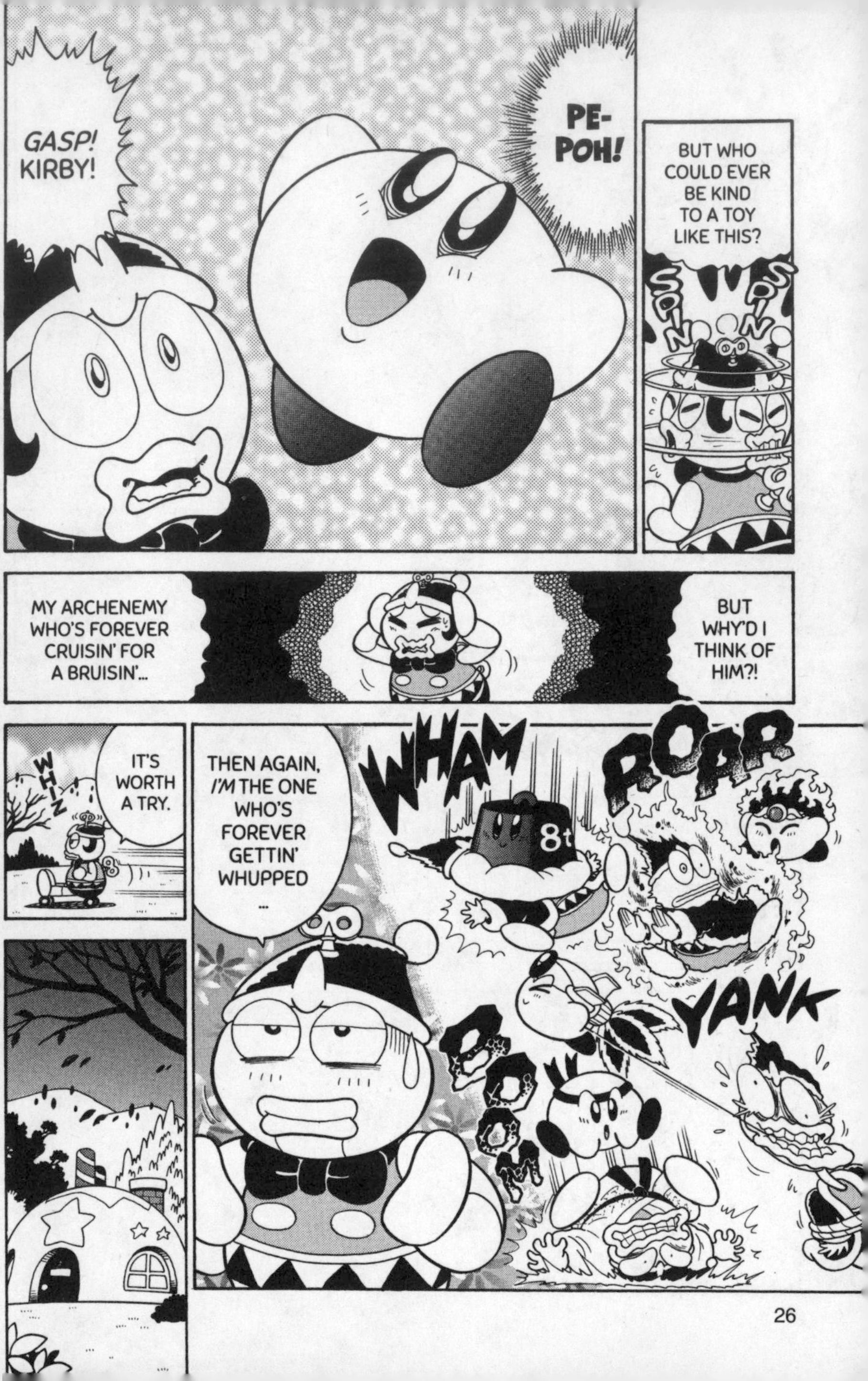
BUT WHO COULD EVER BE KIND TO A TOY LIKE THIS?
SPIN SPIN
PE-POH!
GASP! KIRBY!
BUT WHY'D I THINK OF HIM?!
MY ARCHENEMY WHO'S FOREVER CRUISIN' FOR A BRUISIN'...
ROAR
WHAM
8t
THEN AGAIN, *I'M* THE ONE WHO'S FOREVER GETTIN' WHUPPED ...
YANK
BOOM
IT'S WORTH A TRY.
WHIZ

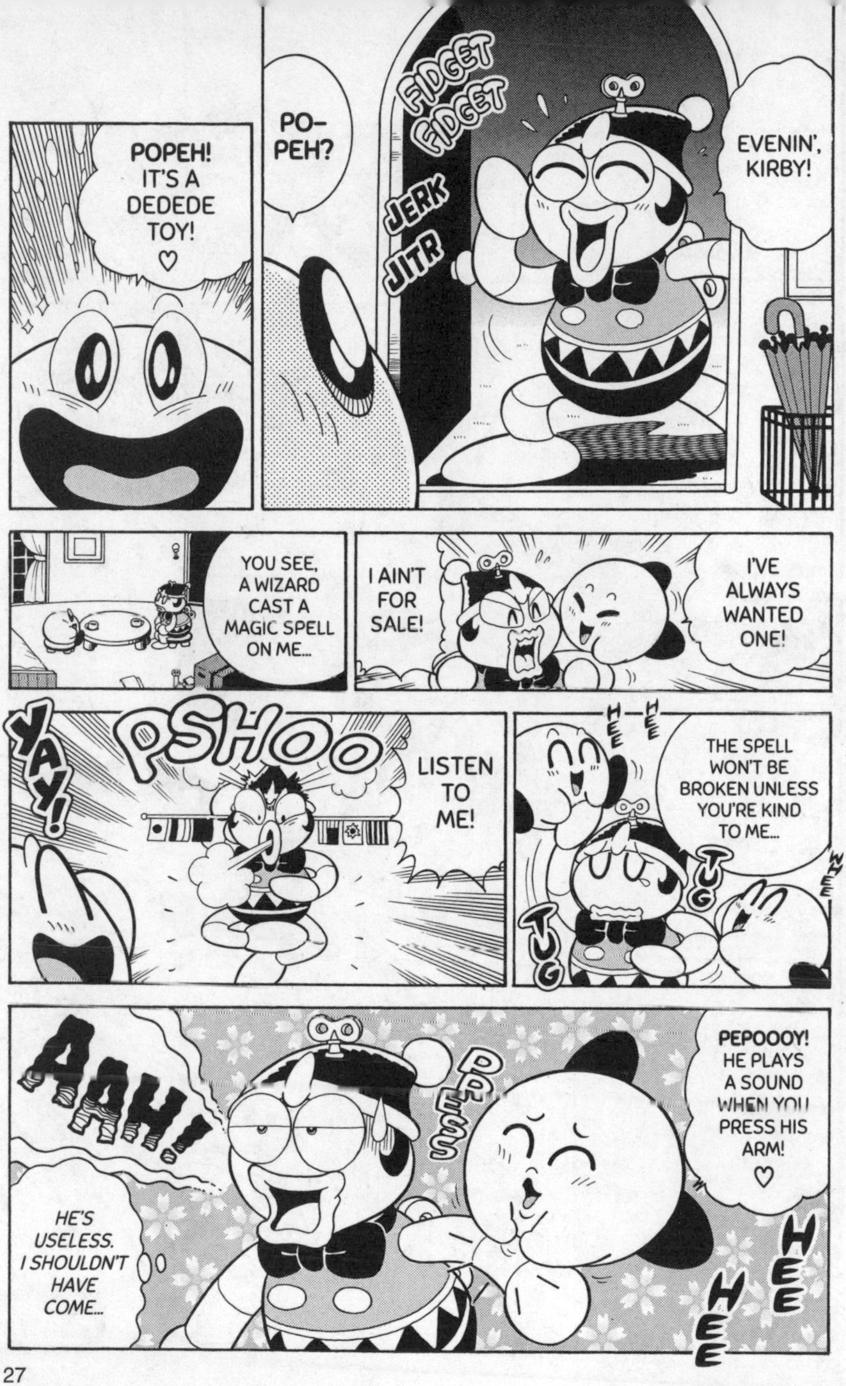
EVENIN', KIRBY!
FIDGET FIDGET
JERK JITR
PO-PEH?
POPEH! IT'S A DEDEDE TOY! ♡
I'VE ALWAYS WANTED ONE!
I AIN'T FOR SALE!
YOU SEE, A WIZARD CAST A MAGIC SPELL ON ME...
HEE HEE
THE SPELL WON'T BE BROKEN UNLESS YOU'RE KIND TO ME...
WHEE
TUG
TUG
LISTEN TO ME!
PSHOO
YAY!
PEPOOOY! HE PLAYS A SOUND WHEN YOU PRESS HIS ARM! ♡
HEE HEE
HEE HEE
PRESS
AAH!
HE'S USELESS. I SHOULDN'T HAVE COME...

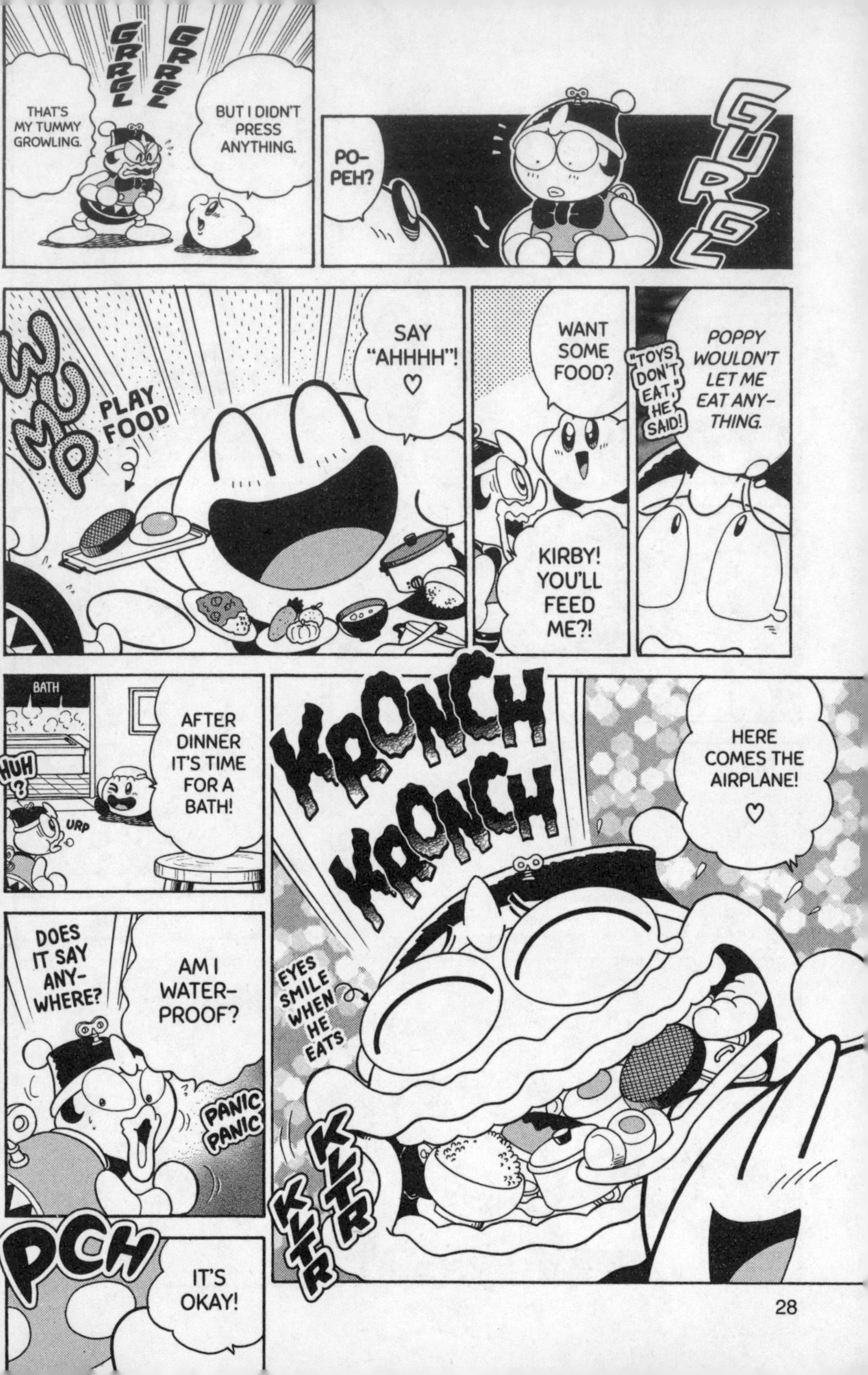
GURGL
PO-PEH?
GRRGL GRRGL
BUT I DIDN'T PRESS ANYTHING.
THAT'S MY TUMMY GROWLING.
POPPY WOULDN'T LET ME EAT ANY-THING.
"TOYS DON'T EAT," HE SAID!
WANT SOME FOOD?
KIRBY! YOU'LL FEED ME?!
SAY "AHHHH"! ♡
WUMP
PLAY FOOD
HERE COMES THE AIRPLANE! ♡
KRONCH KRONCH
EYES SMILE WHEN HE EATS
KLTR KLTR
AFTER DINNER IT'S TIME FOR A BATH!
BATH
HUH?
URP
AM I WATER-PROOF?
DOES IT SAY ANY-WHERE?
PANIC PANIC
PCH
IT'S OKAY!

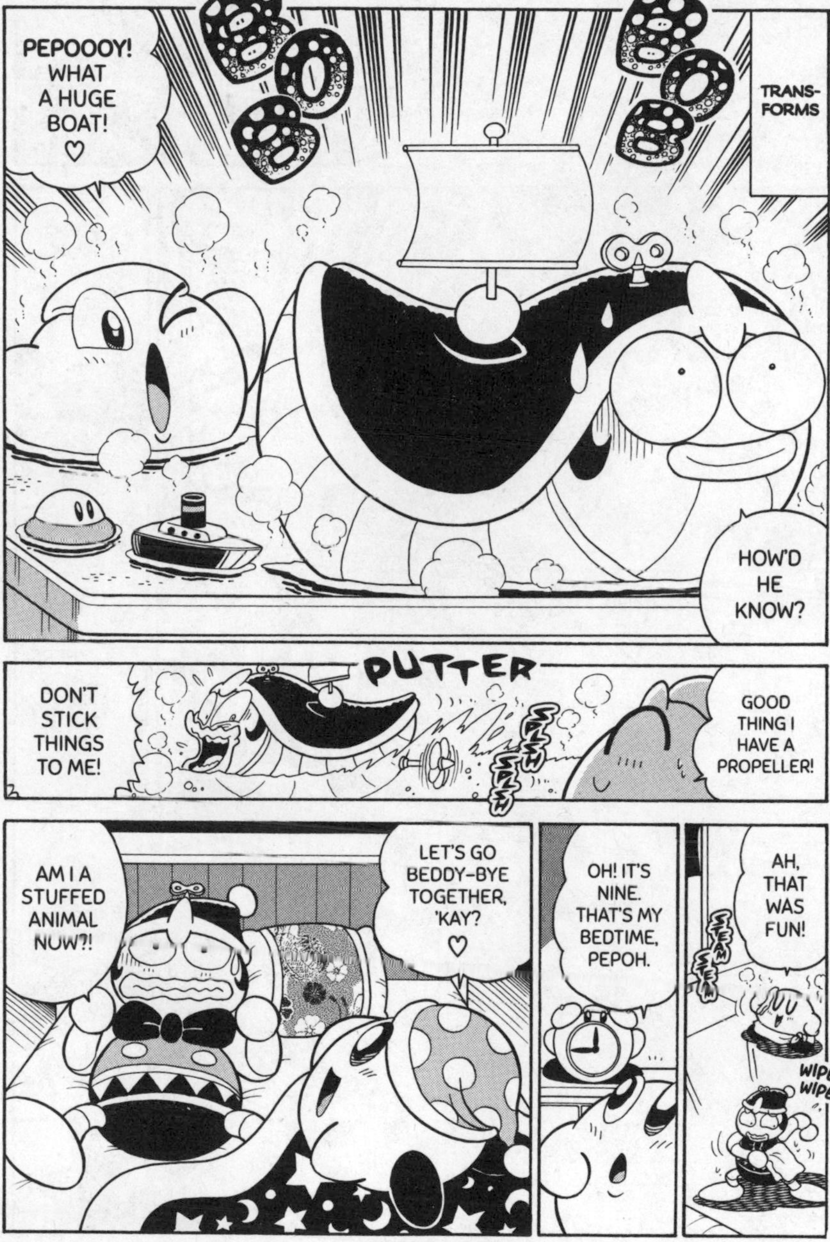
TRANSFORMS
BOB
BOB
PEPOOOY! WHAT A HUGE BOAT! ♡
HOW'D HE KNOW?
GOOD THING I HAVE A PROPELLER!
SPLSH SPLSH
PUTTER
DON'T STICK THINGS TO ME!
AH, THAT WAS FUN!
STEAM STEAM
WIPE WIPE
OH! IT'S NINE. THAT'S MY BEDTIME, PEPOH.
LET'S GO BEDDY-BYE TOGETHER, 'KAY? ♡
AM I A STUFFED ANIMAL NOW?!

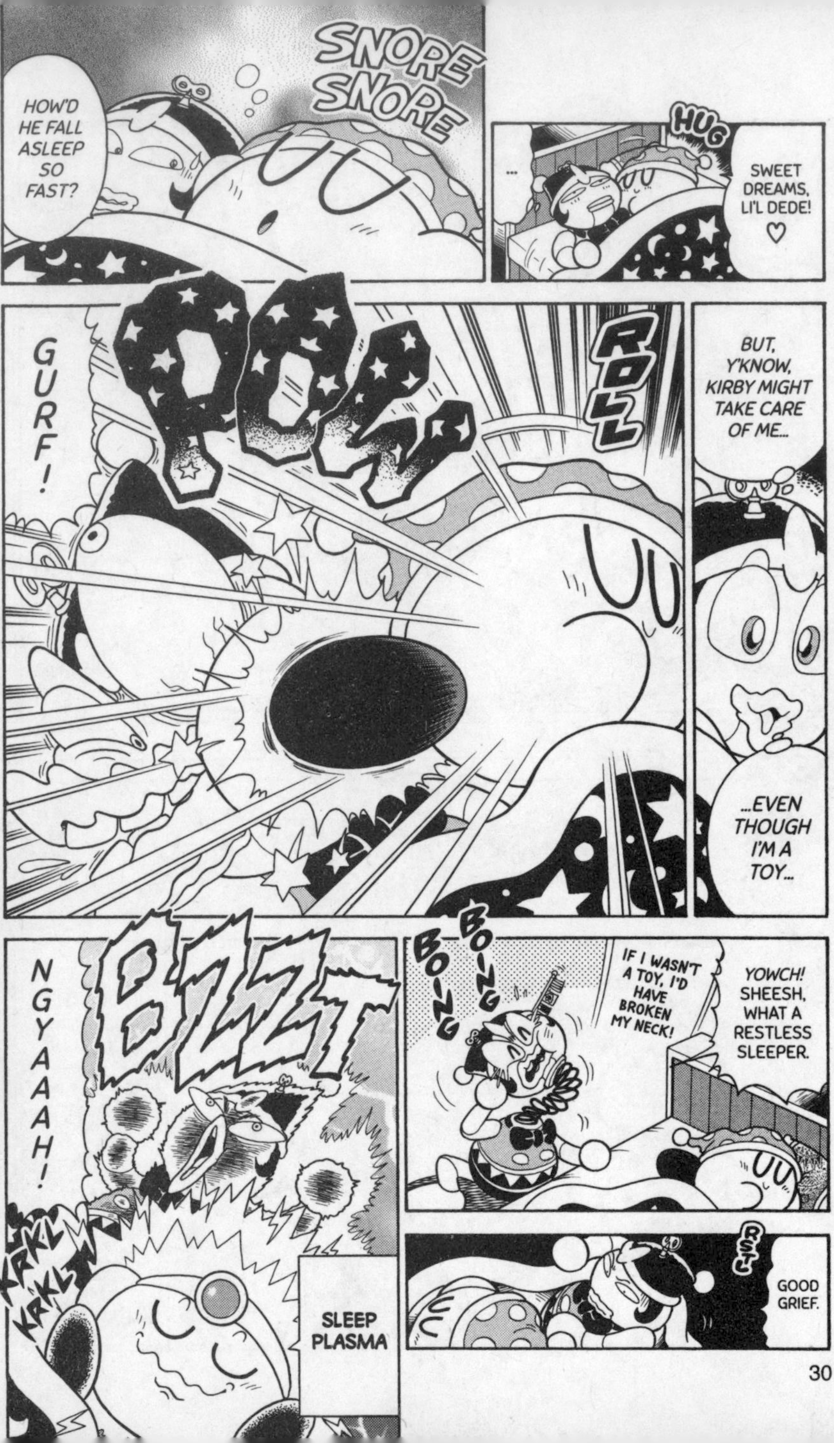
HUG
...
SWEET DREAMS, LI'L DEDE! ♥
SNORE SNORE
HOW'D HE FALL ASLEEP SO FAST?
BUT, Y'KNOW, KIRBY MIGHT TAKE CARE OF ME...
...EVEN THOUGH I'M A TOY...
ROLL
POW
GURF!
YOWCH! SHEESH, WHAT A RESTLESS SLEEPER.
IF I WASN'T A TOY, I'D HAVE BROKEN MY NECK!
BOING
BOING
RSTL
GOOD GRIEF.
BZZT
NGYAAAAH!
KRKL KRKL
SLEEP PLASMA

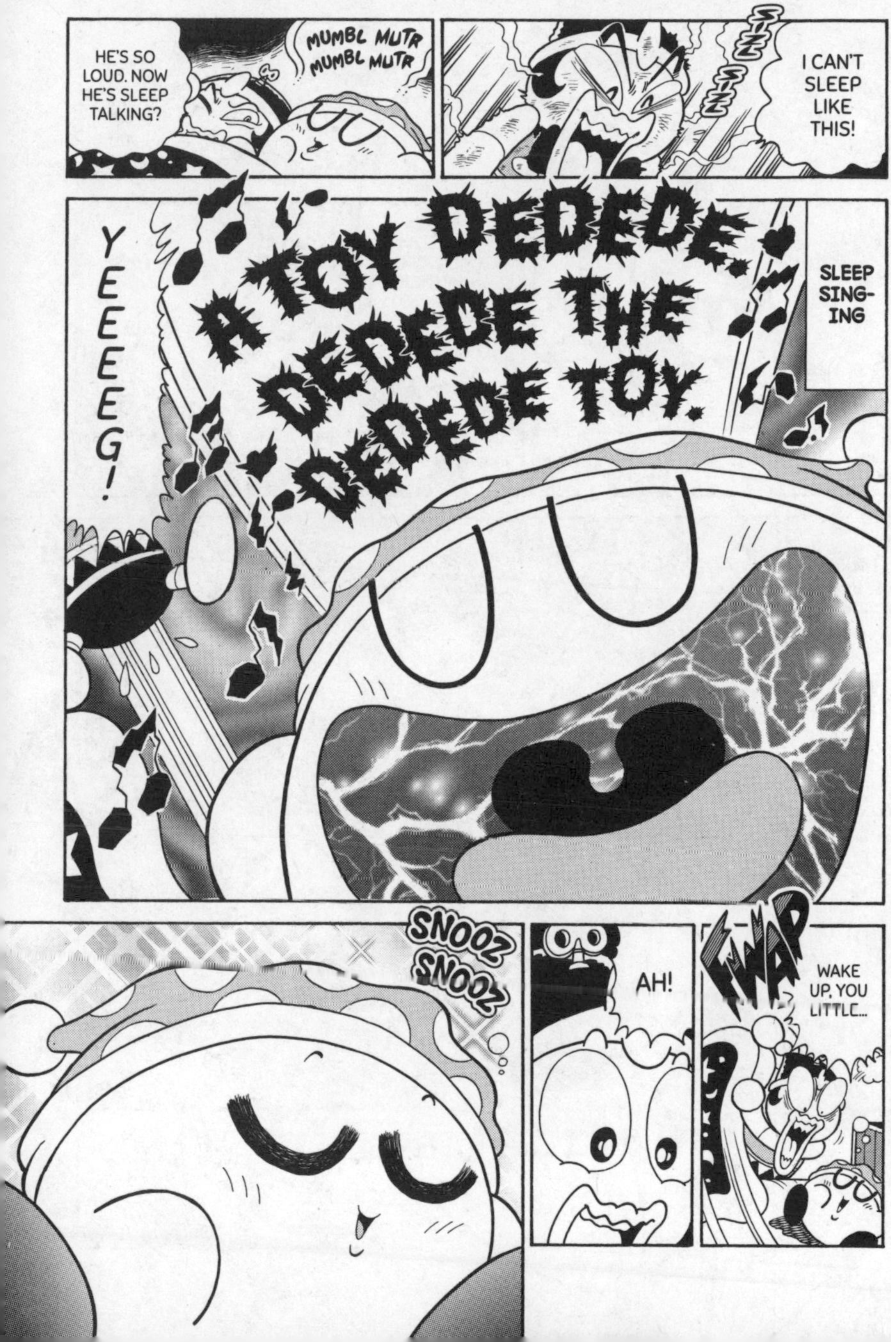
SIZZ
SIZZ
I CAN'T SLEEP LIKE THIS!
MUMBL MUTR MUMBL MUTR
HE'S SO LOUD. NOW HE'S SLEEP TALKING?
SLEEP SINGING
A TOY DEDEDE. DEDEDE THE DEDEDE TOY.
YEEEEEG!
FWAP
WAKE UP, YOU LITTLE...
AH!
SNOOZ SNOOZ

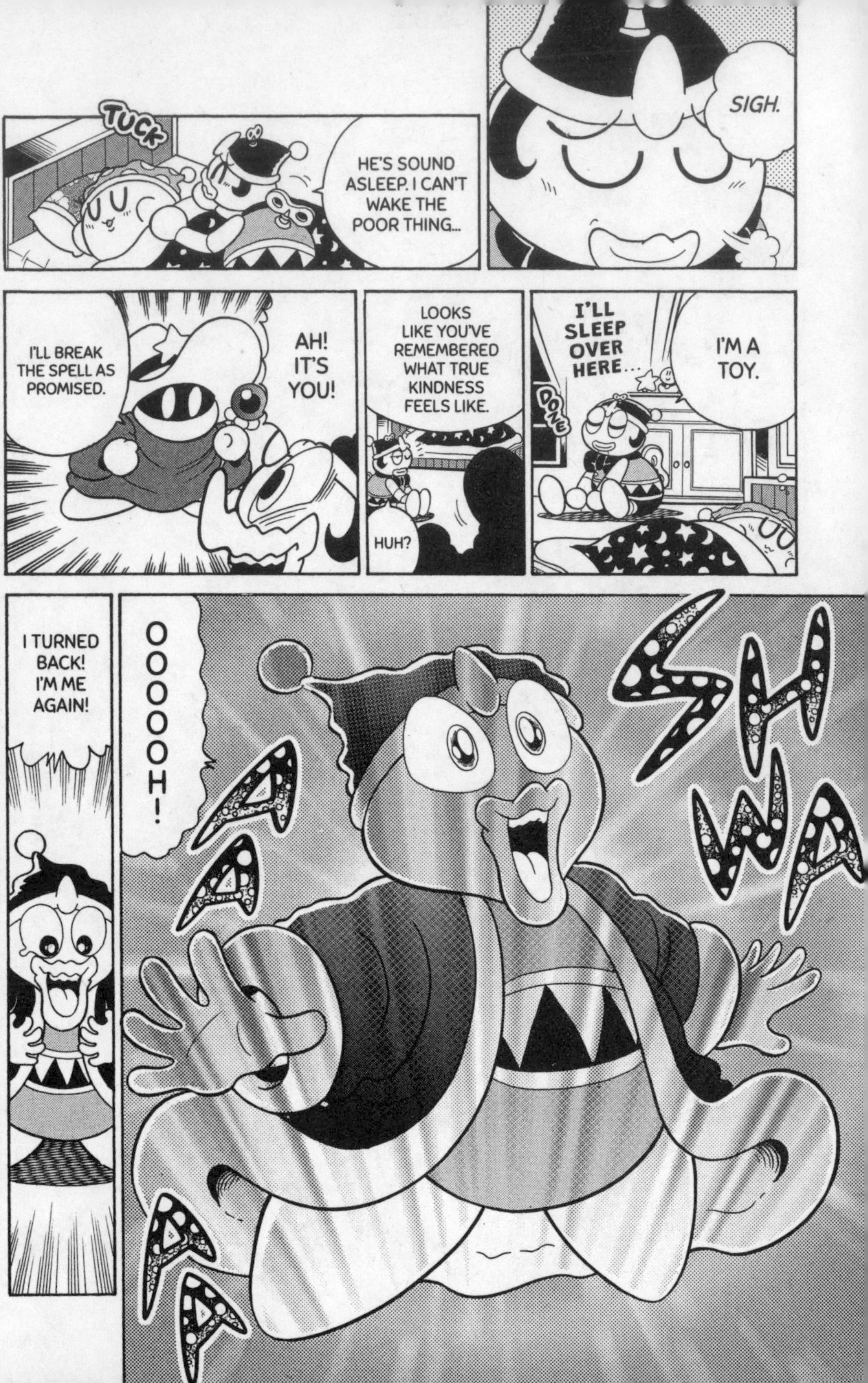
SIGH.
TUCK
HE'S SOUND ASLEEP. I CAN'T WAKE THE POOR THING...
I'M A TOY.
I'LL SLEEP OVER HERE...
DOZE
LOOKS LIKE YOU'VE REMEMBERED WHAT TRUE KINDNESS FEELS LIKE.
HUH?
AH! IT'S YOU!
I'LL BREAK THE SPELL AS PROMISED.
SHWA
OOOOOOH!
I TURNED BACK! I'M ME AGAIN!

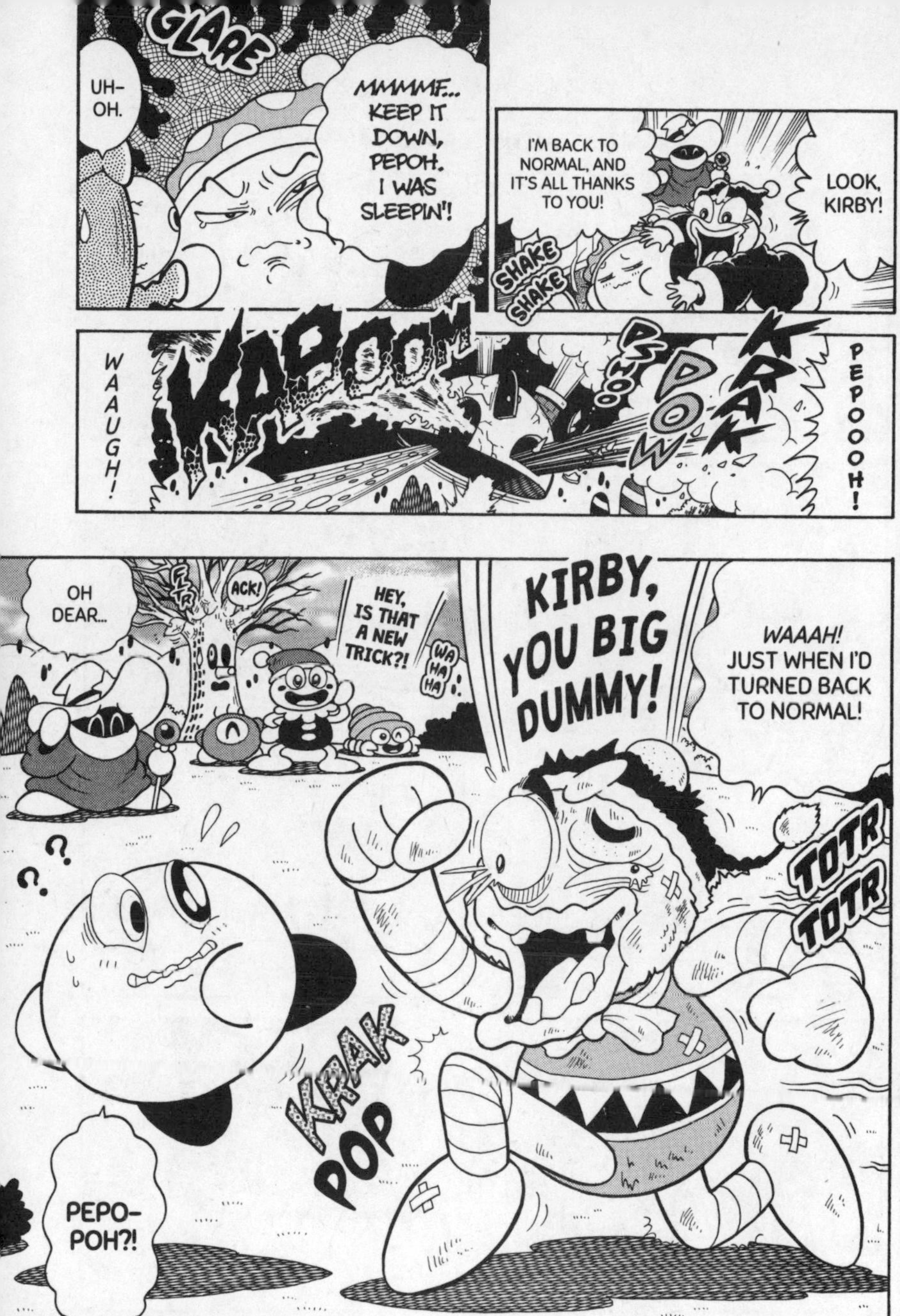
LOOK, KIRBY!
I'M BACK TO NORMAL, AND IT'S ALL THANKS TO YOU!
SHAKE SHAKE
GLARE
MMMMF... KEEP IT DOWN, PEPOH. I WAS SLEEPIN'!
UH-OH.
PEPOOOOH!
KRAK
POW
PSHOO
KABOOM
WAAAUGH!
WAAAH! JUST WHEN I'D TURNED BACK TO NORMAL!
KIRBY, YOU BIG DUMMY!
TOTR TOTR
HEY, IS THAT A NEW TRICK?!
WA HA HA
ACK!
OH DEAR...
KRAK
POP
PEPO-POH?!

MANGA ARTIST: ASSISTANT K

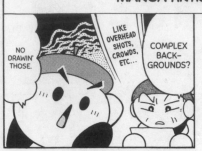

HIKAWA SENSEI, I'M HERE TO HELP, PEPOH!
THANKS, KIRBY!
FIRST, I NEED YOU TO LOOK AT THIS!
WHAT'S THIS? A CONTRACT?
CONTRACT
WHAT DOES IT SAY ABOUT ALL-NIGHTERS?
WON'T DO 'EM.
PICKING UP LUNCH?
NOT ME.
COMPLEX BACKGROUNDS?
LIKE OVERHEAD SHOTS, CROWDS, ETC...
NO DRAWIN' THOSE.
FINISHING TOUCHES?
BLACKS AND WHITE-OUT...
LOUSY AT 'EM.
I'M ASKING FOR $1,000 PER DAY, WITH THREE FREE MEALS AND A NAP INCLUDED!
TREMBL
TREMBL
BEAT IT!
BOMP
PEPOH!

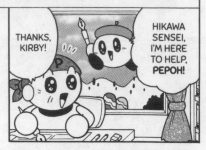

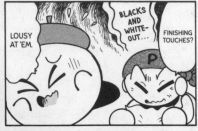

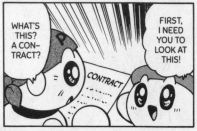

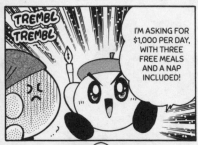

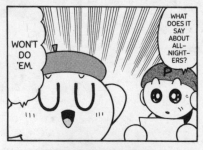

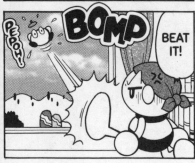

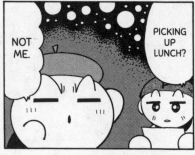

CHAPTER 3: TYPHOON KIRBY MAKES LANDFALL IN DREAM LAND!

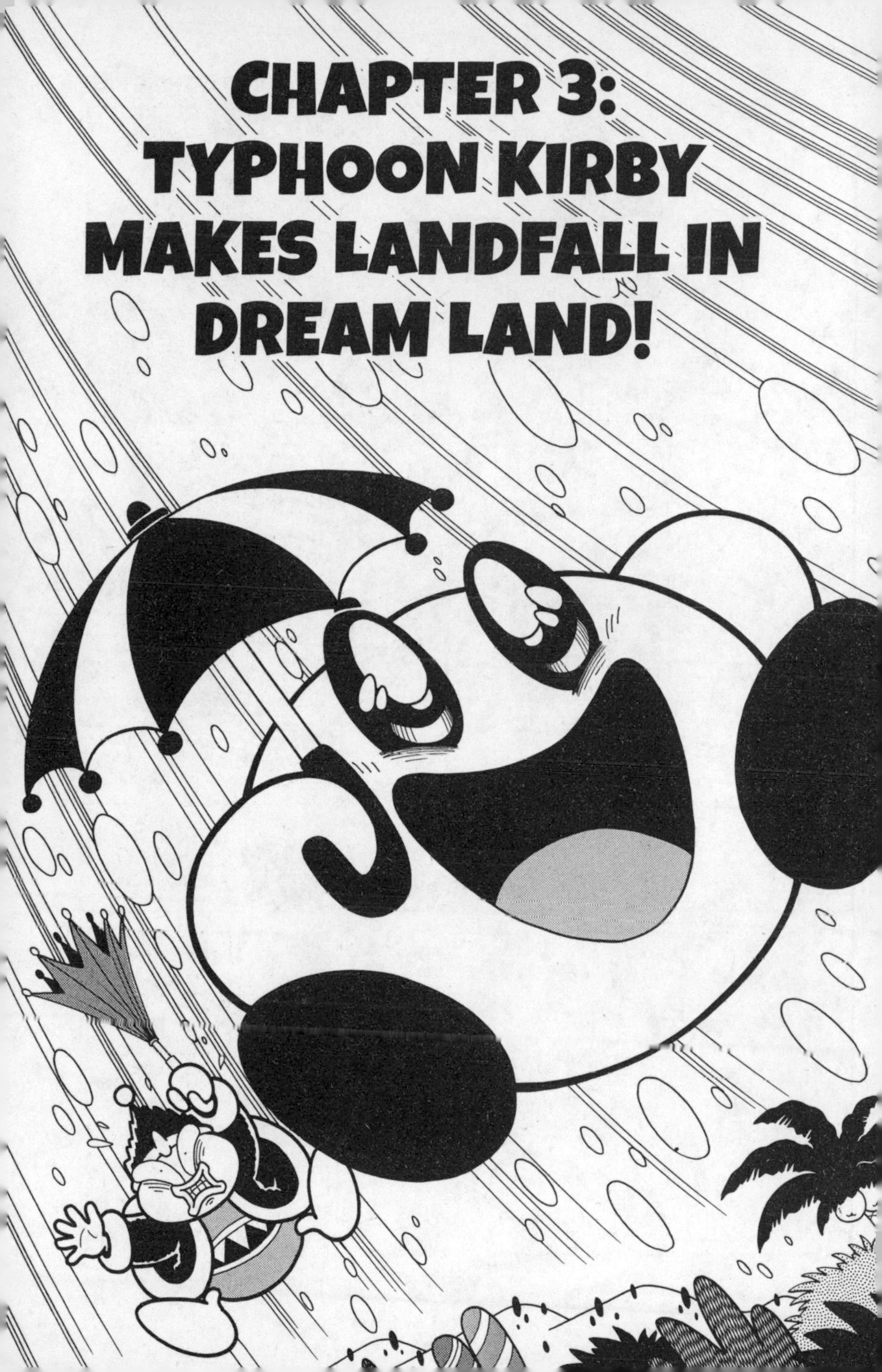

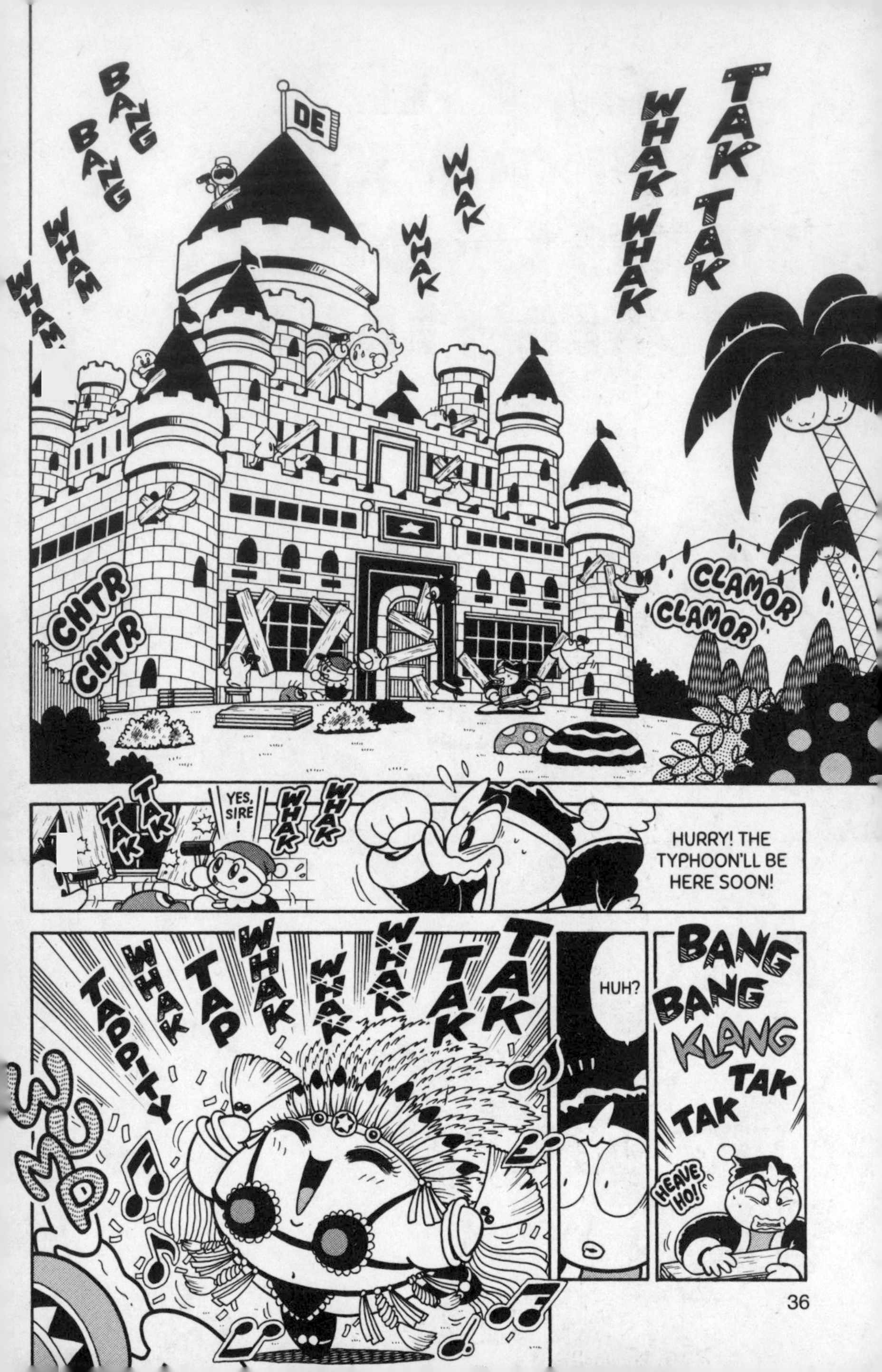
TAK TAK
WHAK WHAK
WHAK WHAK
BANG BANG
WHAM WHAM
CLAMOR CLAMOR
CHTR CHTR
HURRY! THE TYPHOON'LL BE HERE SOON!
WHAK WHAK
YES, SIRE!
TAK TAK
BANG BANG KLANG TAK TAK
HEAVE HO!
HUH?
TAK TAK
WHAK WHAK
WHAK
TAP
WHAK
TAPPITY
WOMP

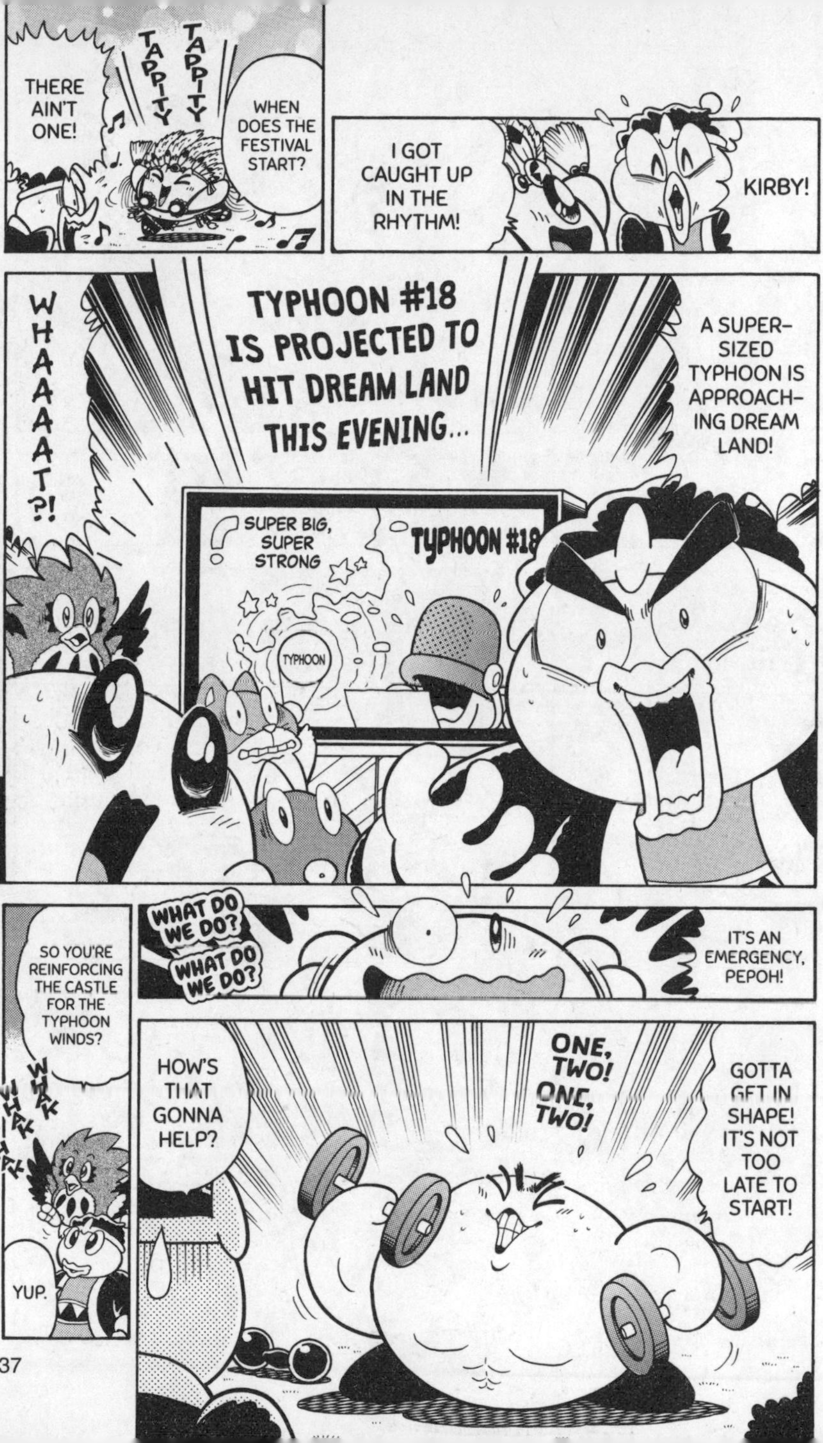
KIRBY!
I GOT CAUGHT UP IN THE RHYTHM!
WHEN DOES THE FESTIVAL START?
TAPPITY TAPPITY
THERE AIN'T ONE!
A SUPER-SIZED TYPHOON IS APPROACHING DREAM LAND!
TYPHOON #18 IS PROJECTED TO HIT DREAM LAND THIS EVENING...
WHAAAAAT?!
TYPHOON #18
SUPER BIG, SUPER STRONG
TYPHOON
IT'S AN EMERGENCY, PEPOH!
WHAT DO WE DO?
WHAT DO WE DO?
GOTTA GET IN SHAPE! IT'S NOT TOO LATE TO START!
ONE, TWO! ONE, TWO!
HOW'S THAT GONNA HELP?
SO YOU'RE REINFORCING THE CASTLE FOR THE TYPHOON WINDS?
WHAK WHAK
THAK
YUP.

AUTHOR'S COMMENT THE STANDARD TYPHOON STORY. IT HAS CLEAN LINES DRAWN WITH A DIP PEN. I WAS DRAWING THE MANGA ALONE AT THIS TIME, SO CHAPTERS WITH LOTS OF BACKGROUND ART WERE ESPECIALLY TOUGH! *(LAUGHS)*

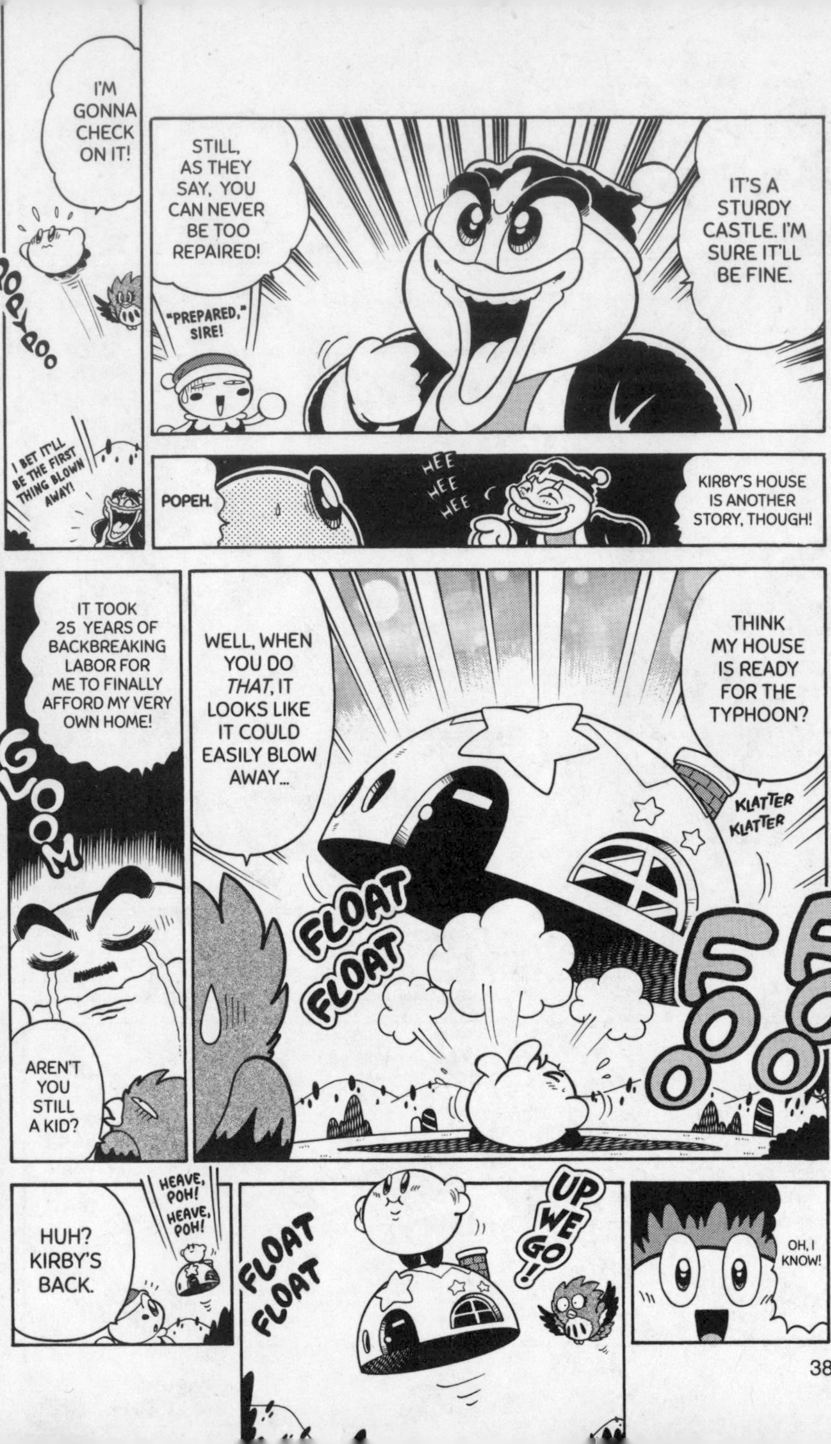
IT'S A STURDY CASTLE. I'M SURE IT'LL BE FINE.
STILL, AS THEY SAY, YOU CAN NEVER BE TOO REPAIRED!
"PREPARED," SIRE!
KIRBY'S HOUSE IS ANOTHER STORY, THOUGH!
HEE HEE HEE
POPEH.
I'M GONNA CHECK ON IT!
POPYPOO
I BET IT'LL BE THE FIRST THING BLOWN AWAY!
THINK MY HOUSE IS READY FOR THE TYPHOON?
KLATTER KLATTER
WELL, WHEN YOU DO *THAT*, IT LOOKS LIKE IT COULD EASILY BLOW AWAY...
FLOAT FLOAT
IT TOOK 25 YEARS OF BACKBREAKING LABOR FOR ME TO FINALLY AFFORD MY VERY OWN HOME!
GLOOM
AREN'T YOU STILL A KID?
OH, I KNOW!
UP WE GO!
FLOAT FLOAT
HEAVE, POH! HEAVE, POH!
HUH? KIRBY'S BACK.

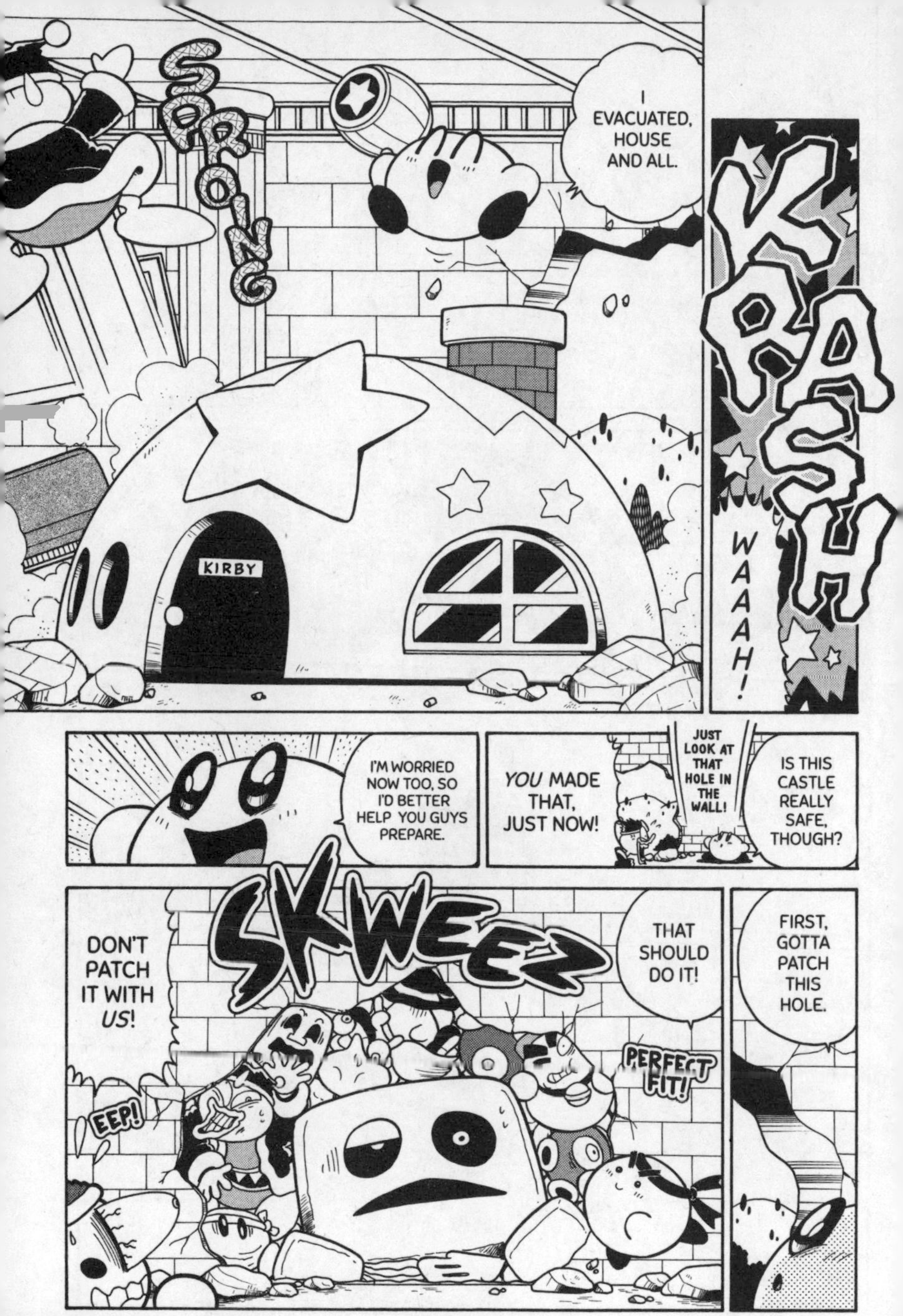
KRASH
WAAAAH!
SPROING
I EVACUATED, HOUSE AND ALL.
KIRBY
IS THIS CASTLE REALLY SAFE, THOUGH?
JUST LOOK AT THAT HOLE IN THE WALL!
YOU MADE THAT, JUST NOW!
I'M WORRIED NOW TOO, SO I'D BETTER HELP YOU GUYS PREPARE.
FIRST, GOTTA PATCH THIS HOLE.
THAT SHOULD DO IT!
SKWEEZ
PERFECT FIT!
DON'T PATCH IT WITH *US*!
EEP!

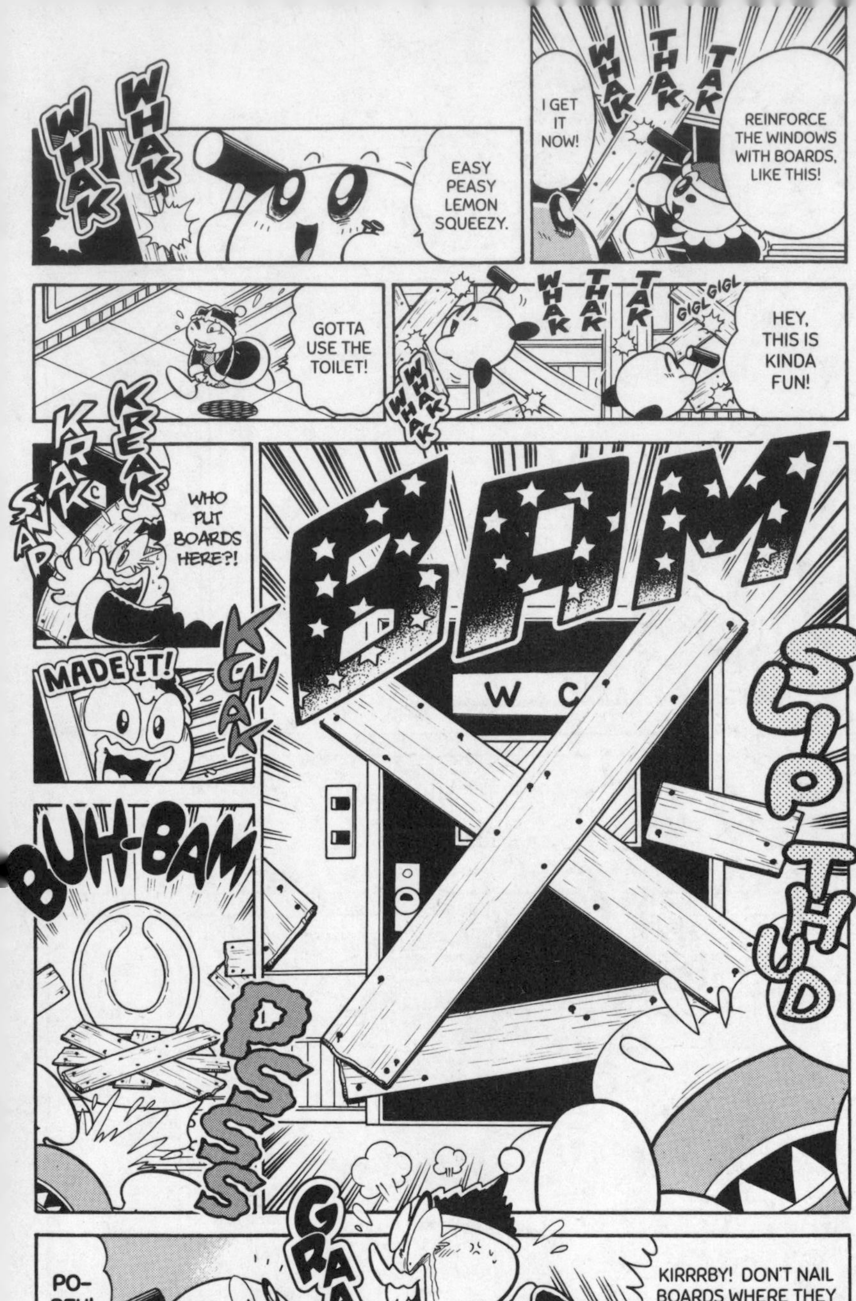
REINFORCE THE WINDOWS WITH BOARDS, LIKE THIS!
TAK
THAK
WHAK
I GET IT NOW!
EASY PEASY LEMON SQUEEZY.
WHAK
WHAK
HEY, THIS IS KINDA FUN!
GIGL GIGL
TAK
THAK
WHAK
WHAK
GOTTA USE THE TOILET!
BAM
W C
SLIP
THUD
PSSS
WHO PUT BOARDS HERE?!
KREAK
KRAK
SNAP
MADE IT!
KCHAK
BUH-BAM
KIRRRBY! DON'T NAIL BOARDS WHERE THEY AREN'T NEEDED!
GRAA
PO-PEH!

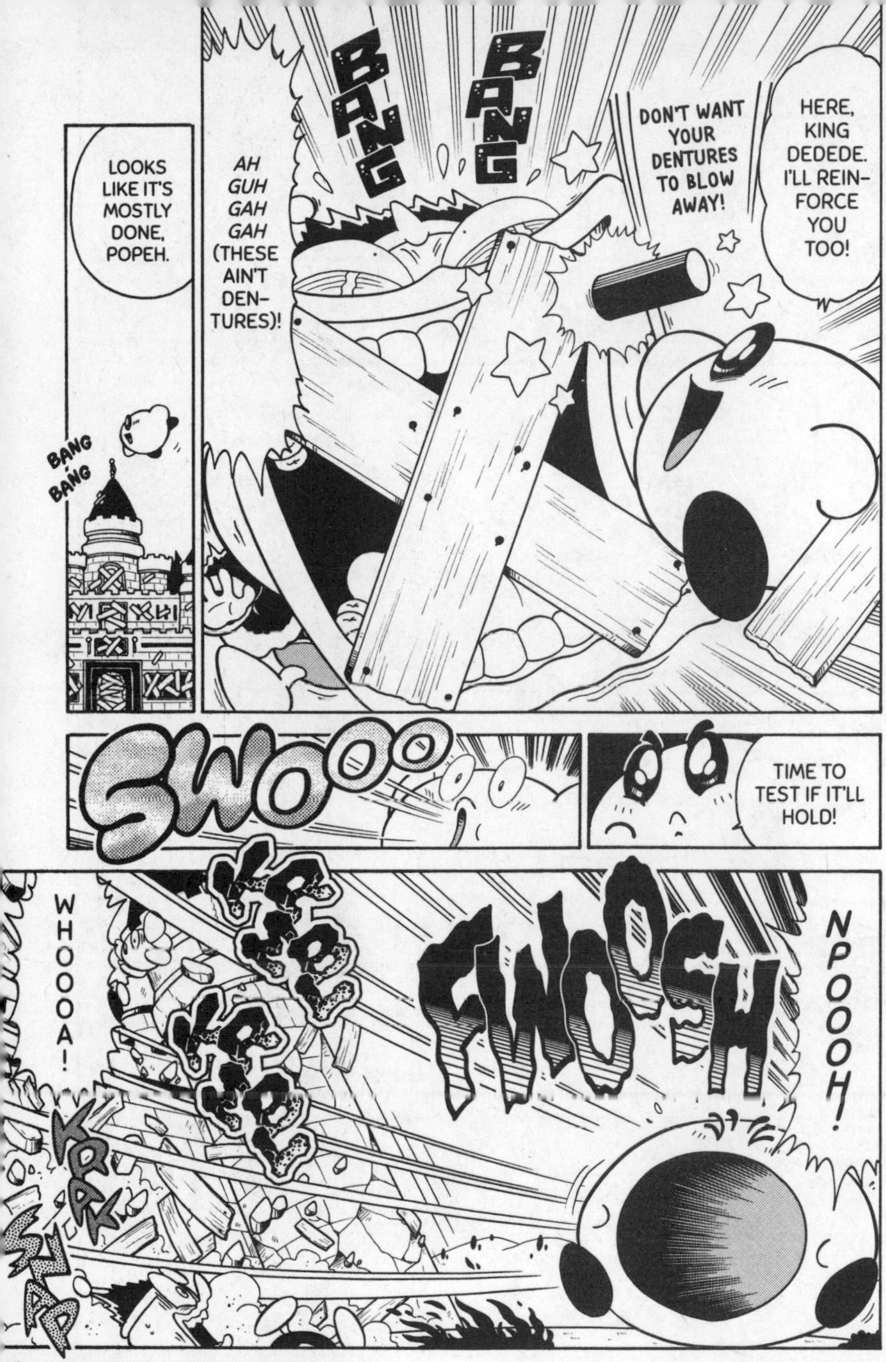
HERE, KING DEDEDE. I'LL REINFORCE YOU TOO!
DON'T WANT YOUR DENTURES TO BLOW AWAY!
BANG
BANG
AH GUH GAH GAH (THESE AIN'T DENTURES)!
LOOKS LIKE IT'S MOSTLY DONE, POPEH.
BANG BANG
TIME TO TEST IF IT'LL HOLD!
SWOOOO
NPOOOOH!
FWOOSH
WHOOOOA!
KRAK
SNAP

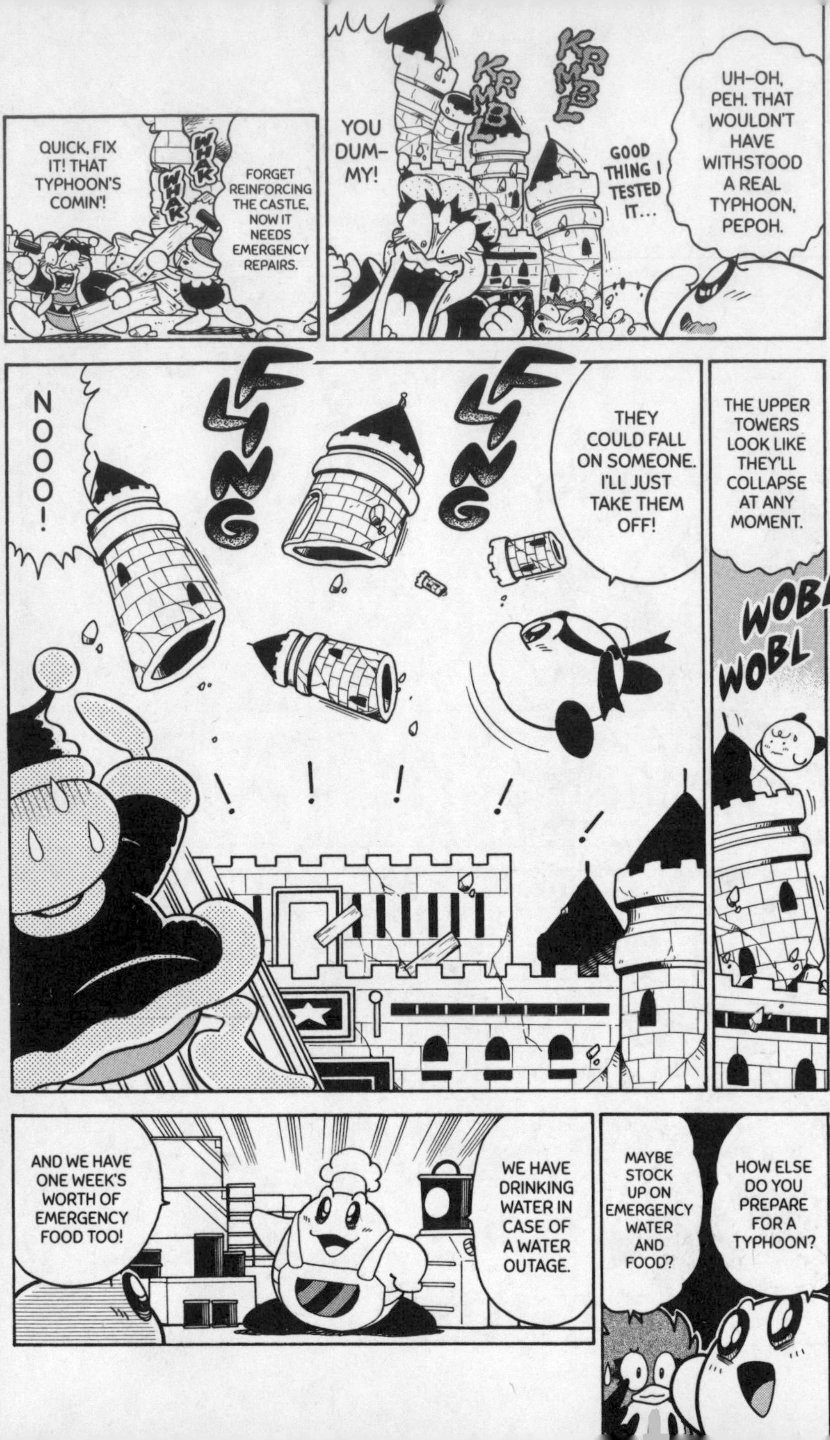
UH-OH, PEH. THAT WOULDN'T HAVE WITHSTOOD A REAL TYPHOON, PEPOH.
GOOD THING I TESTED IT...
KRMBL
KRMBL
YOU DUMMY!
FORGET REINFORCING THE CASTLE, NOW IT NEEDS EMERGENCY REPAIRS.
WHAK
WHAK
QUICK, FIX IT! THAT TYPHOON'S COMIN'!
THE UPPER TOWERS LOOK LIKE THEY'LL COLLAPSE AT ANY MOMENT.
WOBL
WOBL
THEY COULD FALL ON SOMEONE. I'LL JUST TAKE THEM OFF!
FLING
FLING
NOOOO!
! ! ! ! !
HOW ELSE DO YOU PREPARE FOR A TYPHOON?
MAYBE STOCK UP ON EMERGENCY WATER AND FOOD?
WE HAVE DRINKING WATER IN CASE OF A WATER OUTAGE.
AND WE HAVE ONE WEEK'S WORTH OF EMERGENCY FOOD TOO!

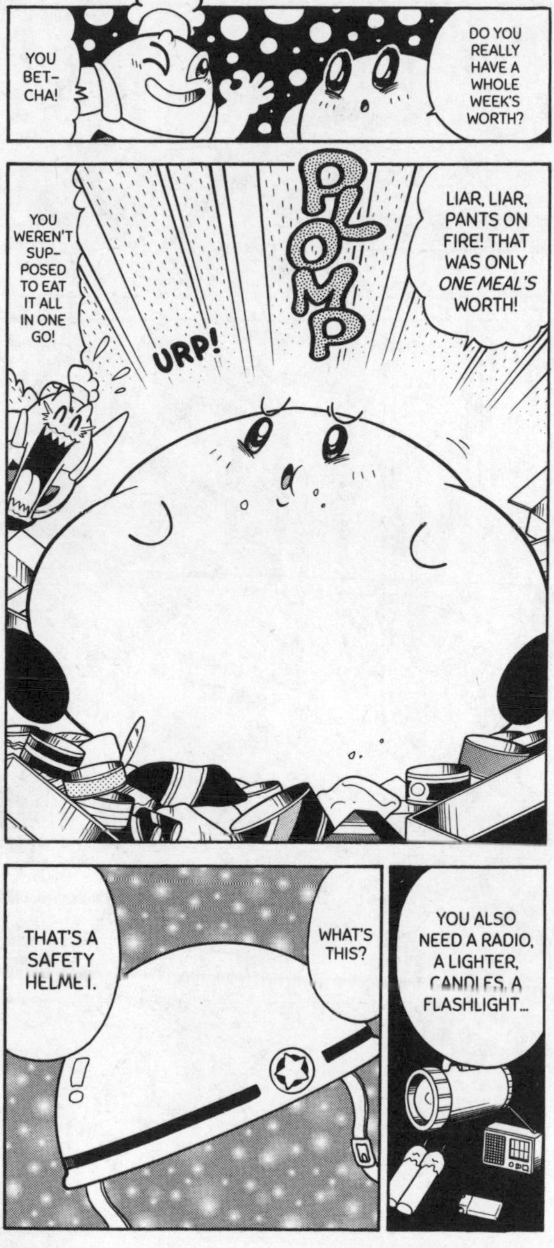
DO YOU REALLY HAVE A WHOLE WEEK'S WORTH?
YOU BET-CHA!
LIAR, LIAR, PANTS ON FIRE! THAT WAS ONLY *ONE MEAL'S* WORTH!
PLOMP
YOU WEREN'T SUP-POSED TO EAT IT ALL IN ONE GO!
URP!
YOU ALSO NEED A RADIO, A LIGHTER, CANDLES, A FLASHLIGHT...
WHAT'S THIS?
THAT'S A SAFETY HELMET.
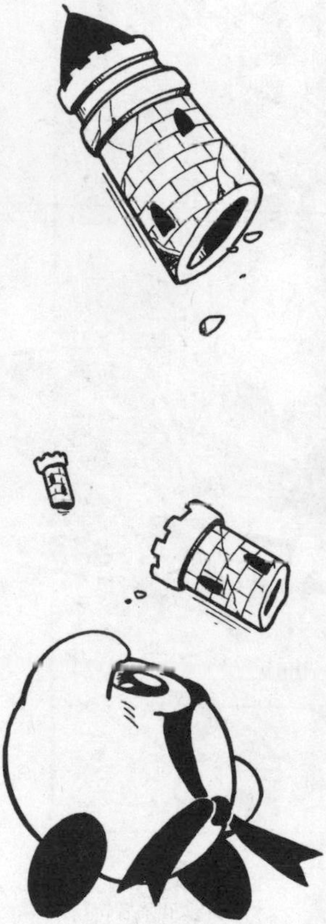

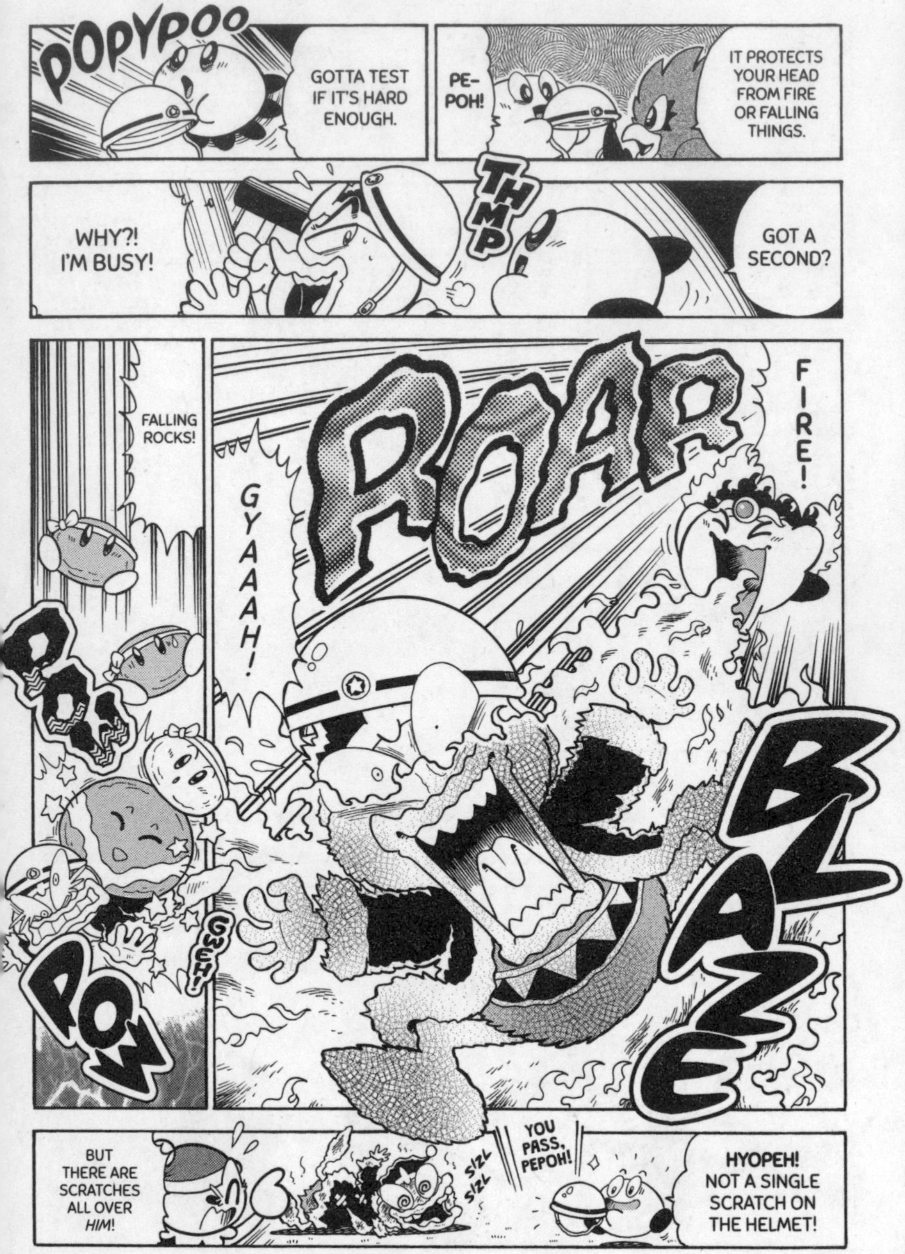
IT PROTECTS YOUR HEAD FROM FIRE OR FALLING THINGS.
PE-POH!
GOTTA TEST IF IT'S HARD ENOUGH.
POPYPOO
GOT A SECOND?
THMP
WHY?! I'M BUSY!
FIRE!
ROAR
GYAAAAH!
BLAZE
FALLING ROCKS!
POW
GWEH!
POW
HYOPEH! NOT A SINGLE SCRATCH ON THE HELMET!
YOU PASS, PEPOH!
S'IZL S'IZL
BUT THERE ARE SCRATCHES ALL OVER *HIM*!

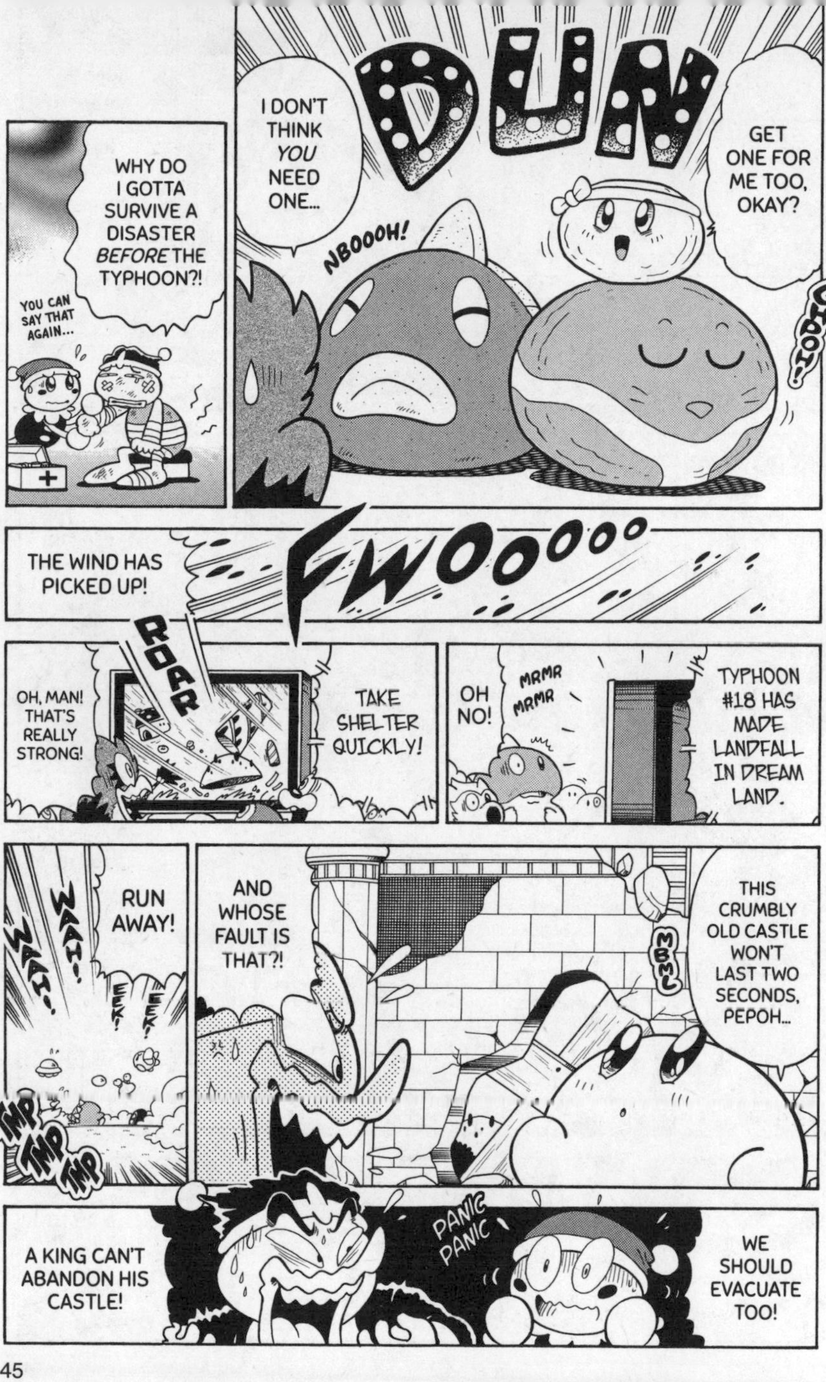
GET ONE FOR ME TOO, OKAY?
CHOOOH!
DUN
I DON'T THINK *YOU* NEED ONE...
NBOOOH!
WHY DO I GOTTA SURVIVE A DISASTER *BEFORE* THE TYPHOON?!
YOU CAN SAY THAT AGAIN...
FWOOOOO
THE WIND HAS PICKED UP!
TYPHOON #18 HAS MADE LANDFALL IN DREAM LAND.
MRMR MRMR
OH NO!
TAKE SHELTER QUICKLY!
ROAR
OH, MAN! THAT'S REALLY STRONG!
THIS CRUMBLY OLD CASTLE WON'T LAST TWO SECONDS, PEPOH...
MBML
AND WHOSE FAULT IS THAT?!
RUN AWAY!
WAAH!
EEK! EEK!
WAAH!
TMP TMP TMP
WE SHOULD EVACUATE TOO!
PANIC PANIC
A KING CAN'T ABANDON HIS CASTLE!

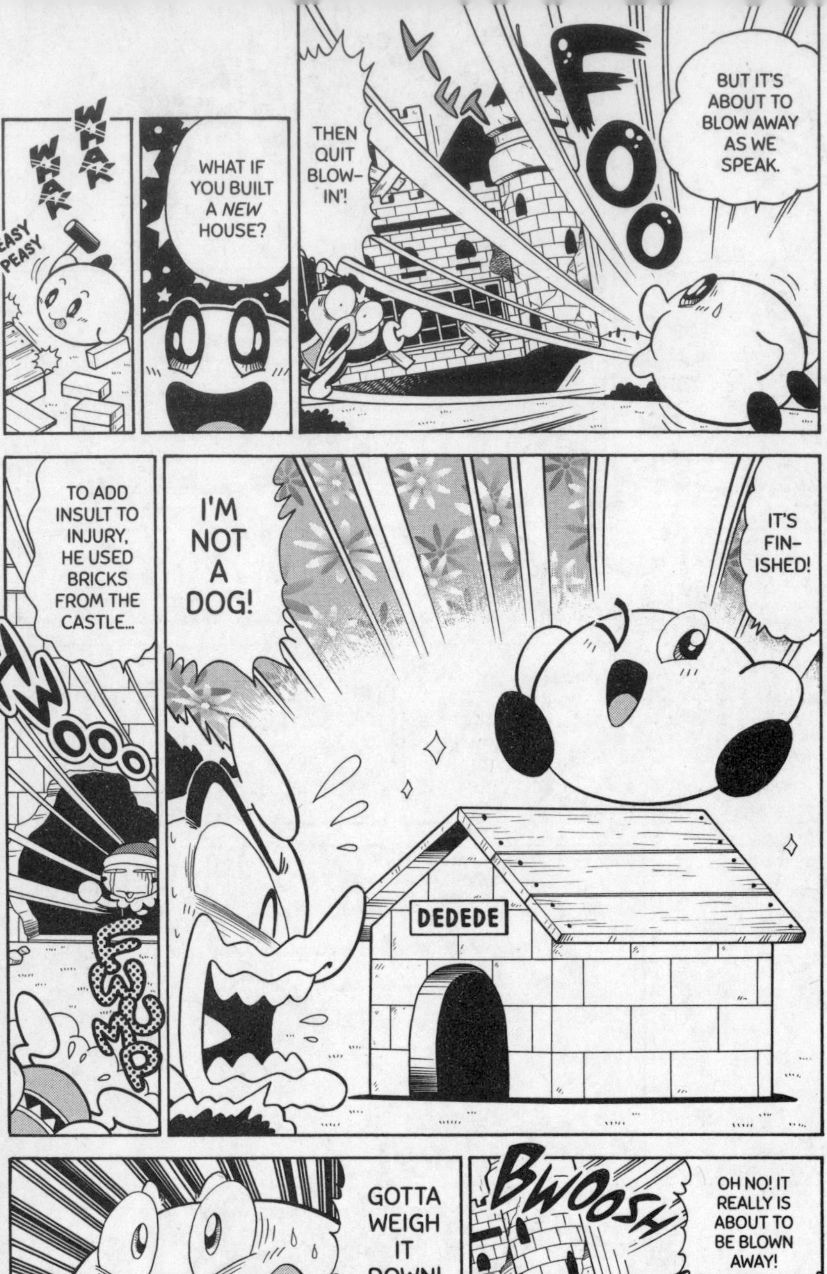
BUT IT'S ABOUT TO BLOW AWAY AS WE SPEAK.
FOOO
THEN QUIT BLOW-IN'!
WHAT IF YOU BUILT A *NEW* HOUSE?
WHAK WHAK
EASY PEASY
IT'S FIN-ISHED!
DEDEDE
I'M NOT A DOG!
TO ADD INSULT TO INJURY, HE USED BRICKS FROM THE CASTLE...
TWOOOO
OH NO! IT REALLY IS ABOUT TO BE BLOWN AWAY!
BWOOSH
TILT
GOTTA WEIGH IT DOWN!

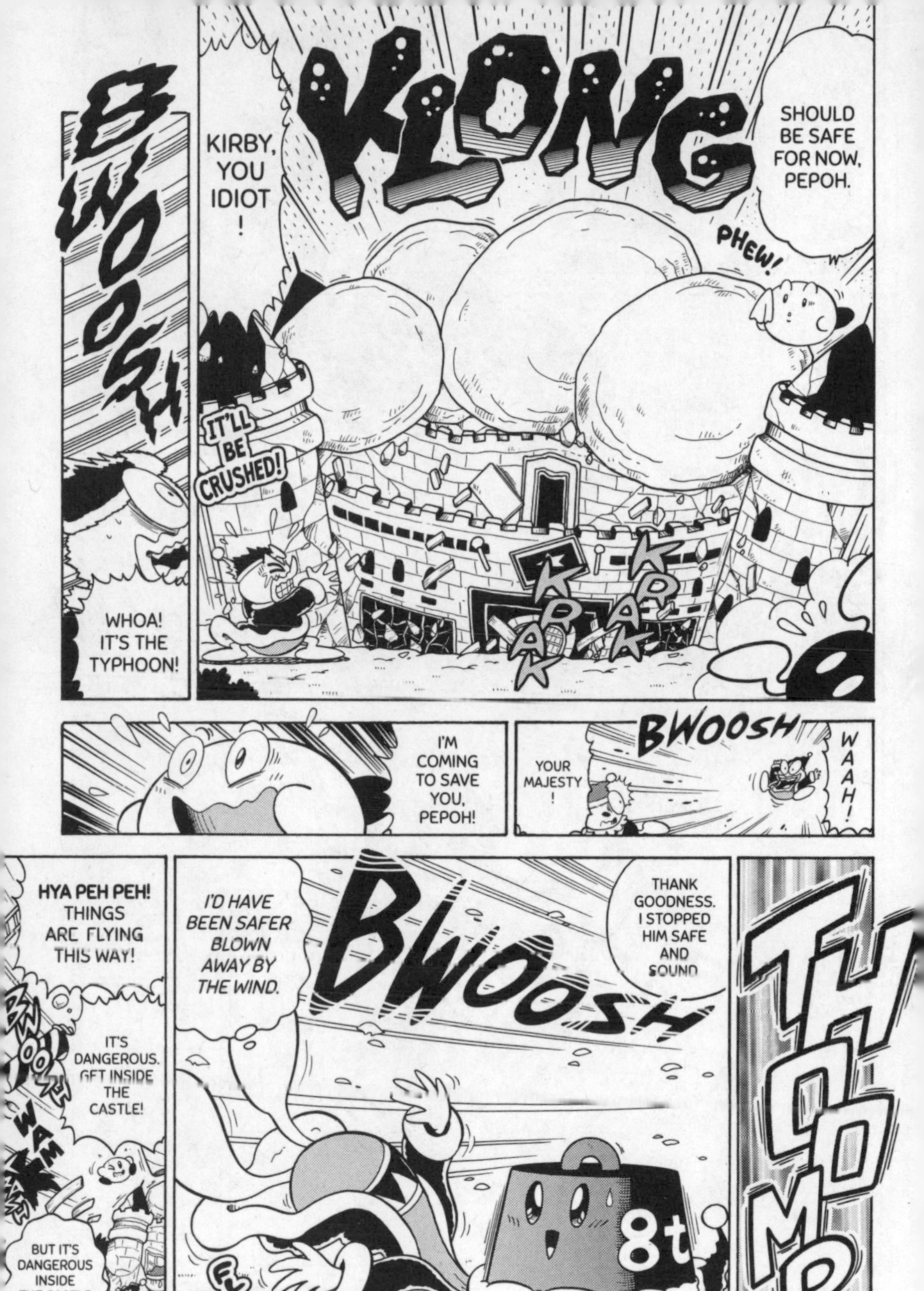
KLONG
SHOULD BE SAFE FOR NOW, PEPOH.
PHEW!
KIRBY, YOU IDIOT!
IT'LL BE CRUSHED!
KRAK
KRAK
BWOOSH
WHOA! IT'S THE TYPHOON!
BWOOSH
WAAAH!
YOUR MAJESTY!
I'M COMING TO SAVE YOU, PEPOH!
THOOOMP
THANK GOODNESS. I STOPPED HIM SAFE AND SOUND
BWOOSH
I'D HAVE BEEN SAFER BLOWN AWAY BY THE WIND.
8t
HYA PEH PEH! THINGS ARE FLYING THIS WAY!
BWOOOSH
IT'S DANGEROUS. GET INSIDE THE CASTLE!
WAM
WAM
BUT IT'S DANGEROUS INSIDE THE CASTLE TOO!

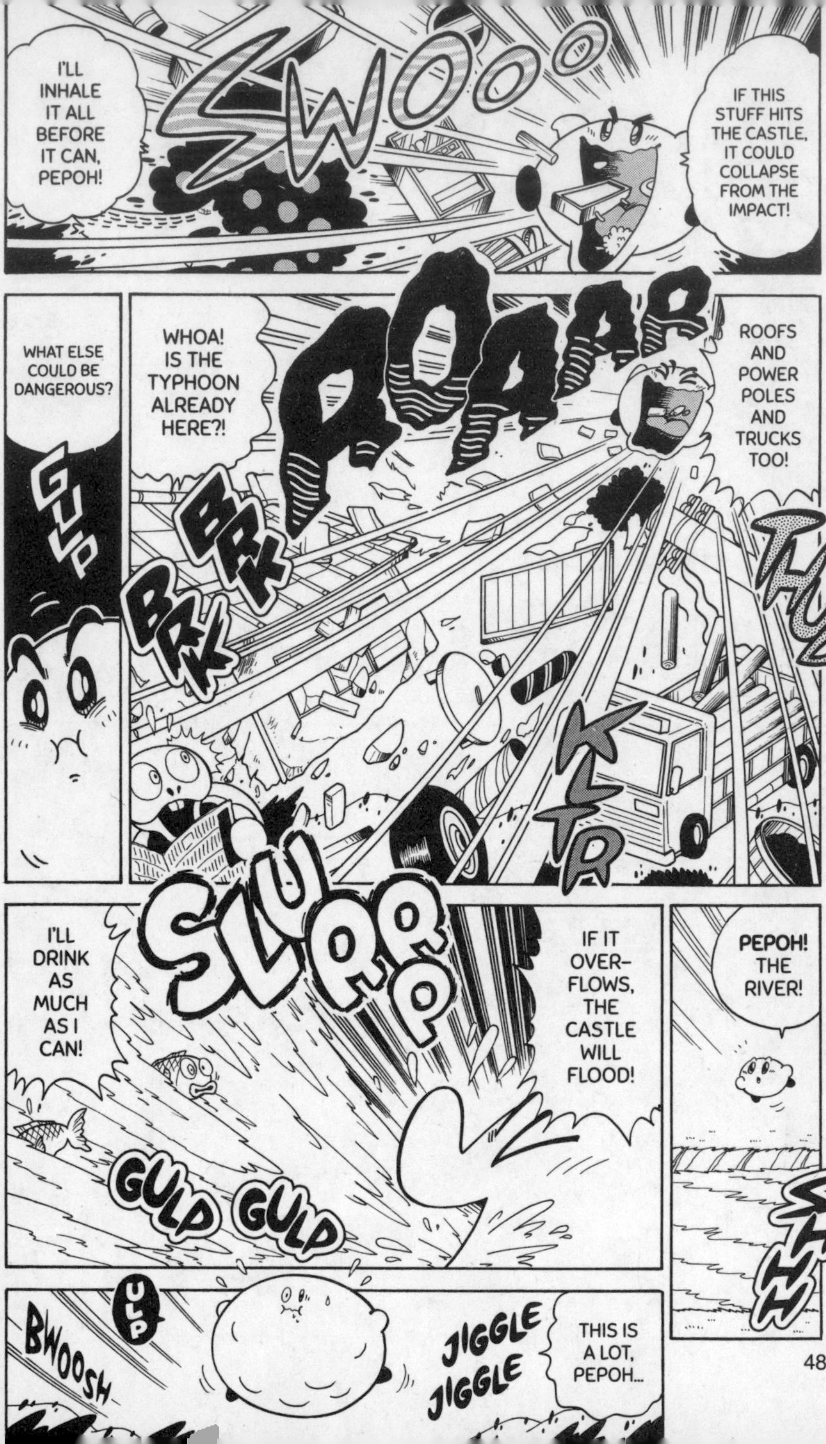
IF THIS STUFF HITS THE CASTLE, IT COULD COLLAPSE FROM THE IMPACT!
SWOOO
I'LL INHALE IT ALL BEFORE IT CAN, PEPOH!
ROOFS AND POWER POLES AND TRUCKS TOO!
ROAAR
WHOA! IS THE TYPHOON ALREADY HERE?!
THUD
BRK
BRK
KLTR
WHAT ELSE COULD BE DANGEROUS?
GULP
PEPOH! THE RIVER!
SHHHH
IF IT OVER-FLOWS, THE CASTLE WILL FLOOD!
SLURP
I'LL DRINK AS MUCH AS I CAN!
GULP GULP
THIS IS A LOT, PEPOH...
JIGGLE JIGGLE
ULP
BWOOSH

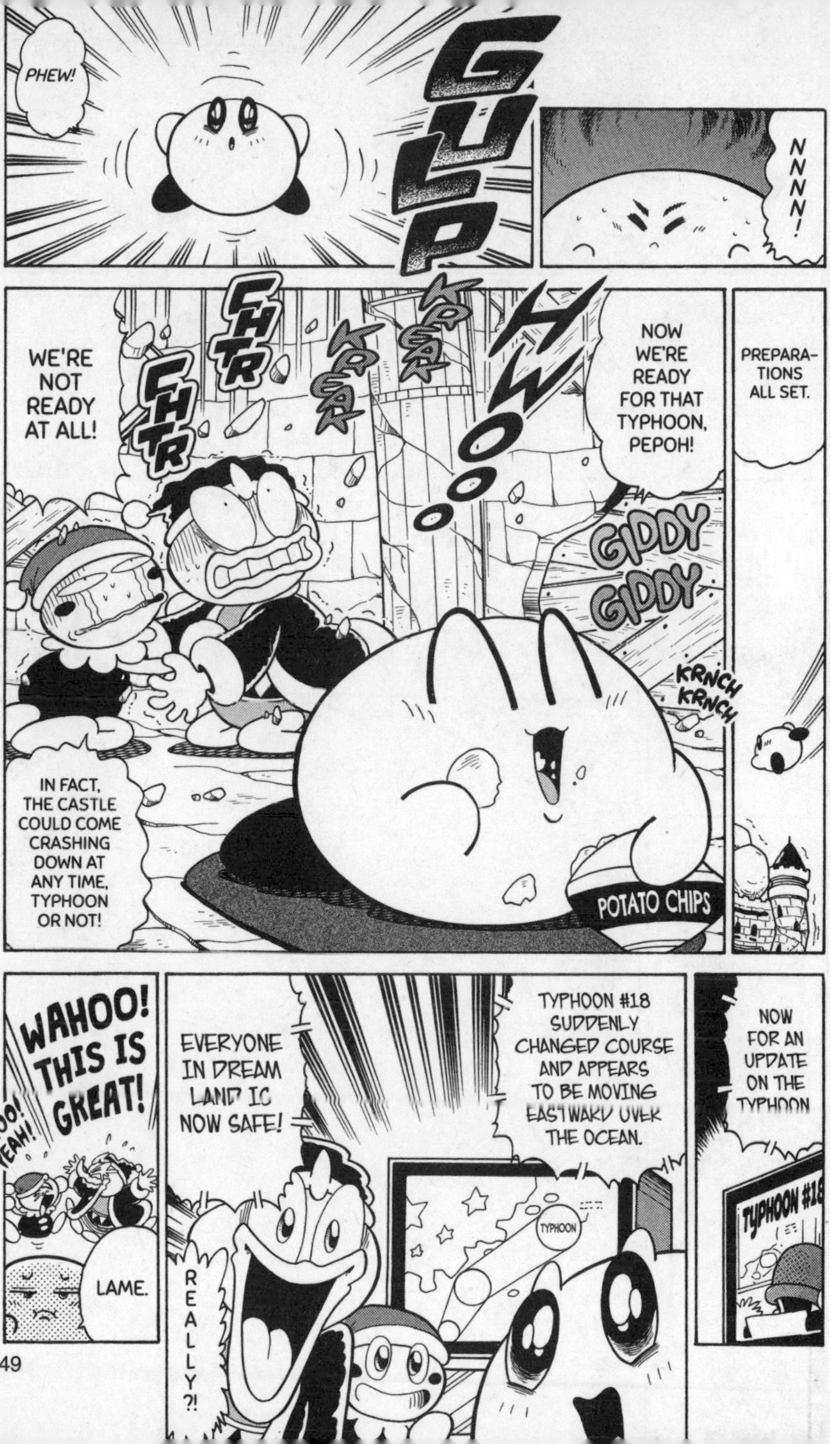
NNNN!
GULP
PHEW!
PREPARATIONS ALL SET.
HWOOOO
KREAK KREAK
NOW WE'RE READY FOR THAT TYPHOON, PEPOH!
GIDDY GIDDY
KRNCH KRNCH
CHTR CHTR
WE'RE NOT READY AT ALL!
IN FACT, THE CASTLE COULD COME CRASHING DOWN AT ANY TIME, TYPHOON OR NOT!
POTATO CHIPS
NOW FOR AN UPDATE ON THE TYPHOON
TYPHOON #18
TYPHOON #18 SUDDENLY CHANGED COURSE AND APPEARS TO BE MOVING EASTWARD OVER THE OCEAN.
EVERYONE IN DREAM LAND IS NOW SAFE!
TYPHOON
REALLY?!
WAHOO! THIS IS GREAT!
WOO! YEAH!
LAME.

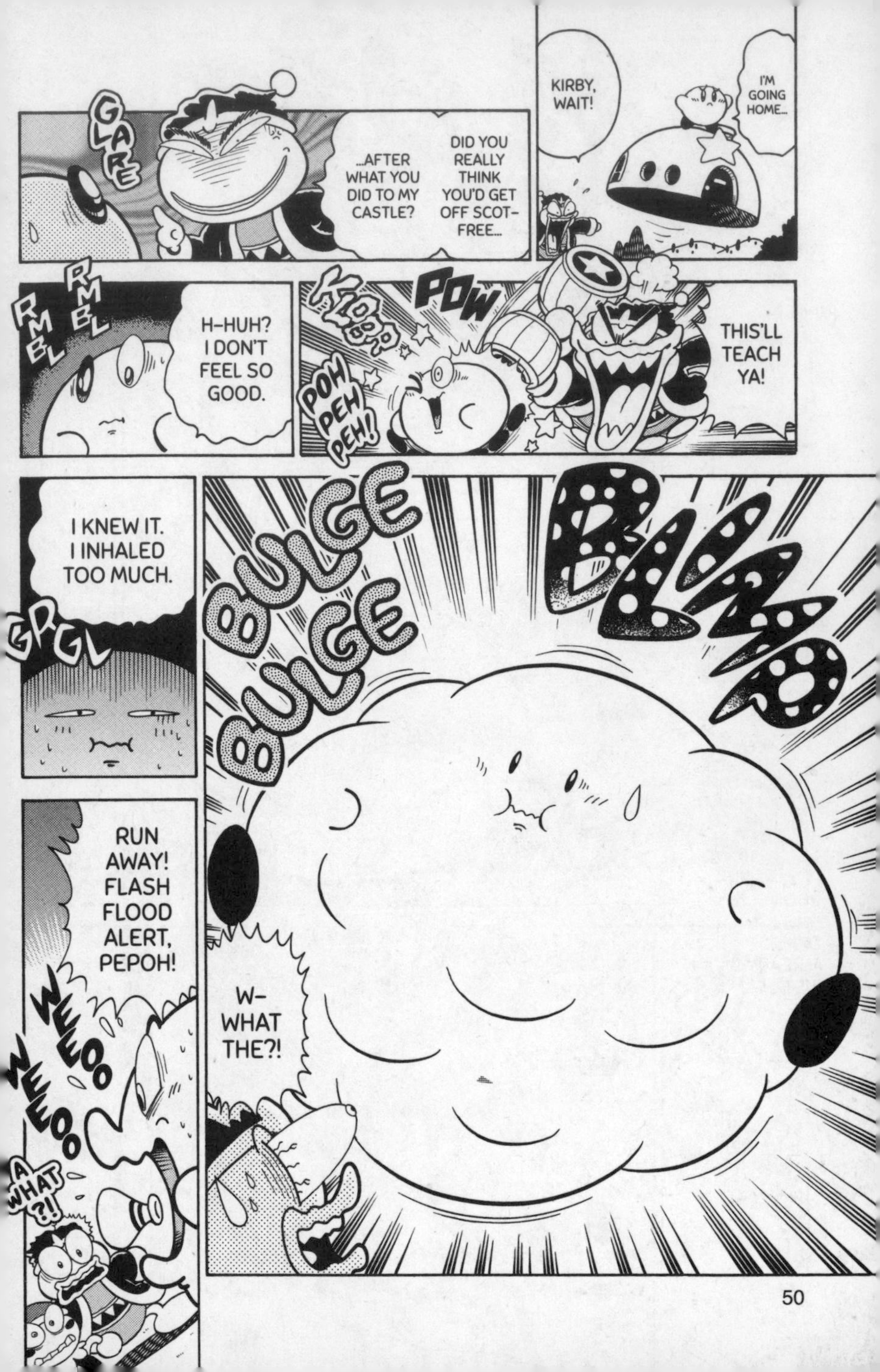
I'M GOING HOME...
KIRBY, WAIT!
DID YOU REALLY THINK YOU'D GET OFF SCOT-FREE...
...AFTER WHAT YOU DID TO MY CASTLE?
GLARE
THIS'LL TEACH YA!
POW
KLOBB
POH PEH PEH!
RMBL RMBL
H-HUH? I DON'T FEEL SO GOOD.
BLIMP
BULGE BULGE
W-WHAT THE?!
I KNEW IT. I INHALED TOO MUCH.
GRGL
RUN AWAY! FLASH FLOOD ALERT, PEPOH!
WEEOO WEEOO
A WHAT?!

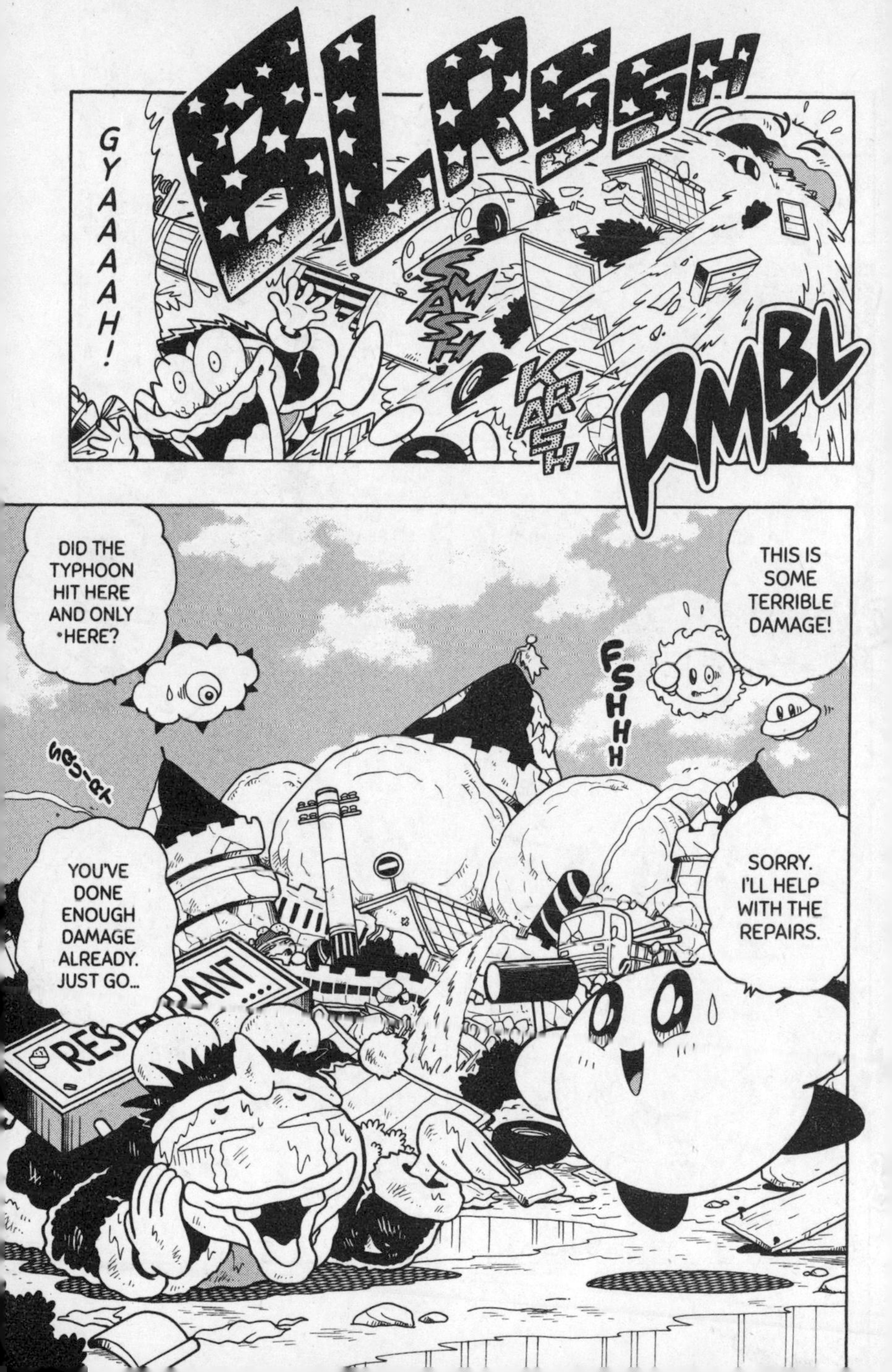
BLRSSH
GYAAAAAH!
SMASH
KRASH
RMBL
THIS IS SOME TERRIBLE DAMAGE!
FSHHH
DID THE TYPHOON HIT HERE AND ONLY HERE?
SORRY. I'LL HELP WITH THE REPAIRS.
YOU'VE DONE ENOUGH DAMAGE ALREADY. JUST GO...

MAKE-BELIEVE BROTHER 1

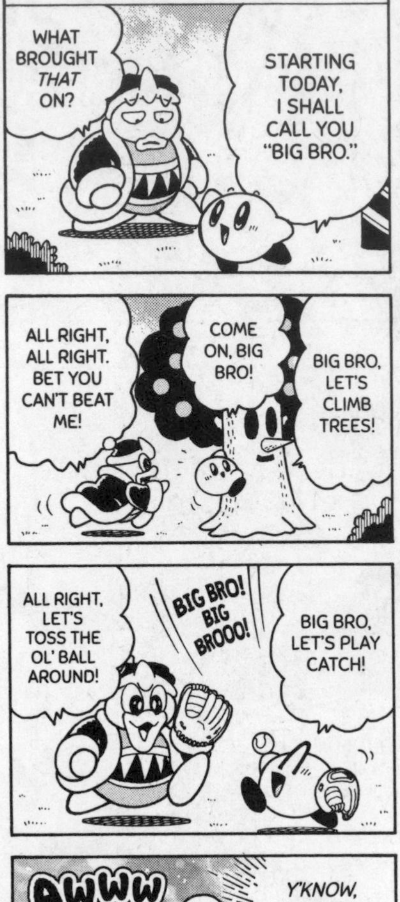
STARTING TODAY, I SHALL CALL YOU "BIG BRO."
WHAT BROUGHT *THAT* ON?
BIG BRO, LET'S CLIMB TREES!
COME ON, BIG BRO!
ALL RIGHT, ALL RIGHT. BET YOU CAN'T BEAT ME!
BIG BRO, LET'S PLAY CATCH!
BIG BRO! BIG BROOO!
ALL RIGHT, LET'S TOSS THE OL' BALL AROUND!
Y'KNOW, I THINK I COULD GET USED TO THIS.
AWWW

MAKE-BELIEVE BROTHER 2

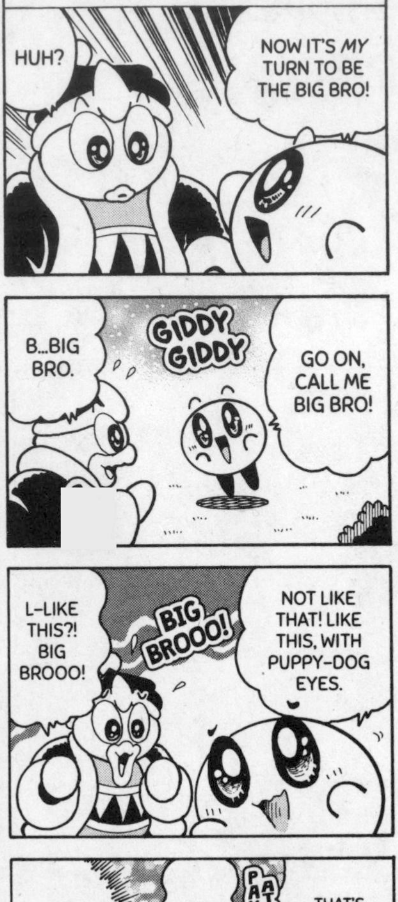
NOW IT'S *MY* TURN TO BE THE BIG BRO!
HUH?
GO ON, CALL ME BIG BRO!
GIDDY GIDDY
B...BIG BRO.
NOT LIKE THAT! LIKE THIS, WITH PUPPY-DOG EYES.
BIG BROOO!
L-LIKE THIS?! BIG BROOO!
THAT'S NOT RIGHT! HOW MANY TIMES DO I HAVE TO TELL YOU?!
PAY ATTENTION!
BIG BROOO !
WIGL WIGL
THIS HAS LOST ITS APPEAL.

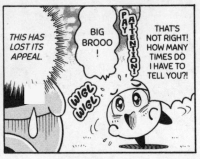

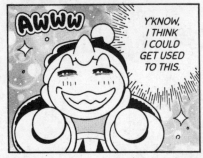

CHAPTER 4: BODY DOUBLE KAPAR, PROTECT KING DEDEDE!

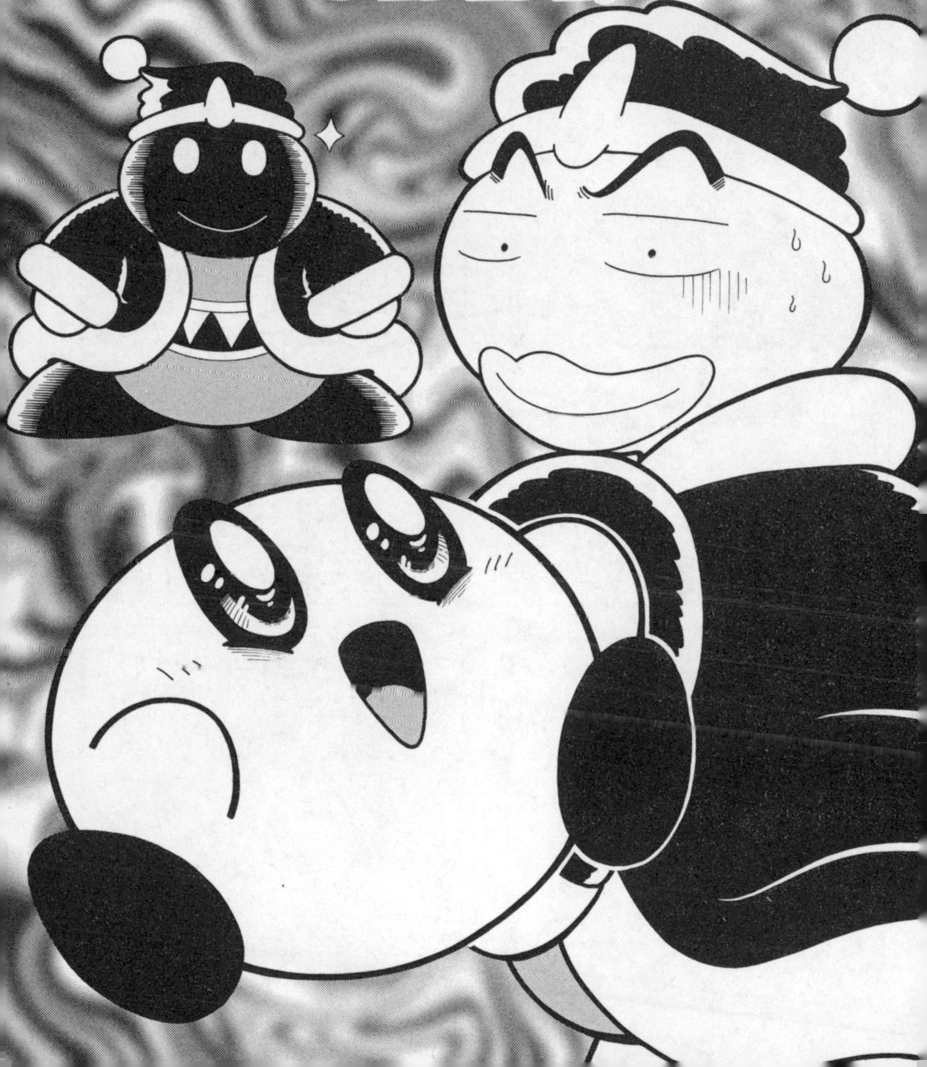

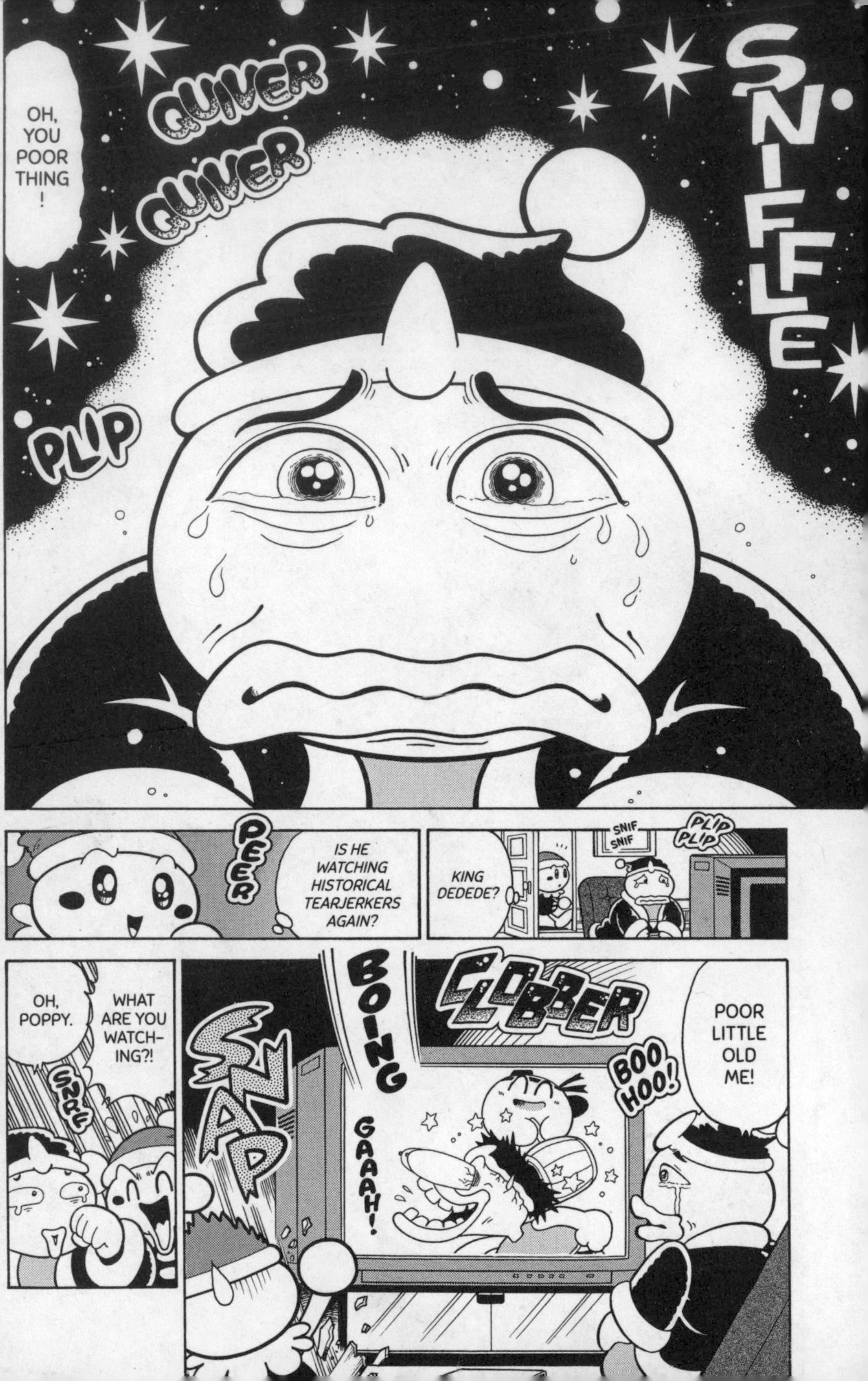
SNIFFLE
QUIVER QUIVER
OH, YOU POOR THING!
PLIP
PLIP PLIP
SNIF SNIF
KING DEDEDE?
IS HE WATCHING HISTORICAL TEARJERKERS AGAIN?
PEER
POOR LITTLE OLD ME!
BOO HOO!
CLOBBER
BOING
SNAP
GAAAH!
WHAT ARE YOU WATCH-ING?!
OH, POPPY.
SNRF

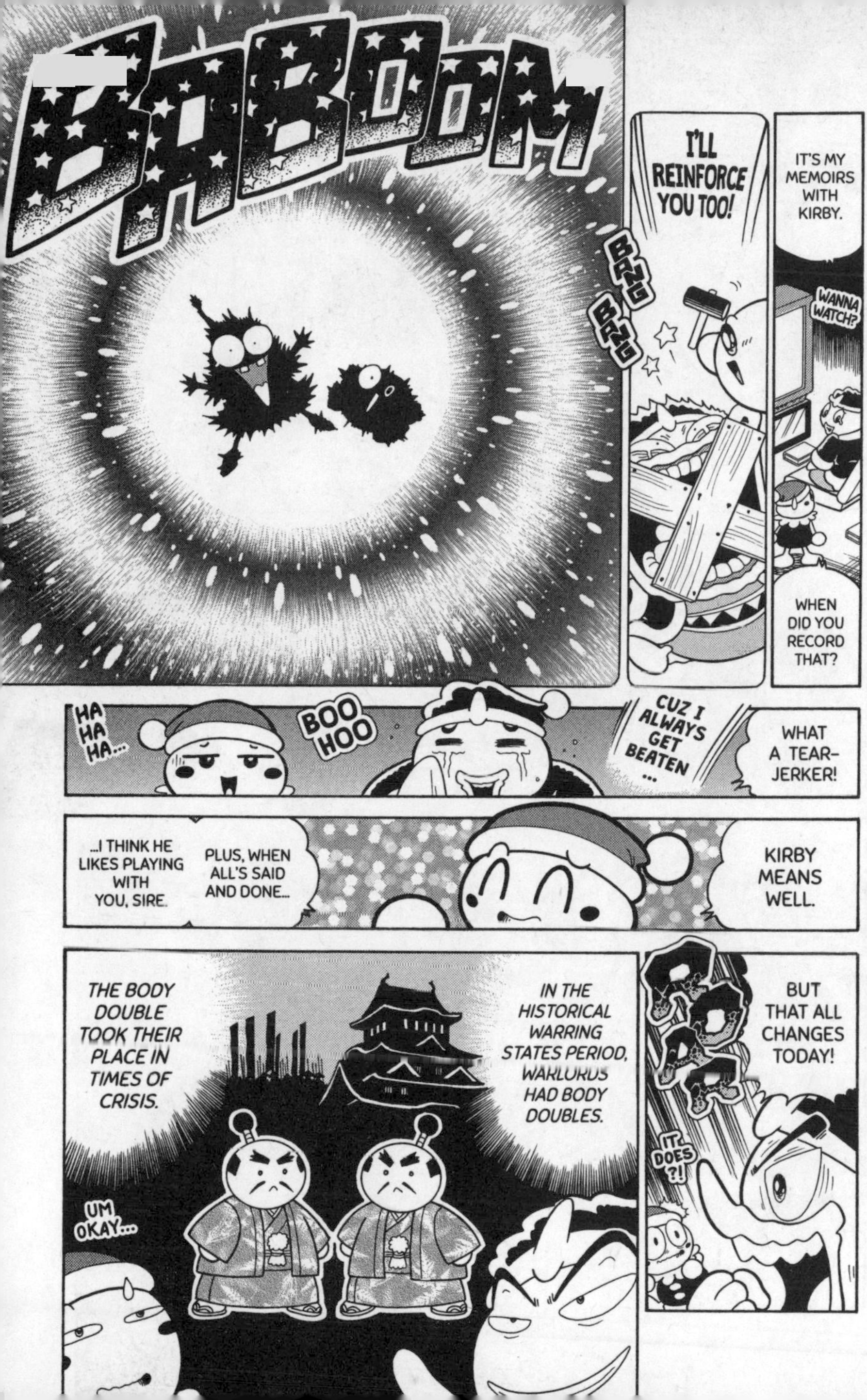
IT'S MY MEMOIRS WITH KIRBY.
WANNA WATCH?
WHEN DID YOU RECORD THAT?
I'LL REINFORCE YOU TOO!
BANG BANG
BABOOM
WHAT A TEAR-JERKER!
CUZ I ALWAYS GET BEATEN...
BOO HOO
HA HA HA...
KIRBY MEANS WELL.
PLUS, WHEN ALL'S SAID AND DONE...
...I THINK HE LIKES PLAYING WITH YOU, SIRE.
BUT THAT ALL CHANGES TODAY!
IT DOES?!
IN THE HISTORICAL WARRING STATES PERIOD, WARLORDS HAD BODY DOUBLES.
THE BODY DOUBLE TOOK THEIR PLACE IN TIMES OF CRISIS.
UM OKAY...

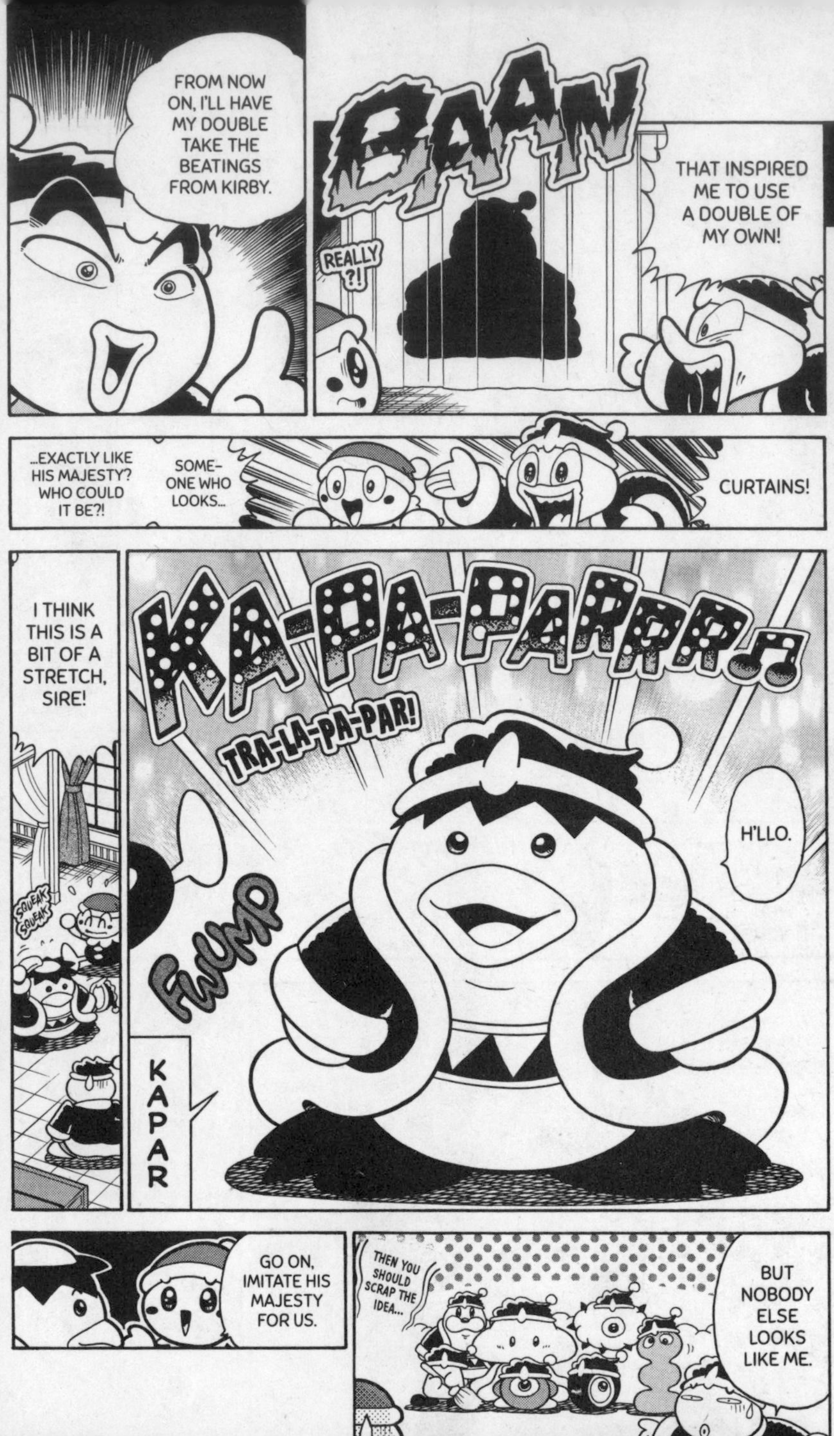
THAT INSPIRED ME TO USE A DOUBLE OF MY OWN!
BAAN
REALLY ?!
FROM NOW ON, I'LL HAVE MY DOUBLE TAKE THE BEATINGS FROM KIRBY.
CURTAINS!
SOME-ONE WHO LOOKS...
...EXACTLY LIKE HIS MAJESTY? WHO COULD IT BE?!
KA-PA-PARRR♫
TRA-LA-PA-PAR!
H'LLO.
FWUMP
KAPAR
I THINK THIS IS A BIT OF A STRETCH, SIRE!
SQUEAK SQUEAK
BUT NOBODY ELSE LOOKS LIKE ME.
THEN YOU SHOULD SCRAP THE IDEA...
GO ON, IMITATE HIS MAJESTY FOR US.

AUTHOR'S COMMENT

WHAT IF SOMEONE WAS REPLACED BY THEIR DOUBLE? SCARY THOUGHT! I HAD A TOUGH TIME ON THIS ONE SINCE THERE WASN'T A CHARACTER WHO RESEMBLED KING DEDEDE.

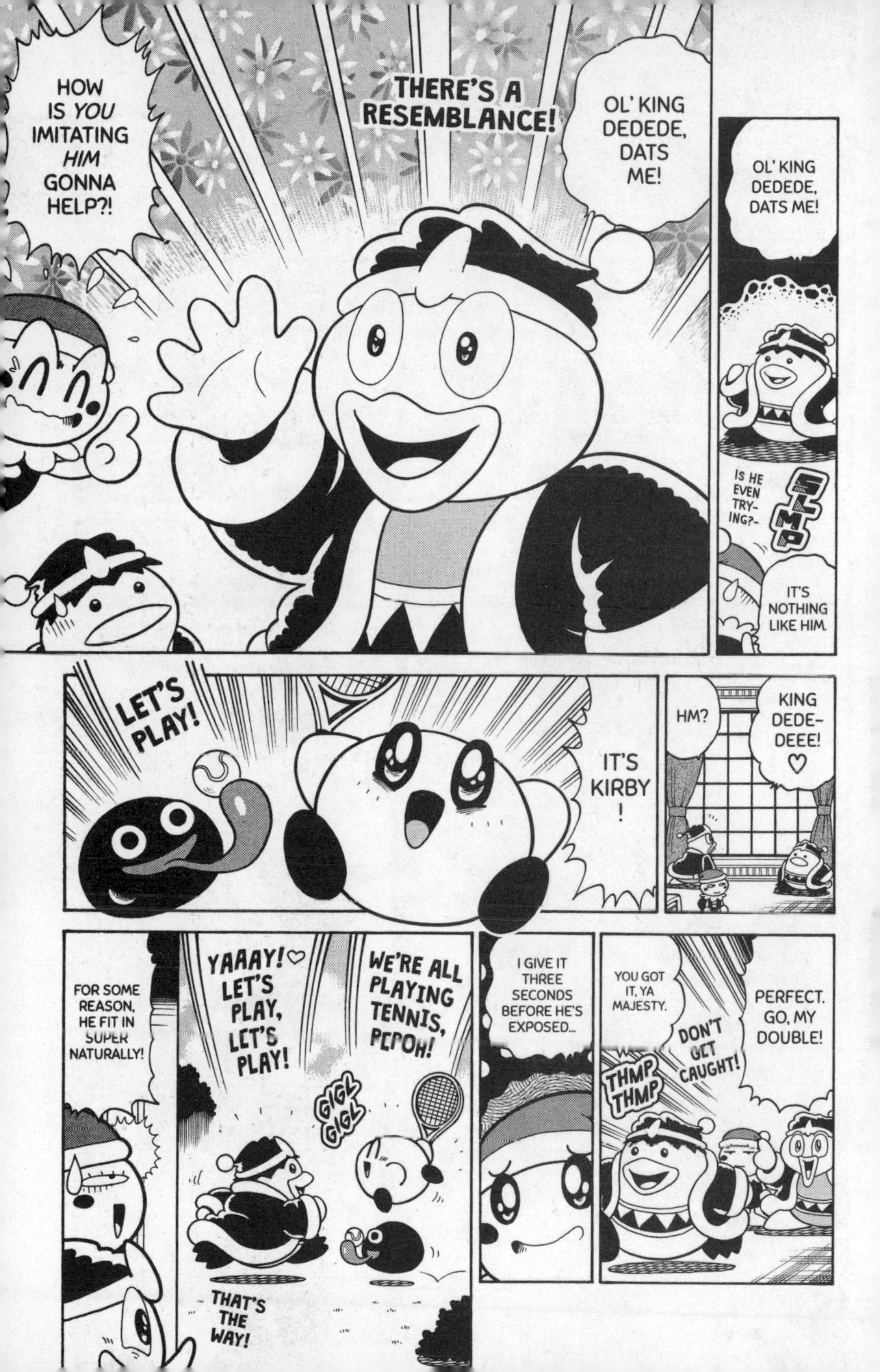
OL' KING DEDEDE, DATS ME!
IS HE EVEN TRYING?-
IT'S NOTHING LIKE HIM.
OL' KING DEDEDE, DATS ME!
THERE'S A RESEMBLANCE!
HOW IS *YOU* IMITATING *HIM* GONNA HELP?!
KING DEDE-DEEE! ♡
HM?
IT'S KIRBY!
LET'S PLAY!
PERFECT. GO, MY DOUBLE!
YOU GOT IT, YA MAJESTY.
DON'T GET CAUGHT!
THMP THMP
I GIVE IT THREE SECONDS BEFORE HE'S EXPOSED...
WE'RE ALL PLAYING TENNIS, PEPOH!
YAAAY! ♡ LET'S PLAY, LET'S PLAY!
GIGL GIGL
THAT'S THE WAY!
FOR SOME REASON, HE FIT IN SUPER NATURALLY!

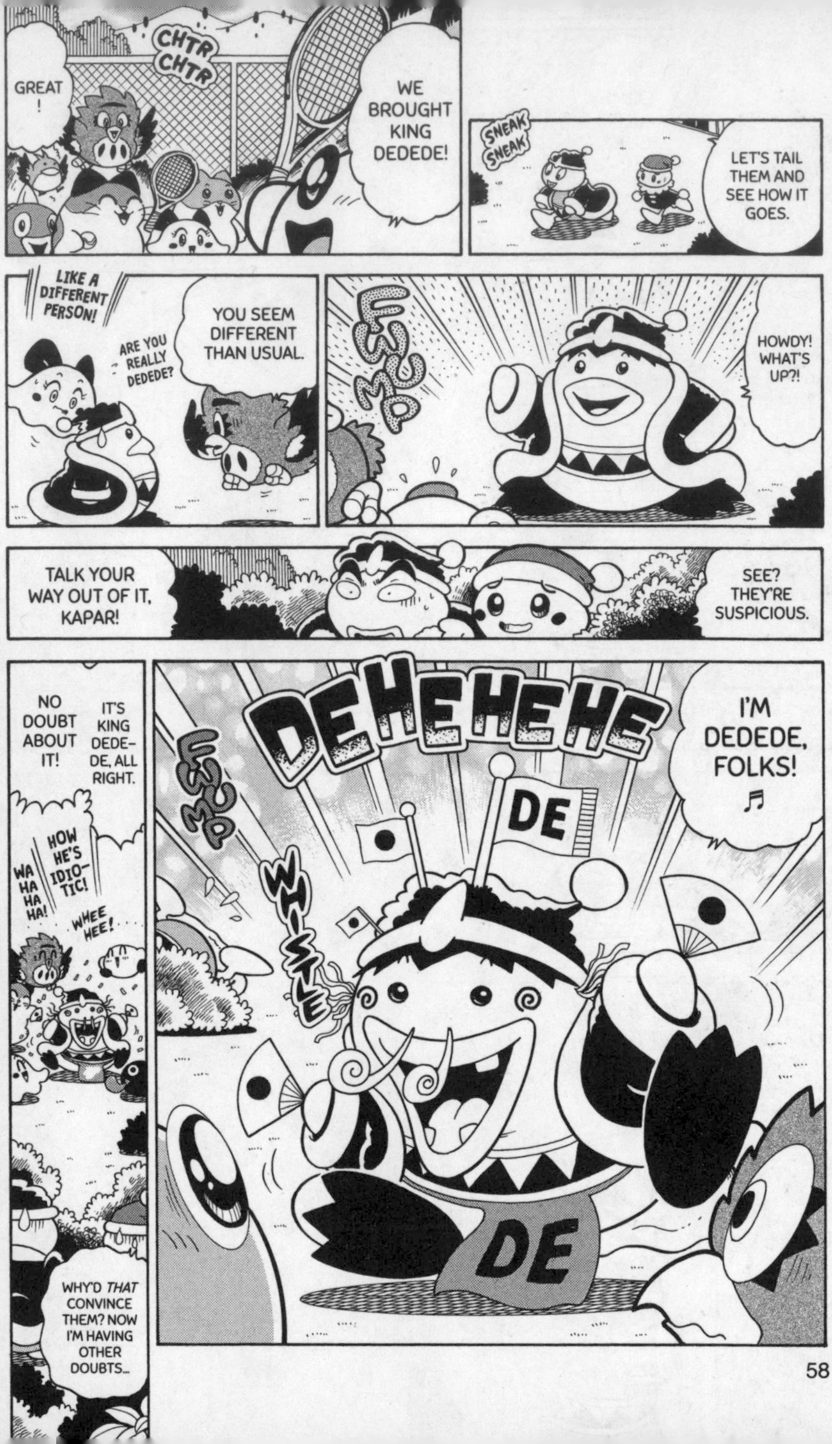
GREAT!
CHTR CHTR
WE BROUGHT KING DEDEDE!
SNEAK SNEAK
LET'S TAIL THEM AND SEE HOW IT GOES.
LIKE A DIFFERENT PERSON!
ARE YOU REALLY DEDEDE?
YOU SEEM DIFFERENT THAN USUAL.
FWUMP
HOWDY! WHAT'S UP?!
TALK YOUR WAY OUT OF IT, KAPAR!
SEE? THEY'RE SUSPICIOUS.
NO DOUBT ABOUT IT!
IT'S KING DEDE-DE, ALL RIGHT.
HOW HE'S IDIOTIC!
WA HA HA HA!
WHEE HEE!
WHY'D THAT CONVINCE THEM? NOW I'M HAVING OTHER DOUBTS...
DEHEHEHE
FWUMP
WHISTLE
DE
I'M DEDEDE, FOLKS! ♬
DE

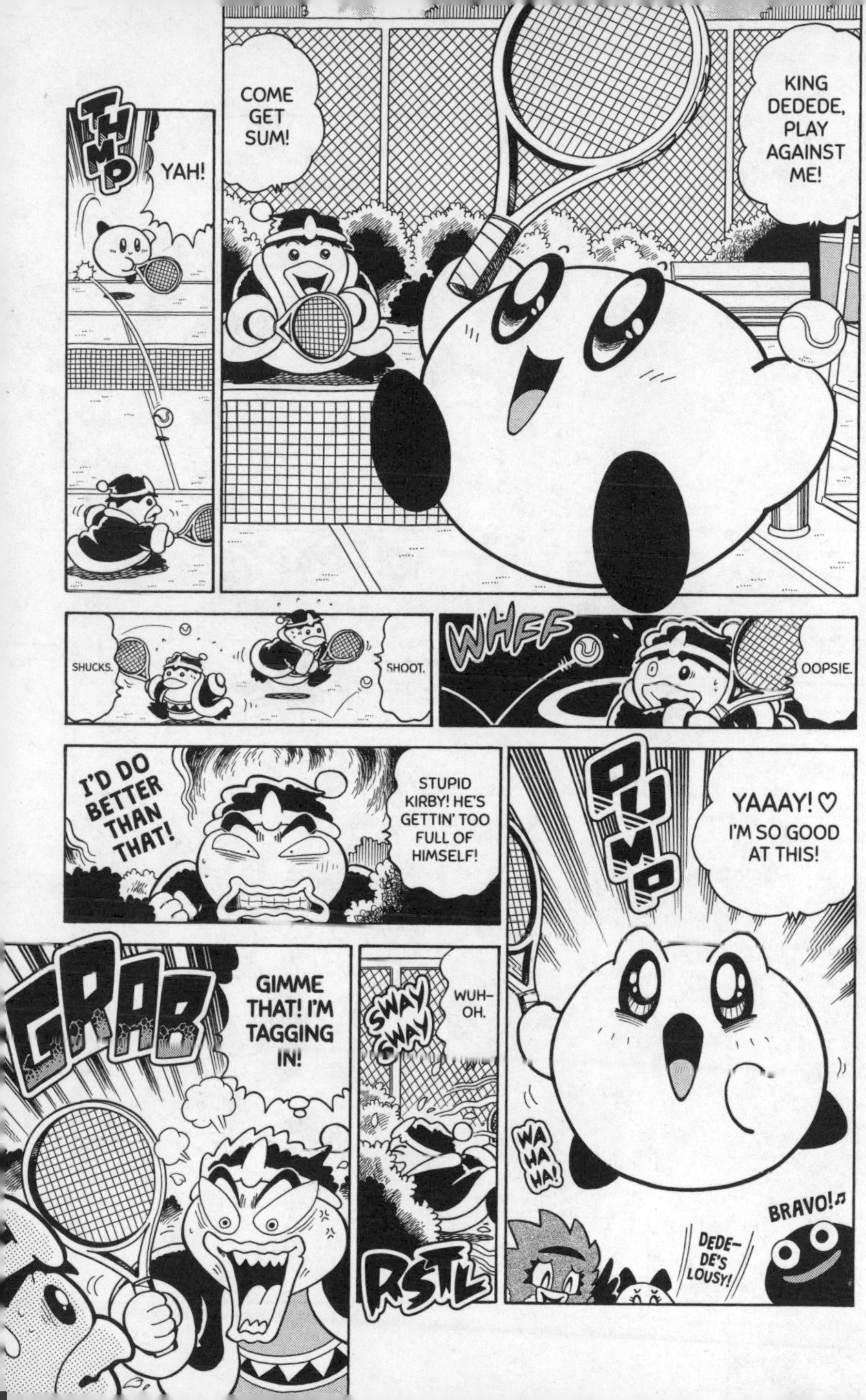
KING DEDEDE, PLAY AGAINST ME!
COME GET SUM!
THMP
YAH!
OOPSIE.
WHFF
SHOOT.
SHUCKS.
PUMP
YAAAY! ♡ I'M SO GOOD AT THIS!
BRAVO!♪
DEDE-DE'S LOUSY!
WA HA HA!
STUPID KIRBY! HE'S GETTIN' TOO FULL OF HIMSELF!
I'D DO BETTER THAN THAT!
WUH-OH.
SWAY SWAY
RSTL
GIMME THAT! I'M TAGGING IN!
GRAB

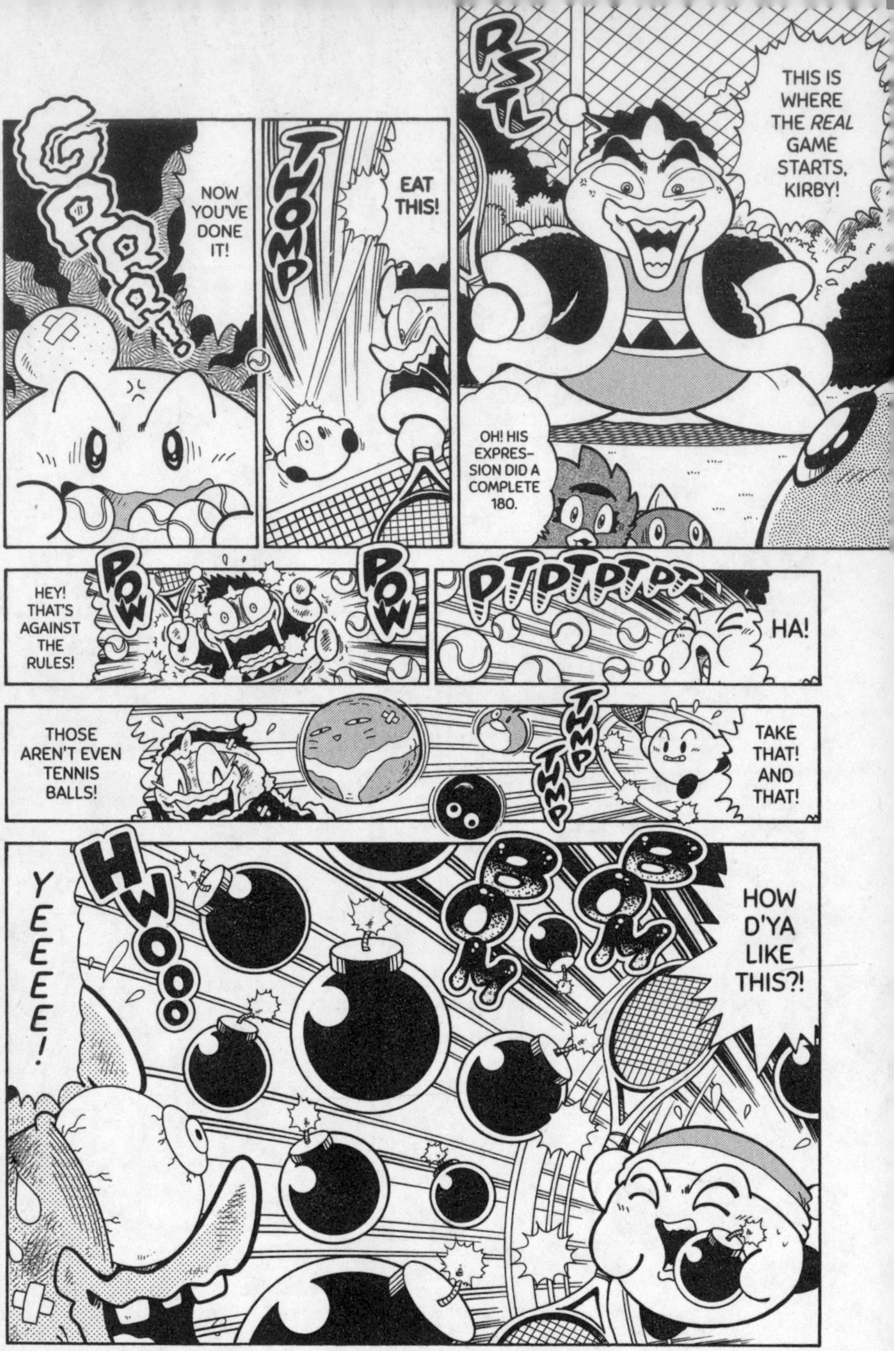
RSTL
THIS IS WHERE THE *REAL* GAME STARTS, KIRBY!
OH! HIS EXPRES-SION DID A COMPLETE 180.
THOMP
EAT THIS!
GRRR!!
NOW YOU'VE DONE IT!
PTPTPTPT
HA!
POW
POW
HEY! THAT'S AGAINST THE RULES!
TAKE THAT! AND THAT!
THMP
THMP
THOSE AREN'T EVEN TENNIS BALLS!
HOW D'YA LIKE THIS?!
BOOM
BOOM
HWOOO
YEEEEE!

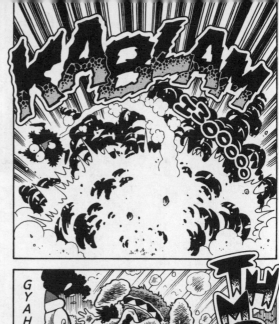

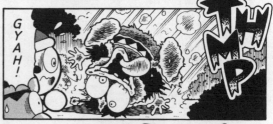

KABLAM
1300000
THUMP
GYAH!
KIRBY!
AH!
I GOT A LITTLE TOO WORKED UP...
SORRY, KING DEDEDE.
IT'S ALL GOOD. I'M FINE! ♡
WOW, NOT A SCRATCH ON HIM!
WHAT A TOUGH GUY!
WHEW!

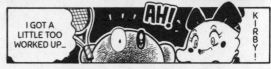

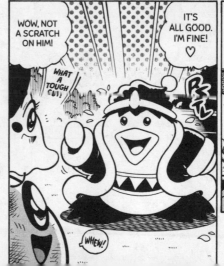

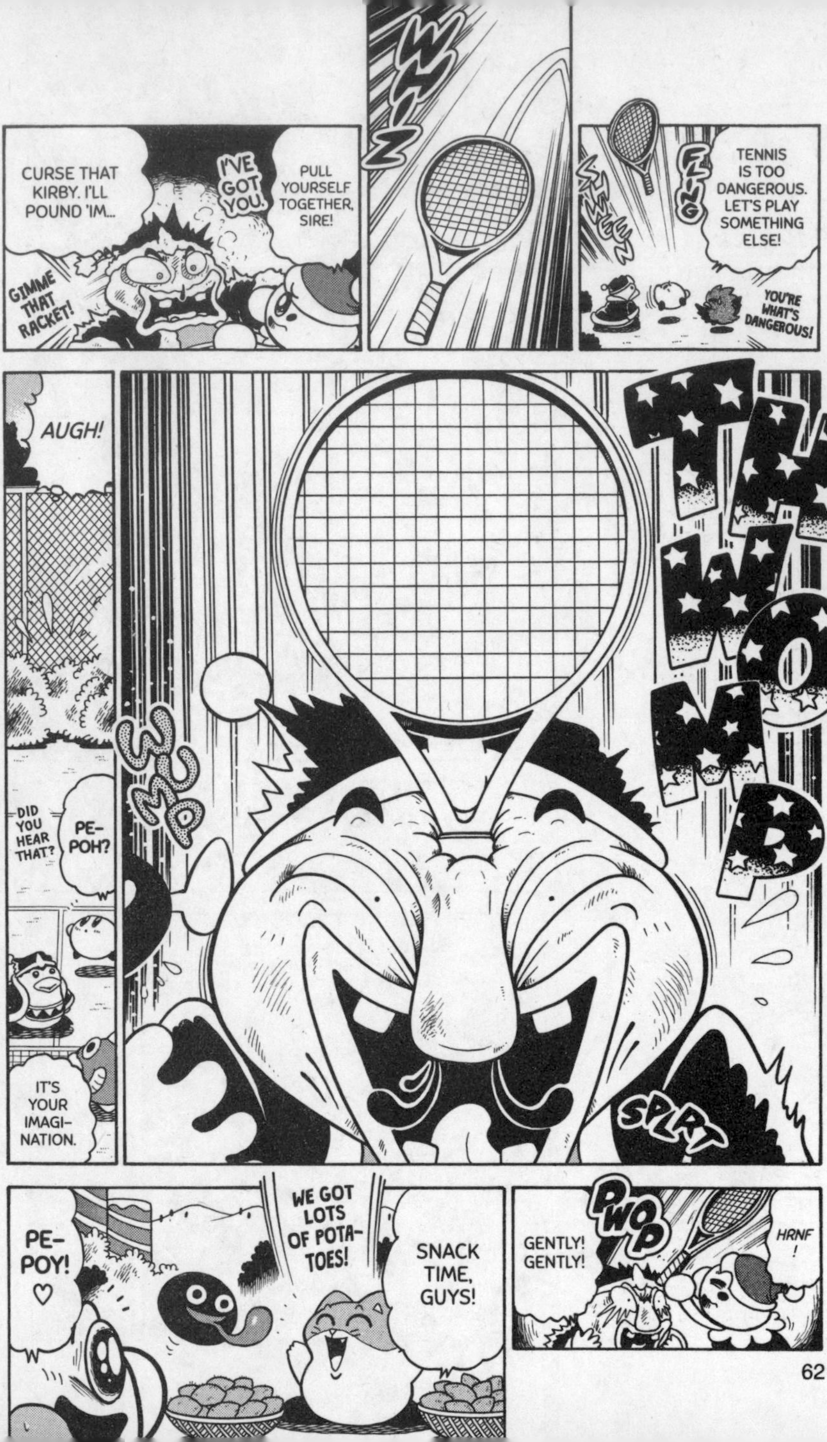
TENNIS IS TOO DANGEROUS. LET'S PLAY SOMETHING ELSE!
FLING
SHWEEN
YOU'RE WHAT'S DANGEROUS!
PULL YOURSELF TOGETHER, SIRE!
I'VE GOT YOU.
CURSE THAT KIRBY. I'LL POUND 'IM...
GIMME THAT RACKET!
THWOMP
SPLRT
AUGH!
PE-POH?
DID YOU HEAR THAT?
IT'S YOUR IMAGINATION.
PWOP
HRNF!
GENTLY! GENTLY!
SNACK TIME, GUYS!
WE GOT LOTS OF POTA-TOES!
PE-POY! ♡

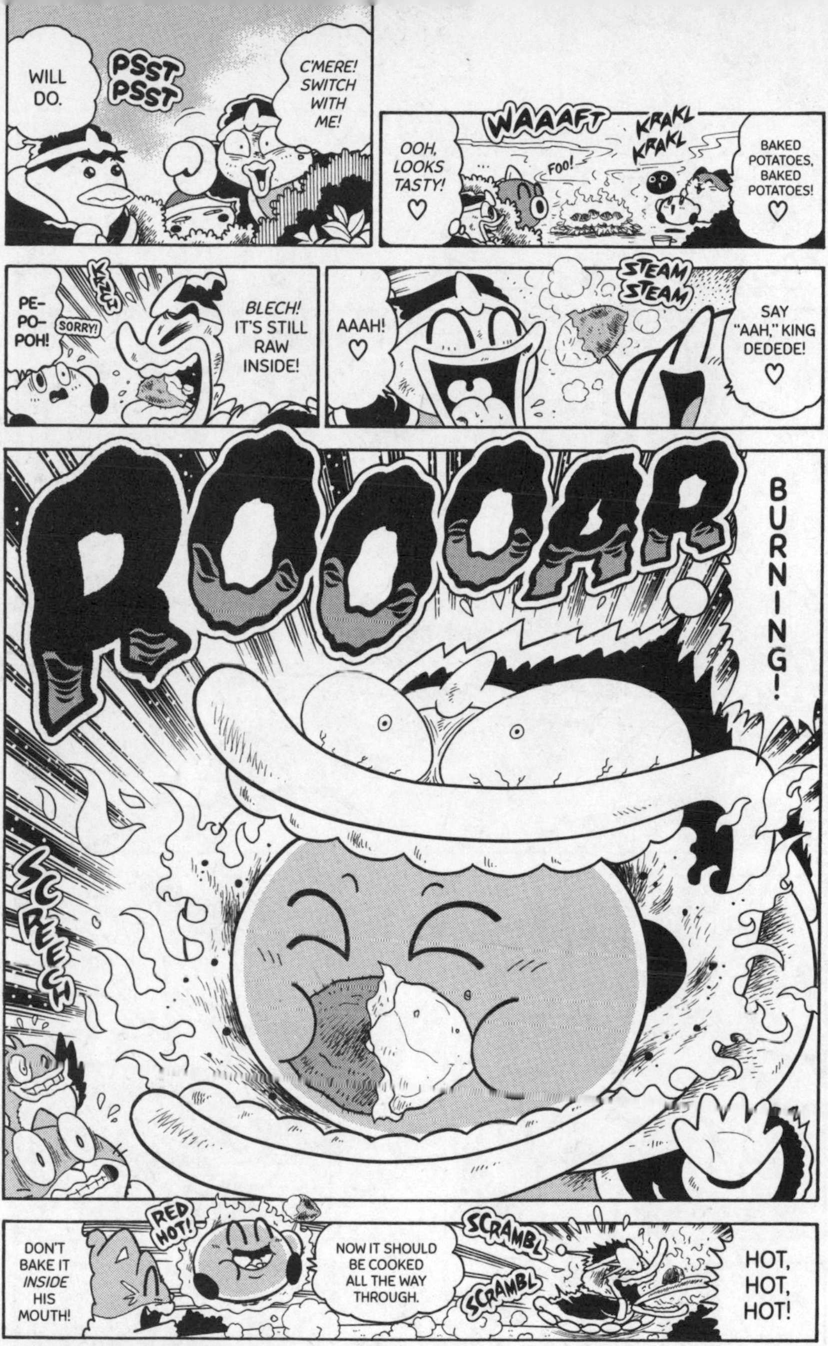
BAKED POTATOES, BAKED POTATOES! ♡
KRAKL KRAKL
FOO!
WAAAFT
OOH, LOOKS TASTY! ♡
...
C'MERE! SWITCH WITH ME!
PSST PSST
WILL DO.
SAY "AAH," KING DEDEDE! ♡
STEAM STEAM
AAAH! ♡
BLECH! IT'S STILL RAW INSIDE!
KRNCH
SORRY!
PE-PO-POH!
BURNING!
ROOOAR
SCREECH
HOT, HOT, HOT!
SCRAMBL
SCRAMBL
NOW IT SHOULD BE COOKED ALL THE WAY THROUGH.
RED HOT!
DON'T BAKE IT *INSIDE* HIS MOUTH!

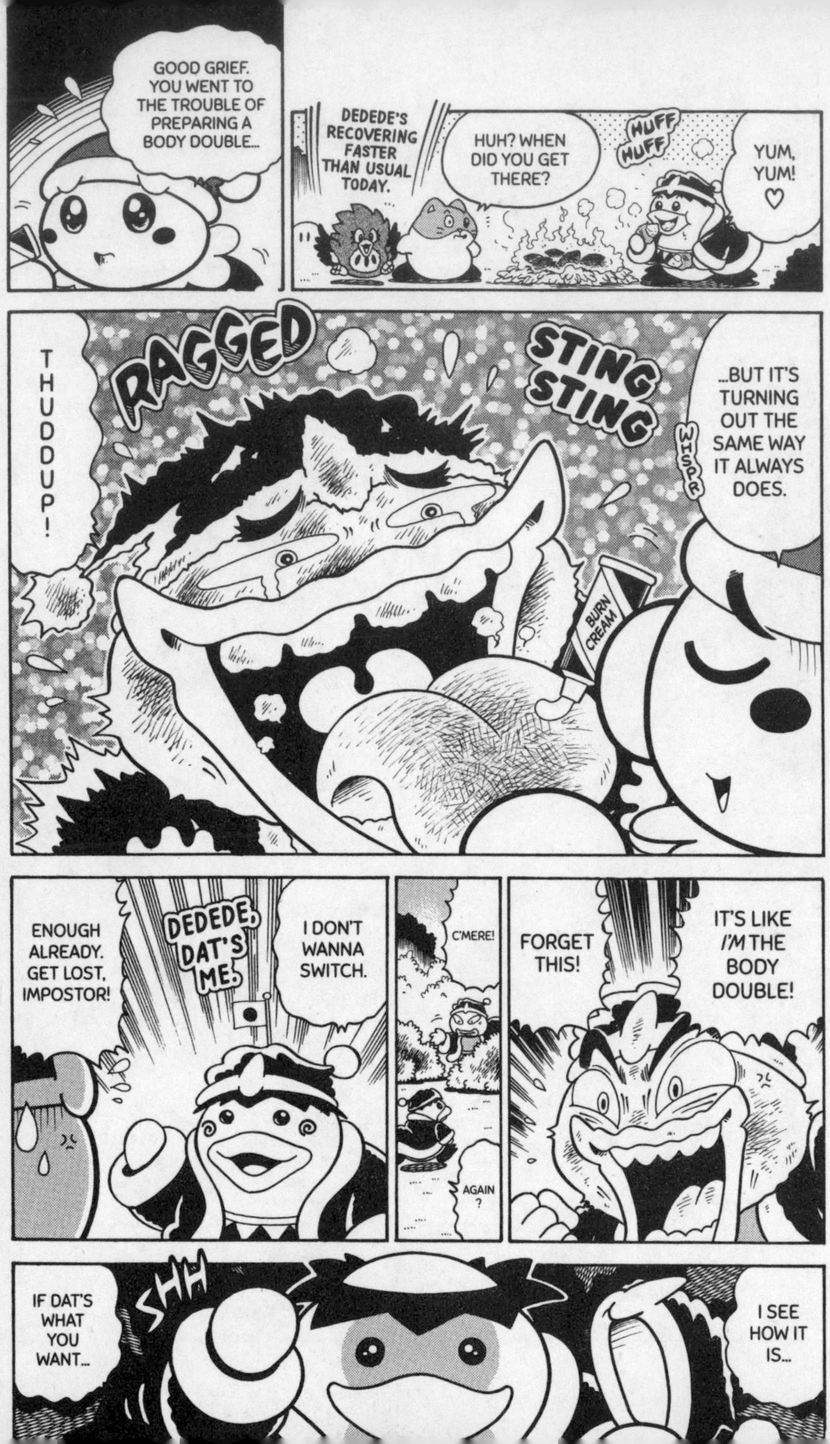
YUM, YUM! ♡
HUFF HUFF
HUH? WHEN DID YOU GET THERE?
DEDEDE'S RECOVERING FASTER THAN USUAL TODAY.
GOOD GRIEF. YOU WENT TO THE TROUBLE OF PREPARING A BODY DOUBLE...
...BUT IT'S TURNING OUT THE SAME WAY IT ALWAYS DOES.
WHSPR
STING STING
RAGGED
THUDDUP!
BURN CREAM
IT'S LIKE *I'M* THE BODY DOUBLE!
FORGET THIS!
C'MERE!
AGAIN?
I DON'T WANNA SWITCH.
DEDEDE, DAT'S ME.
ENOUGH ALREADY. GET LOST, IMPOSTOR!
I SEE HOW IT IS...
SHH
IF DAT'S WHAT YOU WANT...

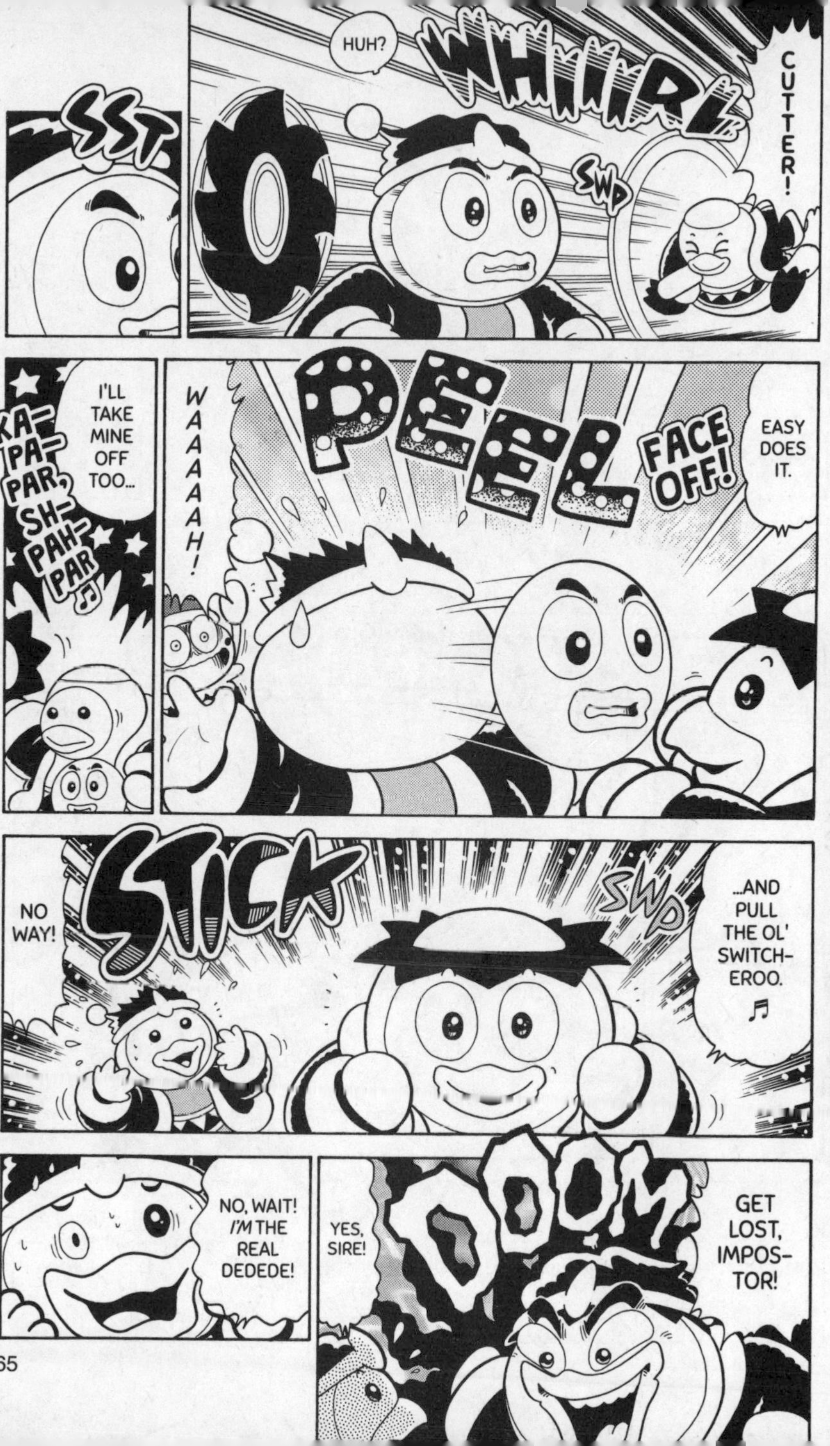
CUTTER!
WHIIIRL
HUH?
SWP
SST
EASY DOES IT.
FACE OFF!
PEEL
WAAAAAAH!
I'LL TAKE MINE OFF TOO...
KA-PA-PAR, SH-PAH-PAR ♫
...AND PULL THE OL' SWITCH-EROO. ♫
SWP
STICK
NO WAY!
GET LOST, IMPOSTOR!
DOOOM
YES, SIRE!
NO, WAIT! *I'M* THE REAL DEDEDE!

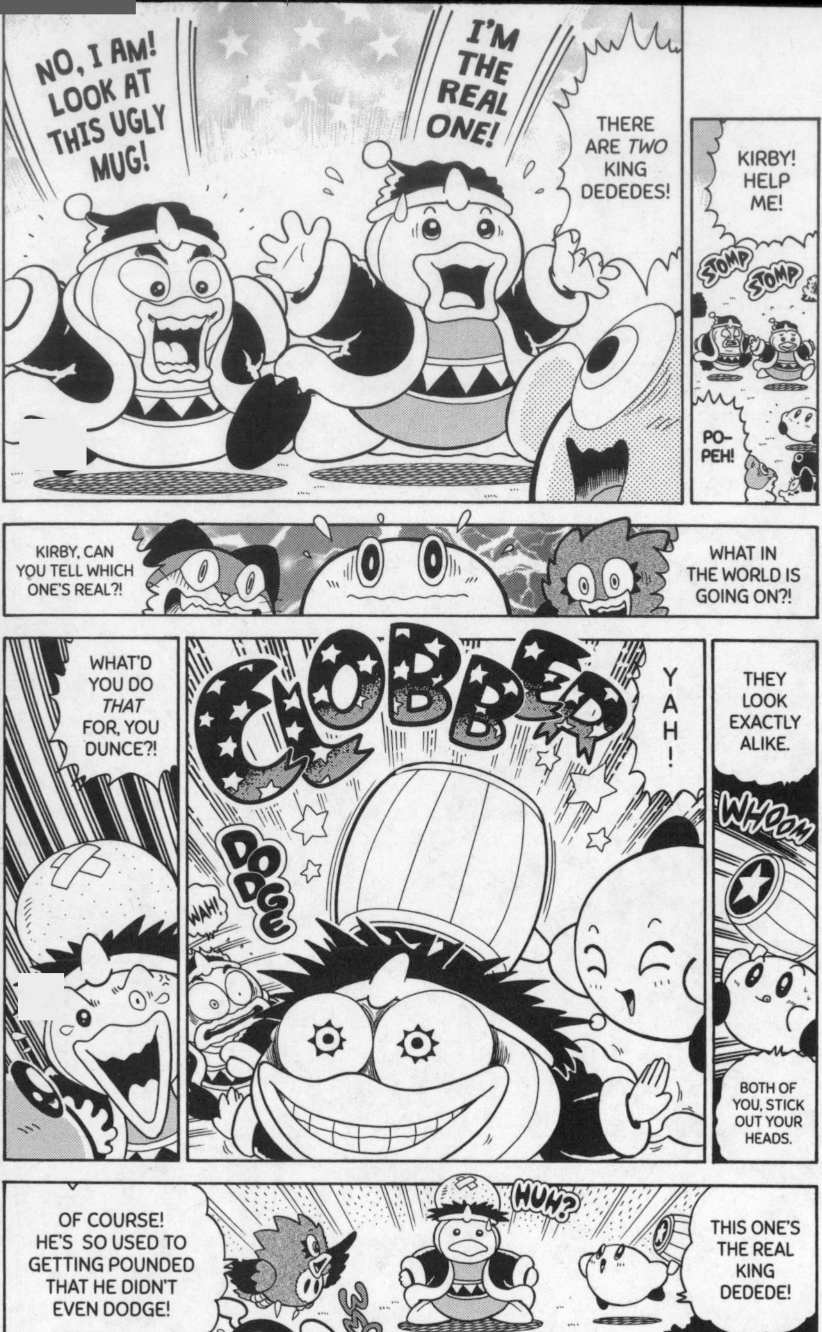
KIRBY! HELP ME!
STOMP
STOMP
PO-PEH!
THERE ARE *TWO* KING DEDEDES!
I'M THE REAL ONE!
NO, I AM! LOOK AT THIS UGLY MUG!
WHAT IN THE WORLD IS GOING ON?!
KIRBY, CAN YOU TELL WHICH ONE'S REAL?!
THEY LOOK EXACTLY ALIKE.
WHOOM
BOTH OF YOU, STICK OUT YOUR HEADS.
YAH!
CLOBBER
DODGE
WAH!
WHAT'D YOU DO *THAT* FOR, YOU DUNCE?!
THIS ONE'S THE REAL KING DEDEDE!
HUH?
OF COURSE! HE'S SO USED TO GETTING POUNDED THAT HE DIDN'T EVEN DODGE!

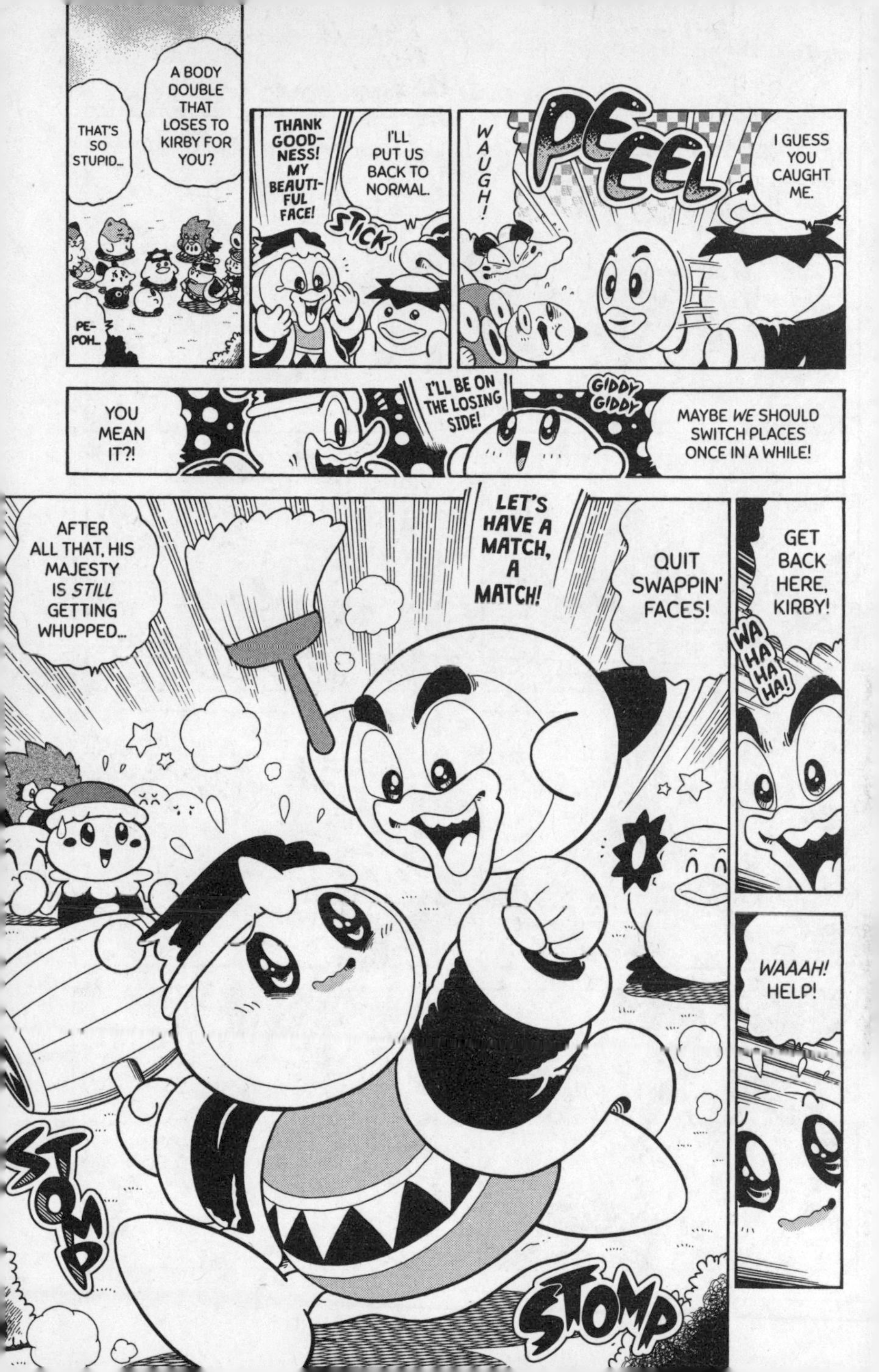
I GUESS YOU CAUGHT ME.
PEEEL
WAUGH!
I'LL PUT US BACK TO NORMAL.
THANK GOODNESS! MY BEAUTIFUL FACE!
STICK
A BODY DOUBLE THAT LOSES TO KIRBY FOR YOU?
THAT'S SO STUPID...
PE-POH...
MAYBE *WE* SHOULD SWITCH PLACES ONCE IN A WHILE!
GIDDY GIDDY
I'LL BE ON THE LOSING SIDE!
YOU MEAN IT?!
GET BACK HERE, KIRBY!
WA HA HA HA!
WAAAH! HELP!
QUIT SWAPPIN' FACES!
LET'S HAVE A MATCH, A MATCH!
AFTER ALL THAT, HIS MAJESTY IS *STILL* GETTING WHUPPED...
STOMP
STOMP

PENNY-PINCHER KIRBY

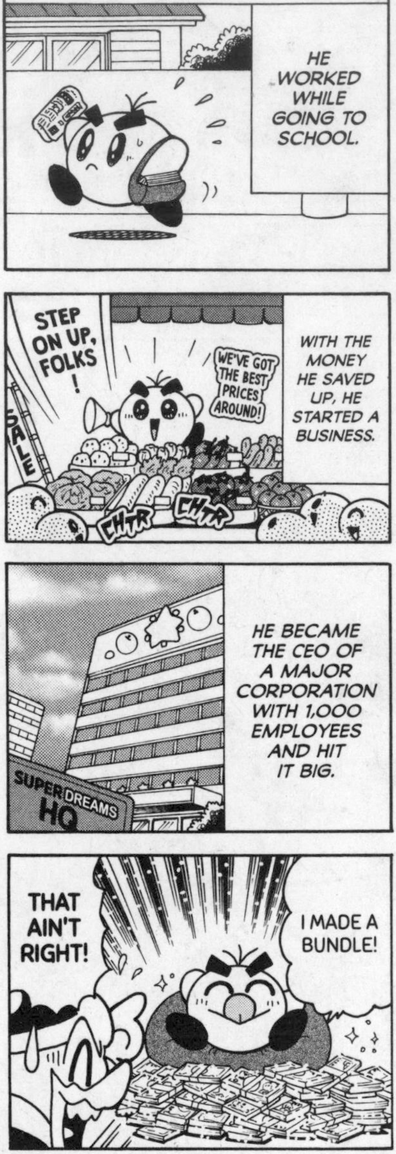
HE WORKED WHILE GOING TO SCHOOL.
WITH THE MONEY HE SAVED UP, HE STARTED A BUSINESS.
STEP ON UP, FOLKS!
WE'VE GOT THE BEST PRICES AROUND!
SALE
CHTR
CHTR
HE BECAME THE CEO OF A MAJOR CORPORATION WITH 1,000 EMPLOYEES AND HIT IT BIG.
SUPER DREAMS HQ
I MADE A BUNDLE!
THAT AIN'T RIGHT!

LITTLE PUN MASTER KIRBY

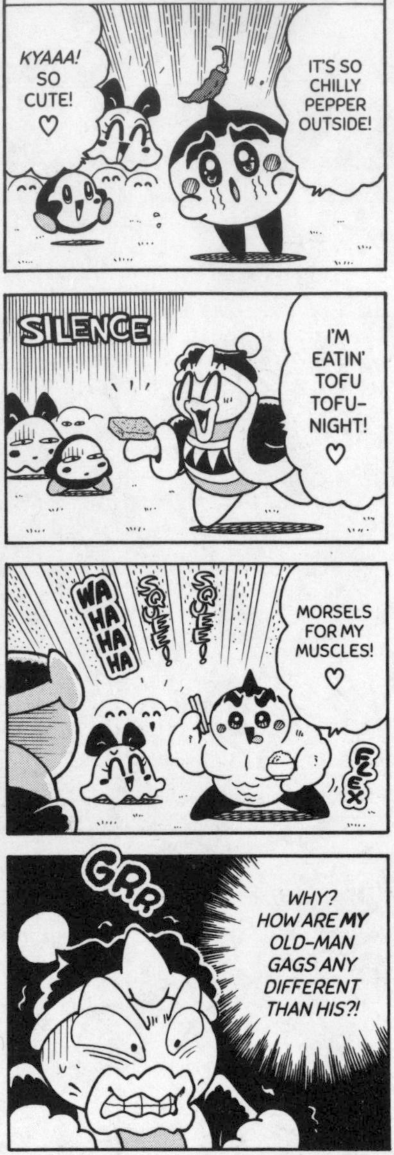
IT'S SO CHILLY PEPPER OUTSIDE!
KYAAA! SO CUTE! ♡
I'M EATIN' TOFU TOFU-NIGHT! ♡
SILENCE
MORSELS FOR MY MUSCLES! ♡
SQUEE!
SQUEE!
WA HA HA HA HA
FLEX
WHY? HOW ARE MY OLD-MAN GAGS ANY DIFFERENT THAN HIS?!
GRR

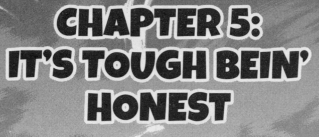

CHAPTER 5: IT'S TOUGH BEIN' HONEST

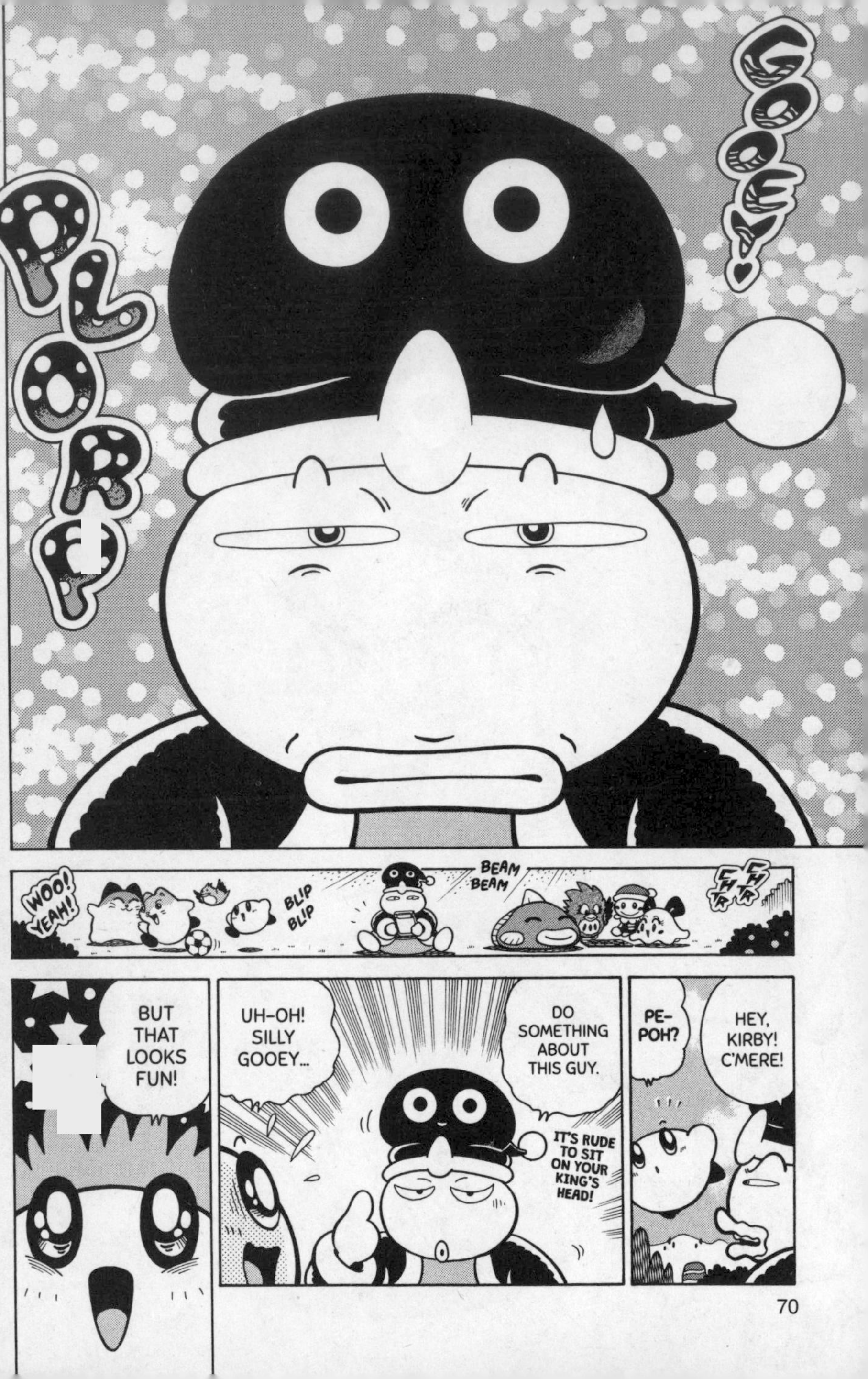
GOOEY♥
PLOP!
CHR CHR
BEAM BEAM
BLIP BLIP
WOO! YEAH!
HEY, KIRBY! C'MERE!
PE-POH?
DO SOMETHING ABOUT THIS GUY.
IT'S RUDE TO SIT ON YOUR KING'S HEAD!
UH-OH! SILLY GOOEY...
BUT THAT LOOKS FUN!

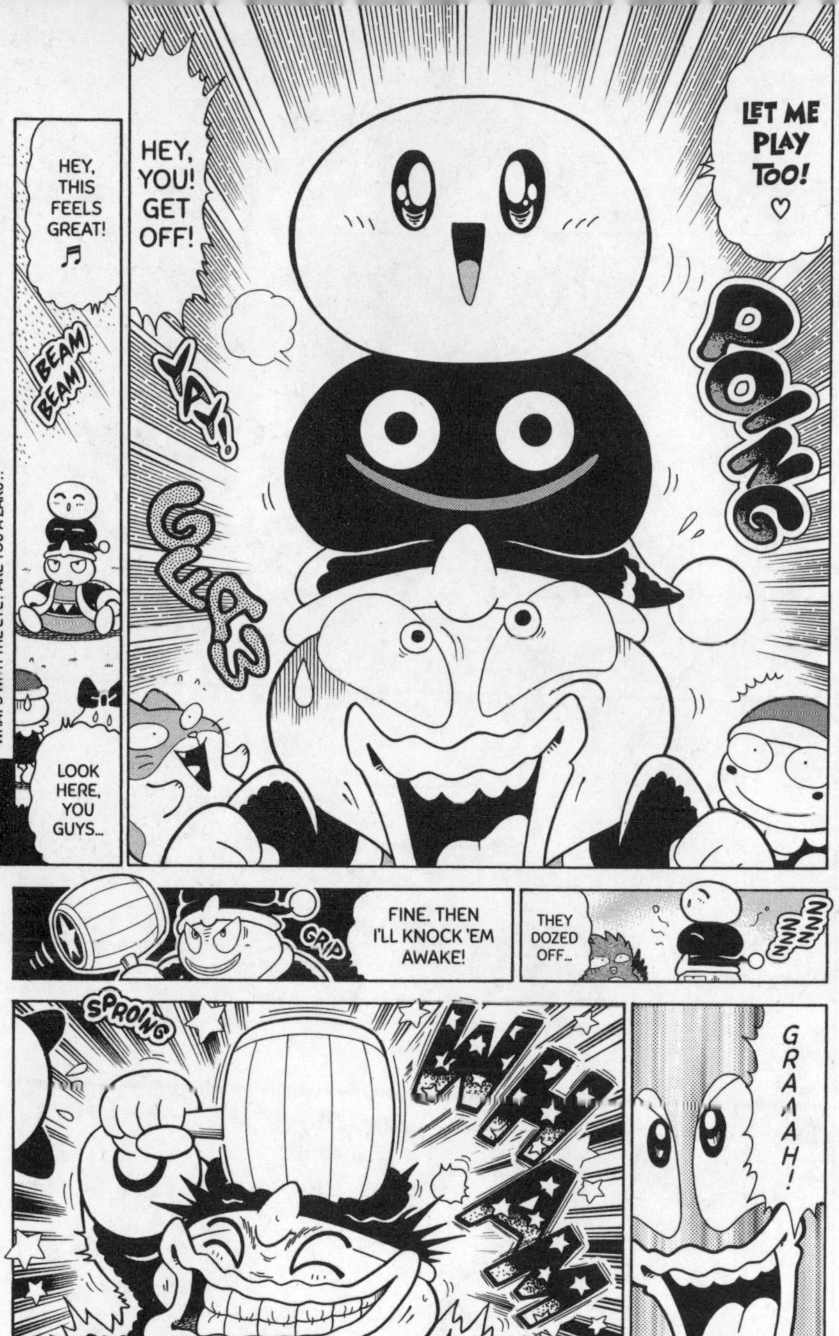
LET ME PLAY TOO! ♡
POING
HEY, YOU! GET OFF!
YAY!
HEY, THIS FEELS GREAT! ♬
BEAM BEAM
LOOK HERE, YOU GUYS...
ZZZ ZZZ
THEY DOZED OFF...
FINE. THEN I'LL KNOCK 'EM AWAKE!
GRIP
GRAAAH!
SPROING

AUTHOR'S COMMENT

MY ROUGH DRAFT FOR THIS STORY GOT APPROVED IN ONE SHOT. IT'S SUCH A BREEZE WHEN CHARACTERS WRITE THE STORY FOR YOU! THE "OUT-OF-STYLE VISOR" LINE WAS ORIGINALLY, "WHAT'S WITH THE EYE? ARE YOU A ZAKU?!"

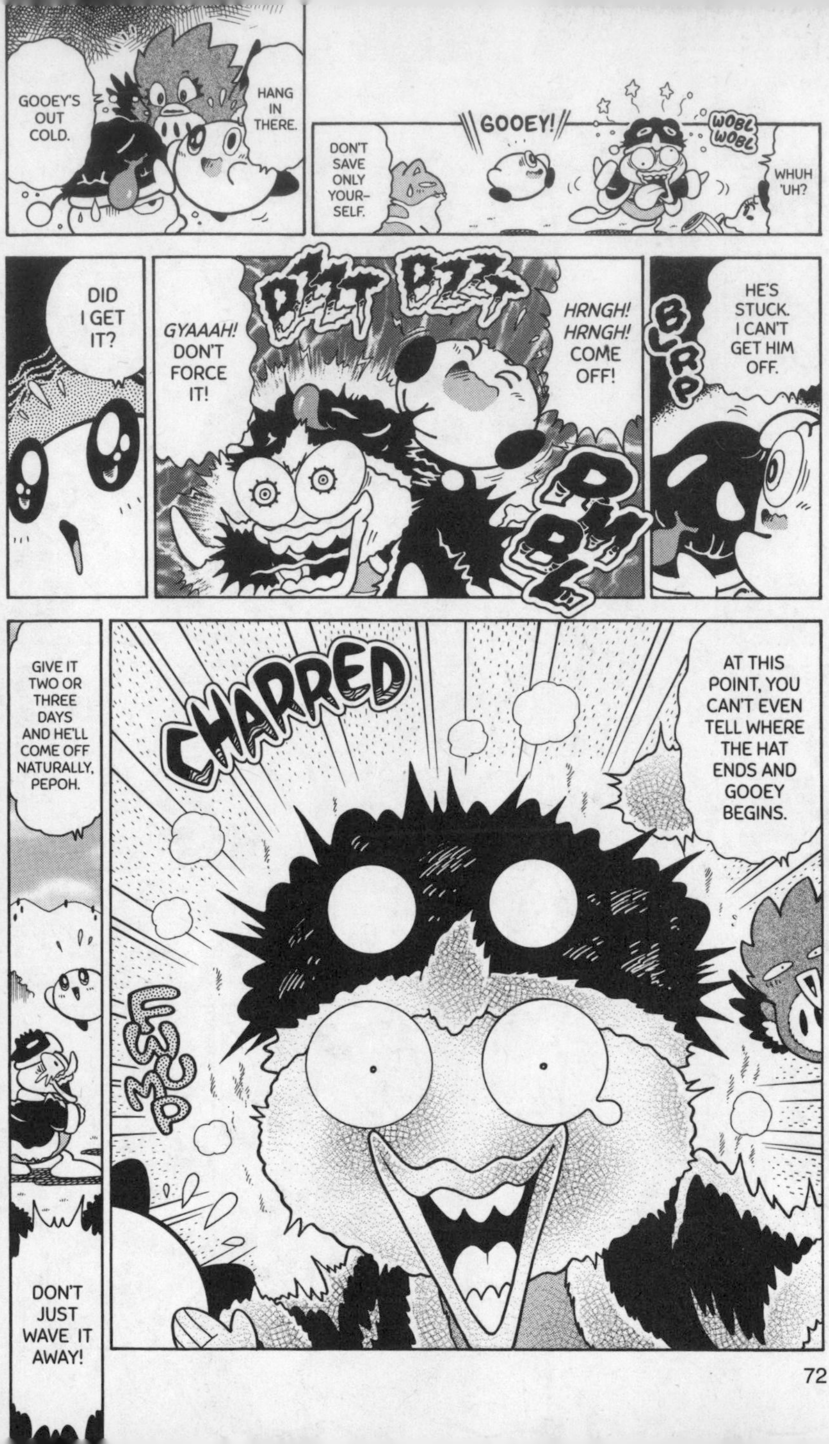
WHUH 'UH?
WOBL WOBL
GOOEY!
DON'T SAVE ONLY YOURSELF.
HANG IN THERE.
GOOEY'S OUT COLD.
HE'S STUCK. I CAN'T GET HIM OFF.
BLRP
HRNGH! HRNGH! COME OFF!
BZZT BZZT
GYAAAH! DON'T FORCE IT!
DID I GET IT?
AT THIS POINT, YOU CAN'T EVEN TELL WHERE THE HAT ENDS AND GOOEY BEGINS.
CHARRED
GIVE IT TWO OR THREE DAYS AND HE'LL COME OFF NATURALLY, PEPOH.
DON'T JUST WAVE IT AWAY!

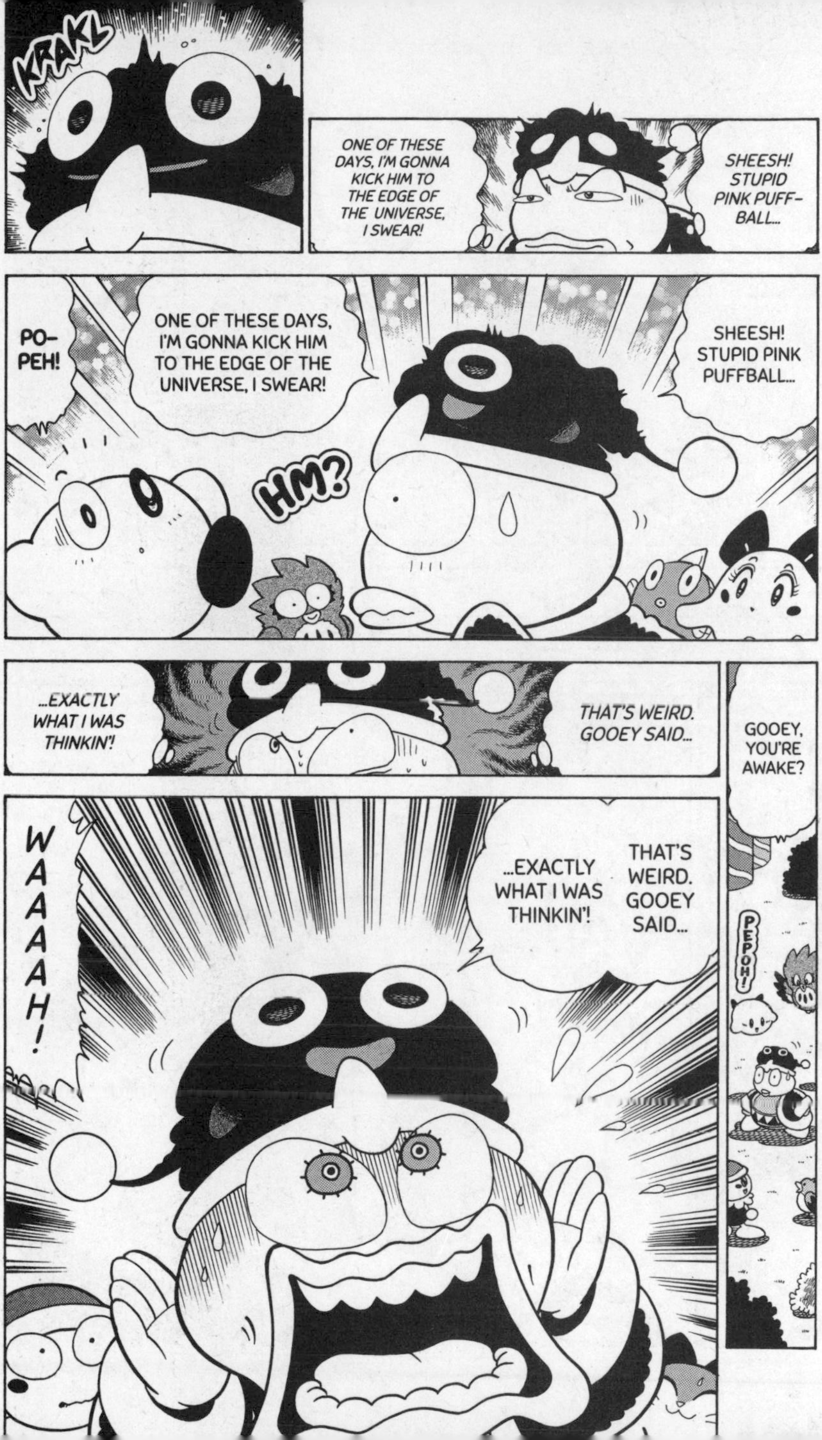
SHEESH! STUPID PINK PUFF-BALL...
ONE OF THESE DAYS, I'M GONNA KICK HIM TO THE EDGE OF THE UNIVERSE, I SWEAR!
KRAKL
SHEESH! STUPID PINK PUFFBALL...
ONE OF THESE DAYS, I'M GONNA KICK HIM TO THE EDGE OF THE UNIVERSE, I SWEAR!
PO-PEH!
HM?
GOOEY, YOU'RE AWAKE?
PEPOH!
THAT'S WEIRD. GOOEY SAID...
...EXACTLY WHAT I WAS THINKIN'!
THAT'S WEIRD. GOOEY SAID...
...EXACTLY WHAT I WAS THINKIN'!
WAAAAAH!

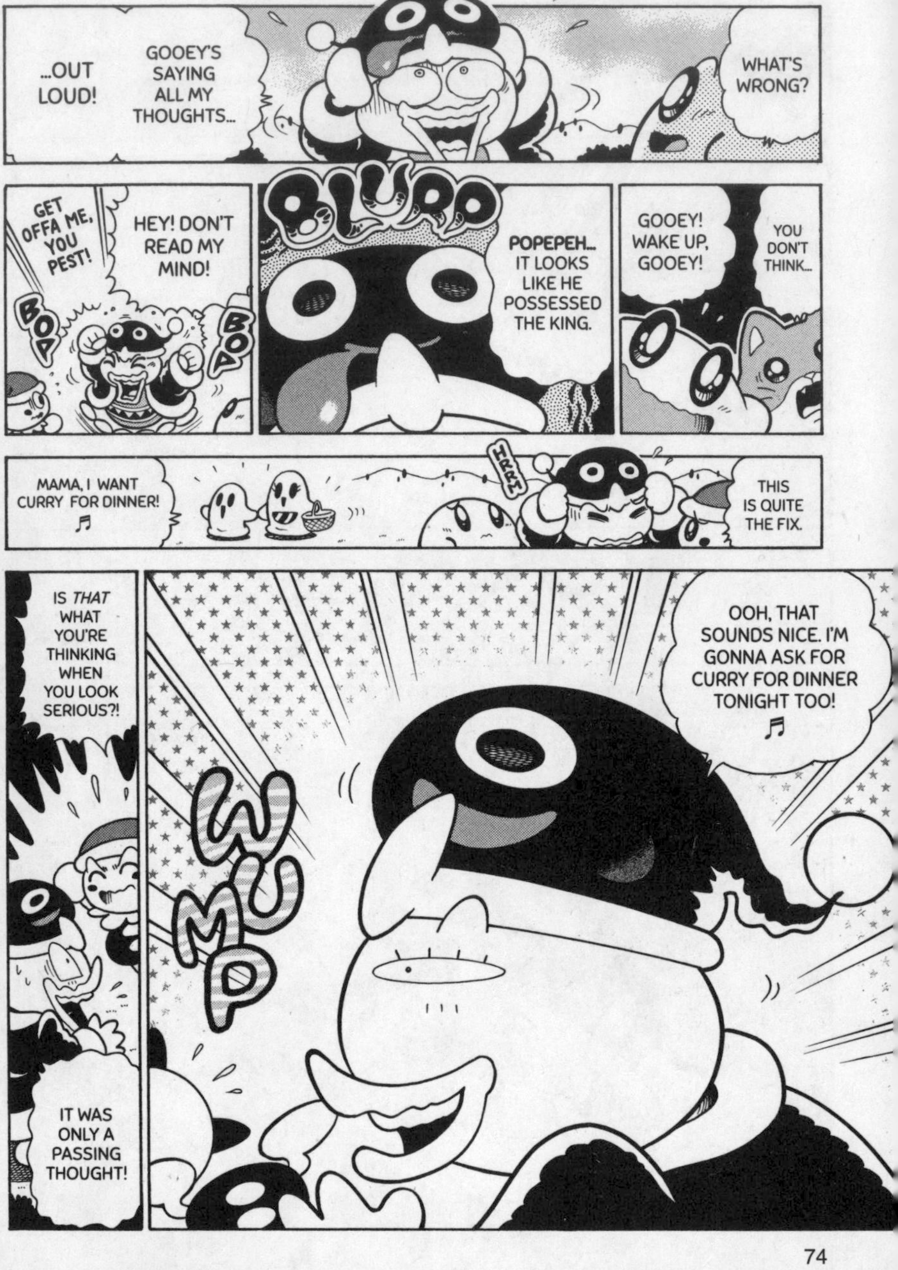
WHAT'S WRONG?
GOOEY'S SAYING ALL MY THOUGHTS...
...OUT LOUD!
YOU DON'T THINK...
GOOEY! WAKE UP, GOOEY!
BLUPP
POPEPEH... IT LOOKS LIKE HE POSSESSED THE KING.
HEY! DON'T READ MY MIND!
GET OFFA ME, YOU PEST!
BOP
BOP
THIS IS QUITE THE FIX.
HRRM
MAMA, I WANT CURRY FOR DINNER! ♬
OOH, THAT SOUNDS NICE. I'M GONNA ASK FOR CURRY FOR DINNER TONIGHT TOO! ♬
WUMP
IS *THAT* WHAT YOU'RE THINKING WHEN YOU LOOK SERIOUS?!
IT WAS ONLY A PASSING THOUGHT!

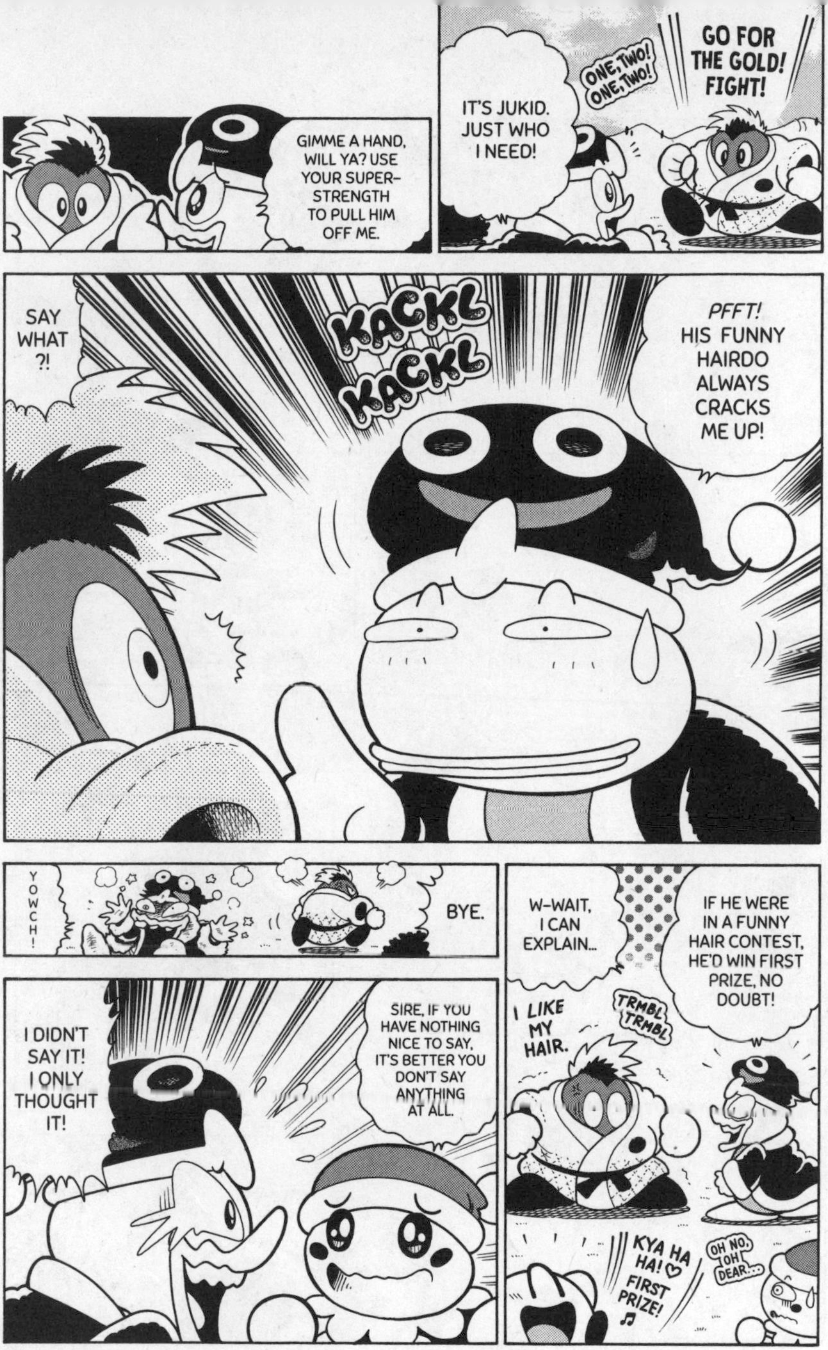

GO FOR THE GOLD! FIGHT!
ONE, TWO! ONE, TWO!
IT'S JUKID. JUST WHO I NEED!
GIMME A HAND, WILL YA? USE YOUR SUPER-STRENGTH TO PULL HIM OFF ME.
PFFT! HIS FUNNY HAIRDO ALWAYS CRACKS ME UP!
KACKL KACKL
SAY WHAT ?!
IF HE WERE IN A FUNNY HAIR CONTEST, HE'D WIN FIRST PRIZE, NO DOUBT!
W-WAIT, I CAN EXPLAIN...
TRMBL TRMBL
I LIKE MY HAIR.
OH NO, OH DEAR...
KYA HA HA! ♡ FIRST PRIZE! ♪
BYE.
YOWCH!
SIRE, IF YOU HAVE NOTHING NICE TO SAY, IT'S BETTER YOU DON'T SAY ANYTHING AT ALL.
I DIDN'T SAY IT! I ONLY THOUGHT IT!

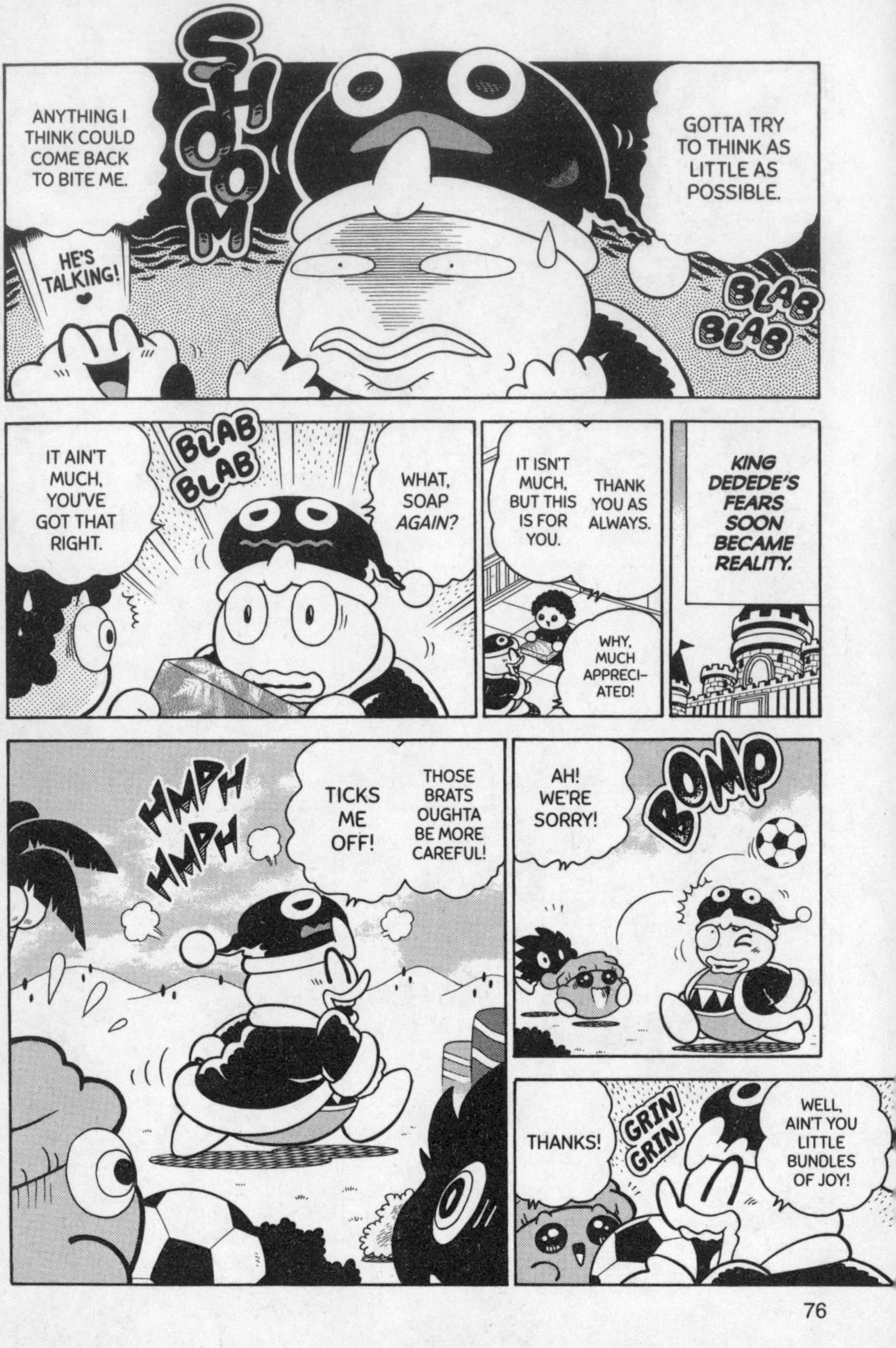
GOTTA TRY TO THINK AS LITTLE AS POSSIBLE.
BLAB BLAB
SHOOM
ANYTHING I THINK COULD COME BACK TO BITE ME.
HE'S TALKING!
KING DEDEDE'S FEARS SOON BECAME REALITY.
THANK YOU AS ALWAYS.
IT ISN'T MUCH, BUT THIS IS FOR YOU.
WHY, MUCH APPRECI-ATED!
WHAT, SOAP *AGAIN?*
BLAB BLAB
IT AIN'T MUCH, YOU'VE GOT THAT RIGHT.
BOMP
AH! WE'RE SORRY!
WELL, AIN'T YOU LITTLE BUNDLES OF JOY!
GRIN GRIN
THANKS!
THOSE BRATS OUGHTA BE MORE CAREFUL!
TICKS ME OFF!
HMPH HMPH

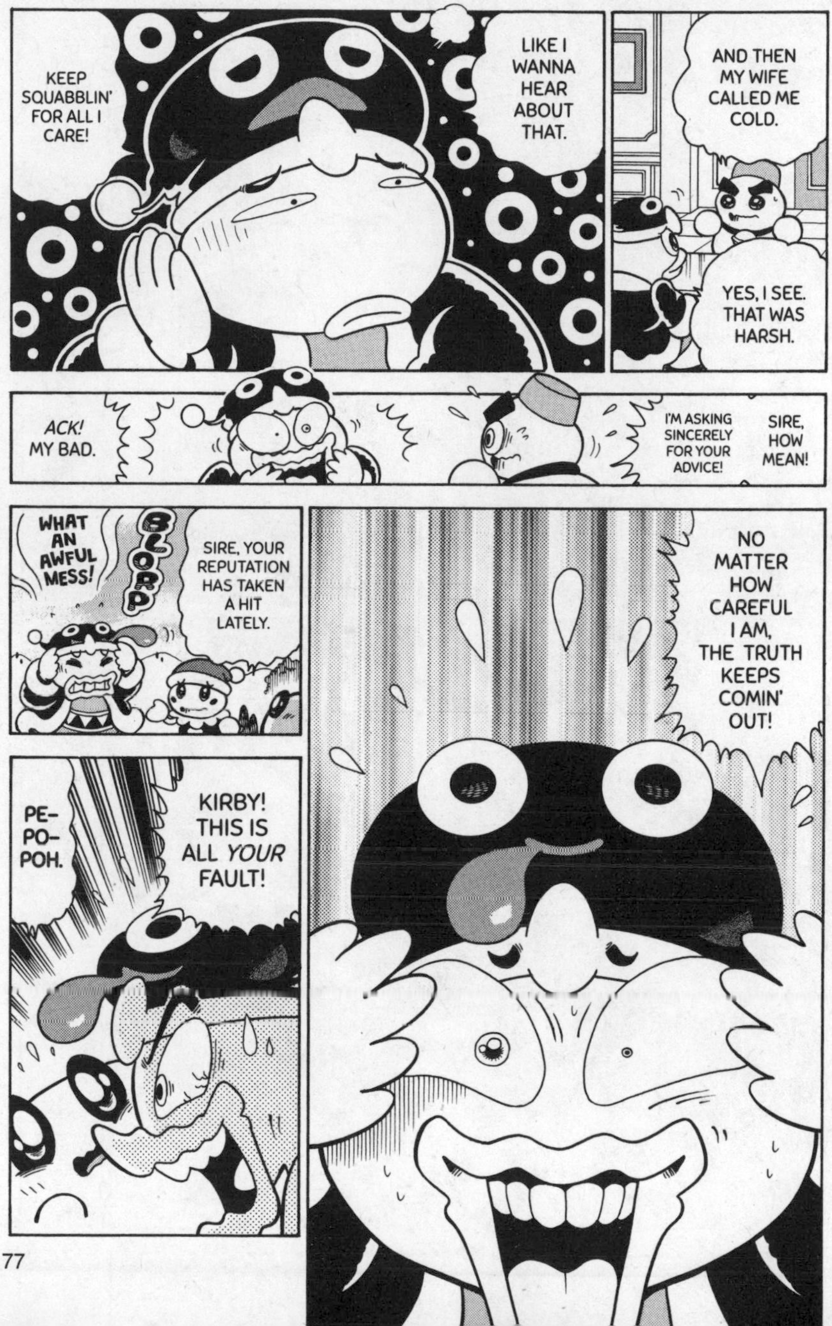
AND THEN MY WIFE CALLED ME COLD.
YES, I SEE. THAT WAS HARSH.
LIKE I WANNA HEAR ABOUT THAT.
KEEP SQUABBLIN' FOR ALL I CARE!
SIRE, HOW MEAN!
I'M ASKING SINCERELY FOR YOUR ADVICE!
ACK! MY BAD.
NO MATTER HOW CAREFUL I AM, THE TRUTH KEEPS COMIN' OUT!
SIRE, YOUR REPUTATION HAS TAKEN A HIT LATELY.
BLORP
WHAT AN AWFUL MESS!
KIRBY! THIS IS ALL *YOUR* FAULT!
PE-PO-POH.

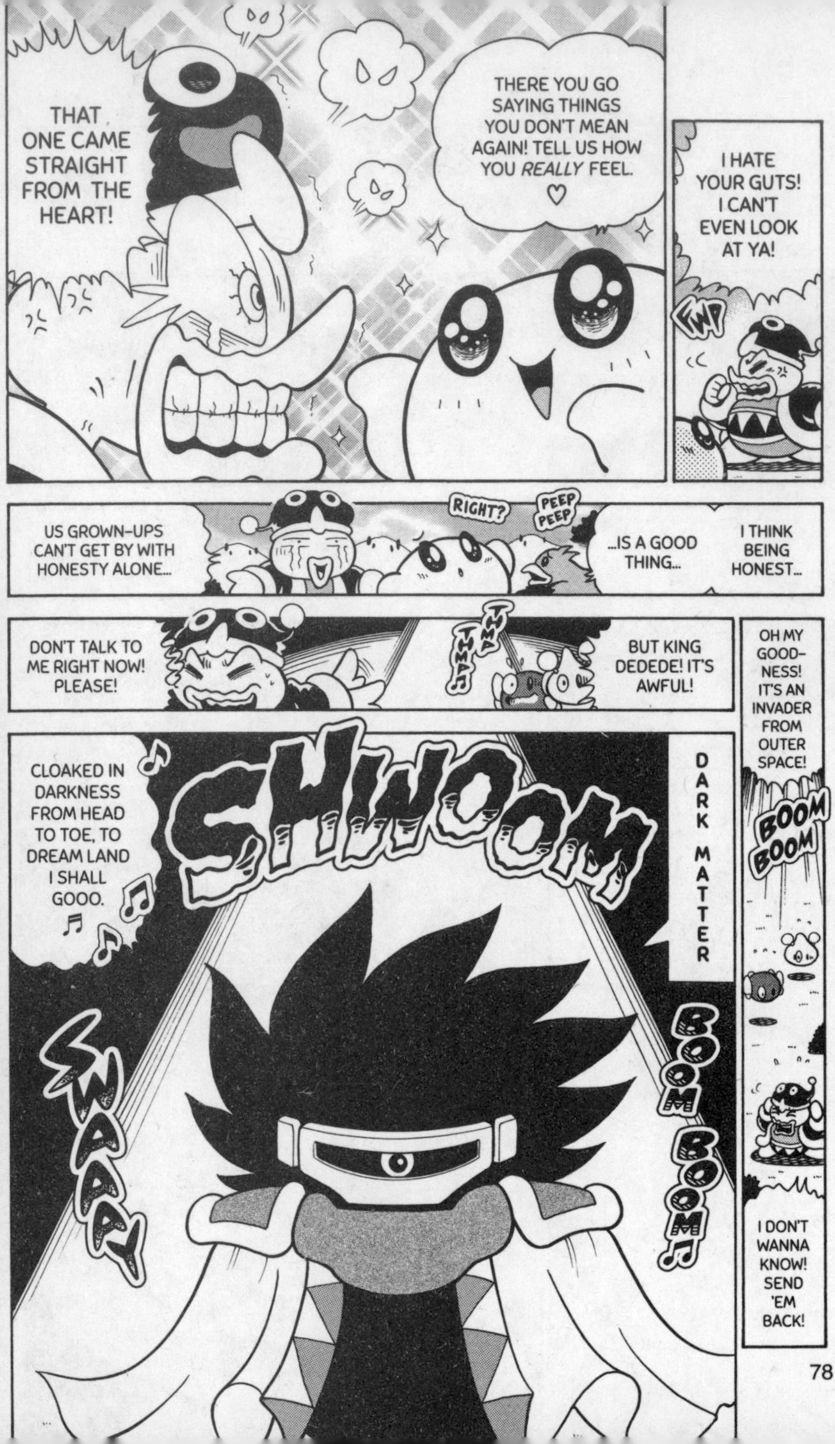
I HATE YOUR GUTS! I CAN'T EVEN LOOK AT YA!
FWP
THERE YOU GO SAYING THINGS YOU DON'T MEAN AGAIN! TELL US HOW YOU *REALLY* FEEL. ♡
THAT ONE CAME STRAIGHT FROM THE HEART!
I THINK BEING HONEST...
...IS A GOOD THING...
PEEP PEEP
RIGHT?
US GROWN-UPS CAN'T GET BY WITH HONESTY ALONE...
OH MY GOODNESS! IT'S AN INVADER FROM OUTER SPACE!
BOOM BOOM
I DON'T WANNA KNOW! SEND 'EM BACK!
BUT KING DEDEDE! IT'S AWFUL!
THMP THMP
DON'T TALK TO ME RIGHT NOW! PLEASE!
DARK MATTER
SHWOOM
CLOAKED IN DARKNESS FROM HEAD TO TOE, TO DREAM LAND I SHALL GOOO.
BOOM BOOM BOOM
SWAAAY

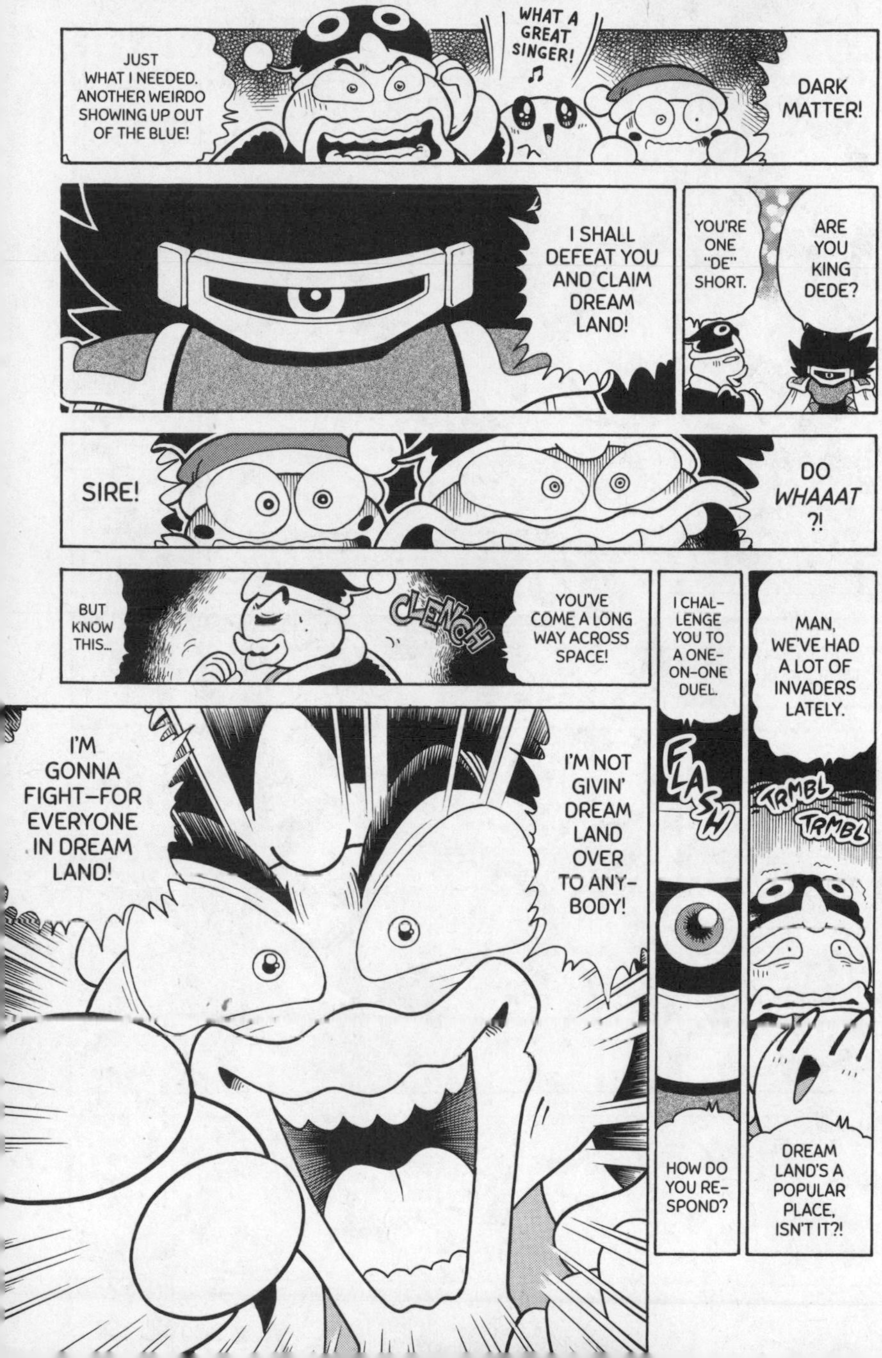
DARK MATTER!
WHAT A GREAT SINGER! ♪
JUST WHAT I NEEDED. ANOTHER WEIRDO SHOWING UP OUT OF THE BLUE!
ARE YOU KING DEDE?
YOU'RE ONE "DE" SHORT.
I SHALL DEFEAT YOU AND CLAIM DREAM LAND!
DO *WHAAAT*?!
SIRE!
MAN, WE'VE HAD A LOT OF INVADERS LATELY.
TRMBL TRMBL
DREAM LAND'S A POPULAR PLACE, ISN'T IT?!
I CHAL-LENGE YOU TO A ONE-ON-ONE DUEL.
FLASH
HOW DO YOU RE-SPOND?
YOU'VE COME A LONG WAY ACROSS SPACE!
CLENCH
BUT KNOW THIS...
I'M NOT GIVIN' DREAM LAND OVER TO ANY-BODY!
I'M GONNA FIGHT—FOR EVERYONE IN DREAM LAND!

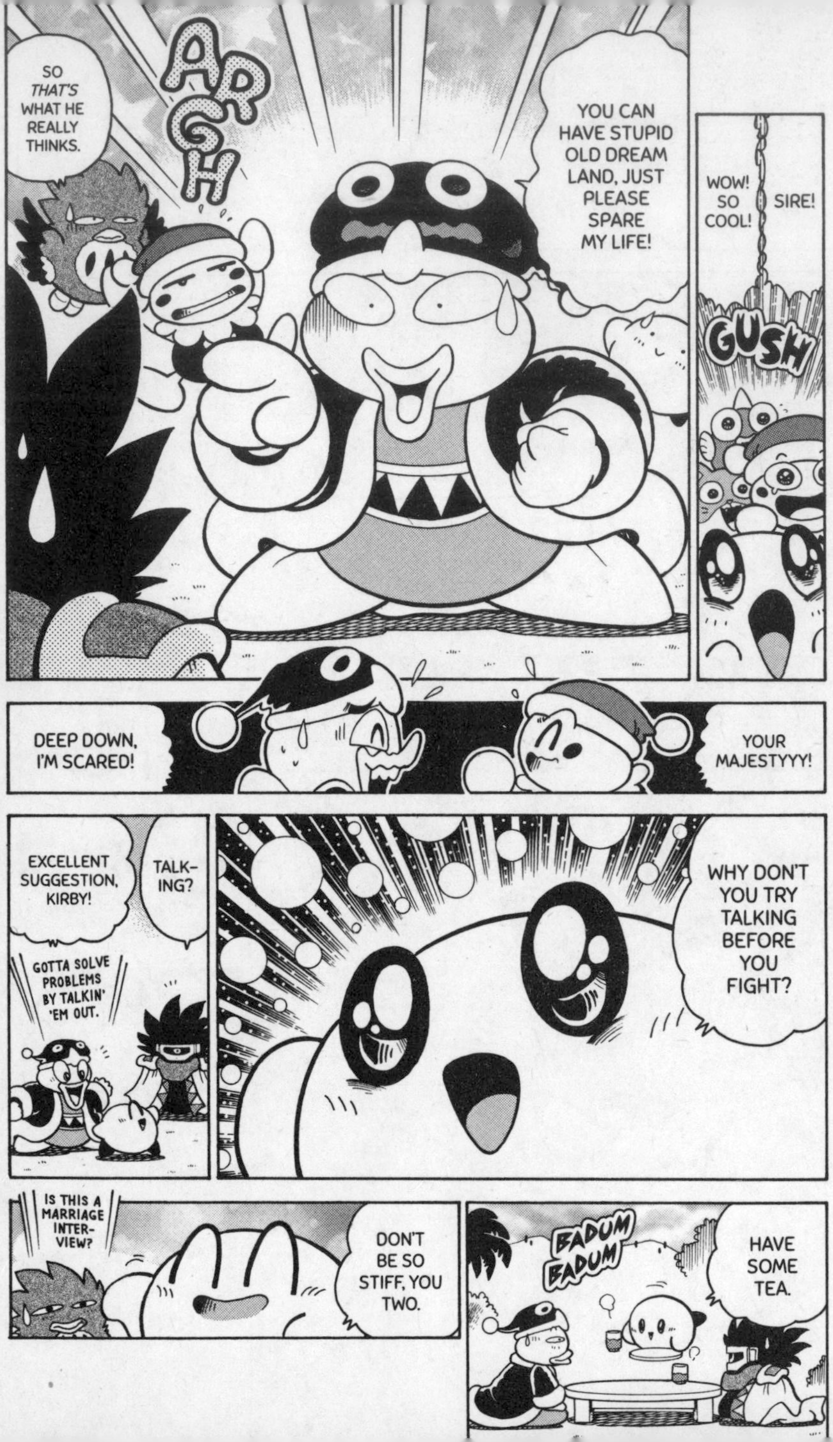
SIRE!
WOW! SO COOL!
GUSH
YOU CAN HAVE STUPID OLD DREAM LAND, JUST PLEASE SPARE MY LIFE!
ARGH
SO THAT'S WHAT HE REALLY THINKS.
YOUR MAJESTYYY!
DEEP DOWN, I'M SCARED!
WHY DON'T YOU TRY TALKING BEFORE YOU FIGHT?
TALK-ING?
EXCELLENT SUGGESTION, KIRBY!
GOTTA SOLVE PROBLEMS BY TALKIN' 'EM OUT.
HAVE SOME TEA.
BADUM BADUM
DON'T BE SO STIFF, YOU TWO.
IS THIS A MARRIAGE INTER-VIEW?

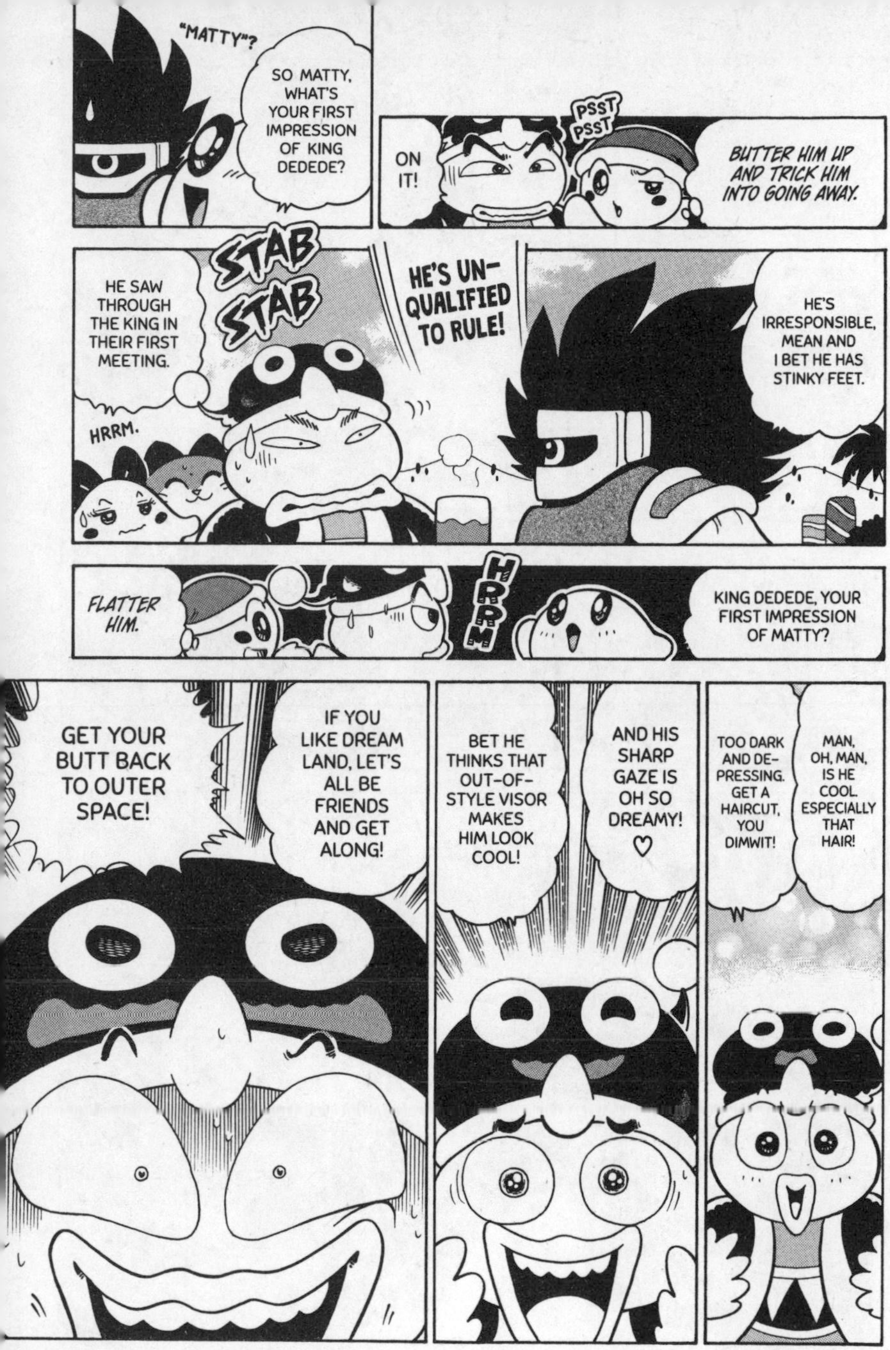
BUTTER HIM UP AND TRICK HIM INTO GOING AWAY.
PSST PSST
ON IT!
"MATTY"?
SO MATTY, WHAT'S YOUR FIRST IMPRESSION OF KING DEDEDE?
HE'S IRRESPONSIBLE, MEAN AND I BET HE HAS STINKY FEET.
HE'S UN-QUALIFIED TO RULE!
STAB STAB
HE SAW THROUGH THE KING IN THEIR FIRST MEETING.
HRRM.
KING DEDEDE, YOUR FIRST IMPRESSION OF MATTY?
HRRM
FLATTER HIM.
MAN, OH, MAN, IS HE COOL. ESPECIALLY THAT HAIR!
TOO DARK AND DE-PRESSING. GET A HAIRCUT, YOU DIMWIT!
AND HIS SHARP GAZE IS OH SO DREAMY! ♡
BET HE THINKS THAT OUT-OF-STYLE VISOR MAKES HIM LOOK COOL!
IF YOU LIKE DREAM LAND, LET'S ALL BE FRIENDS AND GET ALONG!
GET YOUR BUTT BACK TO OUTER SPACE!

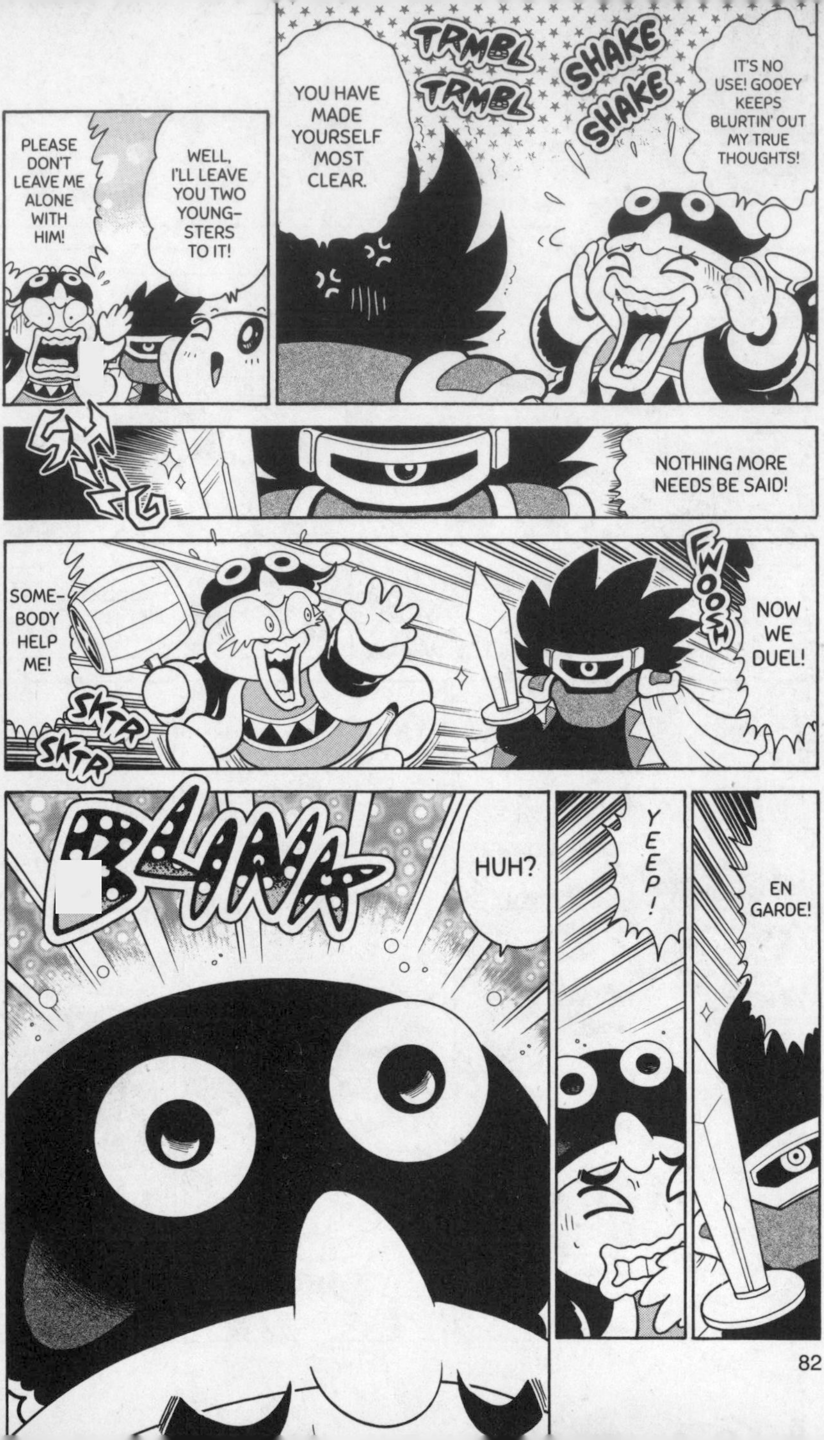
IT'S NO USE! GOOEY KEEPS BLURTIN' OUT MY TRUE THOUGHTS!
SHAKE SHAKE
TRMBL TRMBL
YOU HAVE MADE YOURSELF MOST CLEAR.
WELL, I'LL LEAVE YOU TWO YOUNG-STERS TO IT!
PLEASE DON'T LEAVE ME ALONE WITH HIM!
NOTHING MORE NEEDS BE SAID!
NOW WE DUEL!
FWOOSH
SOME-BODY HELP ME!
SKTR SKTR
EN GARDE!
YEEP!
HUH?
BLINK

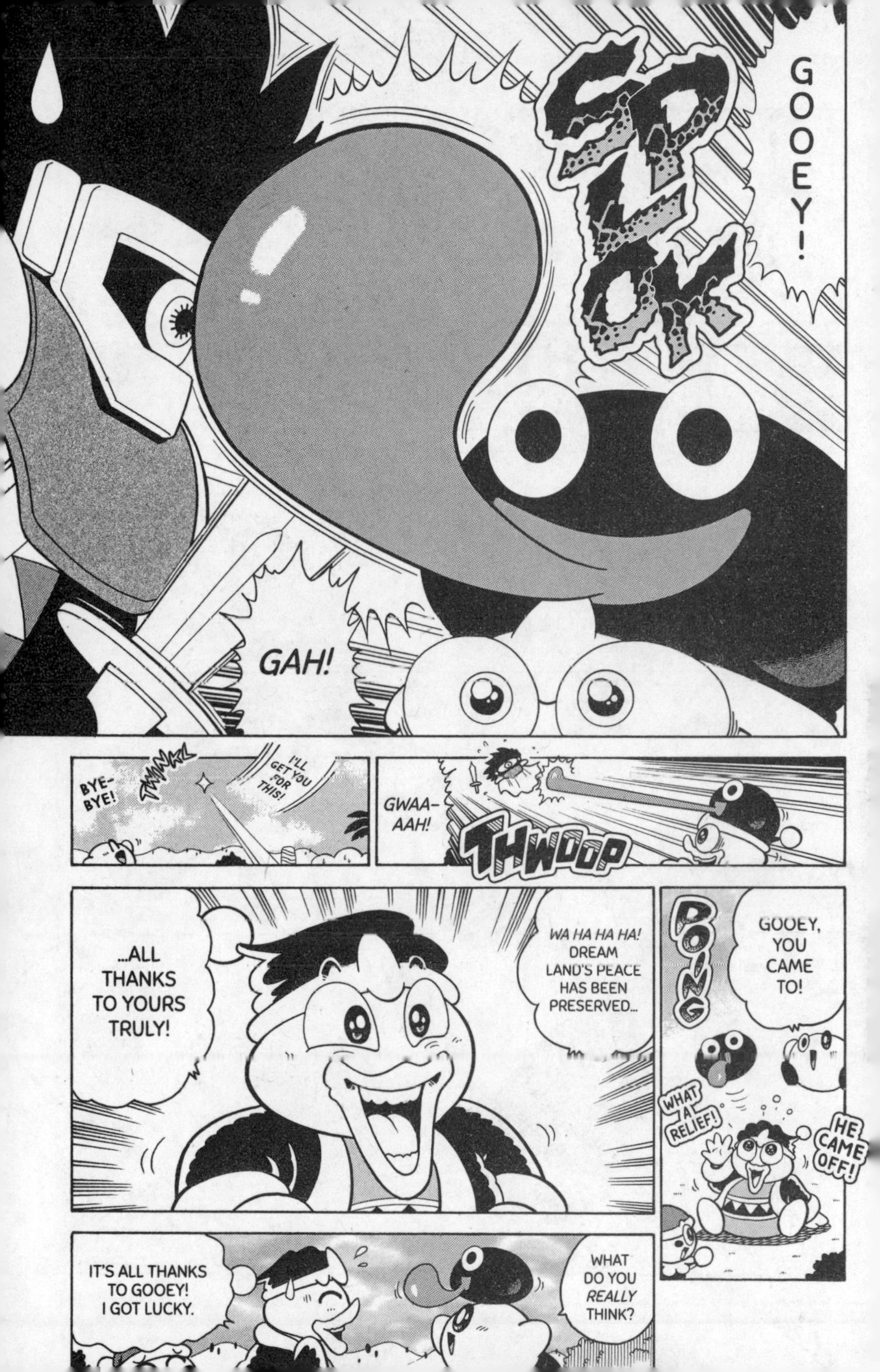
GOOEY!
GAH!
GWAA-AAH!
THWOOP
I'LL GET YOU FOR THIS!
BYE-BYE!
BOING
GOOEY, YOU CAME TO!
HE CAME OFF!
WHAT A RELIEF!
WA HA HA HA! DREAM LAND'S PEACE HAS BEEN PRESERVED...
...ALL THANKS TO YOURS TRULY!
WHAT DO YOU *REALLY* THINK?
IT'S ALL THANKS TO GOOEY! I GOT LUCKY.

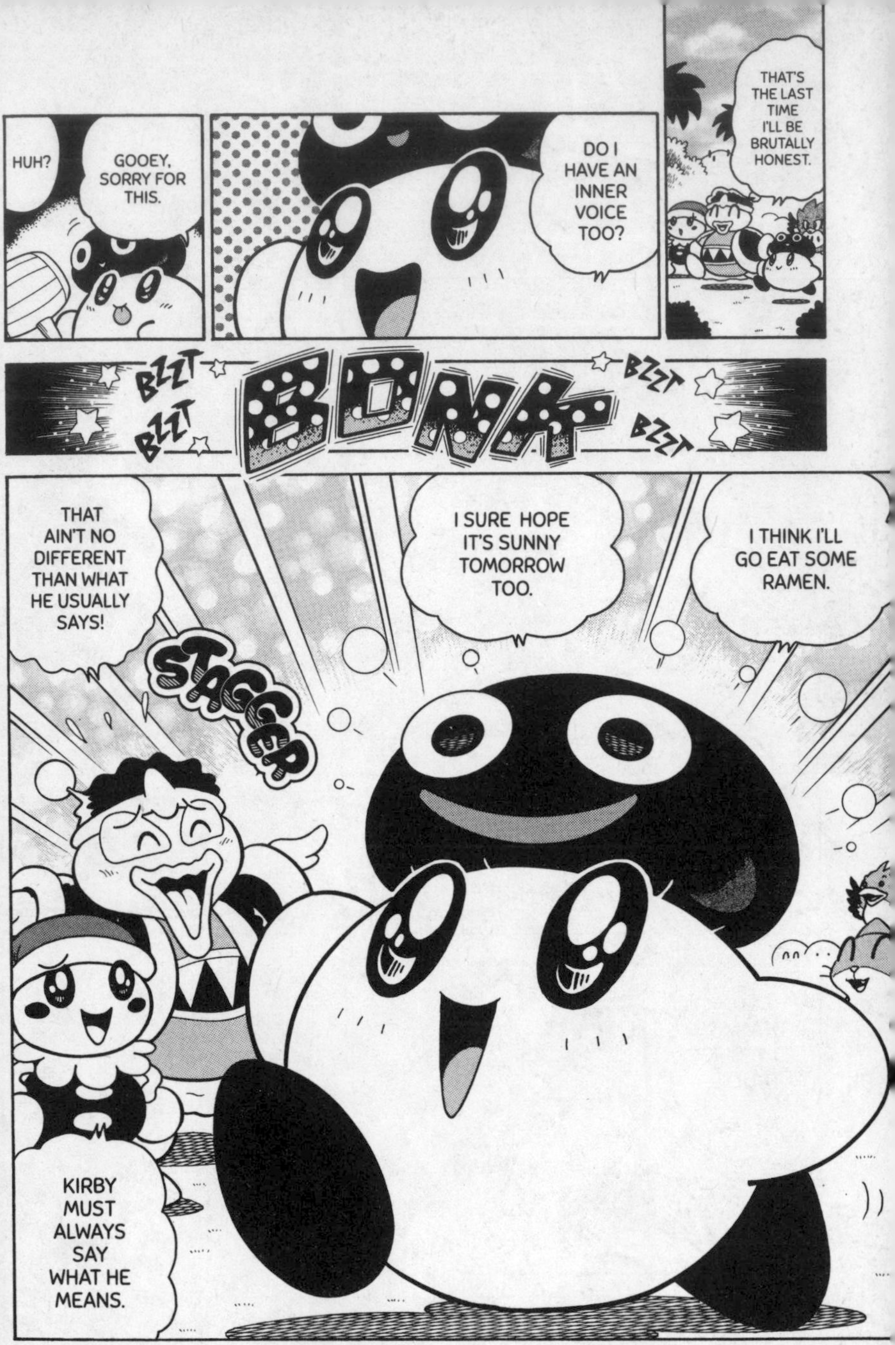
THAT'S THE LAST TIME I'LL BE BRUTALLY HONEST.
DO I HAVE AN INNER VOICE TOO?
GOOEY, SORRY FOR THIS.
HUH?
BZZT
BZZT
BONK
BZZT
BZZT
I THINK I'LL GO EAT SOME RAMEN.
I SURE HOPE IT'S SUNNY TOMORROW TOO.
THAT AIN'T NO DIFFERENT THAN WHAT HE USUALLY SAYS!
STAGGER
KIRBY MUST ALWAYS SAY WHAT HE MEANS.

CHAPTER 6: SPOOKY TALES! WELCOME TO TERROR INN

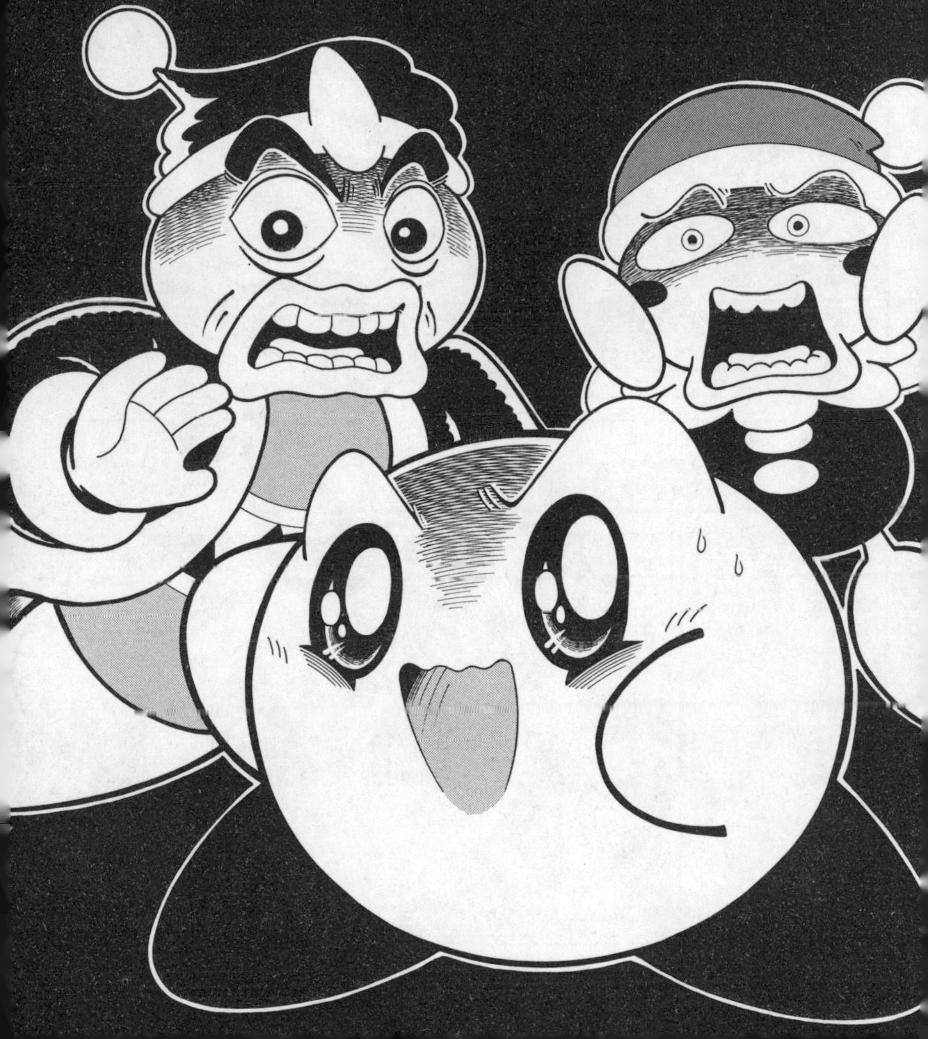

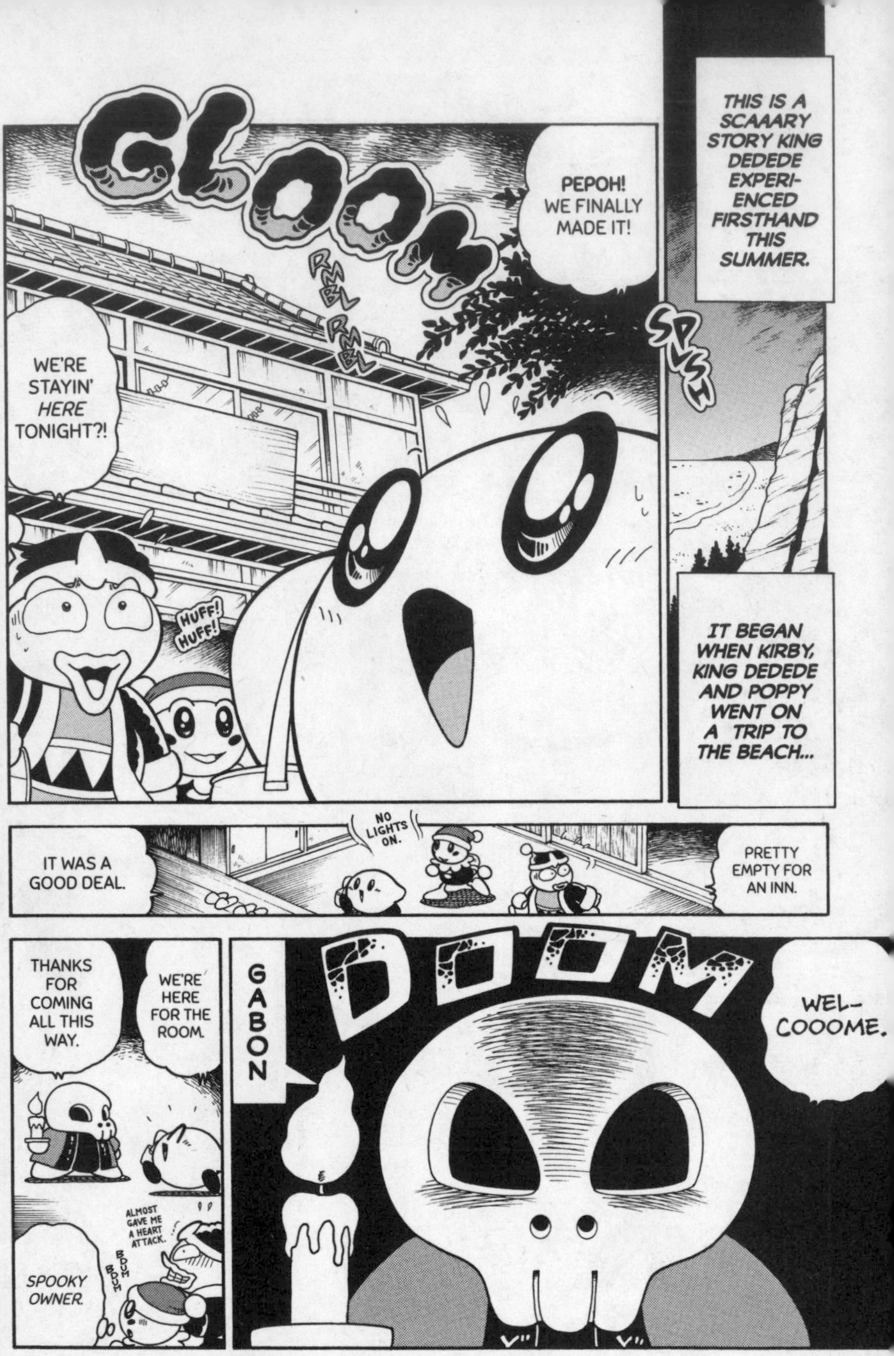
THIS IS A SCAAARY STORY KING DEDEDE EXPERIENCED FIRSTHAND THIS SUMMER.
IT BEGAN WHEN KIRBY, KING DEDEDE AND POPPY WENT ON A TRIP TO THE BEACH...
GLOOM
RMBL RMBL
SPLSH
PEPOH! WE FINALLY MADE IT!
WE'RE STAYIN' *HERE* TONIGHT?!
HUFF! HUFF!
PRETTY EMPTY FOR AN INN.
NO LIGHTS ON.
IT WAS A GOOD DEAL.
DOOM
WEL-COOOME.
GABON
WE'RE HERE FOR THE ROOM.
THANKS FOR COMING ALL THIS WAY.
ALMOST GAVE ME A HEART ATTACK.
BDUM BDUM
SPOOKY OWNER.

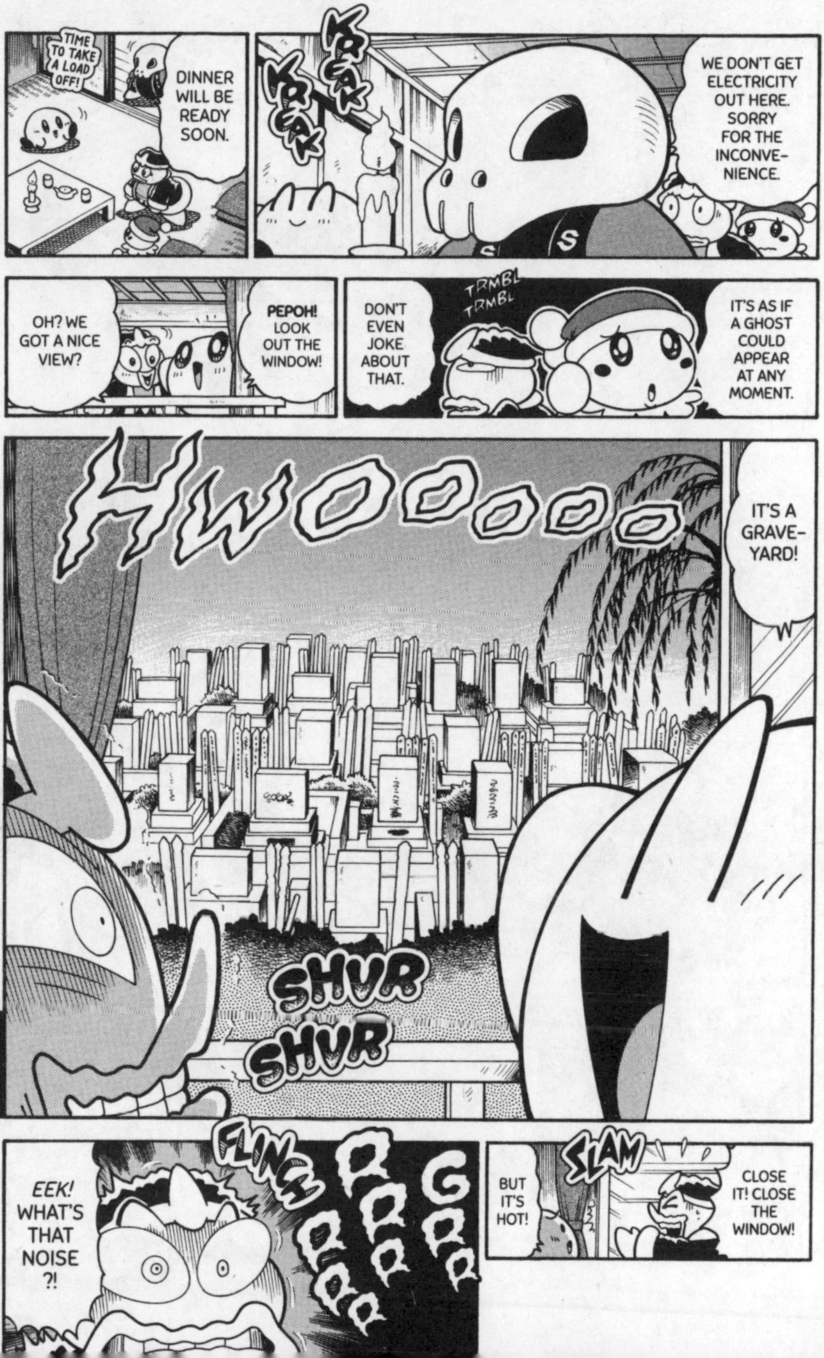

WE DON'T GET ELECTRICITY OUT HERE. SORRY FOR THE INCONVENIENCE.
KRAK KRAK
DINNER WILL BE READY SOON.
TIME TO TAKE A LOAD OFF!
IT'S AS IF A GHOST COULD APPEAR AT ANY MOMENT.
TRMBL TRMBL
DON'T EVEN JOKE ABOUT THAT.
PEPOH! LOOK OUT THE WINDOW!
OH? WE GOT A NICE VIEW?
HWOOOOOO
IT'S A GRAVEYARD!
SHUR SHUR
SLAM
CLOSE IT! CLOSE THE WINDOW!
BUT IT'S HOT!
FLINCH
GRRRRRRR
EEK! WHAT'S THAT NOISE ?!

AUTHOR'S COMMENT

THIS ONE'S AN 8-PAGE SHORT STORY. THE CHARACTERS' QUIRKS REALLY SHINE, AND IT'S A FUN ONE TO REREAD TOO.

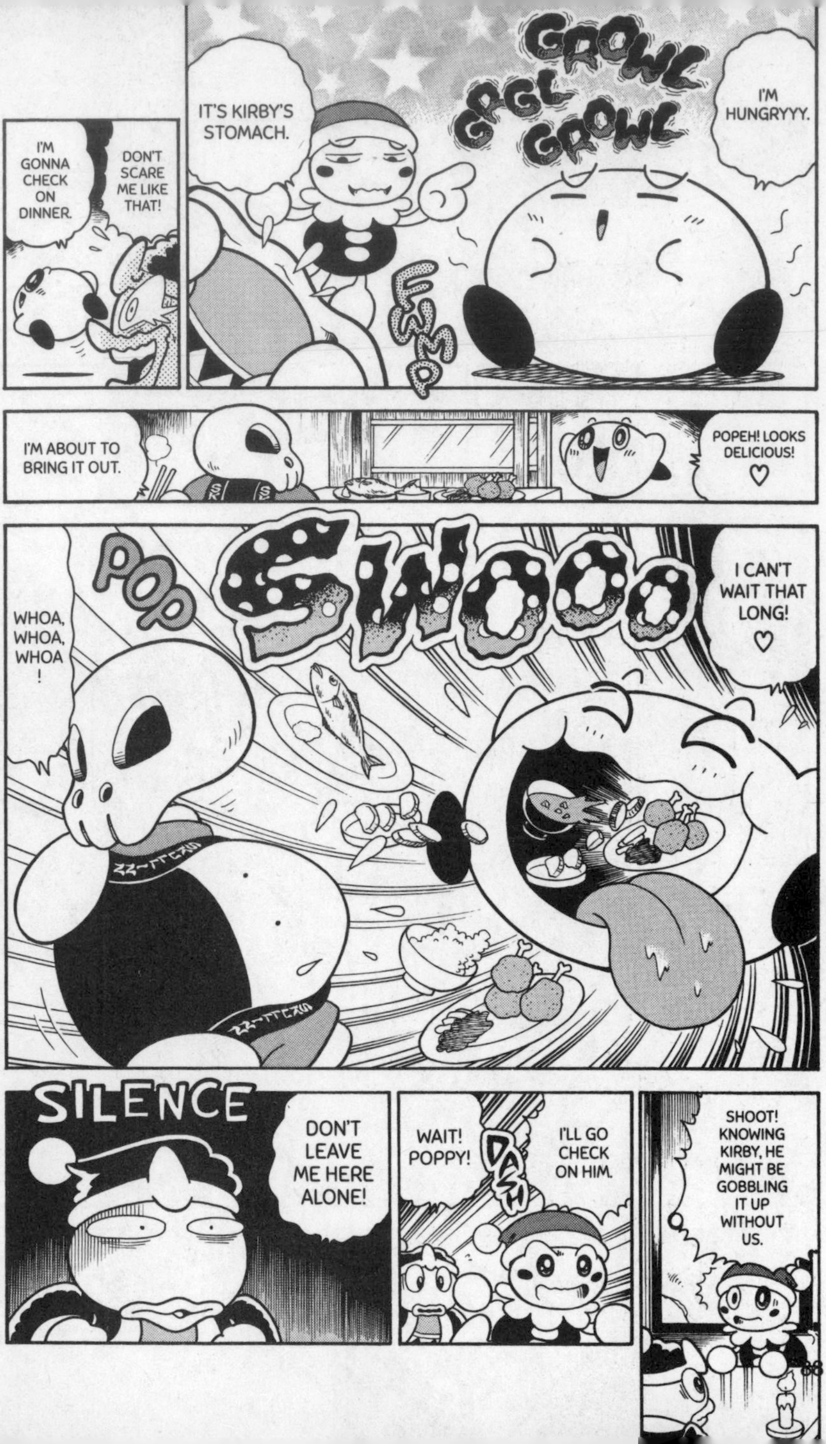

I'M HUNGRYYY.
GROWL GRGL GROWL
IT'S KIRBY'S STOMACH.
FWMP
DON'T SCARE ME LIKE THAT!
I'M GONNA CHECK ON DINNER.
POPEH! LOOKS DELICIOUS! ♡
I'M ABOUT TO BRING IT OUT.
I CAN'T WAIT THAT LONG! ♡
SWOOO
POP
WHOA, WHOA, WHOA!
SHOOT! KNOWING KIRBY, HE MIGHT BE GOBBLING IT UP WITHOUT US.
I'LL GO CHECK ON HIM.
DASH
WAIT! POPPY!
SILENCE
DON'T LEAVE ME HERE ALONE!

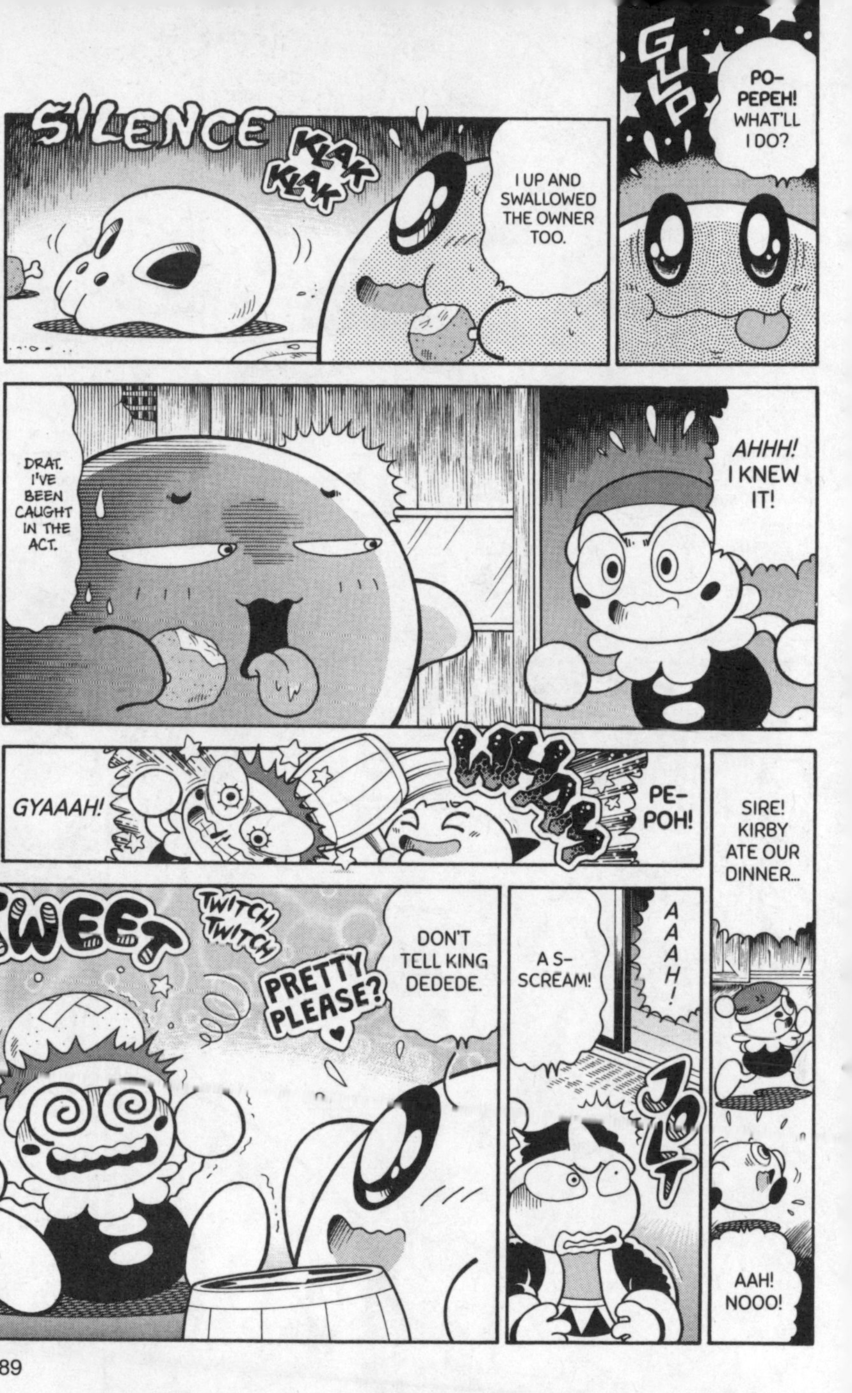
GULP
PO-PEPEH! WHAT'LL I DO?
I UP AND SWALLOWED THE OWNER TOO.
KLAK KLAK
SILENCE
AHHH! I KNEW IT!
DRAT. I'VE BEEN CAUGHT IN THE ACT.
SIRE! KIRBY ATE OUR DINNER...
AAH! NOOO!
PE-POH!
WHAM
GYAAAH!
AAAAH!
A S-SCREAM!
JOLT
DON'T TELL KING DEDEDE.
PRETTY PLEASE?
TWITCH TWITCH
TWEET

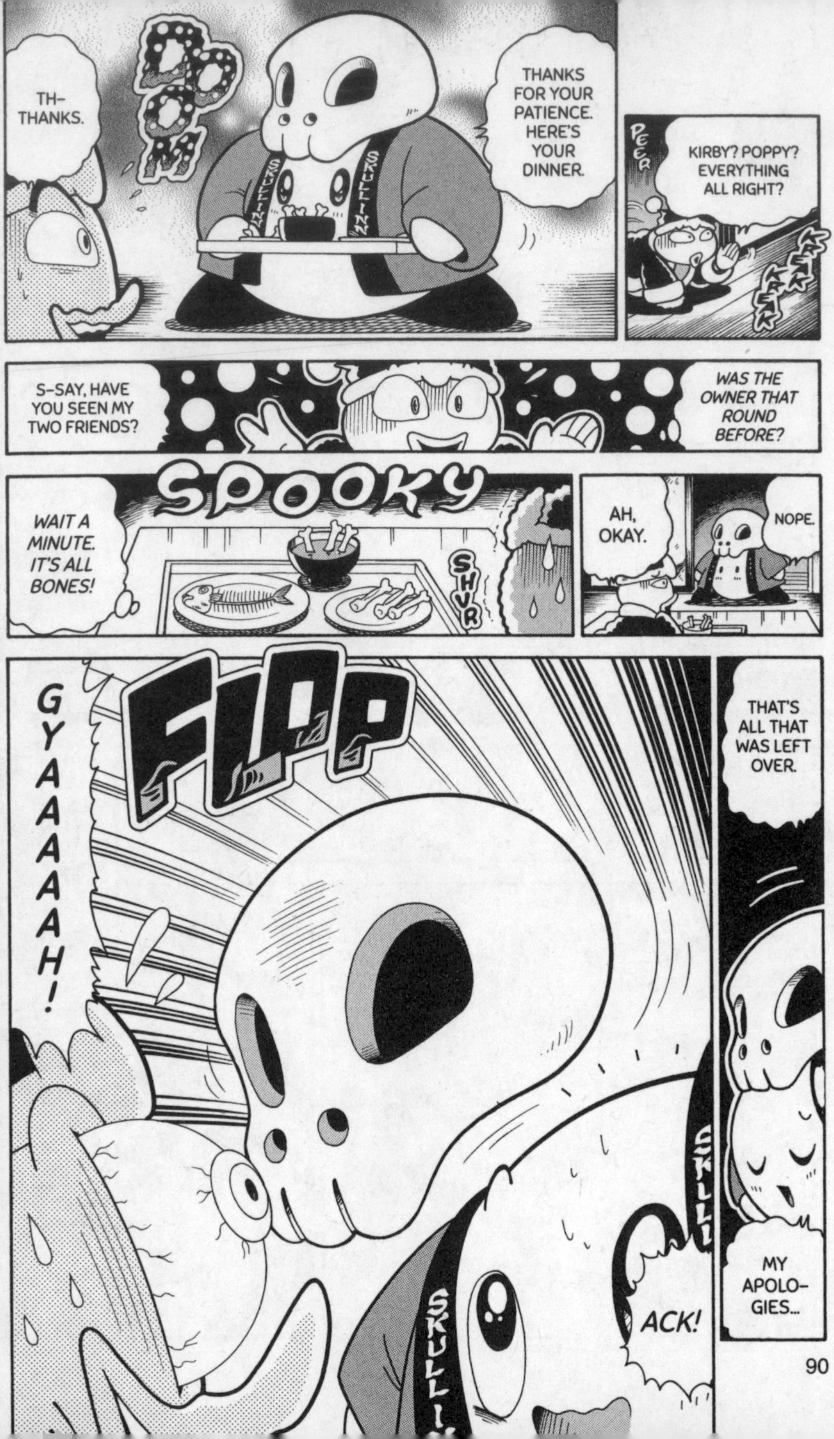
PEER
KIRBY? POPPY? EVERYTHING ALL RIGHT?
KREAK KREAK KREAK
THANKS FOR YOUR PATIENCE. HERE'S YOUR DINNER.
SKULL INN
TH- THANKS.
WAS THE OWNER THAT ROUND BEFORE?
S-SAY, HAVE YOU SEEN MY TWO FRIENDS?
NOPE.
AH, OKAY.
SPOOKY
SHVR
WAIT A MINUTE. IT'S ALL BONES!
THAT'S ALL THAT WAS LEFT OVER.
MY APOLOGIES...
FLOP
ACK!
GYAAAAAAAH!

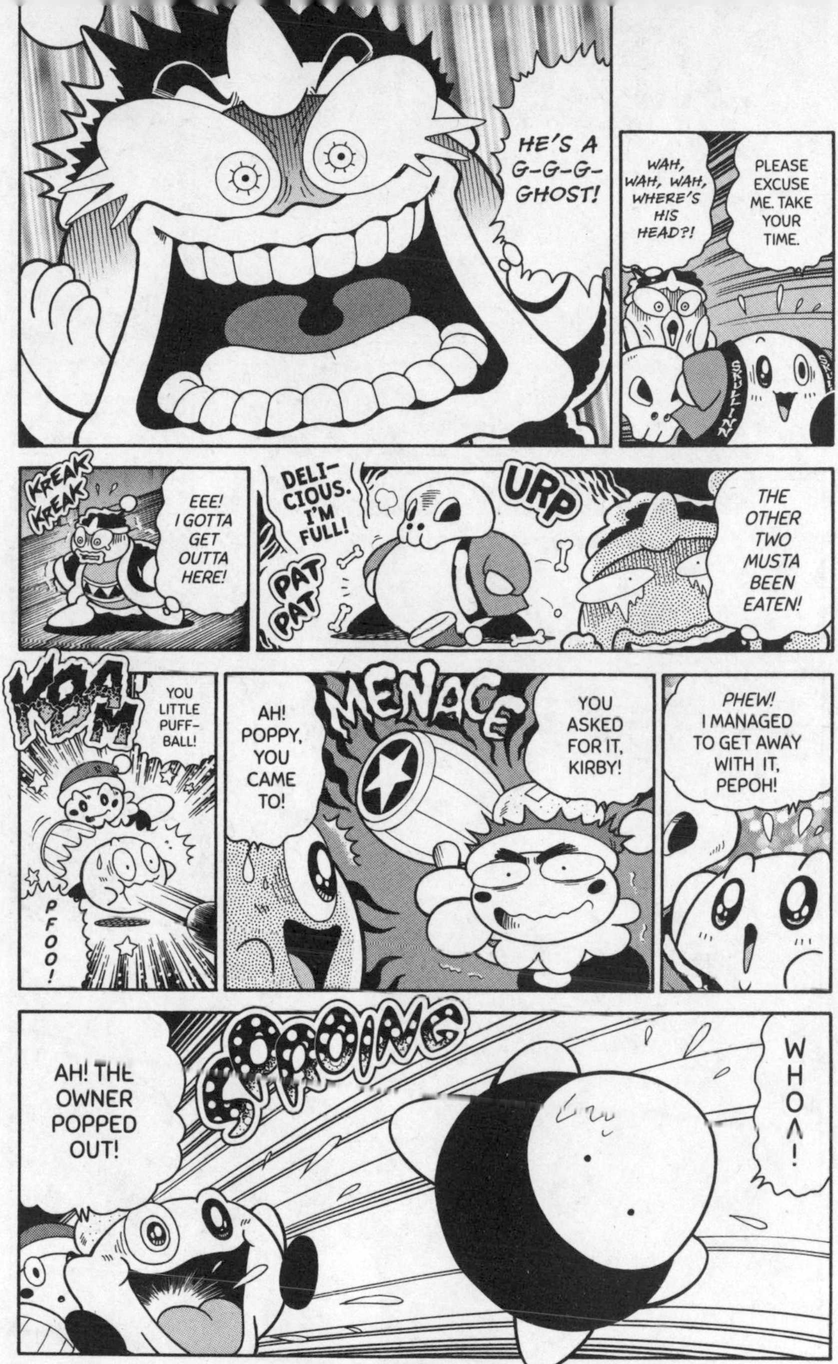
PLEASE EXCUSE ME. TAKE YOUR TIME.
WAH, WAH, WAH, WHERE'S HIS HEAD?!
HE'S A G-G-G-GHOST!
THE OTHER TWO MUSTA BEEN EATEN!
URP
DELI-CIOUS. I'M FULL!
PAT PAT
KREAK KREAK
EEE! I GOTTA GET OUTTA HERE!
PHEW! I MANAGED TO GET AWAY WITH IT, PEPOH!
YOU ASKED FOR IT, KIRBY!
MENACE
AH! POPPY, YOU CAME TO!
YOU LITTLE PUFF-BALL!
PFOOO!
WHOA!
SPROING
AH! THE OWNER POPPED OUT!

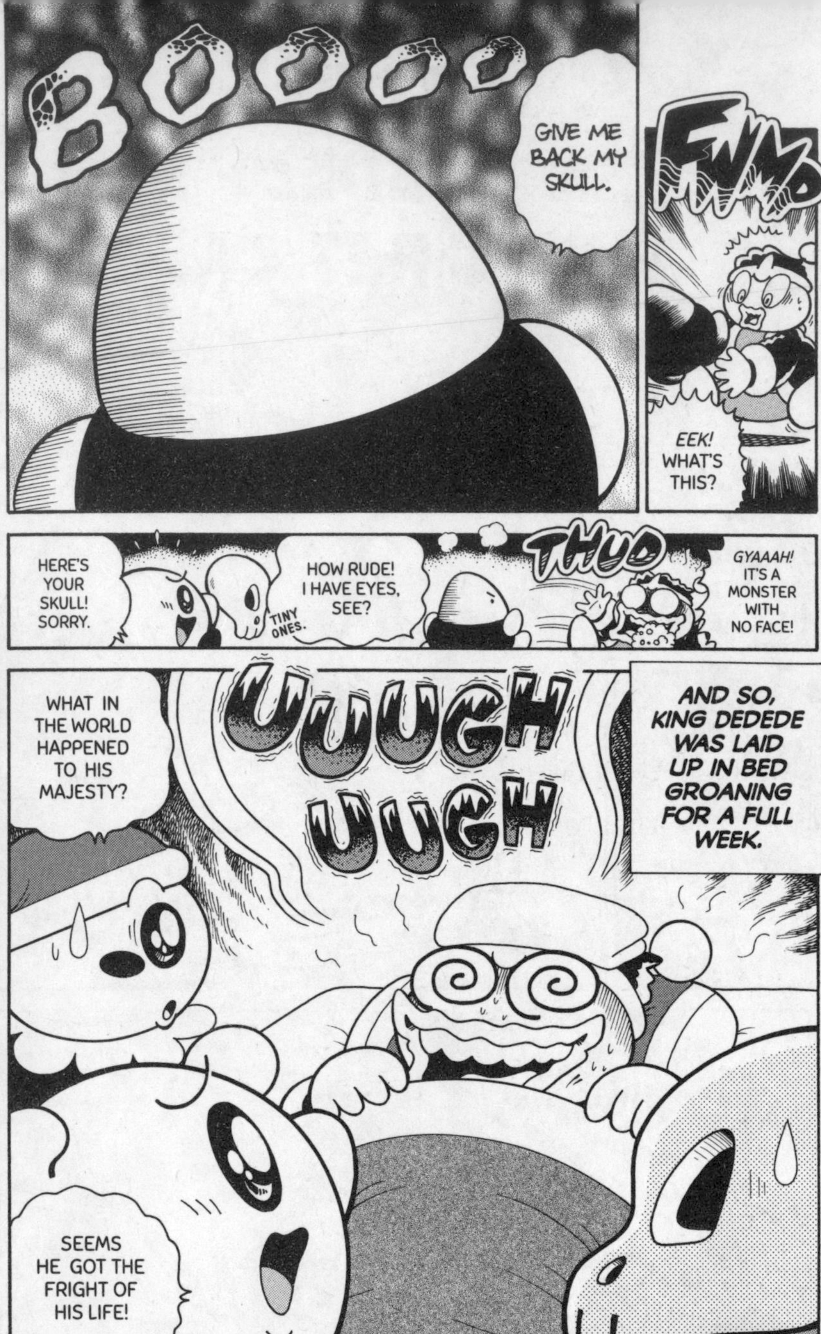
EEK! WHAT'S THIS?
BOOOOO
GIVE ME BACK MY SKULL.
GYAAAH! IT'S A MONSTER WITH NO FACE!
THUD
HOW RUDE! I HAVE EYES, SEE?
TINY ONES.
HERE'S YOUR SKULL! SORRY.
AND SO, KING DEDEDE WAS LAID UP IN BED GROANING FOR A FULL WEEK.
UUUGH UUGH
WHAT IN THE WORLD HAPPENED TO HIS MAJESTY?
SEEMS HE GOT THE FRIGHT OF HIS LIFE!

CHAPTER 7: KING DEDEDE'S ROBOTIC PET CRAZE

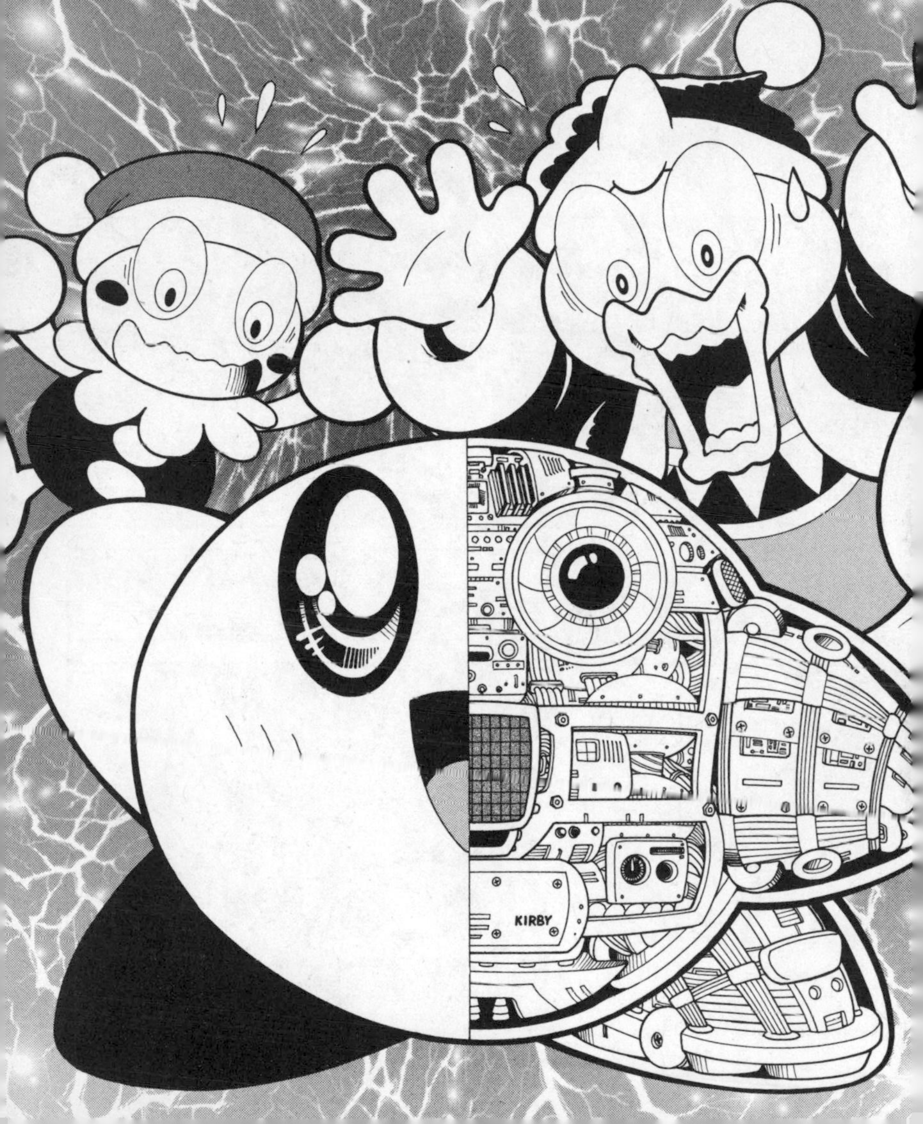
KIRBY

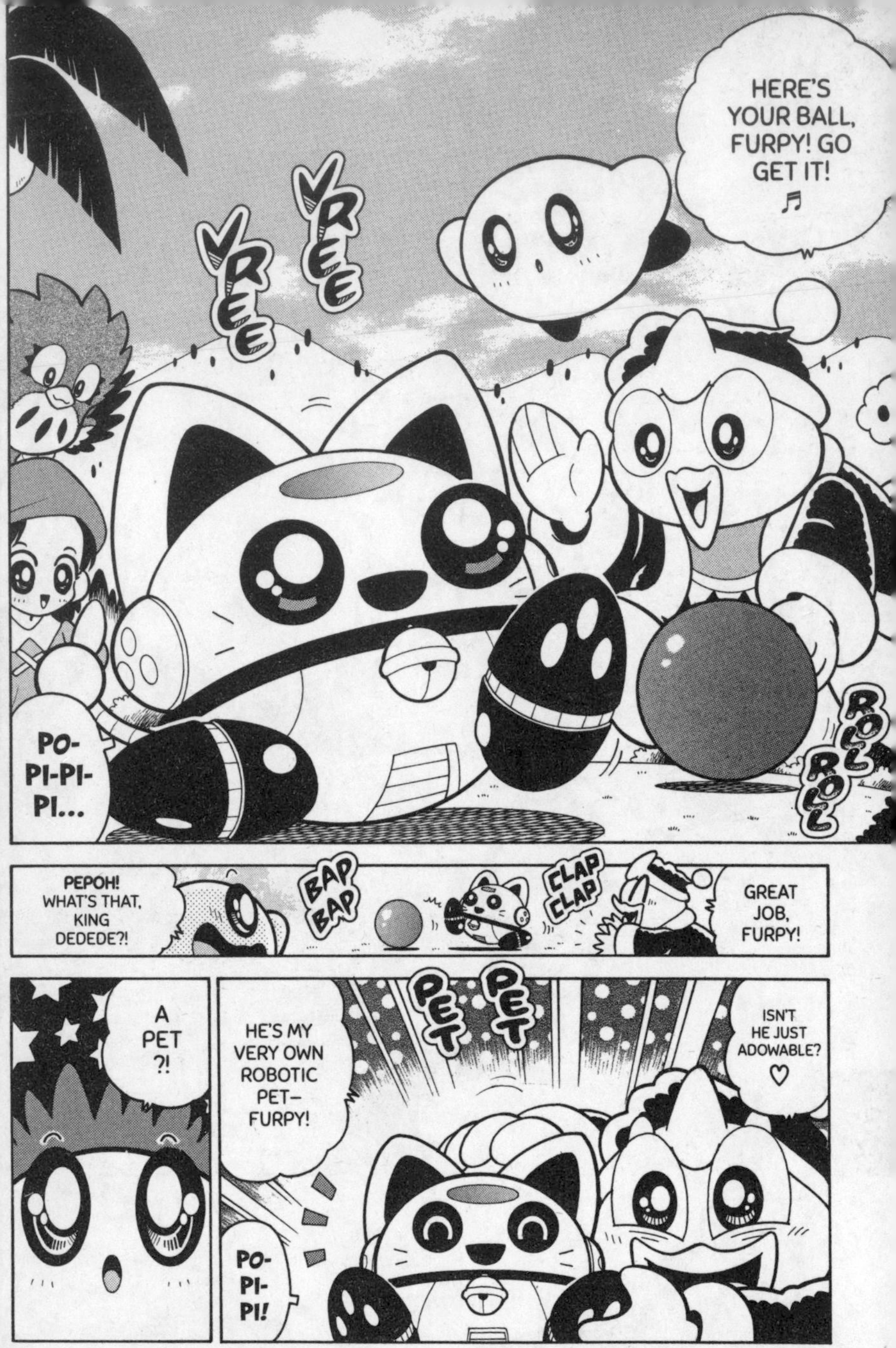
HERE'S YOUR BALL, FURPY! GO GET IT! ♪
VREE VREE
ROLL ROLL
PO-PI-PI-PI...
GREAT JOB, FURPY!
CLAP CLAP
BAP BAP
PEPOH! WHAT'S THAT, KING DEDEDE?!
ISN'T HE JUST ADOWABLE? ♡
PET PET
HE'S MY VERY OWN ROBOTIC PET—FURPY!
PO-PI-PI!
A PET?!

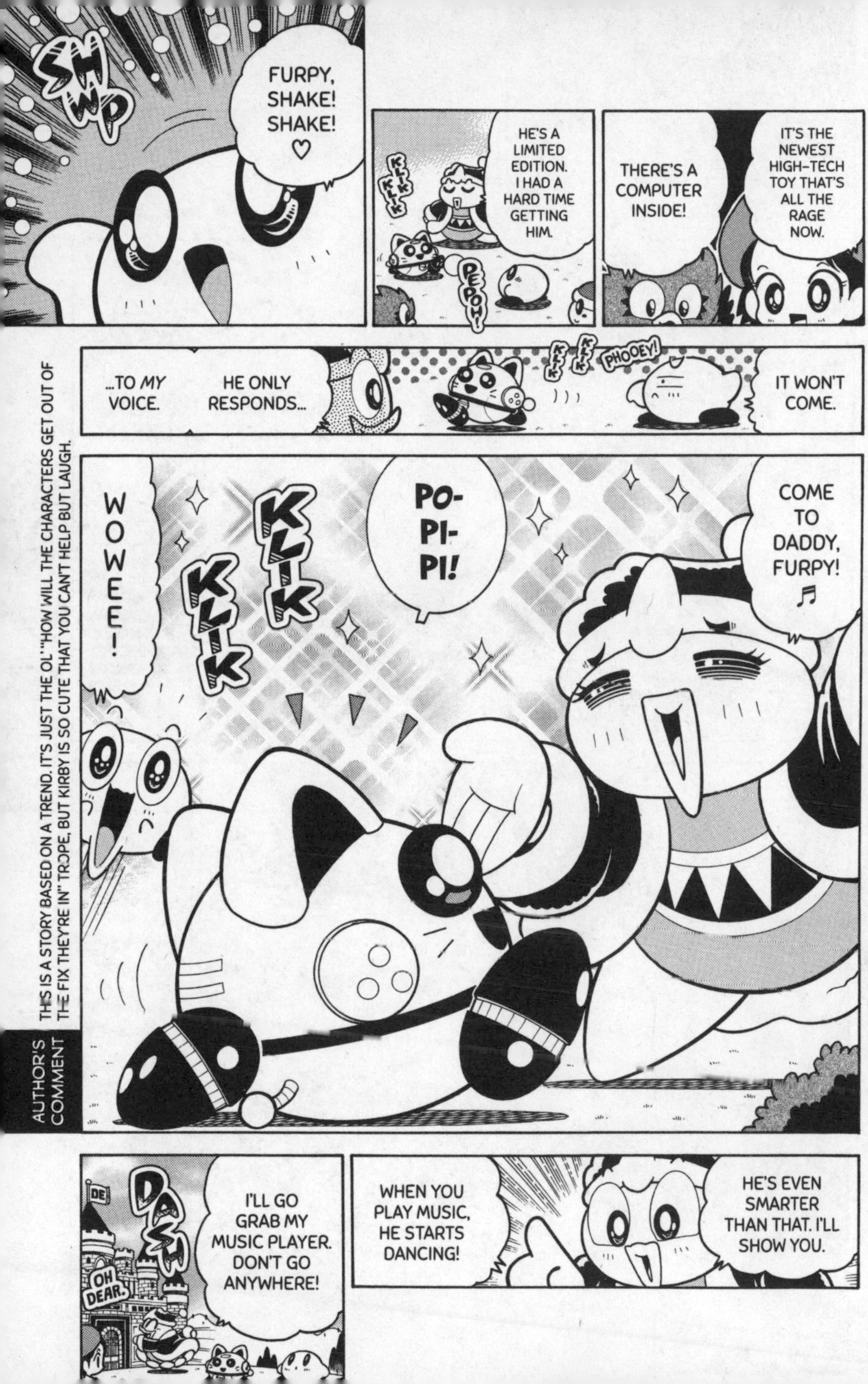
IT'S THE NEWEST HIGH-TECH TOY THAT'S ALL THE RAGE NOW.
THERE'S A COMPUTER INSIDE!
HE'S A LIMITED EDITION. I HAD A HARD TIME GETTING HIM.
KLIK KLIK
PEPOH!
FURPY, SHAKE! SHAKE! ♡
SHWP
IT WON'T COME.
PHOOEY!
KLIK KLIK
HE ONLY RESPONDS...
...TO *MY* VOICE.
COME TO DADDY, FURPY! ♪
PO-PI-PI!
KLIK KLIK
WOWEE!
HE'S EVEN SMARTER THAN THAT. I'LL SHOW YOU.
WHEN YOU PLAY MUSIC, HE STARTS DANCING!
I'LL GO GRAB MY MUSIC PLAYER. DON'T GO ANYWHERE!
DASH
OH DEAR.
DE

AUTHOR'S COMMENT

THIS IS A STORY BASED ON A TREND. IT'S JUST THE OL' "HOW WILL THE CHARACTERS GET OUT OF THE FIX THEY'RE IN" TROPE, BUT KIRBY IS SO CUTE THAT YOU CAN'T HELP BUT LAUGH.

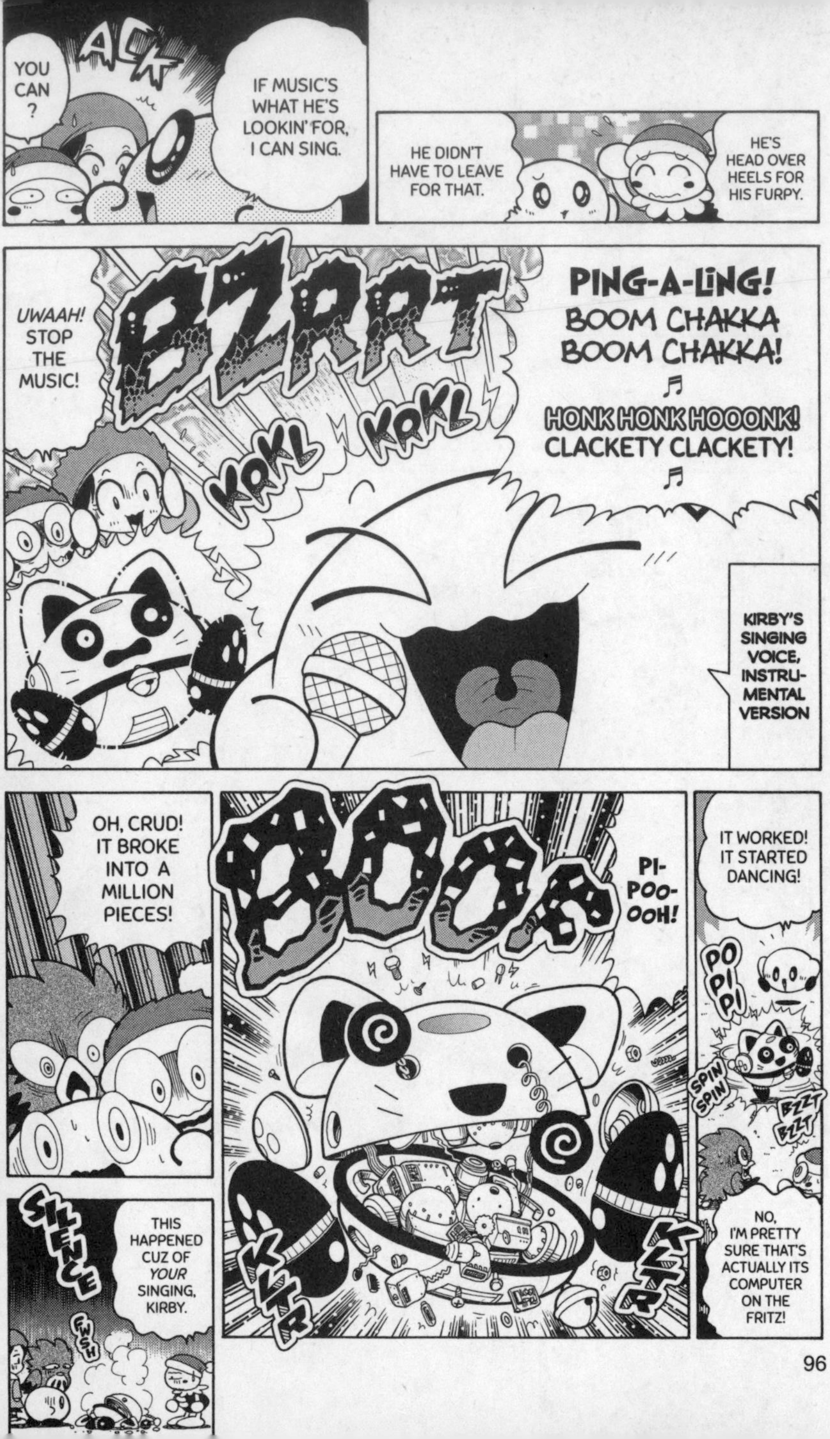
HE'S HEAD OVER HEELS FOR HIS FURPY.
HE DIDN'T HAVE TO LEAVE FOR THAT.
IF MUSIC'S WHAT HE'S LOOKIN' FOR, I CAN SING.
ACK
YOU CAN ?
PING-A-LING! BOOM CHAKKA BOOM CHAKKA! ♬
HONK HONK HOOONK! CLACKETY CLACKETY! ♬
KIRBY'S SINGING VOICE, INSTRUMENTAL VERSION
BZRRT
KOKL KOKL
UWAAH! STOP THE MUSIC!
IT WORKED! IT STARTED DANCING!
POPIPI
SPIN SPIN
BZZT BZZT
NO, I'M PRETTY SURE THAT'S ACTUALLY ITS COMPUTER ON THE FRITZ!
BOOM
PI-POO-OOH!
KLTR
KLTR
OH, CRUD! IT BROKE INTO A MILLION PIECES!
THIS HAPPENED CUZ OF *YOUR* SINGING, KIRBY.
SILENCE
FWSH

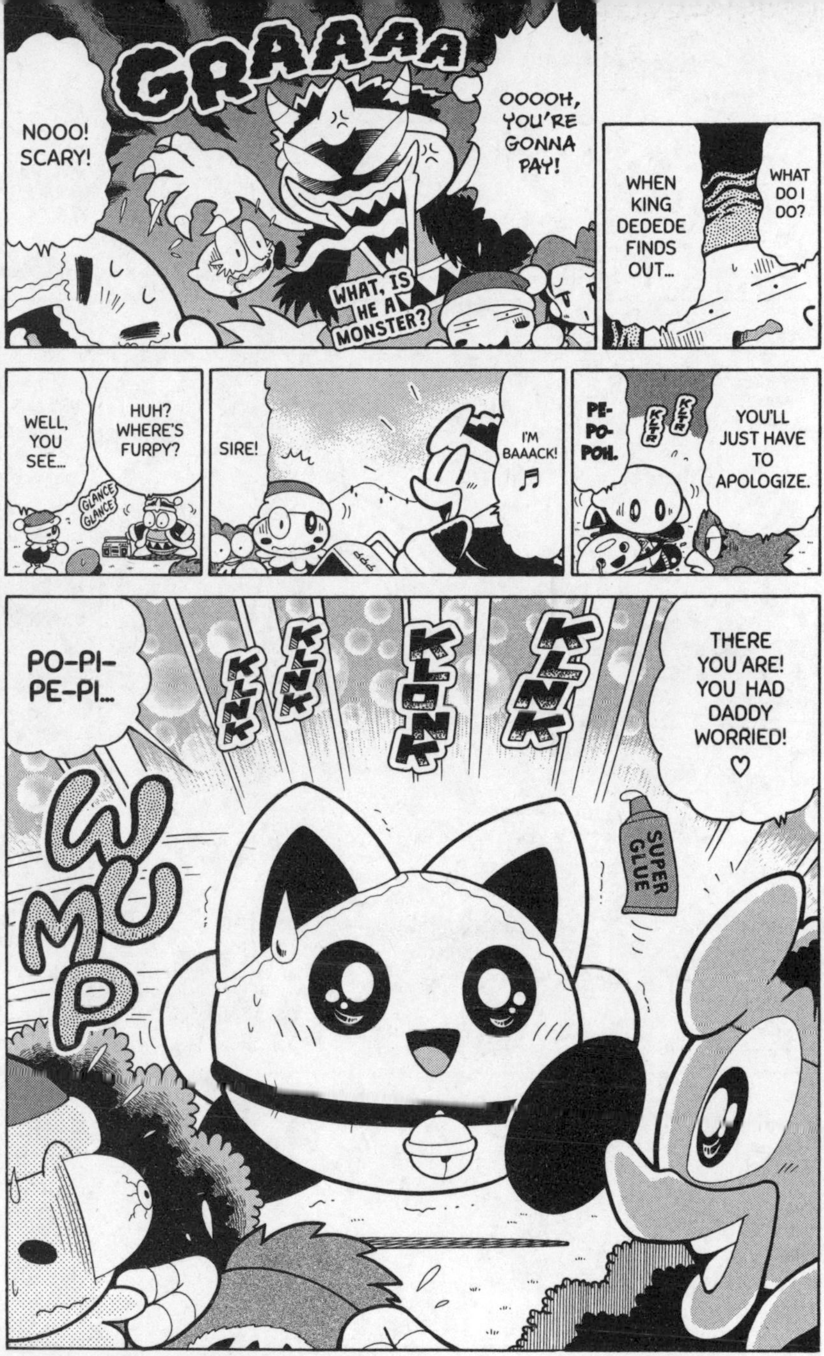
WHAT DO I DO?
WHEN KING DEDEDE FINDS OUT...
GRAAAA
OOOOH, YOU'RE GONNA PAY!
NOOO! SCARY!
WHAT, IS HE A MONSTER?
YOU'LL JUST HAVE TO APOLOGIZE.
KLTR KLTR
PE-PO-POH.
I'M BAAACK! ♪
SIRE!
HUH? WHERE'S FURPY?
WELL, YOU SEE...
GLANCE GLANCE
THERE YOU ARE! YOU HAD DADDY WORRIED! ♡
KLINK
KLONK
KLINK
KLINK
PO-PI-PE-PI...
SUPER GLUE
WUMP

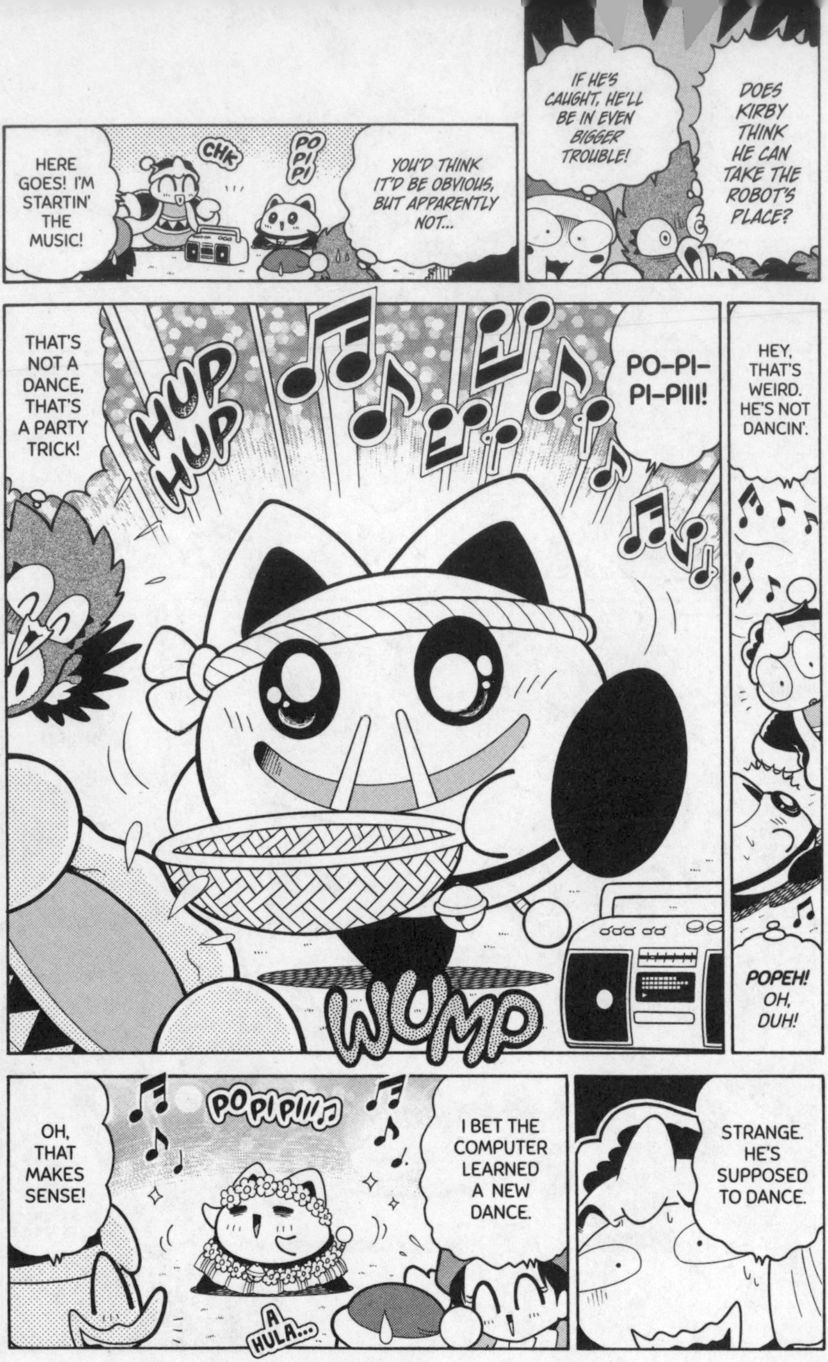
DOES KIRBY THINK HE CAN TAKE THE ROBOT'S PLACE?
IF HE'S CAUGHT, HE'LL BE IN EVEN BIGGER TROUBLE!
YOU'D THINK IT'D BE OBVIOUS, BUT APPARENTLY NOT...
PO PI PI
CHK
HERE GOES! I'M STARTIN' THE MUSIC!
HEY, THAT'S WEIRD. HE'S NOT DANCIN'.
POPEH! OH, DUH!
PO-PI-PI-PIII!
HUP HUP
THAT'S NOT A DANCE, THAT'S A PARTY TRICK!
WUMP
STRANGE. HE'S SUPPOSED TO DANCE.
I BET THE COMPUTER LEARNED A NEW DANCE.
POPIPIII
OH, THAT MAKES SENSE!
A HULA...

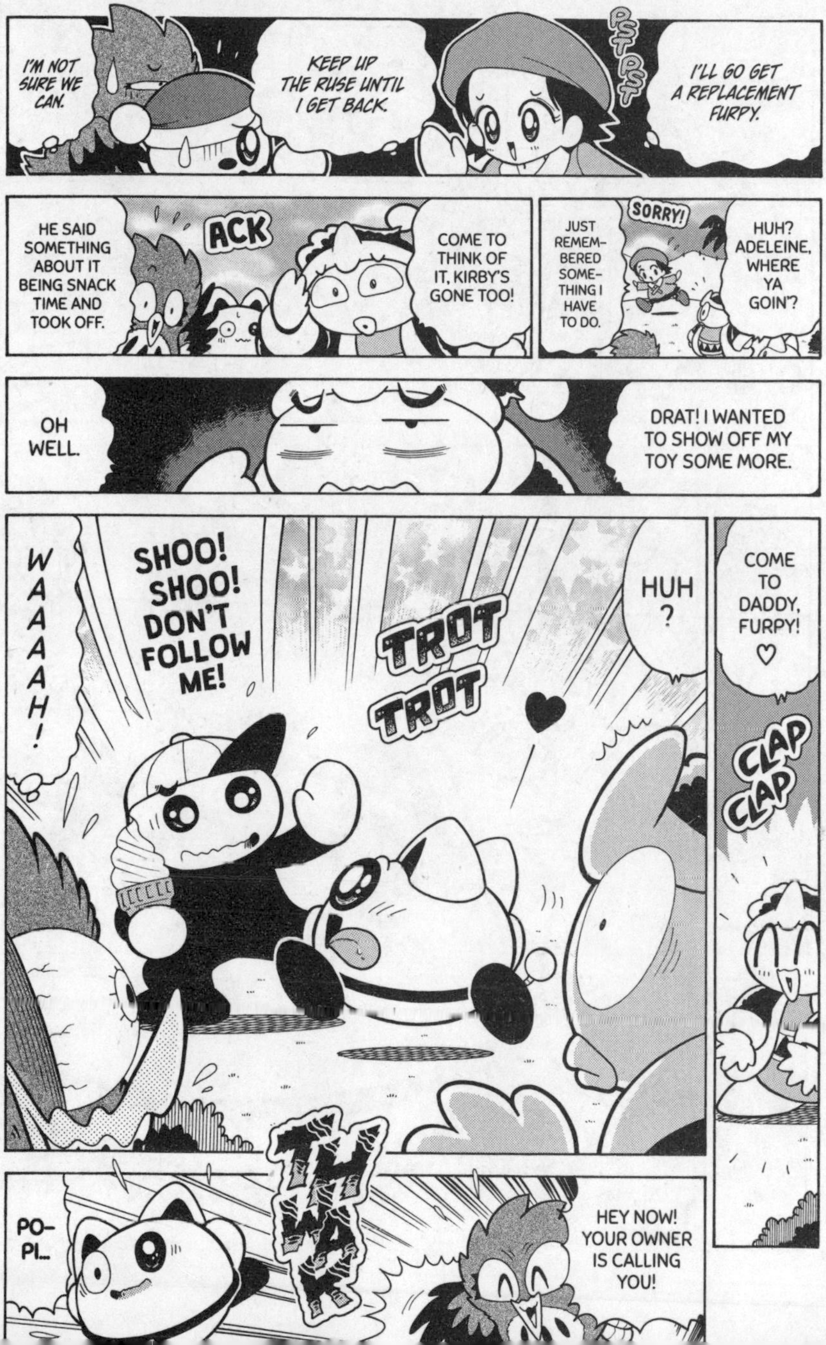
I'LL GO GET A REPLACEMENT FURPY.
PST PST
KEEP UP THE RUSE UNTIL I GET BACK.
I'M NOT SURE WE CAN.
HUH? ADELEINE, WHERE YA GOIN'?
SORRY!
JUST REMEMBERED SOMETHING I HAVE TO DO.
COME TO THINK OF IT, KIRBY'S GONE TOO!
ACK
HE SAID SOMETHING ABOUT IT BEING SNACK TIME AND TOOK OFF.
DRAT! I WANTED TO SHOW OFF MY TOY SOME MORE.
OH WELL.
COME TO DADDY, FURPY! ♡
CLAP CLAP
HUH?
TROT TROT
SHOO! SHOO! DON'T FOLLOW ME!
WAAAAAH!
HEY NOW! YOUR OWNER IS CALLING YOU!
THWA
PO-PI...

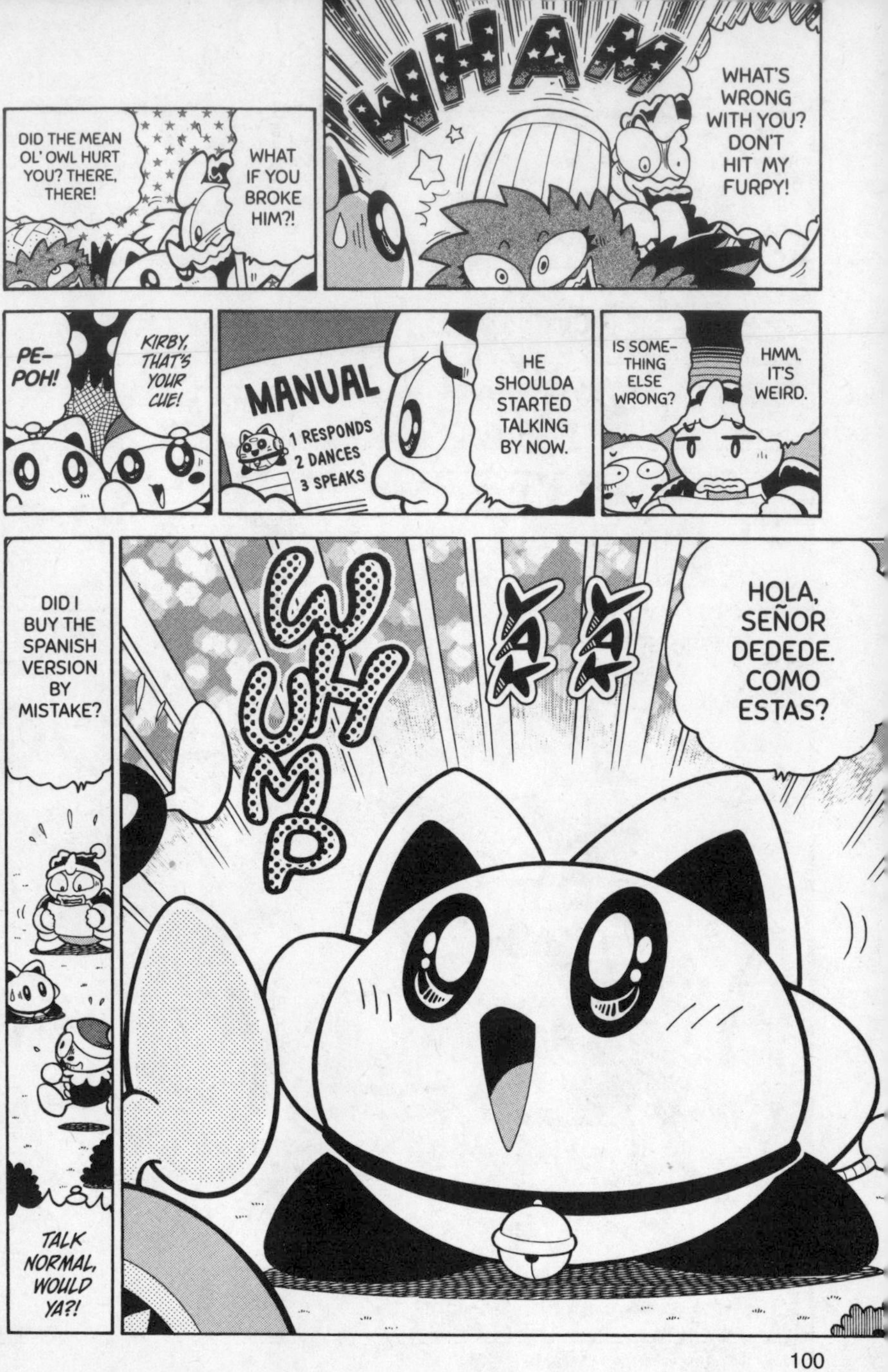
WHAM
WHAT'S WRONG WITH YOU? DON'T HIT MY FURPY!
WHAT IF YOU BROKE HIM?!
DID THE MEAN OL' OWL HURT YOU? THERE, THERE!
HMM. IT'S WEIRD.
IS SOME-THING ELSE WRONG?
HE SHOULDA STARTED TALKING BY NOW.
MANUAL
1 RESPONDS
2 DANCES
3 SPEAKS
KIRBY, THAT'S YOUR CUE!
PE-POH!
HOLA, SEÑOR DEDEDE. COMO ESTAS?
WUHMP
DID I BUY THE SPANISH VERSION BY MISTAKE?
TALK NORMAL, WOULD YA?!

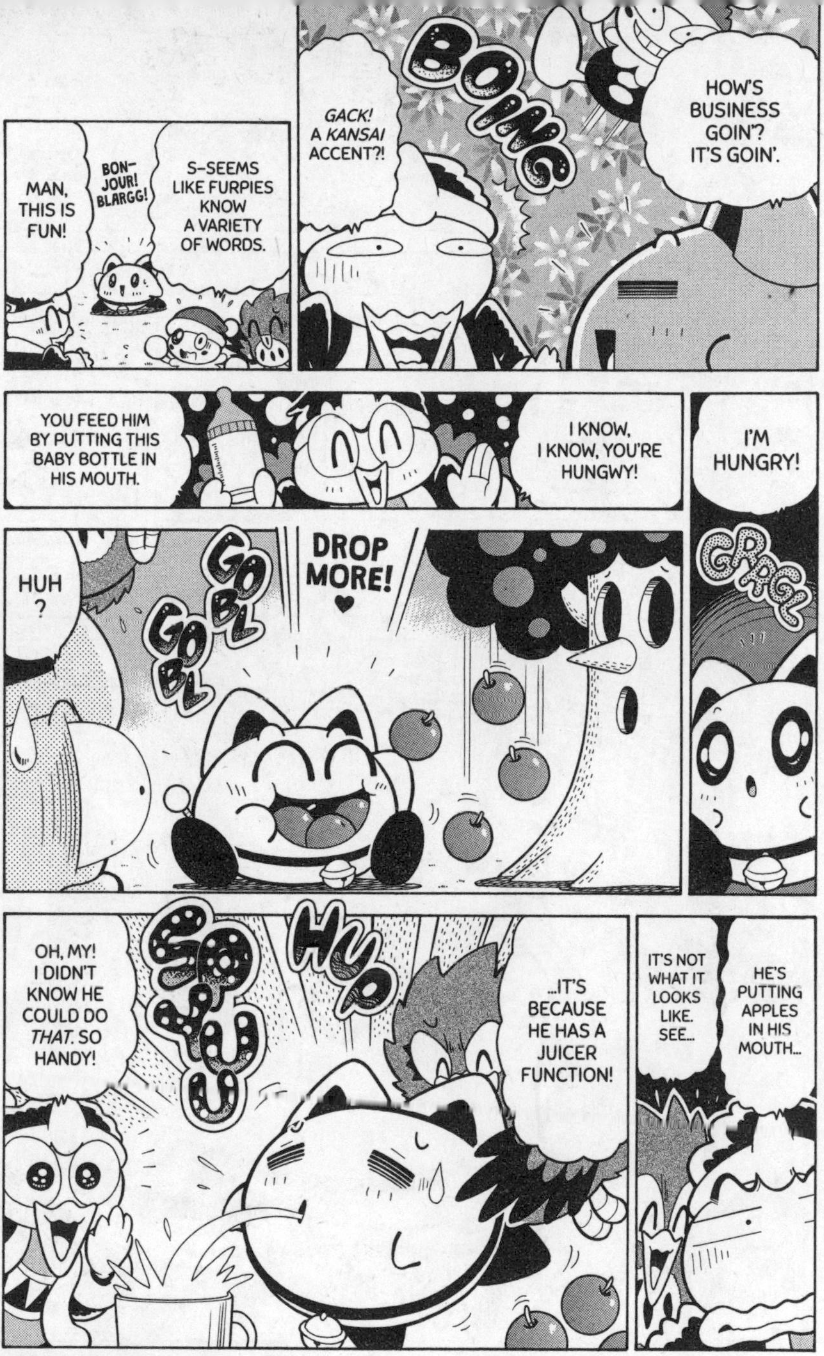
HOW'S BUSINESS GOIN'? IT'S GOIN'.
BOING
GACK! A KANSAI ACCENT?!
S-SEEMS LIKE FURPIES KNOW A VARIETY OF WORDS.
BON-JOUR! BLARGG!
MAN, THIS IS FUN!
I'M HUNGRY!
GRRGL
I KNOW, I KNOW, YOU'RE HUNGWY!
YOU FEED HIM BY PUTTING THIS BABY BOTTLE IN HIS MOUTH.
DROP MORE! ♥
GOBL GOBL
HUH?
HE'S PUTTING APPLES IN HIS MOUTH...
IT'S NOT WHAT IT LOOKS LIKE. SEE...
HUP
...IT'S BECAUSE HE HAS A JUICER FUNCTION!
SPLUU
OH, MY! I DIDN'T KNOW HE COULD DO *THAT*. SO HANDY!

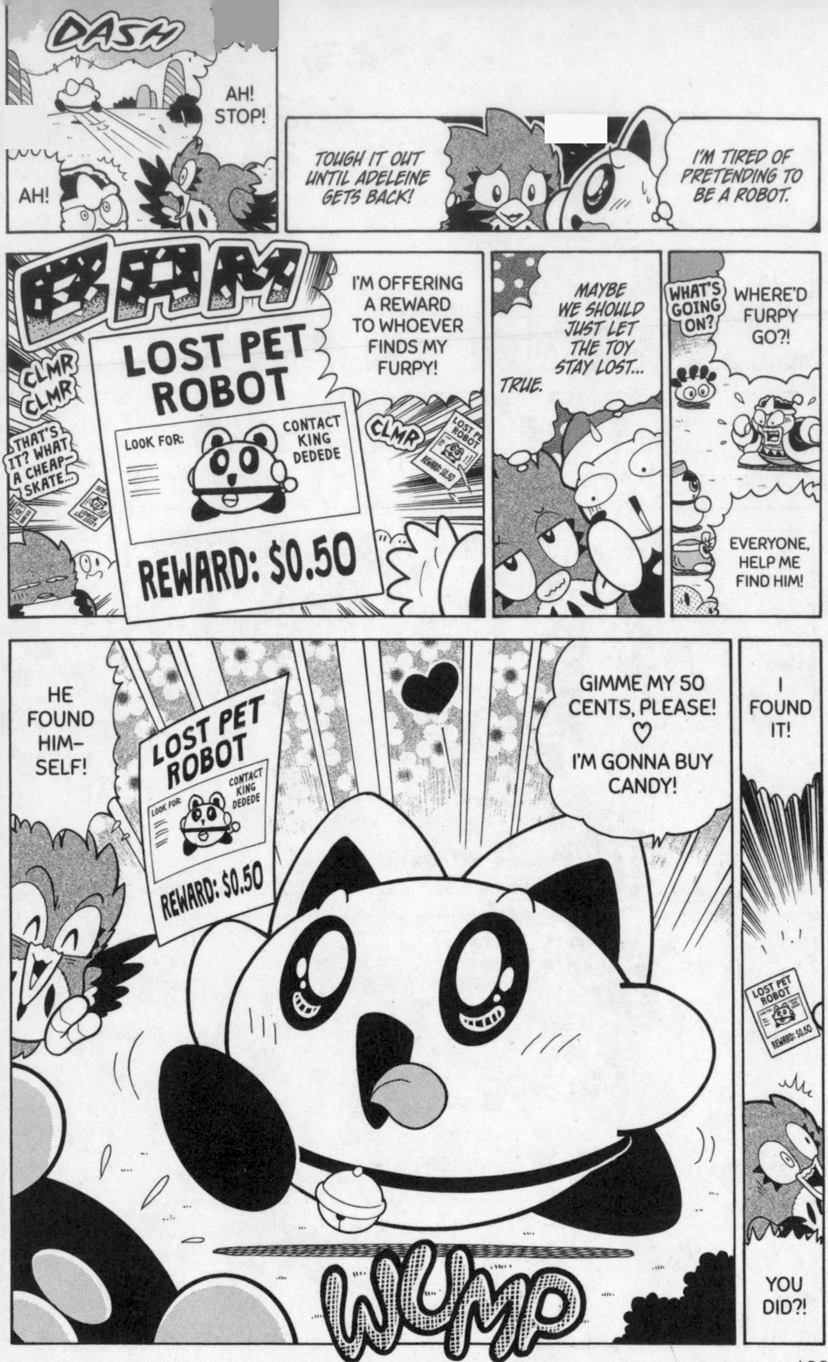
I'M TIRED OF PRETENDING TO BE A ROBOT.
TOUGH IT OUT UNTIL ADELEINE GETS BACK!
DASH
AH! STOP!
AH!
WHERE'D FURPY GO?!
WHAT'S GOING ON?
EVERYONE, HELP ME FIND HIM!
MAYBE WE SHOULD JUST LET THE TOY STAY LOST...
TRUE.
I'M OFFERING A REWARD TO WHOEVER FINDS MY FURPY!
BAM
LOST PET ROBOT
LOOK FOR:
CONTACT KING DEDEDE
REWARD: $0.50
CLMR
CLMR CLMR
THAT'S IT? WHAT A CHEAP-SKATE...
I FOUND IT!
YOU DID?!
GIMME MY 50 CENTS, PLEASE! ♡
I'M GONNA BUY CANDY!
HE FOUND HIM-SELF!
LOST PET ROBOT
LOOK FOR:
CONTACT KING DEDEDE
REWARD: $0.50
WUMP

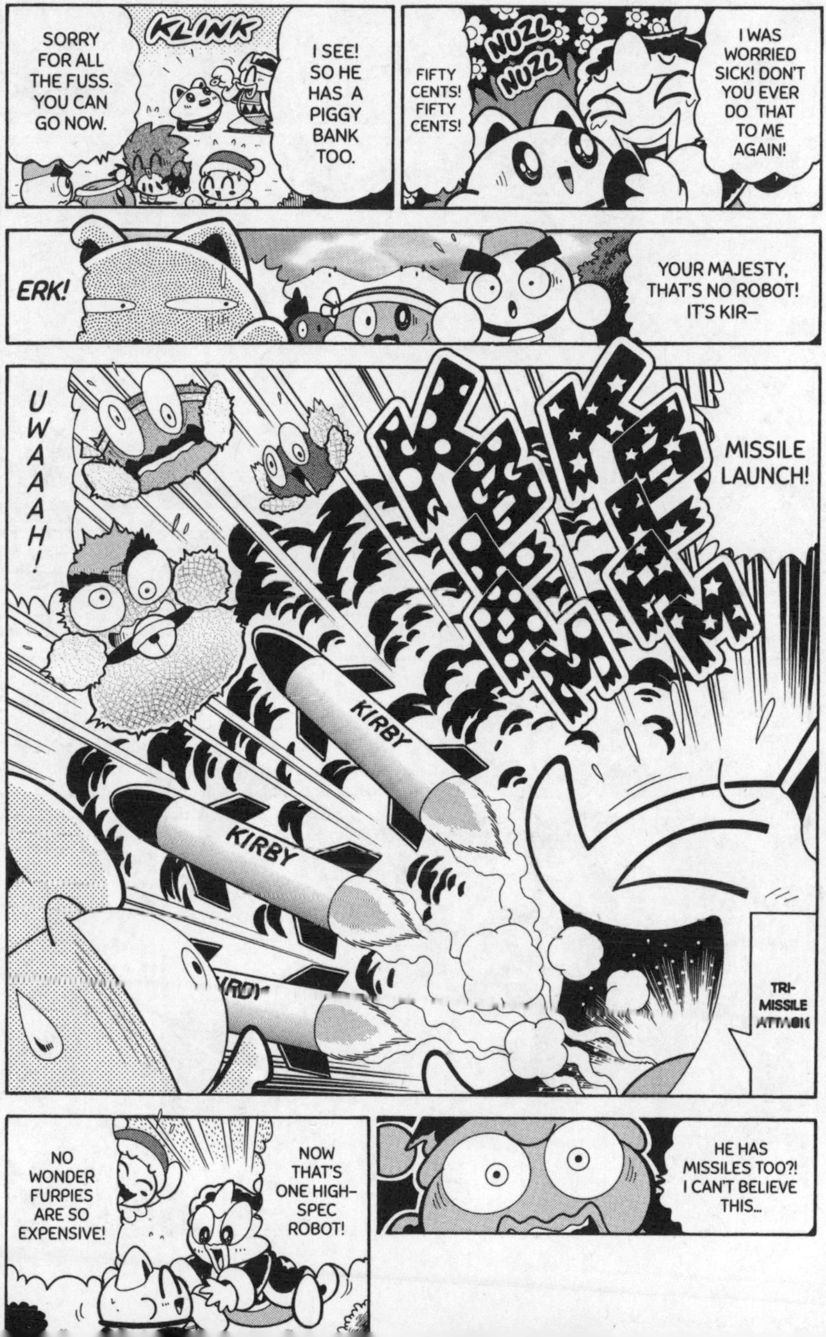
I WAS WORRIED SICK! DON'T YOU EVER DO THAT TO ME AGAIN!
NUZZ NUZZ
FIFTY CENTS! FIFTY CENTS!
I SEE! SO HE HAS A PIGGY BANK TOO.
KLINK
SORRY FOR ALL THE FUSS. YOU CAN GO NOW.
YOUR MAJESTY, THAT'S NO ROBOT! IT'S KIR–
ERK!
MISSILE LAUNCH!
UWAAAAH!
KIRBY
KIRBY
TRI-MISSILE
HE HAS MISSILES TOO?! I CAN'T BELIEVE THIS...
NOW THAT'S ONE HIGH-SPEC ROBOT!
NO WONDER FURPIES ARE SO EXPENSIVE!

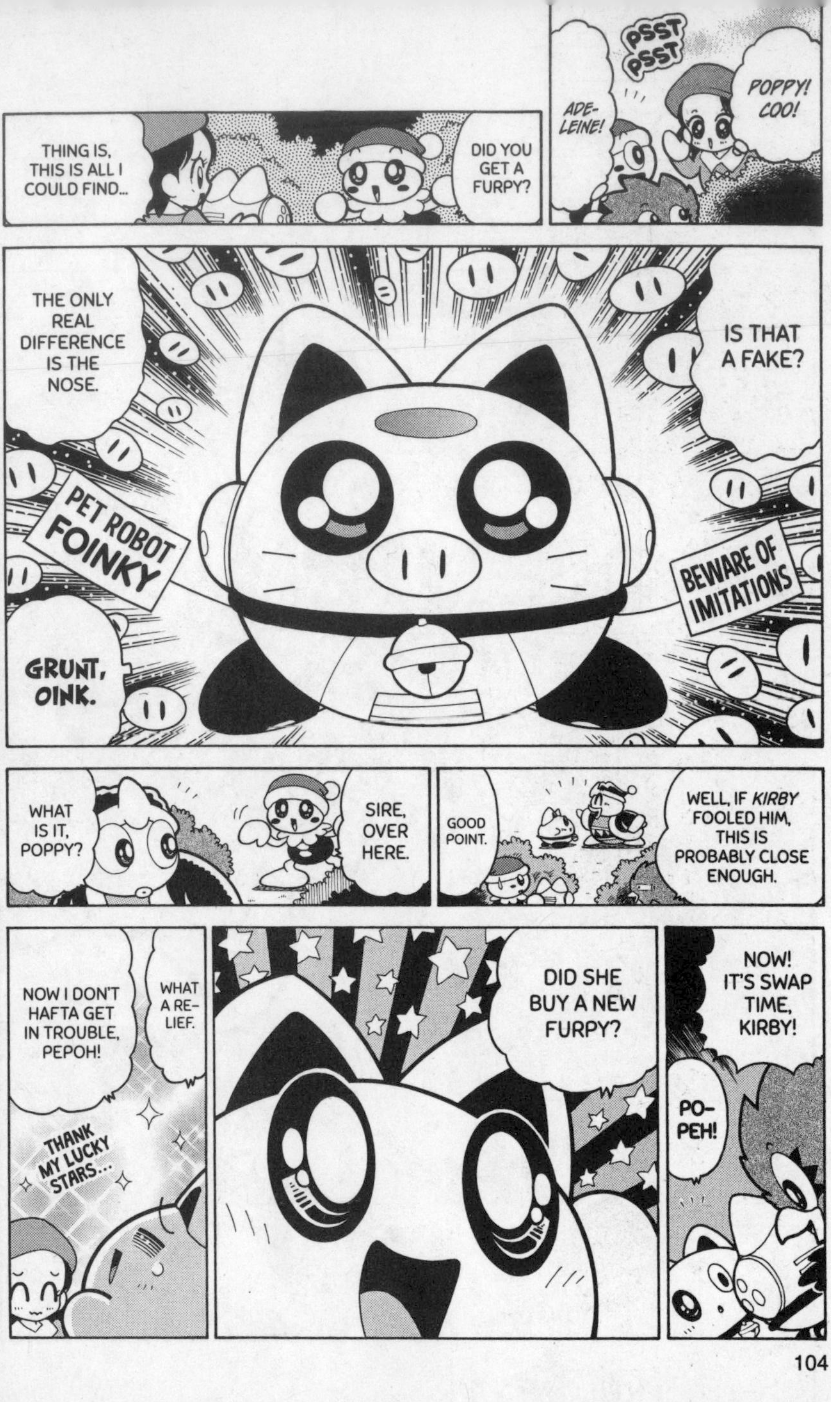
PSST PSST
POPPY! COO!
ADE-LEINE!
DID YOU GET A FURPY?
THING IS, THIS IS ALL I COULD FIND...
IS THAT A FAKE?
THE ONLY REAL DIFFERENCE IS THE NOSE.
BEWARE OF IMITATIONS
PET ROBOT FOINKY
GRUNT, OINK.
WELL, IF *KIRBY* FOOLED HIM, THIS IS PROBABLY CLOSE ENOUGH.
GOOD POINT.
SIRE, OVER HERE.
WHAT IS IT, POPPY?
NOW! IT'S SWAP TIME, KIRBY!
PO-PEH!
DID SHE BUY A NEW FURPY?
WHAT A RE-LIEF.
NOW I DON'T HAFTA GET IN TROUBLE, PEPOH!
THANK MY LUCKY STARS...

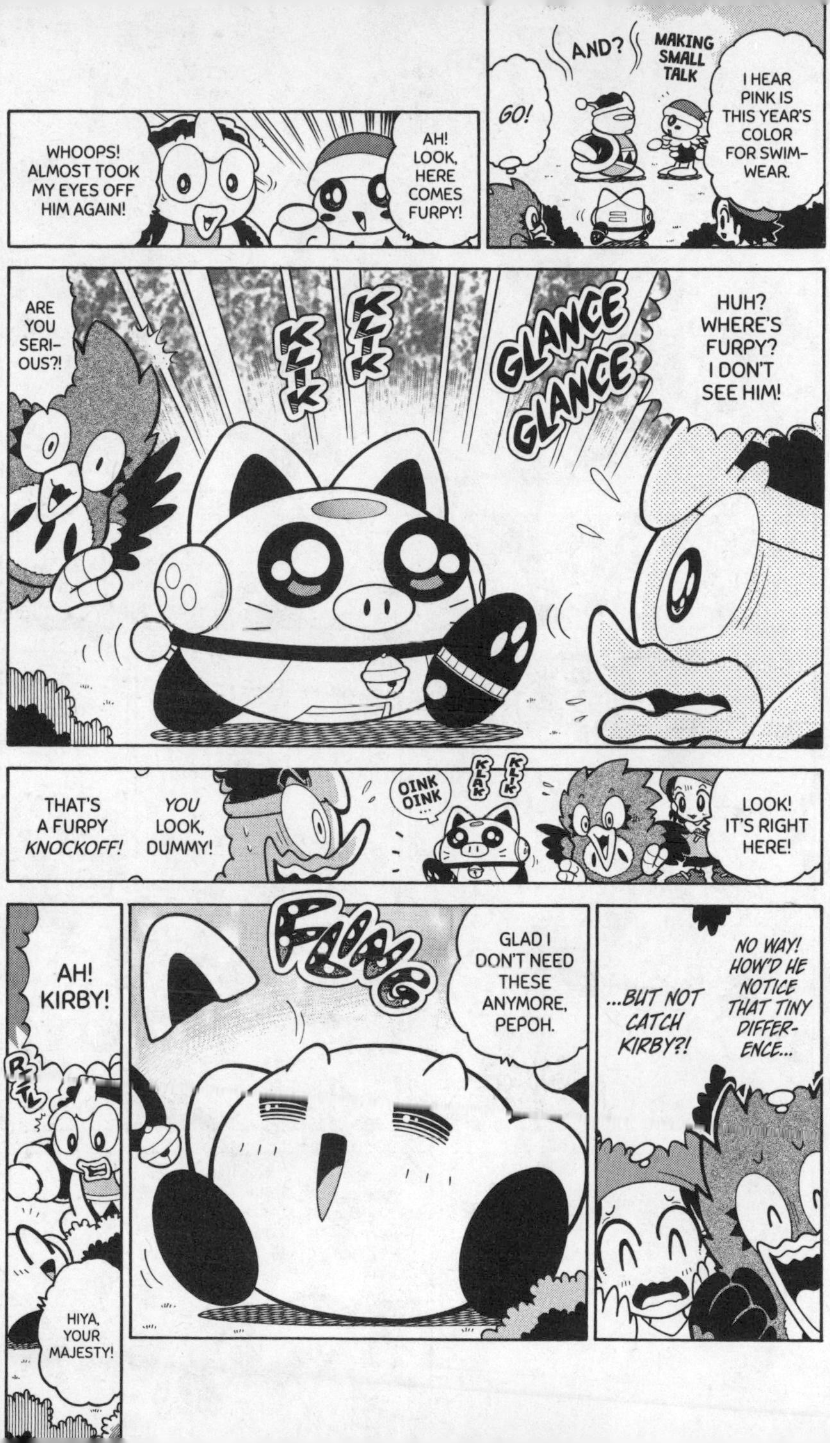
I HEAR PINK IS THIS YEAR'S COLOR FOR SWIM-WEAR.
MAKING SMALL TALK
AND?
GO!
AH! LOOK, HERE COMES FURPY!
WHOOPS! ALMOST TOOK MY EYES OFF HIM AGAIN!
HUH? WHERE'S FURPY? I DON'T SEE HIM!
GLANCE GLANCE
KLIK KLIK
ARE YOU SERI-OUS?!
LOOK! IT'S RIGHT HERE!
KLIK KLAK
OINK OINK
YOU LOOK, DUMMY!
THAT'S A FURPY *KNOCKOFF!*
NO WAY! HOW'D HE NOTICE THAT TINY DIFFER-ENCE...
...BUT NOT CATCH KIRBY?!
GLAD I DON'T NEED THESE ANYMORE, PEPOH.
FLING
AH! KIRBY!
HIYA, YOUR MAJESTY!

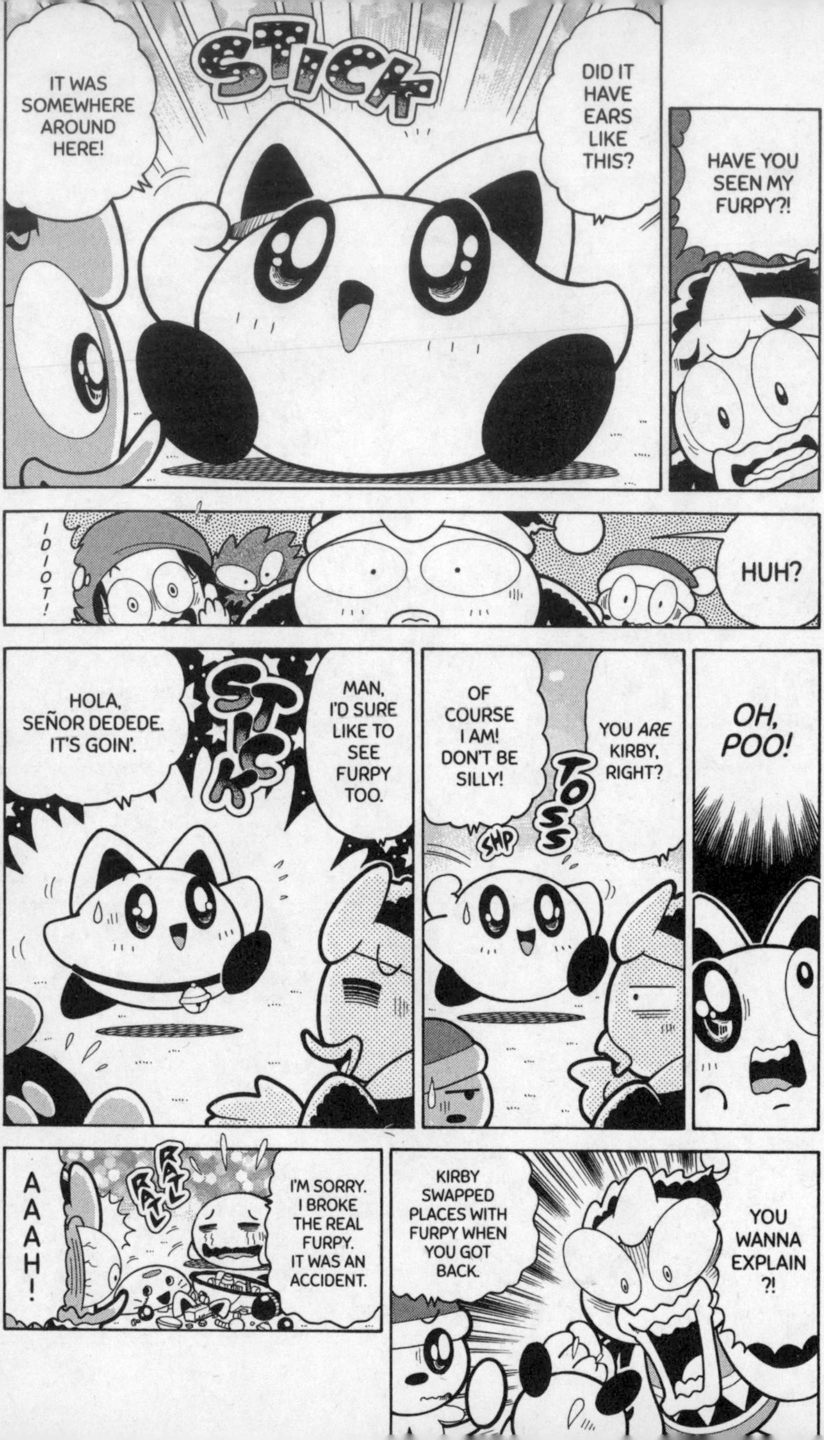
HAVE YOU SEEN MY FURPY?!
DID IT HAVE EARS LIKE THIS?
STICK
IT WAS SOMEWHERE AROUND HERE!
HUH?
IDIOT!
OH, POO!
YOU *ARE* KIRBY, RIGHT?
TOSS
OF COURSE I AM! DON'T BE SILLY!
SHP
MAN, I'D SURE LIKE TO SEE FURPY TOO.
STICK
HOLA, SEÑOR DEDEDE. IT'S GOIN'.
YOU WANNA EXPLAIN?!
KIRBY SWAPPED PLACES WITH FURPY WHEN YOU GOT BACK.
I'M SORRY. I BROKE THE REAL FURPY. IT WAS AN ACCIDENT.
RATL
RATL
AAAH!

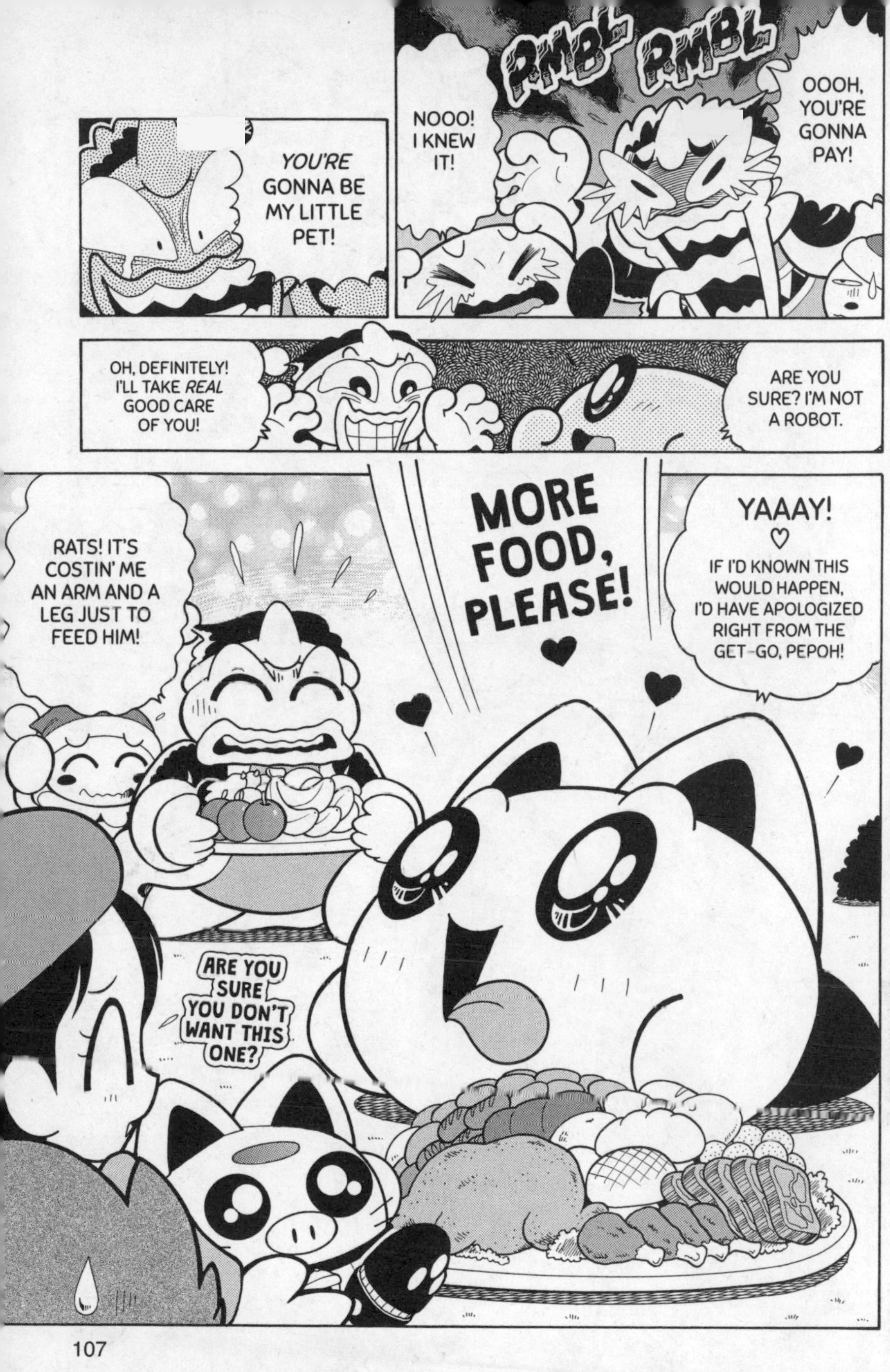
RMBL RMBL
OOOH, YOU'RE GONNA PAY!
NOOO! I KNEW IT!
YOU'RE GONNA BE MY LITTLE PET!
ARE YOU SURE? I'M NOT A ROBOT.
OH, DEFINITELY! I'LL TAKE *REAL* GOOD CARE OF YOU!
YAAAY! ♡
IF I'D KNOWN THIS WOULD HAPPEN, I'D HAVE APOLOGIZED RIGHT FROM THE GET-GO, PEPOH!
MORE FOOD, PLEASE!
RATS! IT'S COSTIN' ME AN ARM AND A LEG JUST TO FEED HIM!
ARE YOU SURE YOU DON'T WANT THIS ONE?

CHAPTER 8: THE COMFORTS OF THE 22ND CENTURY!

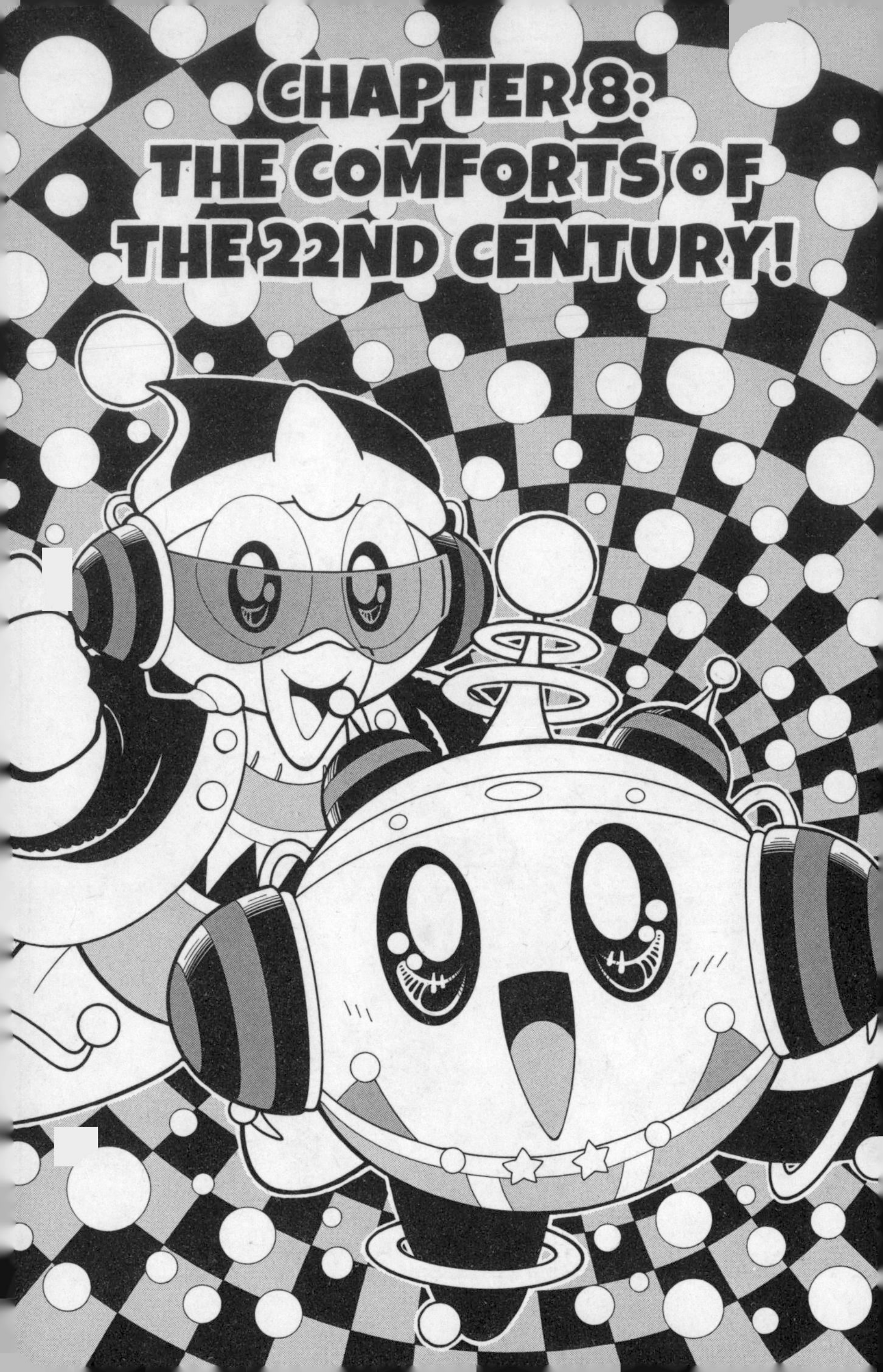

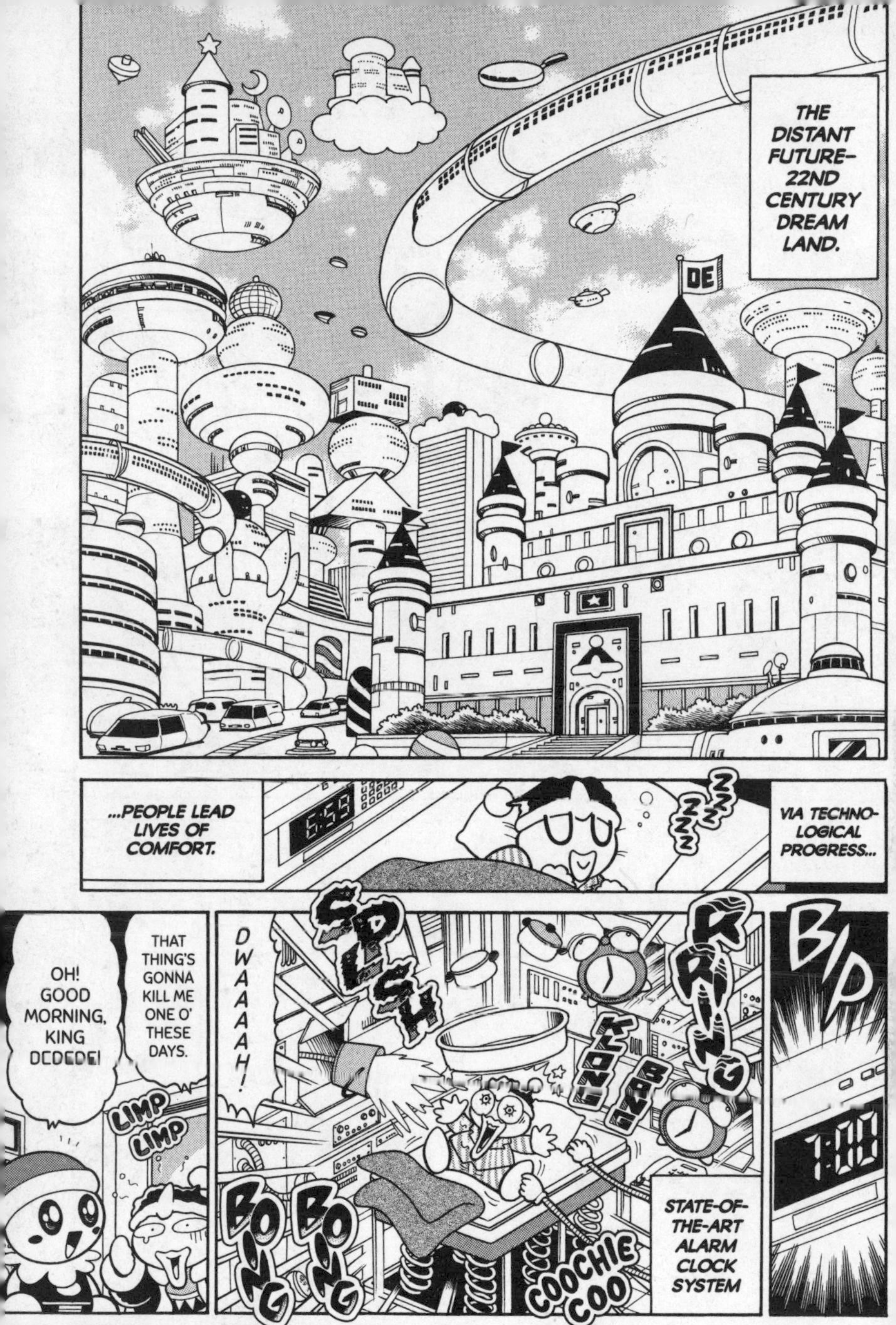
THE DISTANT FUTURE— 22ND CENTURY DREAM LAND.
DE
VIA TECHNO-LOGICAL PROGRESS...
ZZZ ZZZ
6:59
...PEOPLE LEAD LIVES OF COMFORT.
BIP
7:00
RRING
STATE-OF-THE-ART ALARM CLOCK SYSTEM
KLONG
BANG
SPLISH
DWAAAAAH!
BOING
BOING
COOCHIE COO
THAT THING'S GONNA KILL ME ONE O' THESE DAYS.
OH! GOOD MORNING, KING DEDEDE!
LIMP LIMP

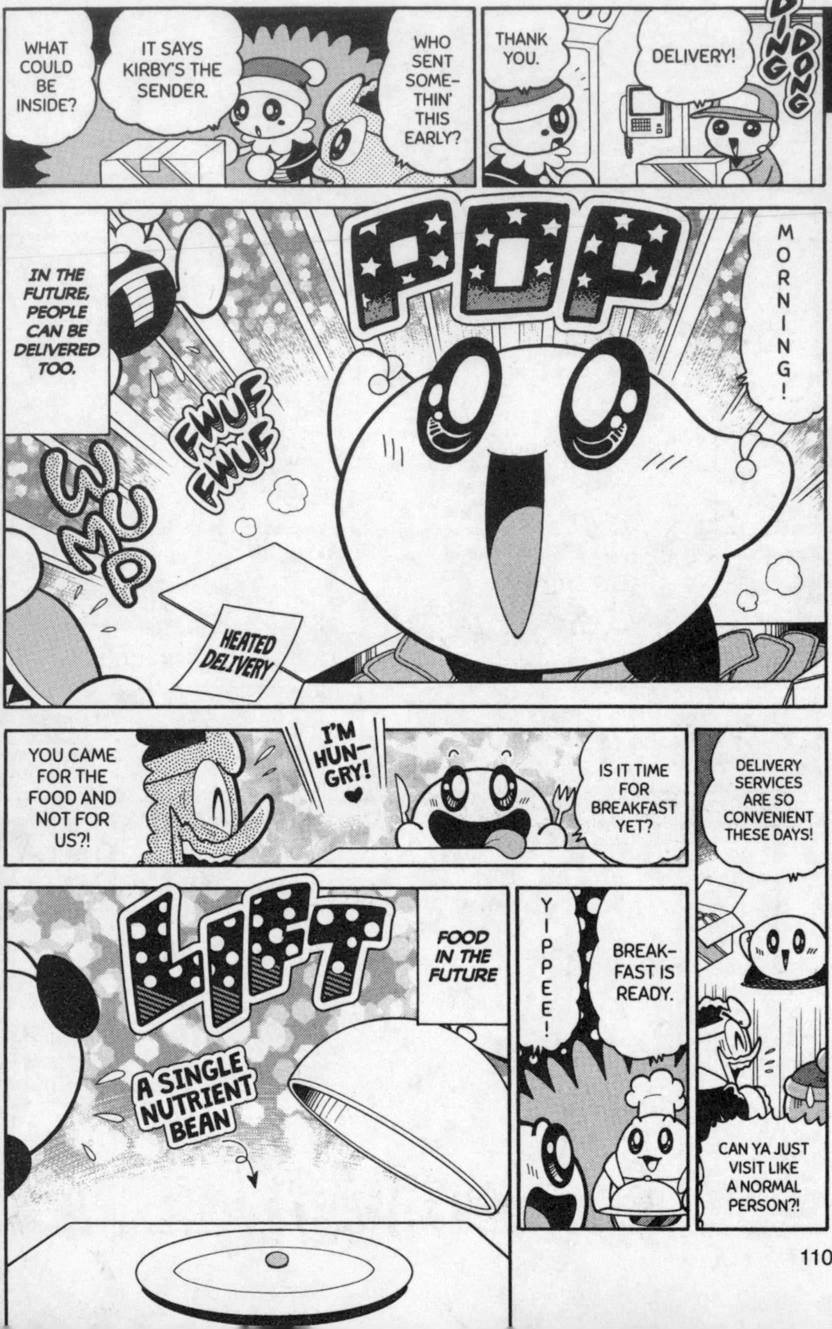
DING DONG
DELIVERY!
THANK YOU.
WHO SENT SOME-THIN' THIS EARLY?
IT SAYS KIRBY'S THE SENDER.
WHAT COULD BE INSIDE?
MORNING!
POP
IN THE FUTURE, PEOPLE CAN BE DELIVERED TOO.
FWUF FWUF
WUMP
HEATED DELIVERY
DELIVERY SERVICES ARE SO CONVENIENT THESE DAYS!
CAN YA JUST VISIT LIKE A NORMAL PERSON?!
IS IT TIME FOR BREAKFAST YET?
I'M HUN-GRY!
YOU CAME FOR THE FOOD AND NOT FOR US?!
BREAK-FAST IS READY.
YIPPEE!
FOOD IN THE FUTURE
LIFT
A SINGLE NUTRIENT BEAN

AUTHOR'S COMMENT
THIS STORY FOLLOWS THE TYPICAL FORMULA, BUT MY ASSISTANTS' ART SKILLS MADE IT A HIGHLY POLISHED CHAPTER.

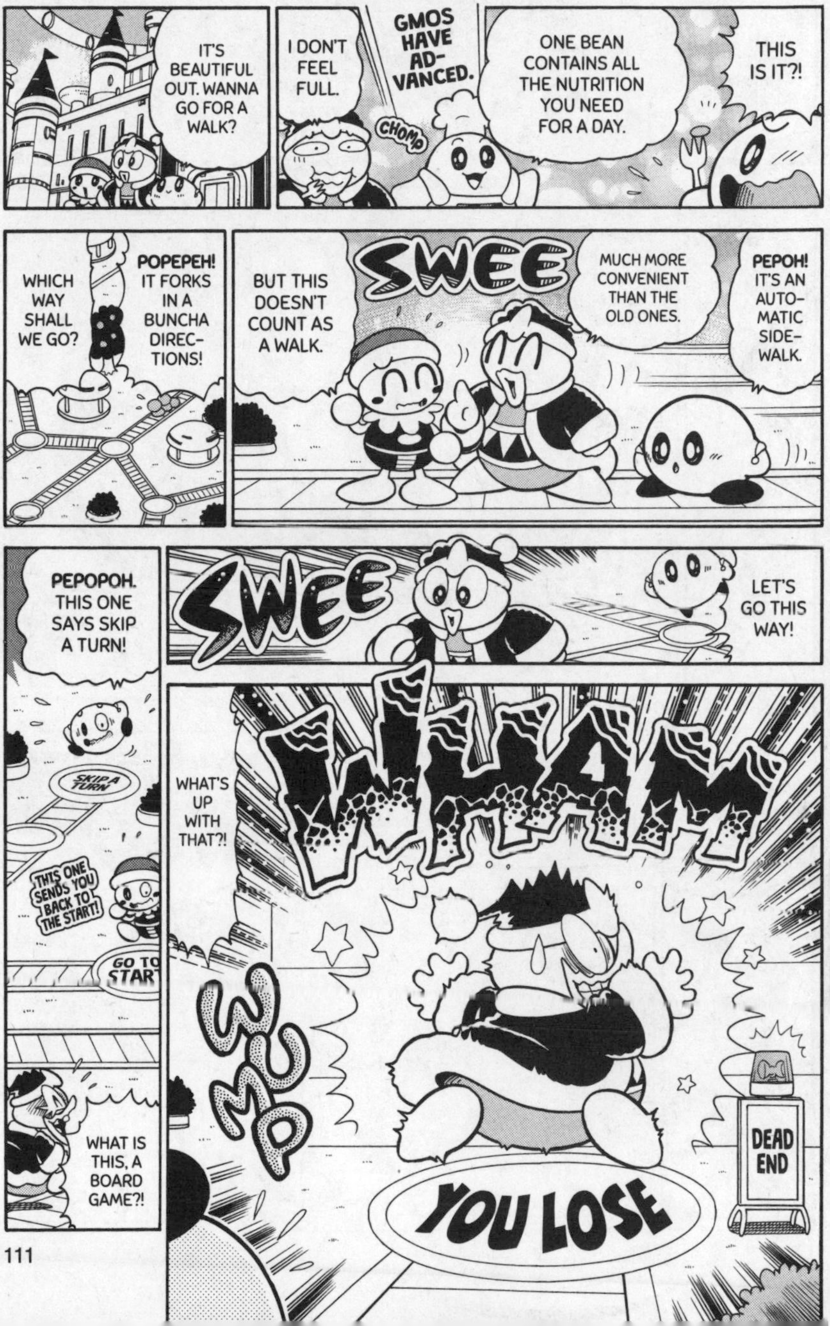
THIS IS IT?!
ONE BEAN CONTAINS ALL THE NUTRITION YOU NEED FOR A DAY.
GMOS HAVE AD-VANCED.
CHOMP
I DON'T FEEL FULL.
IT'S BEAUTIFUL OUT. WANNA GO FOR A WALK?
PEPOH! IT'S AN AUTO-MATIC SIDE-WALK.
MUCH MORE CONVENIENT THAN THE OLD ONES.
SWEE
BUT THIS DOESN'T COUNT AS A WALK.
POPEPEH! IT FORKS IN A BUNCHA DIREC-TIONS!
WHICH WAY SHALL WE GO?
LET'S GO THIS WAY!
SWEE
WHAM
WHAT'S UP WITH THAT?!
DEAD END
WUMP
YOU LOSE
PEPOPOH. THIS ONE SAYS SKIP A TURN!
SKIP A TURN
THIS ONE SENDS YOU BACK TO THE START!
GO TO START
WHAT IS THIS, A BOARD GAME?!

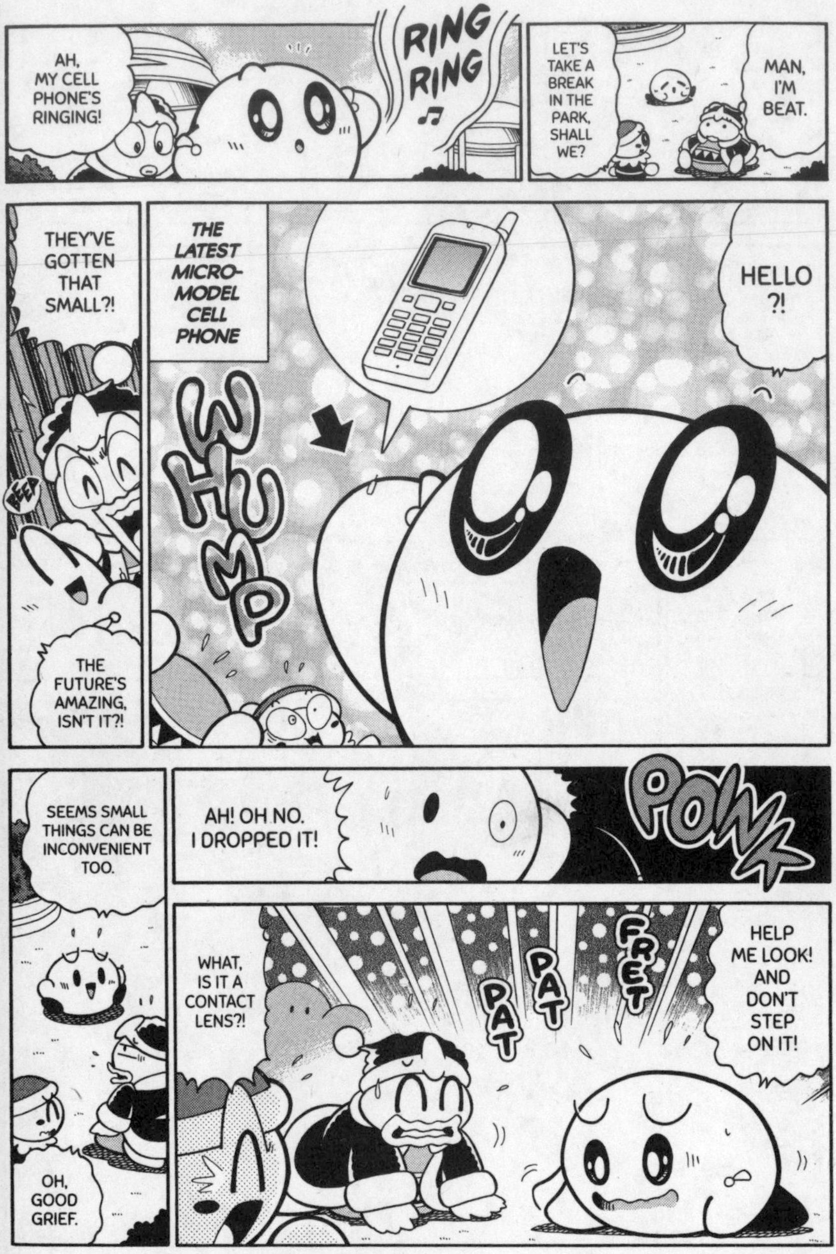
MAN, I'M BEAT.
LET'S TAKE A BREAK IN THE PARK, SHALL WE?
RING RING ♪
AH, MY CELL PHONE'S RINGING!
HELLO?!
THE LATEST MICRO-MODEL CELL PHONE
WHUMP
THEY'VE GOTTEN THAT SMALL?!
BEEP
THE FUTURE'S AMAZING, ISN'T IT?!
POINK
AH! OH NO. I DROPPED IT!
HELP ME LOOK! AND DON'T STEP ON IT!
FRET
PAT PAT
WHAT, IS IT A CONTACT LENS?!
SEEMS SMALL THINGS CAN BE INCONVENIENT TOO.
OH, GOOD GRIEF.

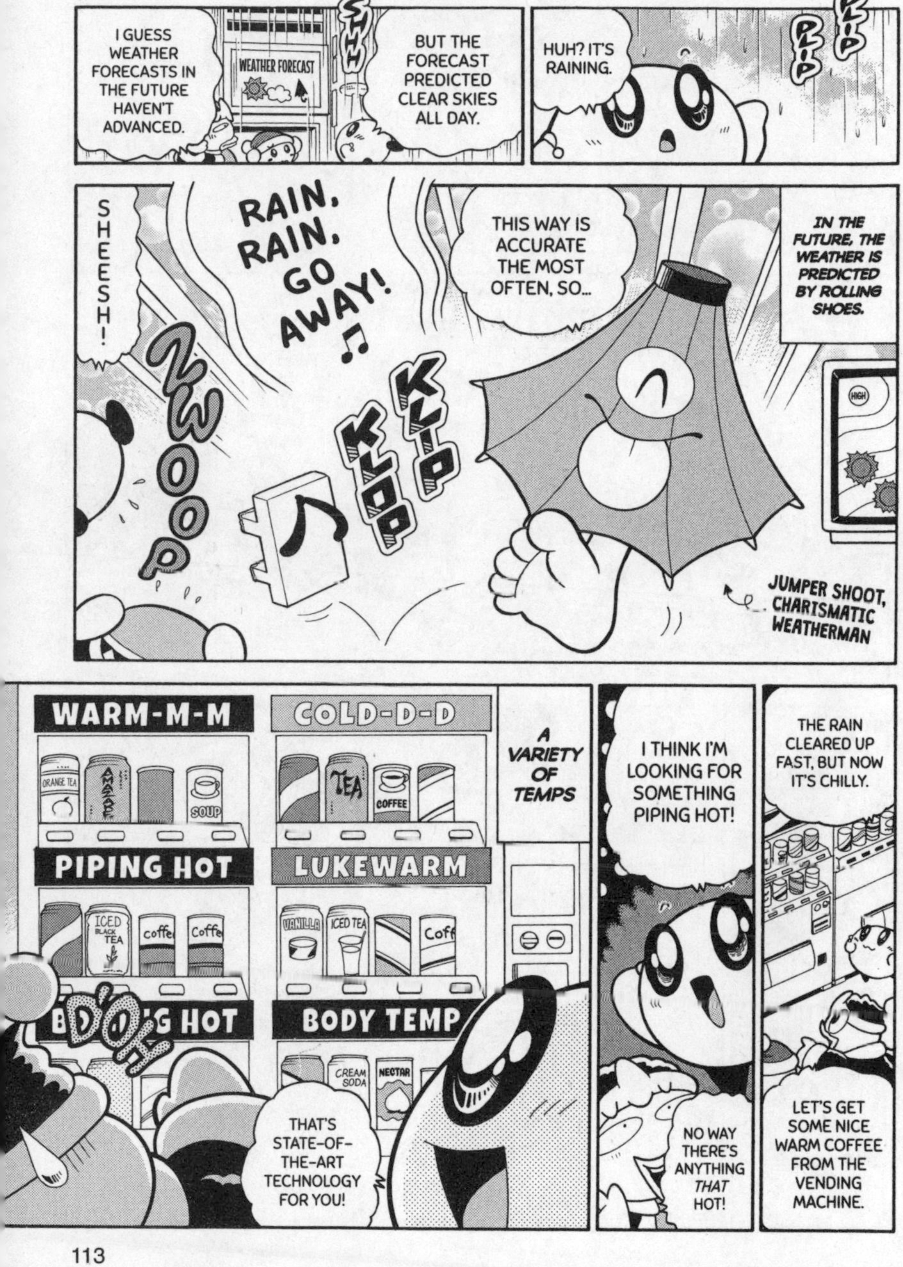
PLIP
PLIP
HUH? IT'S RAINING.
SHHH
BUT THE FORECAST PREDICTED CLEAR SKIES ALL DAY.
WEATHER FORECAST
I GUESS WEATHER FORECASTS IN THE FUTURE HAVEN'T ADVANCED.
IN THE FUTURE, THE WEATHER IS PREDICTED BY ROLLING SHOES.
HIGH
THIS WAY IS ACCURATE THE MOST OFTEN, SO...
RAIN, RAIN, GO AWAY! ♫
SHEESH!
KLIP
KLOP
NWOOP
JUMPER SHOOT, CHARTSMATIC WEATHERMAN
THE RAIN CLEARED UP FAST, BUT NOW IT'S CHILLY.
LET'S GET SOME NICE WARM COFFEE FROM THE VENDING MACHINE.
I THINK I'M LOOKING FOR SOMETHING PIPING HOT!
NO WAY THERE'S ANYTHING *THAT* HOT!
A VARIETY OF TEMPS
COLD-D-D
WARM-M-M
ORANGE TEA
AMAZAKE
SOUP
TEA
COFFEE
LUKEWARM
PIPING HOT
ICED BLACK TEA
VANILLA
ICED TEA
BODY TEMP
D'OH
CREAM SODA
NECTAR
THAT'S STATE-OF-THE-ART TECHNOLOGY FOR YOU!

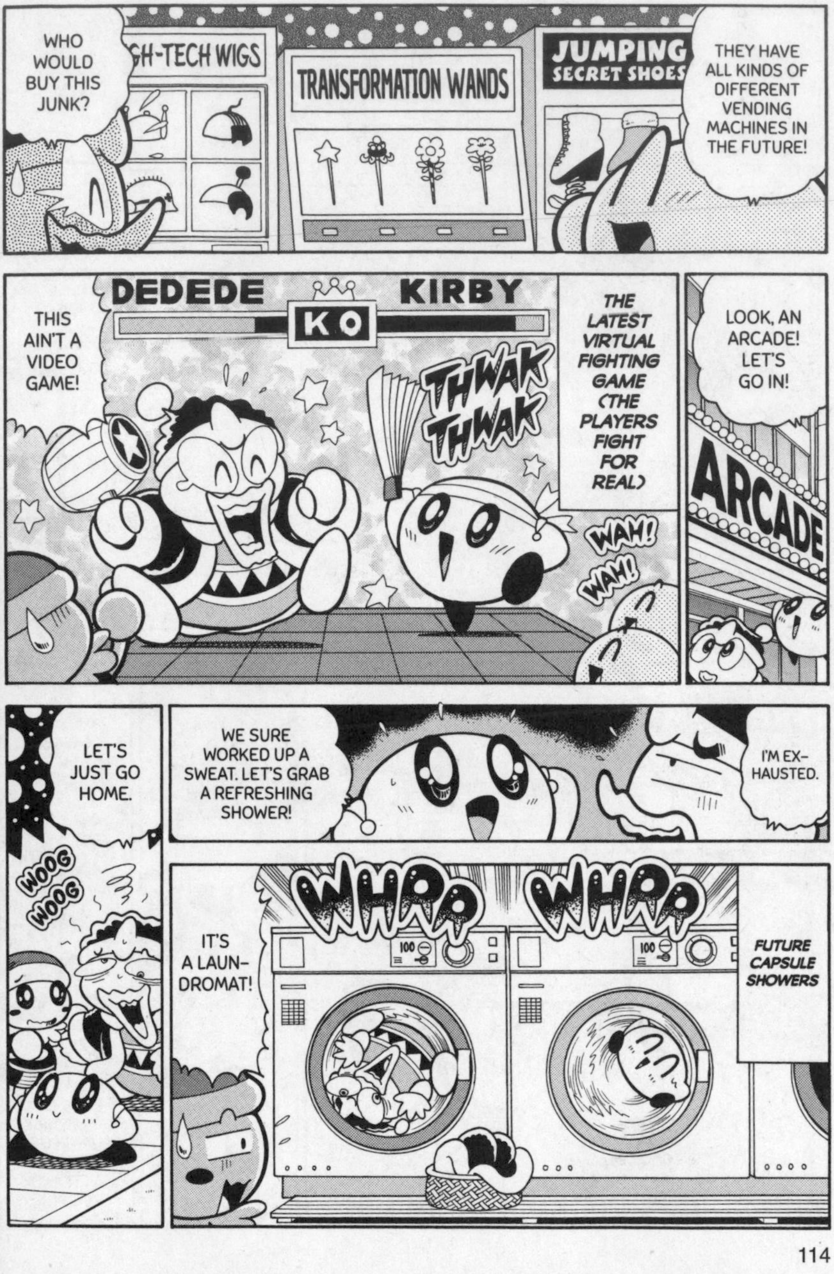
THEY HAVE ALL KINDS OF DIFFERENT VENDING MACHINES IN THE FUTURE!
JUMPING SECRET SHOES
TRANSFORMATION WANDS
GH-TECH WIGS
WHO WOULD BUY THIS JUNK?
LOOK, AN ARCADE! LET'S GO IN!
ARCADE
THE LATEST VIRTUAL FIGHTING GAME (THE PLAYERS FIGHT FOR REAL)
KIRBY
DEDEDE
KO
THWAK THWAK
WAH! WAH!
THIS AIN'T A VIDEO GAME!
I'M EX-HAUSTED.
WE SURE WORKED UP A SWEAT. LET'S GRAB A REFRESHING SHOWER!
FUTURE CAPSULE SHOWERS
WHRR WHRR
IT'S A LAUN-DROMAT!
LET'S JUST GO HOME.
WOOG WOOG

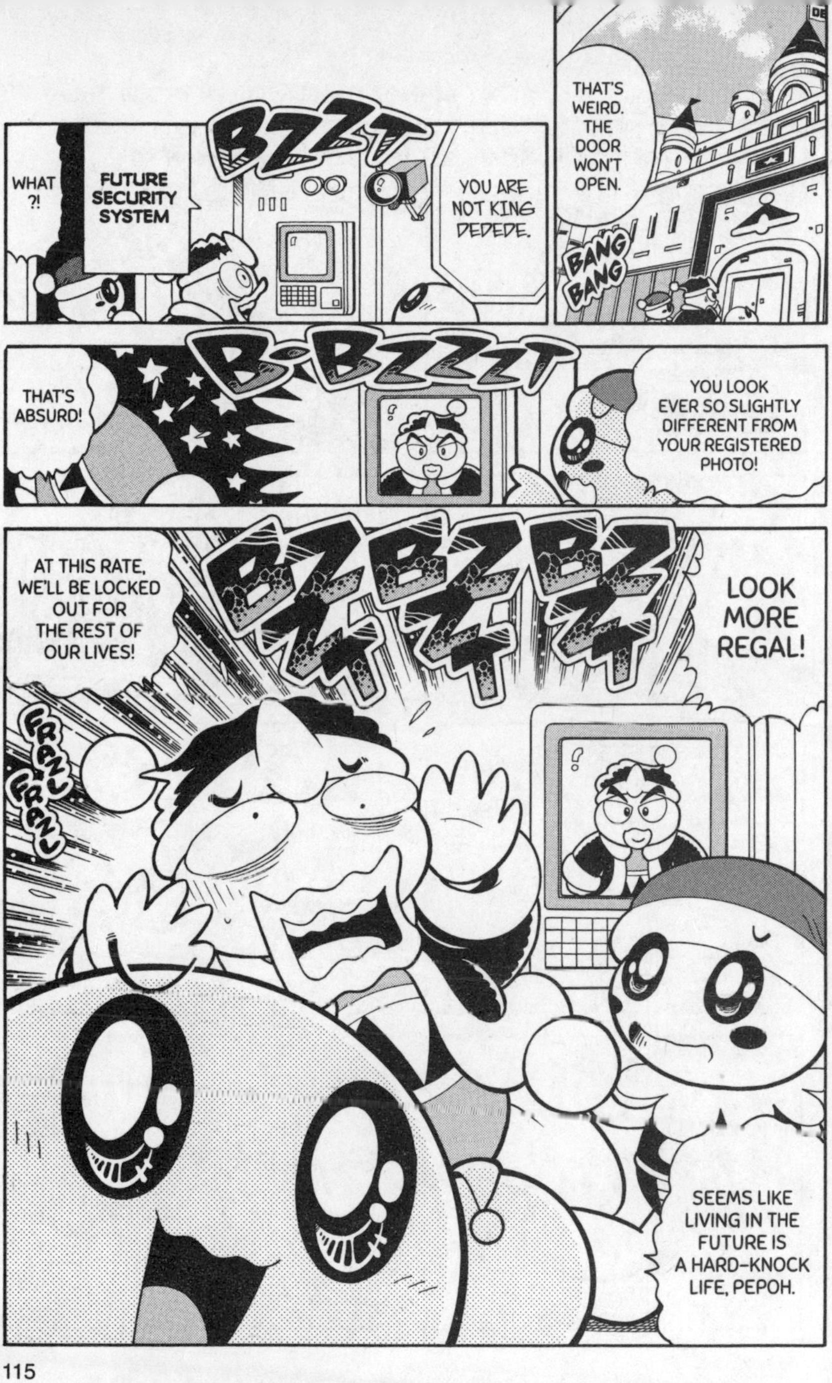
THAT'S WEIRD. THE DOOR WON'T OPEN.
BANG BANG
BZZT
YOU ARE NOT KING DEDEDE.
FUTURE SECURITY SYSTEM
WHAT ?!
YOU LOOK EVER SO SLIGHTLY DIFFERENT FROM YOUR REGISTERED PHOTO!
B-BZZZT
THAT'S ABSURD!
LOOK MORE REGAL!
BZBZBZ
AT THIS RATE, WE'LL BE LOCKED OUT FOR THE REST OF OUR LIVES!
SEEMS LIKE LIVING IN THE FUTURE IS A HARD-KNOCK LIFE, PEPOH.

MARIO KIRBY

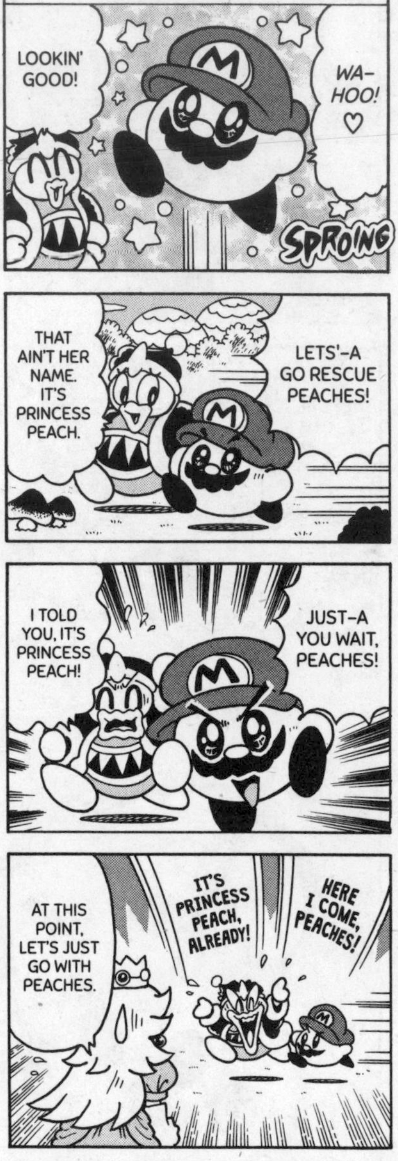
WA-HOO! ♡
LOOKIN' GOOD!
SPROING
LETS'-A GO RESCUE PEACHES!
THAT AIN'T HER NAME. IT'S PRINCESS PEACH.
JUST-A YOU WAIT, PEACHES!
I TOLD YOU, IT'S PRINCESS PEACH!
HERE I COME, PEACHES!
IT'S PRINCESS PEACH, ALREADY!
AT THIS POINT, LET'S JUST GO WITH PEACHES.

MINI FOUR-WHEEL KIRBY

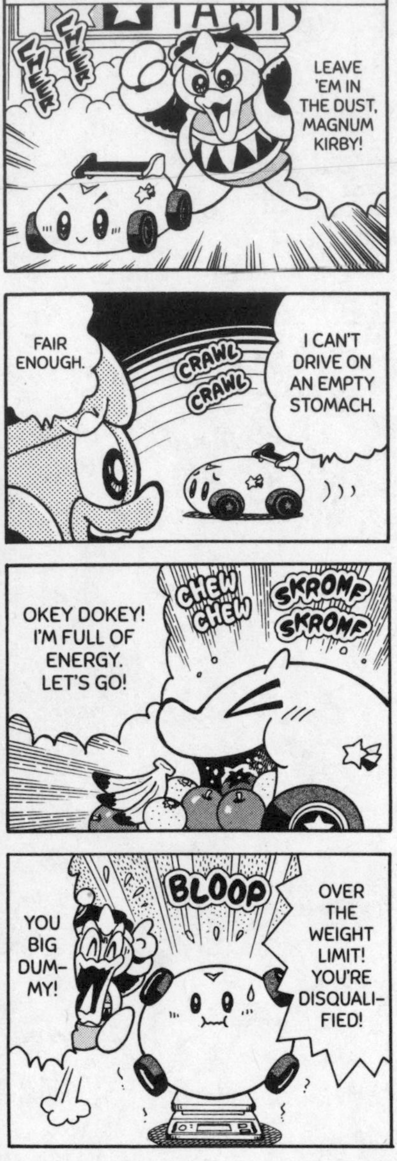
LEAVE 'EM IN THE DUST, MAGNUM KIRBY!
CHEER CHEER
I CAN'T DRIVE ON AN EMPTY STOMACH.
CRAWL CRAWL
FAIR ENOUGH.
SKROMF SKROMF
CHEW CHEW
OKEY DOKEY! I'M FULL OF ENERGY. LET'S GO!
OVER THE WEIGHT LIMIT! YOU'RE DISQUALI-FIED!
BLOOP
YOU BIG DUM-MY!

CHAPTER 9: THE HEART-POUNDING VERY REAL GAME OF LIFE

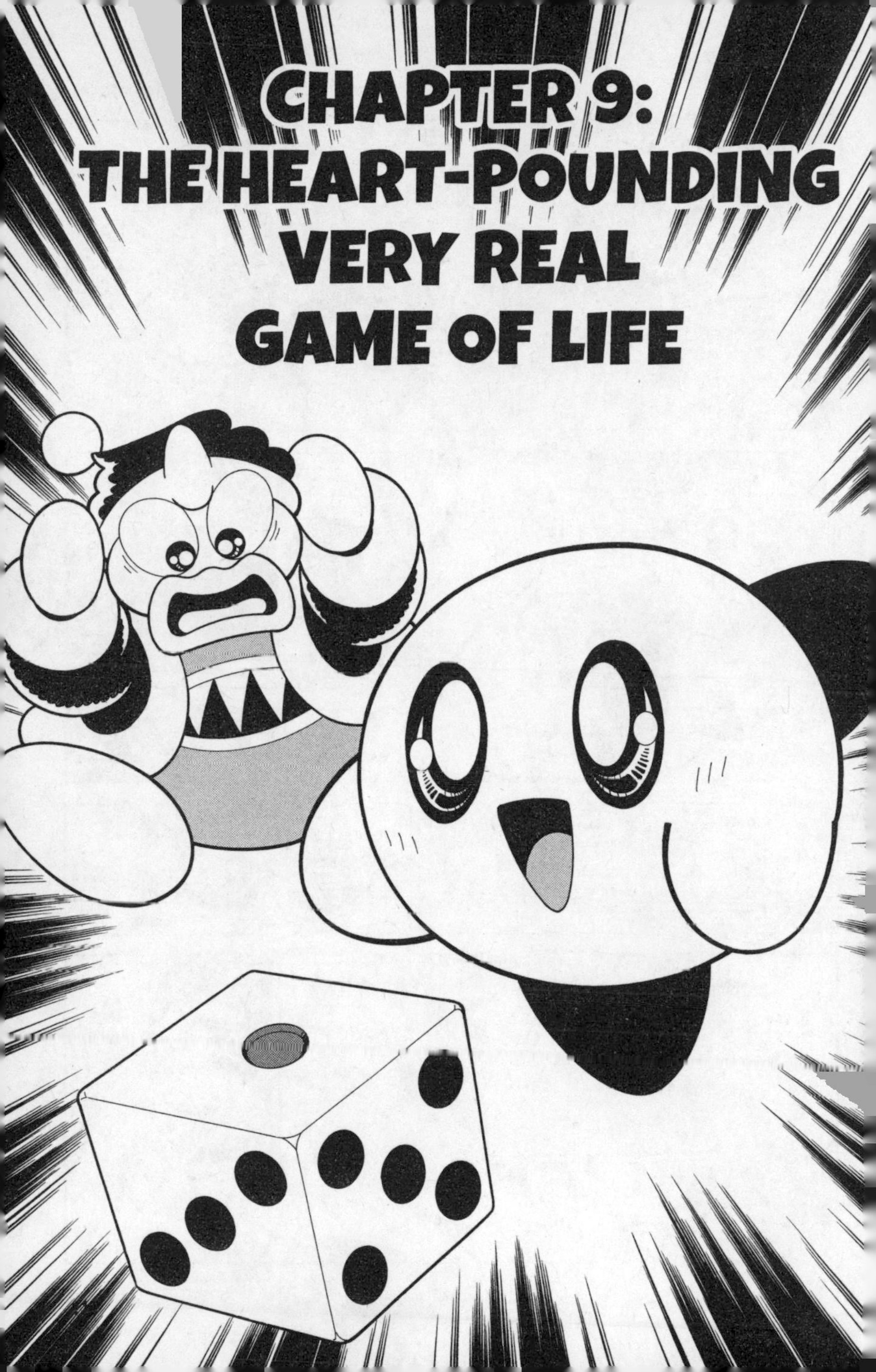

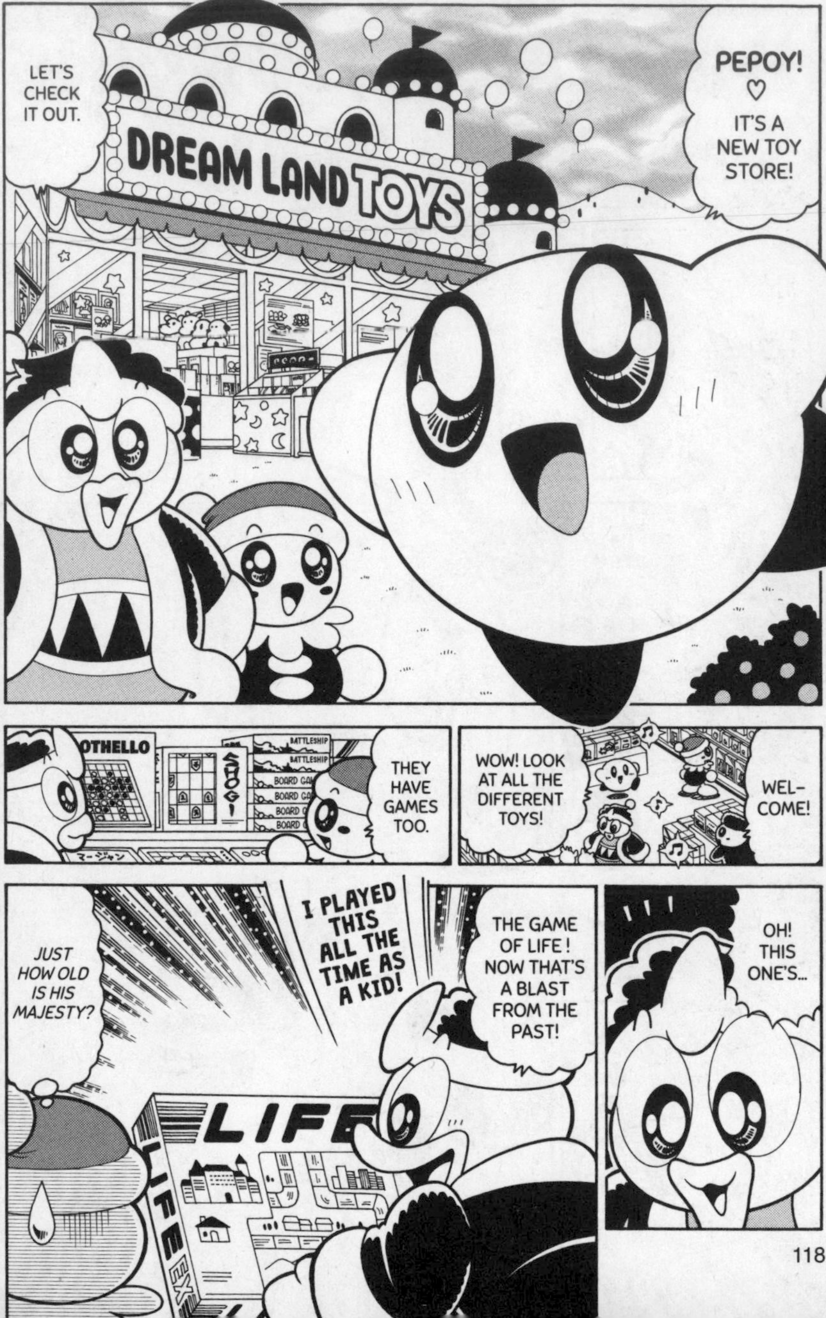
PEPOY! ♡ IT'S A NEW TOY STORE!
LET'S CHECK IT OUT.
DREAM LAND TOYS
WEL-COME!
WOW! LOOK AT ALL THE DIFFERENT TOYS!
THEY HAVE GAMES TOO.
OTHELLO
BATTLESHIP
BATTLESHIP
SHOGI
OH! THIS ONE'S...
THE GAME OF LIFE! NOW THAT'S A BLAST FROM THE PAST!
I PLAYED THIS ALL THE TIME AS A KID!
JUST HOW OLD IS HIS MAJESTY?
LIFE

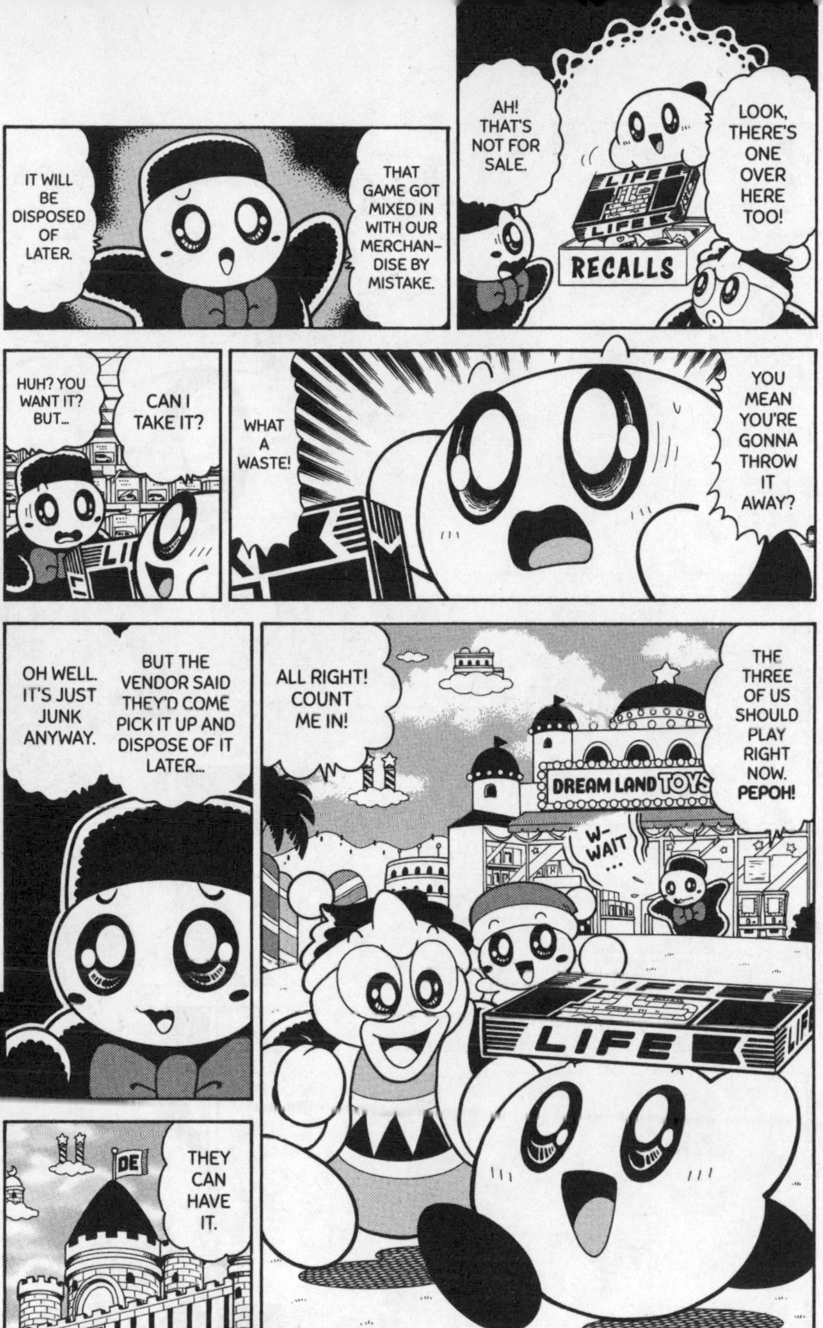
LOOK, THERE'S ONE OVER HERE TOO!
AH! THAT'S NOT FOR SALE.
LIFE
RECALLS
THAT GAME GOT MIXED IN WITH OUR MERCHANDISE BY MISTAKE.
IT WILL BE DISPOSED OF LATER.
YOU MEAN YOU'RE GONNA THROW IT AWAY?
WHAT A WASTE!
CAN I TAKE IT?
HUH? YOU WANT IT? BUT...
THE THREE OF US SHOULD PLAY RIGHT NOW. **PEPOH!**
ALL RIGHT! COUNT ME IN!
W-WAIT...
DREAM LAND TOYS
LIFE
BUT THE VENDOR SAID THEY'D COME PICK IT UP AND DISPOSE OF IT LATER...
OH WELL. IT'S JUST JUNK ANYWAY.
DE
THEY CAN HAVE IT.

AUTHOR'S COMMENT

THE NOSTALGIC GAME OF LIFE. IS THERE ANYONE WHO HASN'T PLAYED IT? IT WAS EXCITING COMING UP WITH EACH SPACE'S DIRECTIONS.

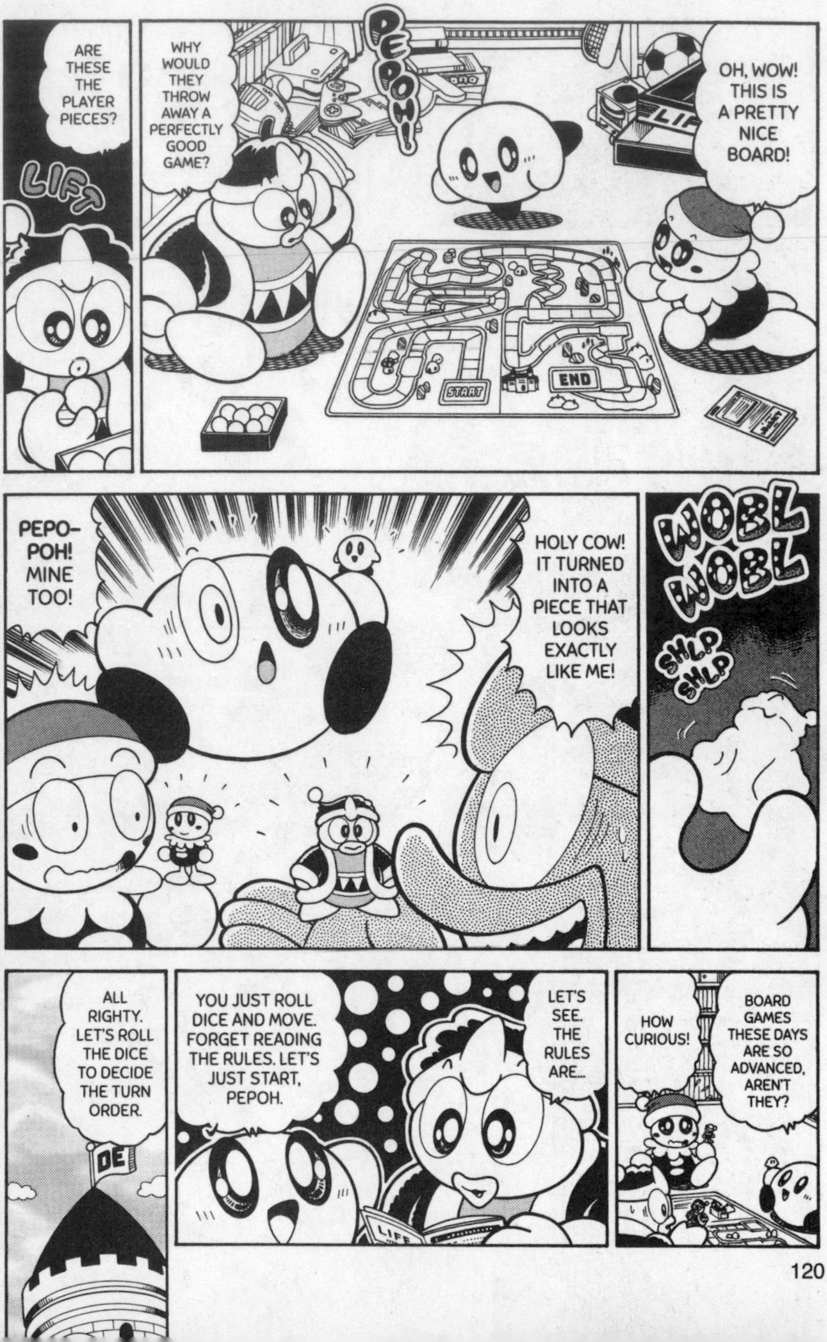
OH, WOW! THIS IS A PRETTY NICE BOARD!
PEPOH!
WHY WOULD THEY THROW AWAY A PERFECTLY GOOD GAME?
ARE THESE THE PLAYER PIECES?
LIFT
WOBL WOBL
SHLP SHLP
HOLY COW! IT TURNED INTO A PIECE THAT LOOKS EXACTLY LIKE ME!
PEPO-POH! MINE TOO!
BOARD GAMES THESE DAYS ARE SO ADVANCED, AREN'T THEY?
HOW CURIOUS!
LET'S SEE. THE RULES ARE...
YOU JUST ROLL DICE AND MOVE. FORGET READING THE RULES. LET'S JUST START, PEPOH.
ALL RIGHTY. LET'S ROLL THE DICE TO DECIDE THE TURN ORDER.

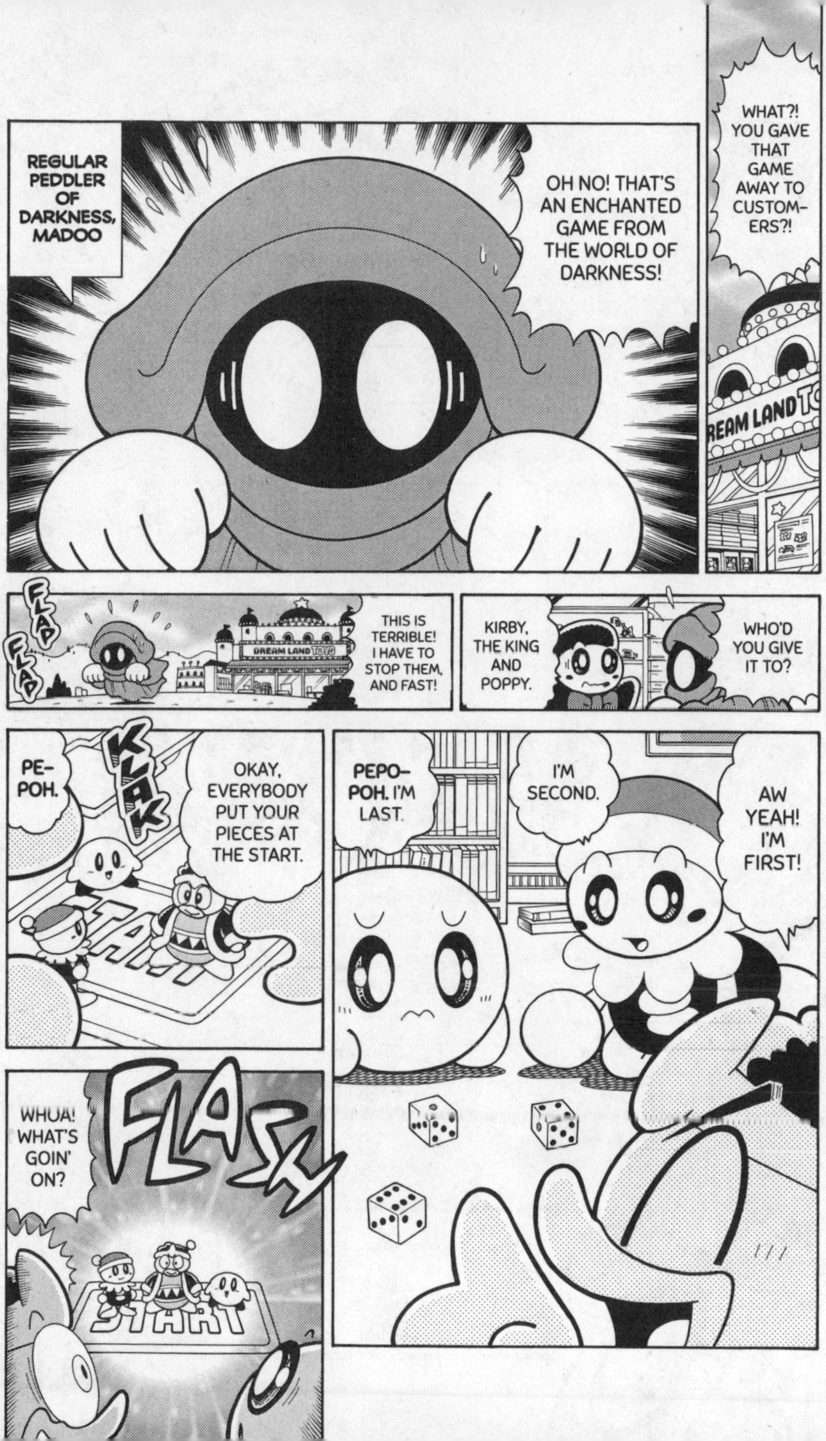
WHAT?! YOU GAVE THAT GAME AWAY TO CUSTOM-ERS?!
DREAM LAND TO
OH NO! THAT'S AN ENCHANTED GAME FROM THE WORLD OF DARKNESS!
REGULAR PEDDLER OF DARKNESS, MADOO
WHO'D YOU GIVE IT TO?
KIRBY, THE KING AND POPPY.
THIS IS TERRIBLE! I HAVE TO STOP THEM, AND FAST!
DREAM LAND TOYS
FLAP
FLAP
AW YEAH! I'M FIRST!
I'M SECOND.
PEPO-POH. I'M LAST.
OKAY, EVERYBODY PUT YOUR PIECES AT THE START.
KLAK
PE-POH.
START
FLASH
WHUA! WHAT'S GOIN' ON?
START

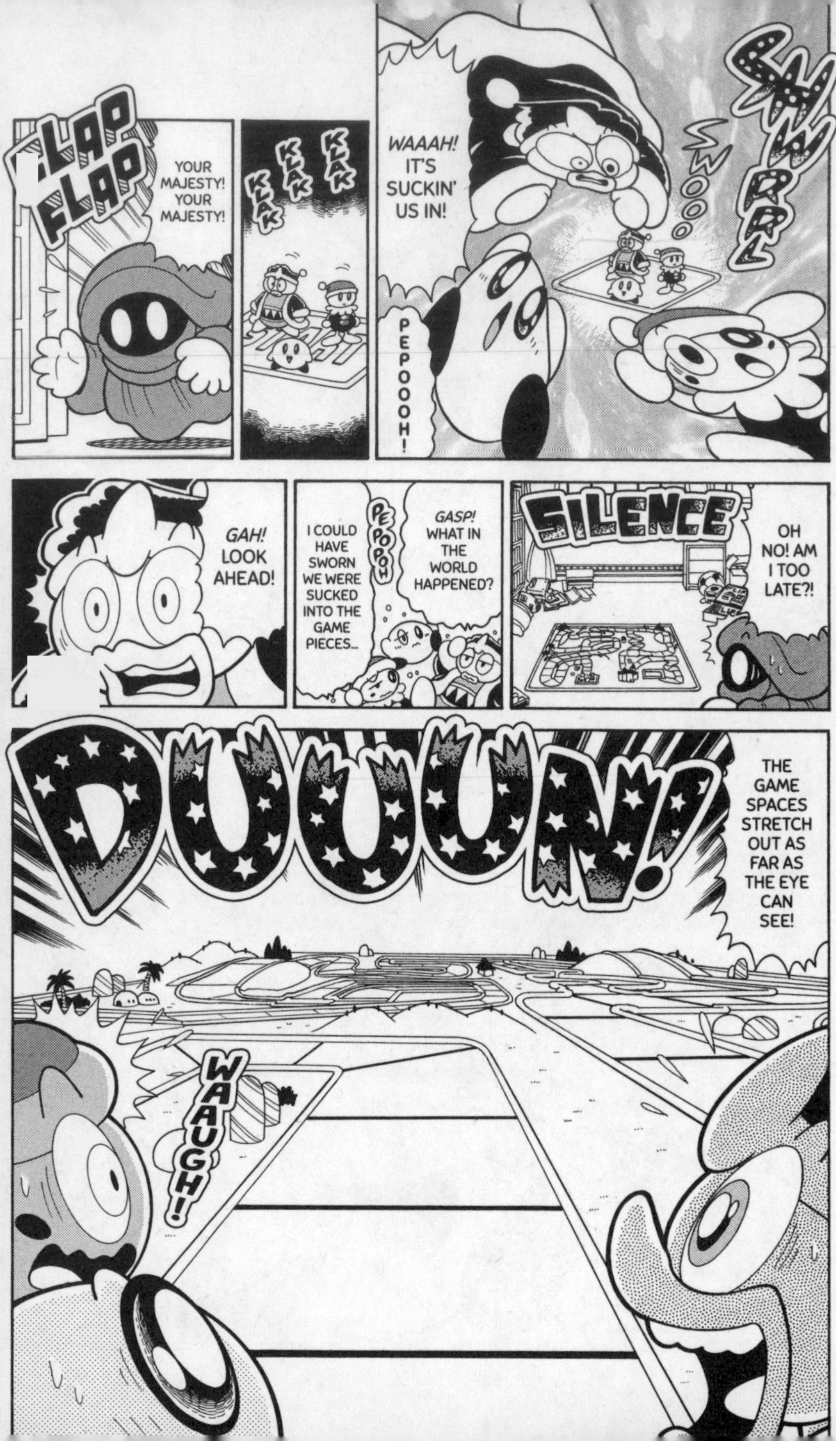
FLAP FLAP
YOUR MAJESTY! YOUR MAJESTY!
KLAK KLAK KLAK
WAAAH! IT'S SUCKIN' US IN!
SWWRRL
SWOOOO
PEPOOOOH!
GAH! LOOK AHEAD!
GASP! WHAT IN THE WORLD HAPPENED?
PEPOPOH
I COULD HAVE SWORN WE WERE SUCKED INTO THE GAME PIECES...
SILENCE
OH NO! AM I TOO LATE?!
DUUUN!
THE GAME SPACES STRETCH OUT AS FAR AS THE EYE CAN SEE!
WAAUGH!

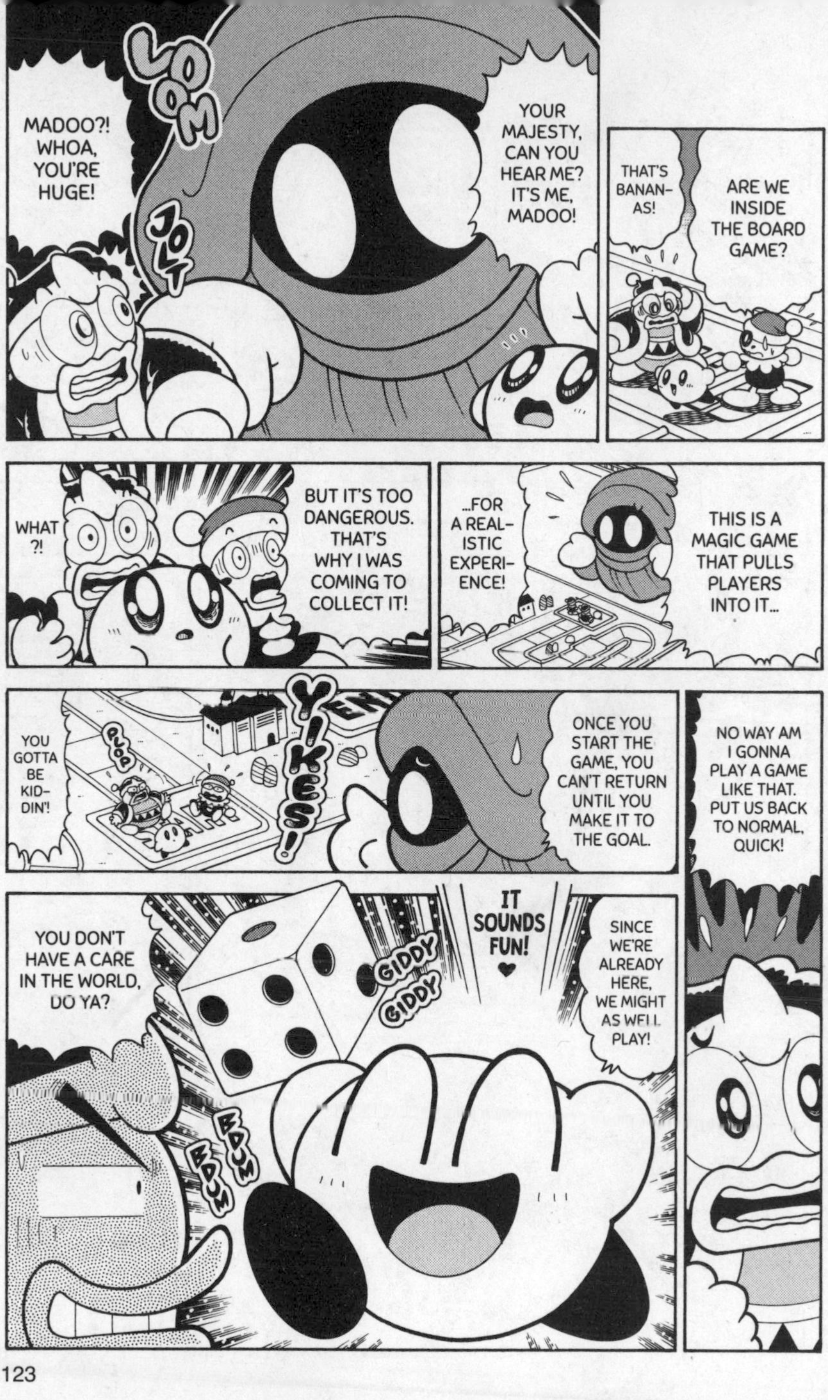
ARE WE INSIDE THE BOARD GAME?
THAT'S BANAN-AS!
YOUR MAJESTY, CAN YOU HEAR ME? IT'S ME, MADOO!
LOOM
JOLT
MADOO?! WHOA, YOU'RE HUGE!
THIS IS A MAGIC GAME THAT PULLS PLAYERS INTO IT...
...FOR A REAL-ISTIC EXPERI-ENCE!
BUT IT'S TOO DANGEROUS. THAT'S WHY I WAS COMING TO COLLECT IT!
WHAT ?!
NO WAY AM I GONNA PLAY A GAME LIKE THAT. PUT US BACK TO NORMAL, QUICK!
ONCE YOU START THE GAME, YOU CAN'T RETURN UNTIL YOU MAKE IT TO THE GOAL.
YIKES!
PLOP
YOU GOTTA BE KID-DIN'!
SINCE WE'RE ALREADY HERE, WE MIGHT AS WELL PLAY!
IT SOUNDS FUN! ♥
GIDDY GIDDY
YOU DON'T HAVE A CARE IN THE WORLD, DO YA?
BDUM BDUM

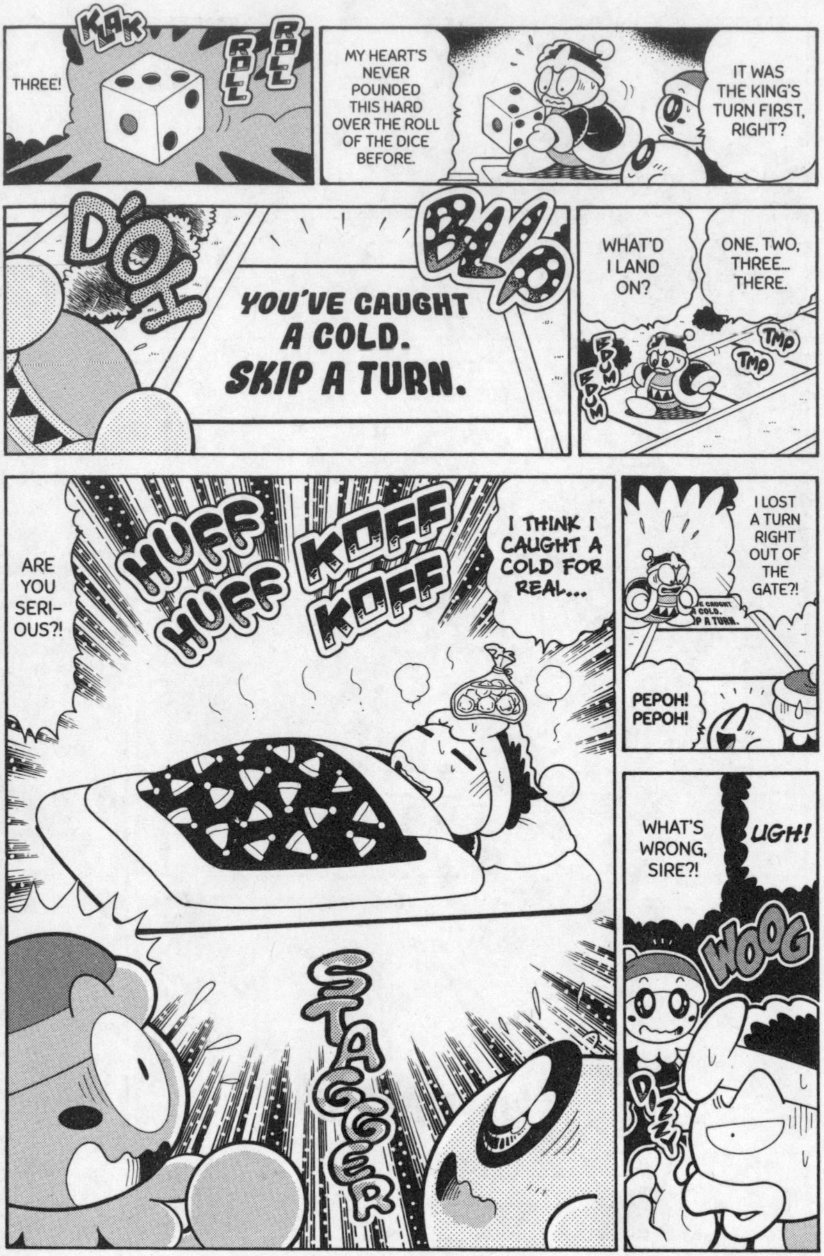
IT WAS THE KING'S TURN FIRST, RIGHT?
MY HEART'S NEVER POUNDED THIS HARD OVER THE ROLL OF THE DICE BEFORE.
KLAK
ROLL ROLL
THREE!
ONE, TWO, THREE... THERE.
WHAT'D I LAND ON?
TMP TMP
BDUM BDUM
BLIP
YOU'VE CAUGHT A COLD. SKIP A TURN.
D'OH
I LOST A TURN RIGHT OUT OF THE GATE?!
PEPOH! PEPOH!
UGH!
WHAT'S WRONG, SIRE?!
WOOG
DIZZY
I THINK I CAUGHT A COLD FOR REAL...
KOFF KOFF
HUFF HUFF
ARE YOU SERI-OUS?!
STAGGER

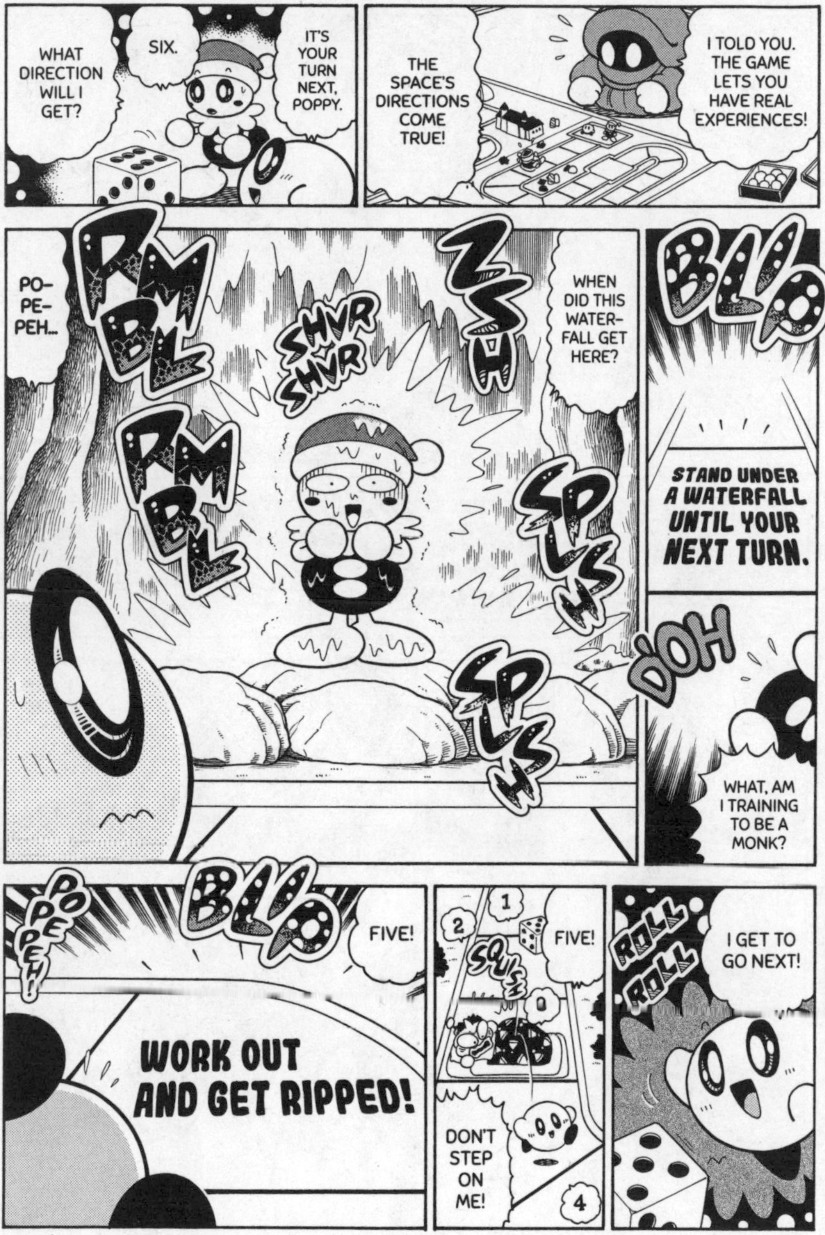
I TOLD YOU. THE GAME LETS YOU HAVE REAL EXPERIENCES!
THE SPACE'S DIRECTIONS COME TRUE!
IT'S YOUR TURN NEXT, POPPY.
SIX.
WHAT DIRECTION WILL I GET?
BLIP
STAND UNDER A WATERFALL UNTIL YOUR NEXT TURN.
DOH
WHAT, AM I TRAINING TO BE A MONK?
WHEN DID THIS WATERFALL GET HERE?
SHVR SHVR
RMMBL
RMMBL
PO-PE-PEH...
SPLSH
SPLSH
ROLL ROLL
I GET TO GO NEXT!
FIVE!
1
2
SQUISH
DON'T STEP ON ME!
4
FIVE!
BLIP
POPEPEH!
WORK OUT AND GET RIPPED!

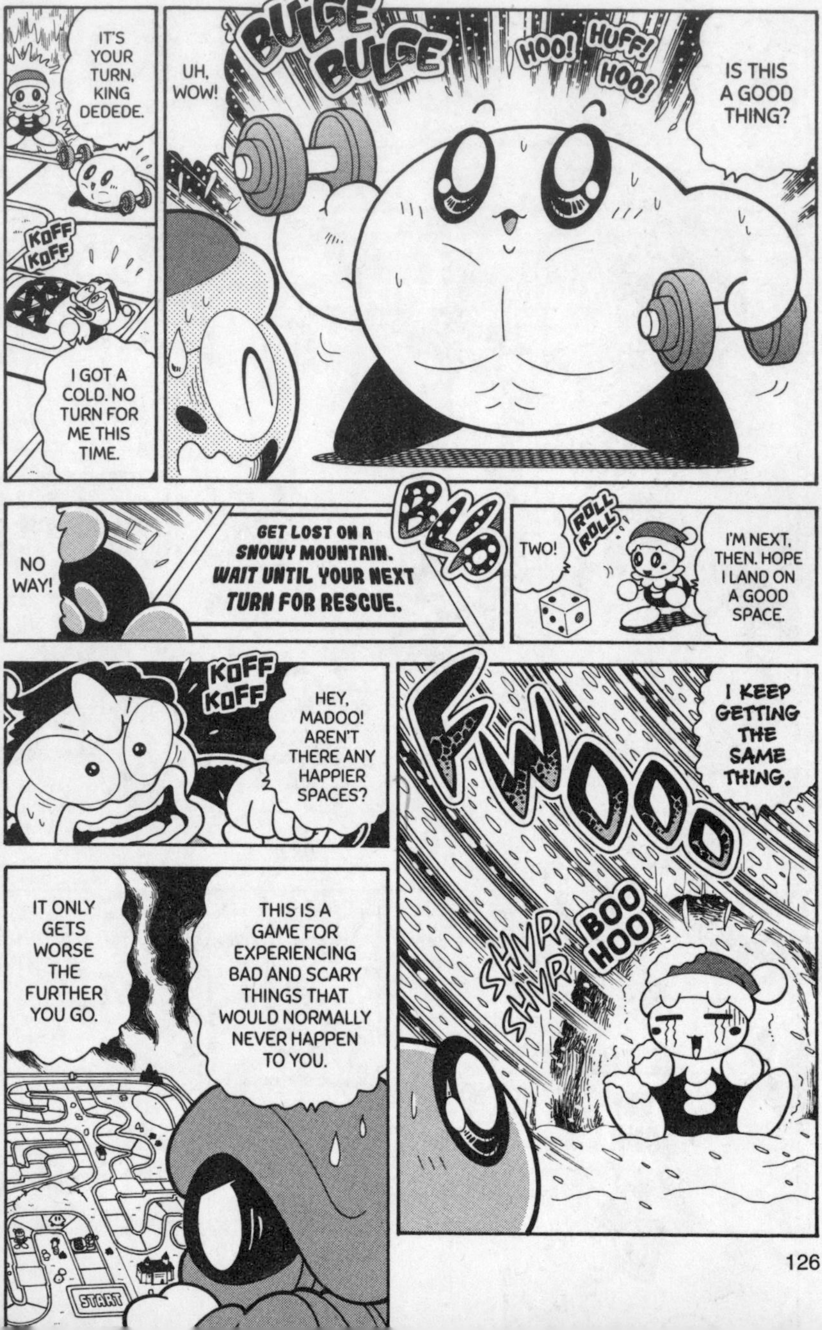
BULGE BULGE
HOO! HUFF! HOO!
IS THIS A GOOD THING?
UH, WOW!
IT'S YOUR TURN, KING DEDEDE.
KOFF KOFF
I GOT A COLD. NO TURN FOR ME THIS TIME.
I'M NEXT, THEN. HOPE I LAND ON A GOOD SPACE.
ROLL ROLL
TWO!
GET LOST ON A SNOWY MOUNTAIN. WAIT UNTIL YOUR NEXT TURN FOR RESCUE.
NO WAY!
FWOOO
I KEEP GETTING THE SAME THING.
BOO HOO
SHVR SHVR
KOFF KOFF
HEY, MADOO! AREN'T THERE ANY HAPPIER SPACES?
THIS IS A GAME FOR EXPERIENCING BAD AND SCARY THINGS THAT WOULD NORMALLY NEVER HAPPEN TO YOU.
IT ONLY GETS WORSE THE FURTHER YOU GO.
START

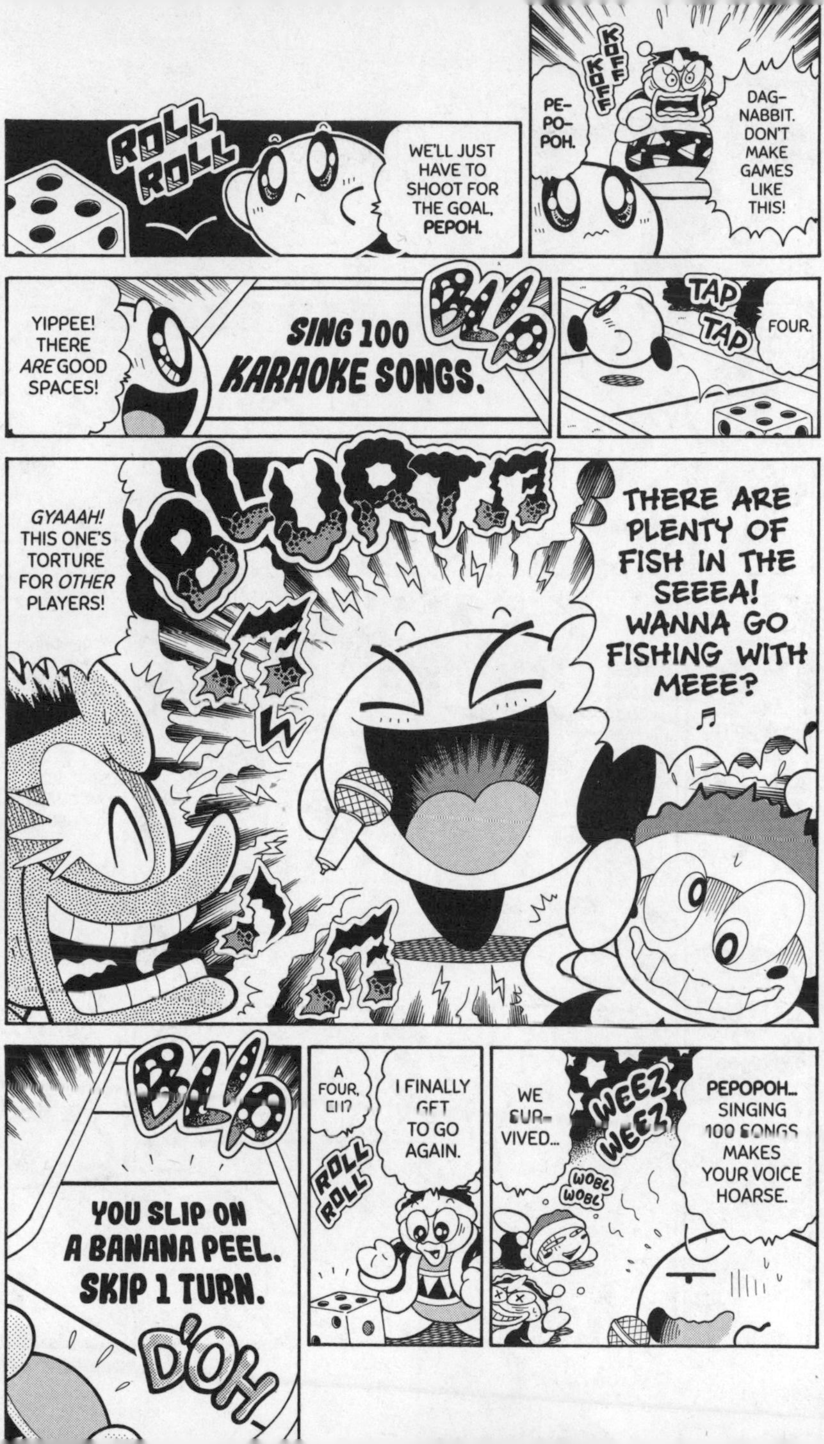
DAG-NABBIT. DON'T MAKE GAMES LIKE THIS!
KOFF KOFF
PE-PO-POH.
ROLL ROLL
WE'LL JUST HAVE TO SHOOT FOR THE GOAL, PEPOH.
FOUR.
TAP TAP
BLIP
SING 100 KARAOKE SONGS.
YIPPEE! THERE ARE GOOD SPACES!
THERE ARE PLENTY OF FISH IN THE SEEEA! WANNA GO FISHING WITH MEEE? ♬
BLURT!!
GYAAAH! THIS ONE'S TORTURE FOR OTHER PLAYERS!
PEPOPOH... SINGING 100 SONGS MAKES YOUR VOICE HOARSE.
WEEZ WEEZ
WE SURVIVED...
WOBL WOBL
I FINALLY GET TO GO AGAIN.
A FOUR, EH?
ROLL ROLL
BLIP
YOU SLIP ON A BANANA PEEL. SKIP 1 TURN.
D'OH

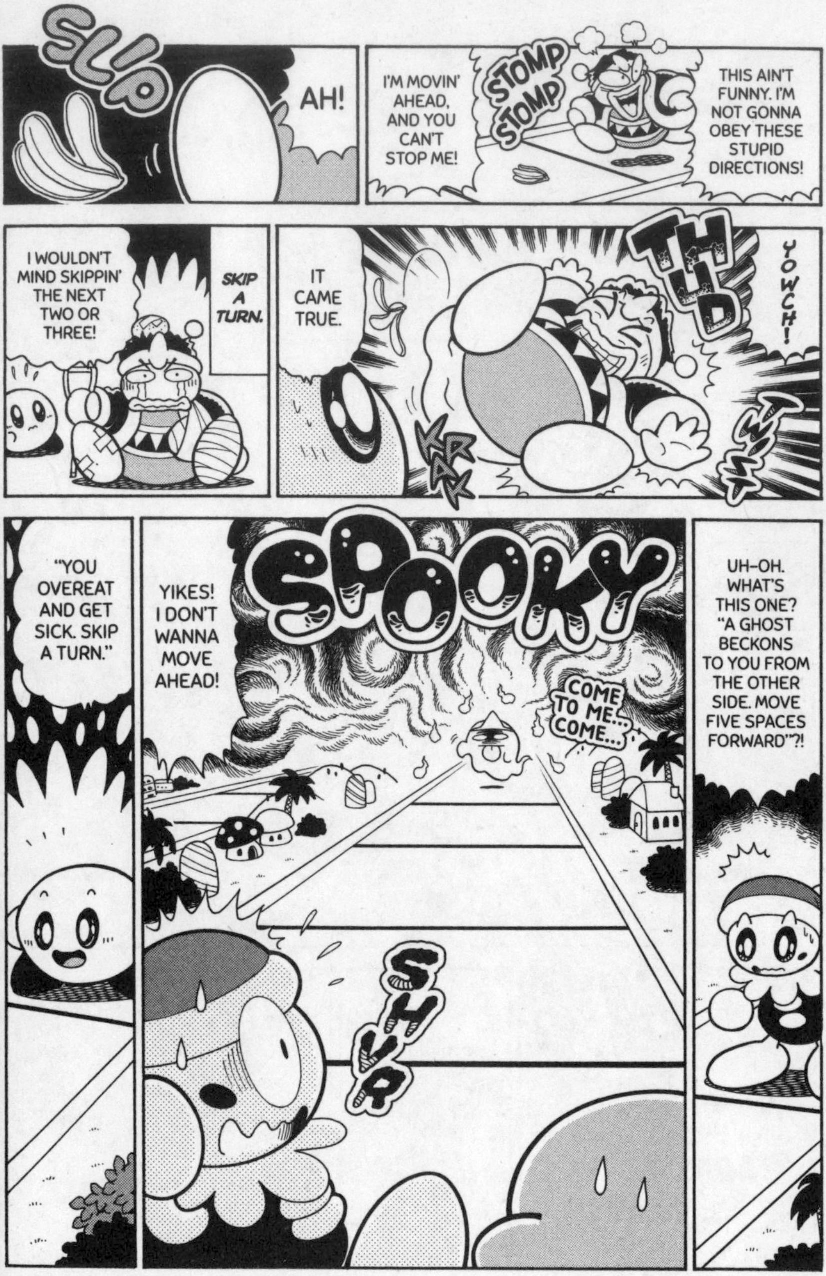
THIS AIN'T FUNNY. I'M NOT GONNA OBEY THESE STUPID DIRECTIONS!
STOMP STOMP
I'M MOVIN' AHEAD, AND YOU CAN'T STOP ME!
AH!
SLIP
YOWCH!
THUD
IT CAME TRUE.
KRAK
SKIP A TURN.
I WOULDN'T MIND SKIPPIN' THE NEXT TWO OR THREE!
UH-OH. WHAT'S THIS ONE? "A GHOST BECKONS TO YOU FROM THE OTHER SIDE. MOVE FIVE SPACES FORWARD"?!
SPOOKY
YIKES! I DON'T WANNA MOVE AHEAD!
COME TO ME... COME...
SHVR
"YOU OVEREAT AND GET SICK. SKIP A TURN."

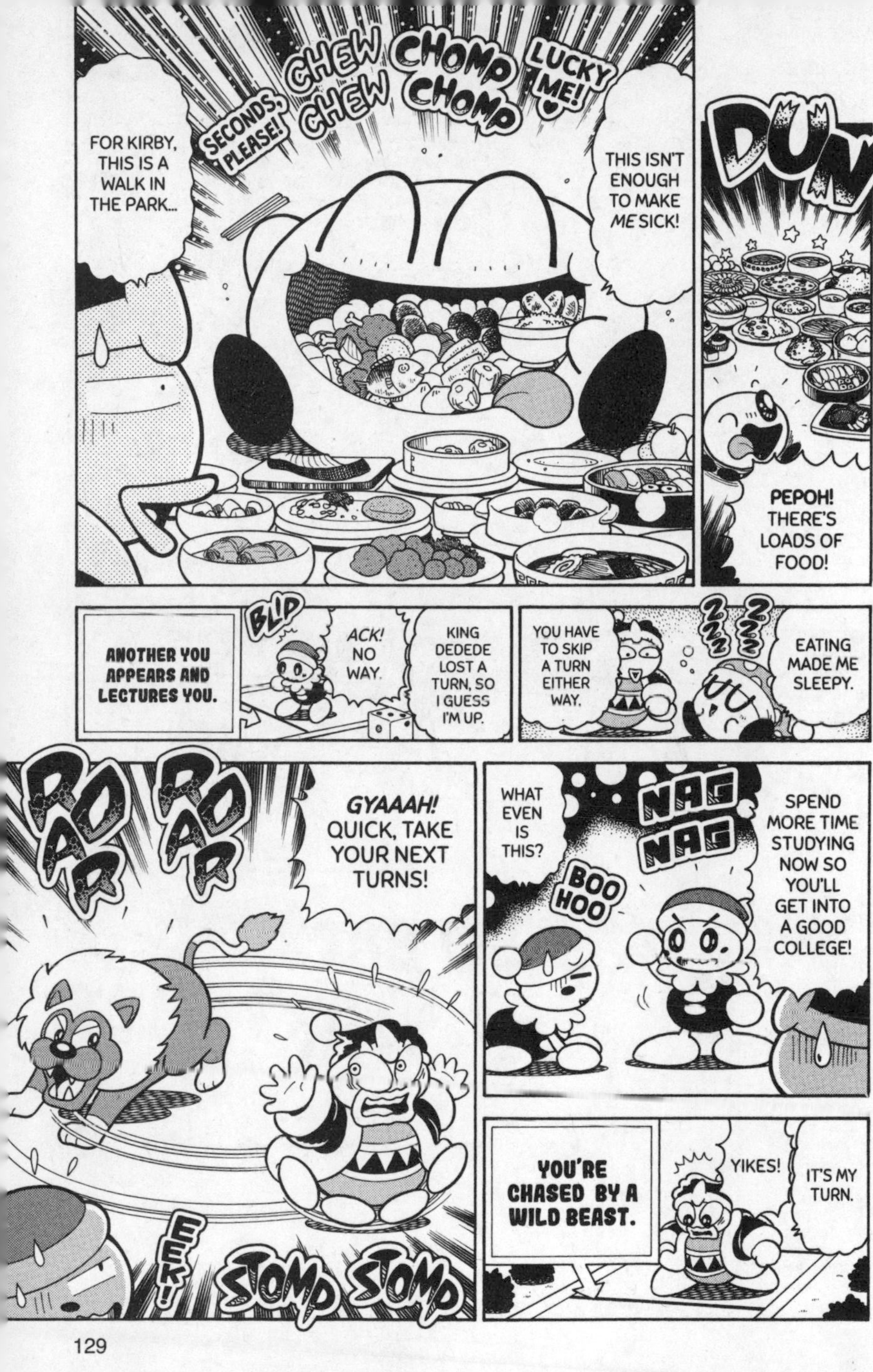
DUN
PEPOH! THERE'S LOADS OF FOOD!
LUCKY ME!♥
CHOMP CHOMP
CHEW CHEW
SECONDS, PLEASE!
THIS ISN'T ENOUGH TO MAKE *ME* SICK!
FOR KIRBY, THIS IS A WALK IN THE PARK...
EATING MADE ME SLEEPY.
ZZZ ZZZ
YOU HAVE TO SKIP A TURN EITHER WAY.
KING DEDEDE LOST A TURN, SO I GUESS I'M UP.
ACK! NO WAY.
BLIP
ANOTHER YOU APPEARS AND LECTURES YOU.
SPEND MORE TIME STUDYING NOW SO YOU'LL GET INTO A GOOD COLLEGE!
NAG NAG
BOO HOO
WHAT EVEN IS THIS?
IT'S MY TURN.
YIKES!
YOU'RE CHASED BY A WILD BEAST.
GYAAAH! QUICK, TAKE YOUR NEXT TURNS!
ROAR ROAR
EEK!
STOMP STOMP

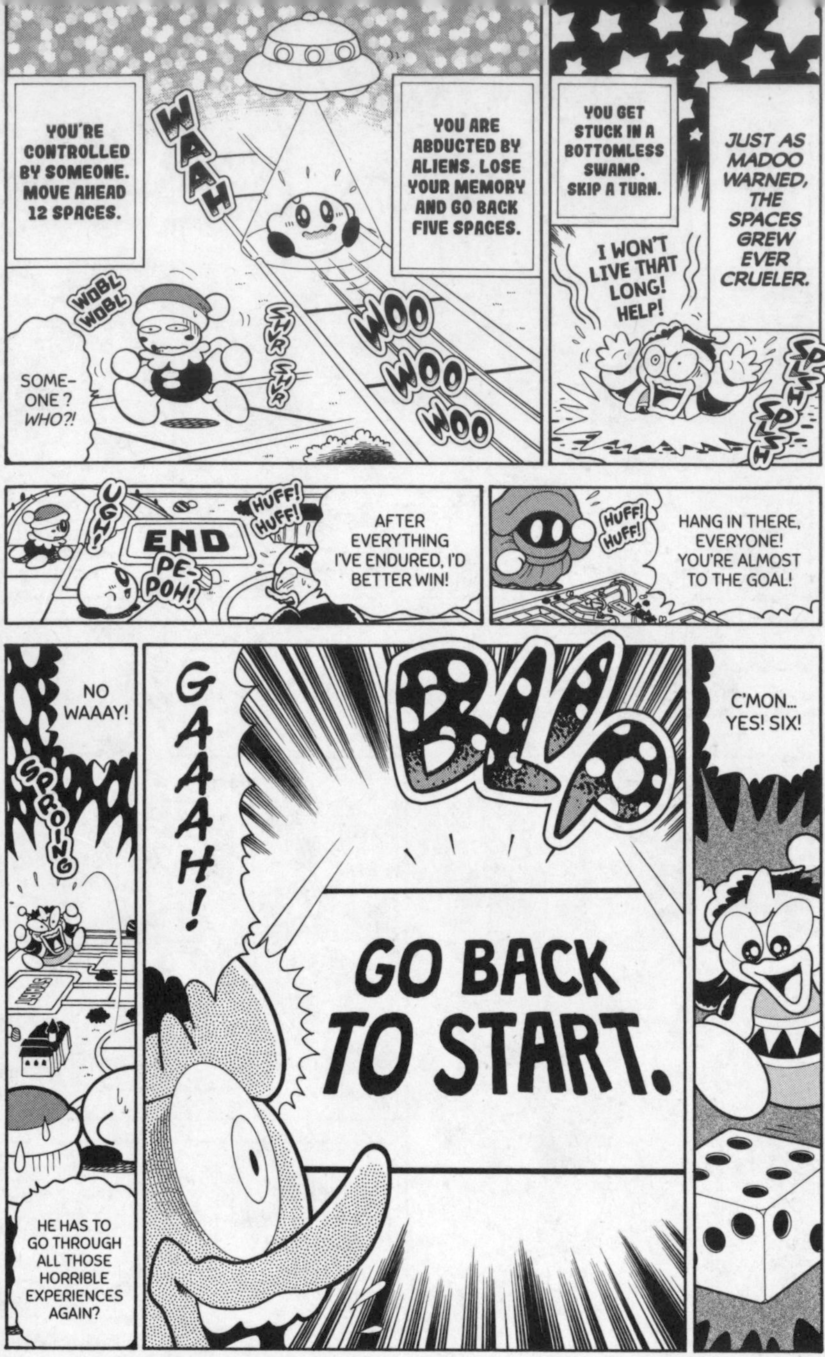
JUST AS MADOO WARNED, THE SPACES GREW EVER CRUELER.
YOU GET STUCK IN A BOTTOMLESS SWAMP. SKIP A TURN.
I WON'T LIVE THAT LONG! HELP!
SPLSH SPLSH
YOU ARE ABDUCTED BY ALIENS. LOSE YOUR MEMORY AND GO BACK FIVE SPACES.
WAAAH
WOO WOO WOO
YOU'RE CONTROLLED BY SOMEONE. MOVE AHEAD 12 SPACES.
WOBL WOBL
SHR SHR
SOME-ONE? WHO?!
HANG IN THERE, EVERYONE! YOU'RE ALMOST TO THE GOAL!
HUFF! HUFF!
AFTER EVERYTHING I'VE ENDURED, I'D BETTER WIN!
HUFF! HUFF!
UGH!
END
PE-POH!
C'MON... YES! SIX!
GAAAAH!
GO BACK TO START.
NO WAAAY!
SPROING
START
HE HAS TO GO THROUGH ALL THOSE HORRIBLE EXPERIENCES AGAIN?

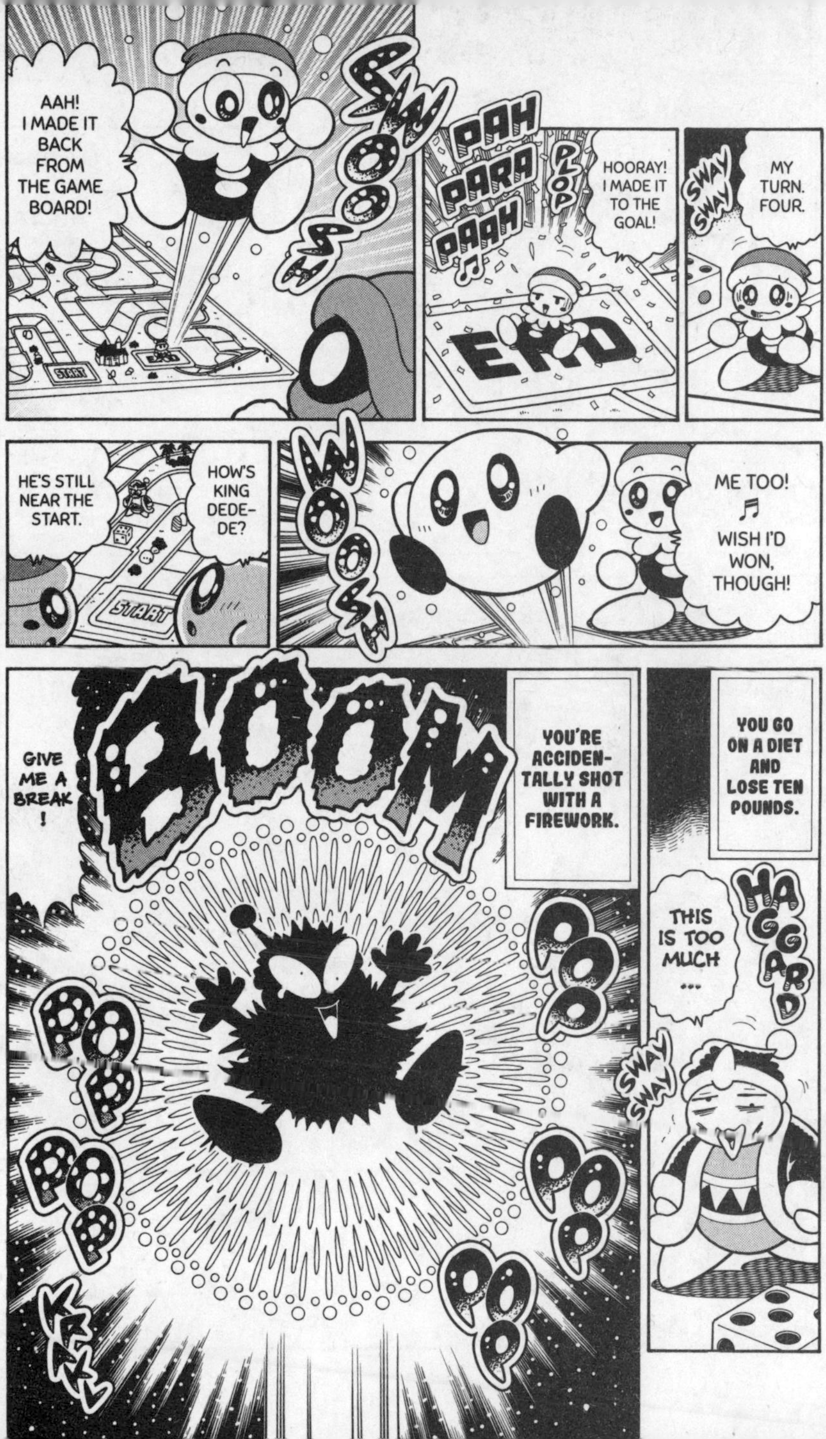
SWAY SWAY
MY TURN. FOUR.
PAH PARA PAAH ♪
PLOP
HOORAY! I MADE IT TO THE GOAL!
END
SWOOSH
AAH! I MADE IT BACK FROM THE GAME BOARD!
START
ME TOO! ♪ WISH I'D WON, THOUGH!
WOOSH
HOW'S KING DEDEDE?
HE'S STILL NEAR THE START.
START
YOU GO ON A DIET AND LOSE TEN POUNDS.
HAGGARD
THIS IS TOO MUCH...
SWAY SWAY
YOU'RE ACCIDENTALLY SHOT WITH A FIREWORK.
BOOM
GIVE ME A BREAK!
POP POP
POP POP
POP POP
POP POP

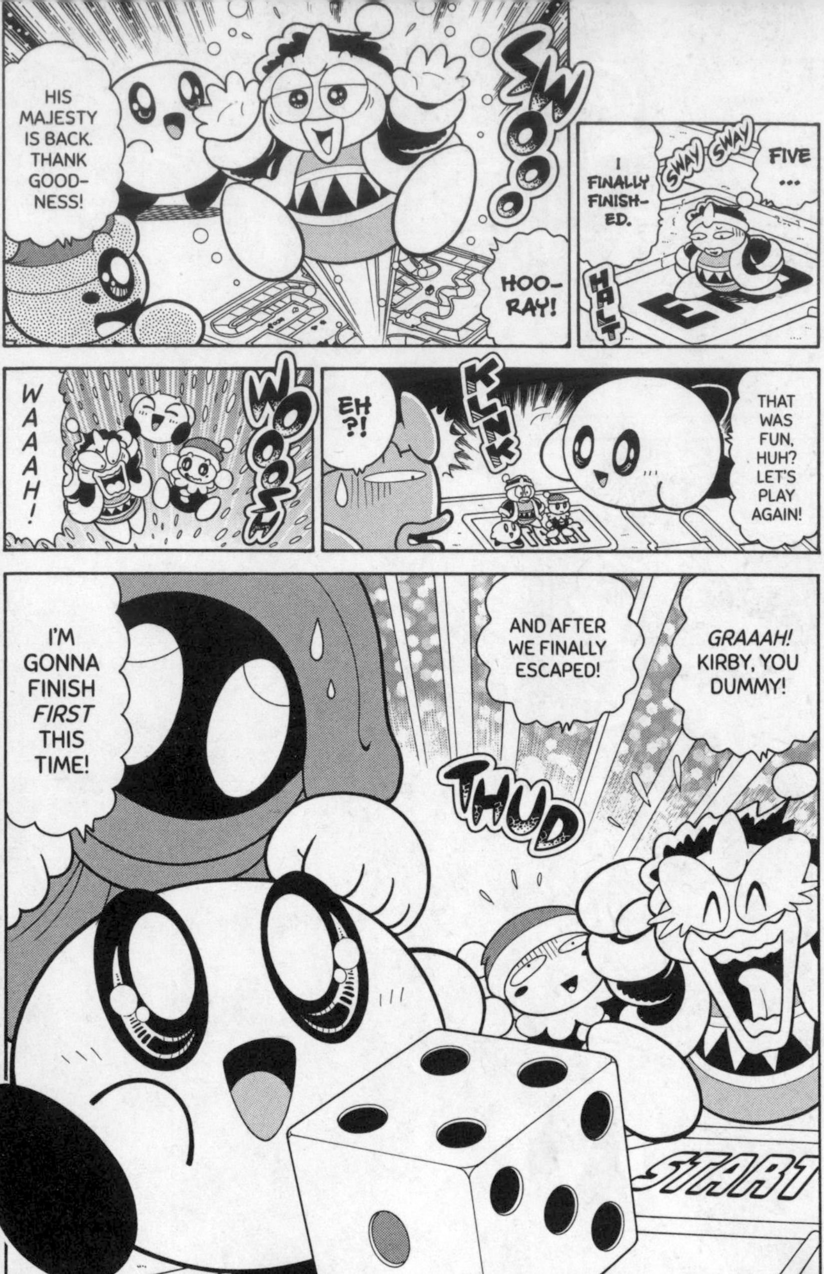
FIVE ...
SWAY SWAY
I FINALLY FINISH-ED.
HALT
SWOOOO
HOO-RAY!
HIS MAJESTY IS BACK. THANK GOOD-NESS!
THAT WAS FUN, HUH? LET'S PLAY AGAIN!
KLNK
EH?!
WOOOSH
WAAAAH!
GRAAAH! KIRBY, YOU DUMMY!
AND AFTER WE FINALLY ESCAPED!
THUD
I'M GONNA FINISH *FIRST* THIS TIME!
START

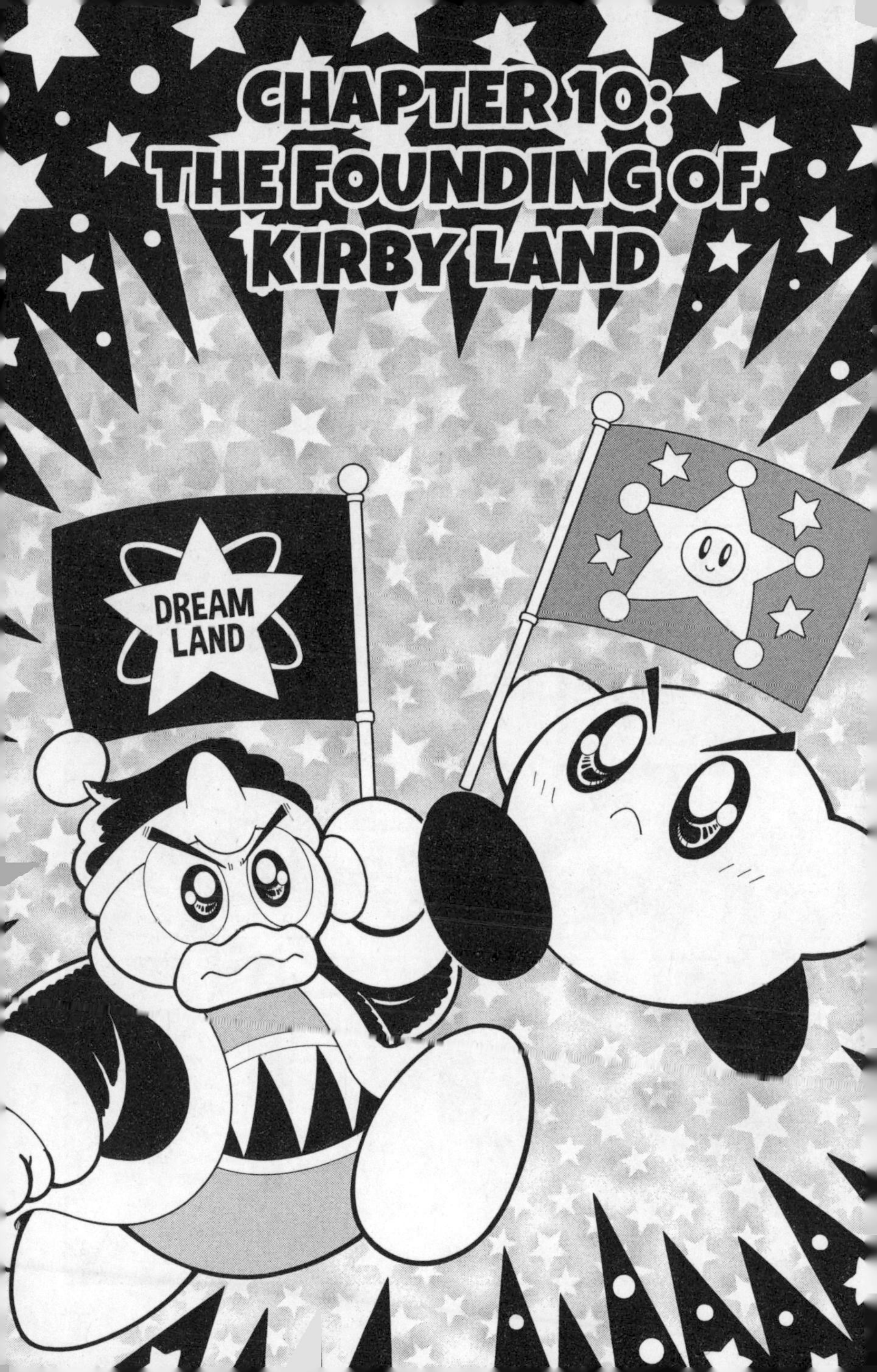
CHAPTER 10:
THE FOUNDING OF KIRBY LAND
DREAM LAND

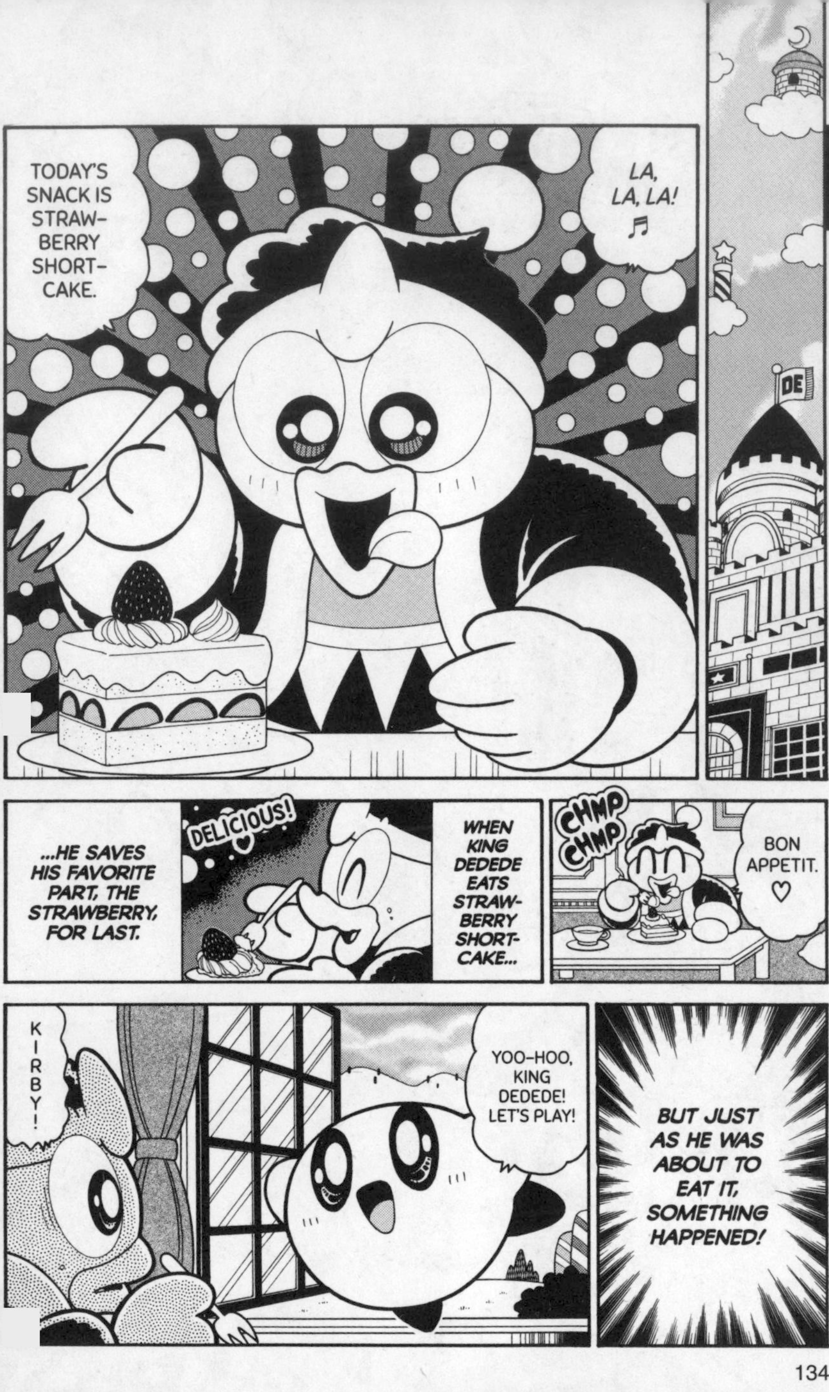
LA, LA, LA! ♪
TODAY'S SNACK IS STRAWBERRY SHORTCAKE.
BON APPETIT. ♡
CHMP CHMP
WHEN KING DEDEDE EATS STRAWBERRY SHORTCAKE...
DELICIOUS! ♡
...HE SAVES HIS FAVORITE PART, THE STRAWBERRY, FOR LAST.
BUT JUST AS HE WAS ABOUT TO EAT IT, SOMETHING HAPPENED!
YOO-HOO, KING DEDEDE! LET'S PLAY!
KIRBY!

AUTHOR'S COMMENT

IN ANY AGE, WARS CAN BE TRIGGERED BY SMALL INCIDENTS. WILL THERE EVER COME A DAY WHEN THE NOTION OF NATIONS NO LONGER EXISTS?

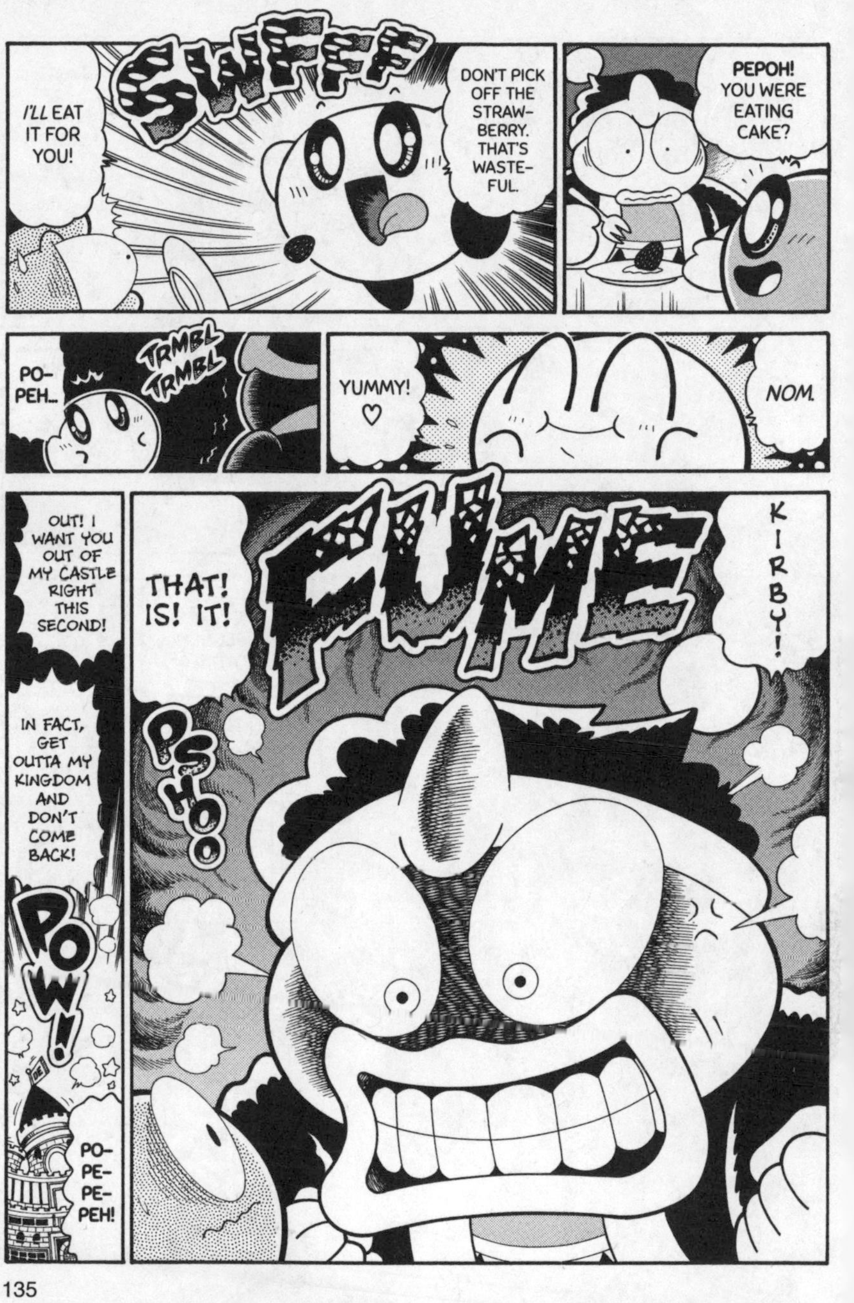
PEPOH! YOU WERE EATING CAKE?
DON'T PICK OFF THE STRAW-BERRY. THAT'S WASTE-FUL.
SWFFF
I'LL EAT IT FOR YOU!
NOM.
YUMMY! ♡
TRMBL TRMBL
PO-PEH...
KIRBY!
FUME
THAT! IS! IT!
PSHOO
OUT! I WANT YOU OUT OF MY CASTLE RIGHT THIS SECOND!
IN FACT, GET OUTTA MY KINGDOM AND DON'T COME BACK!
POW!
PO-PE-PE-PEH!

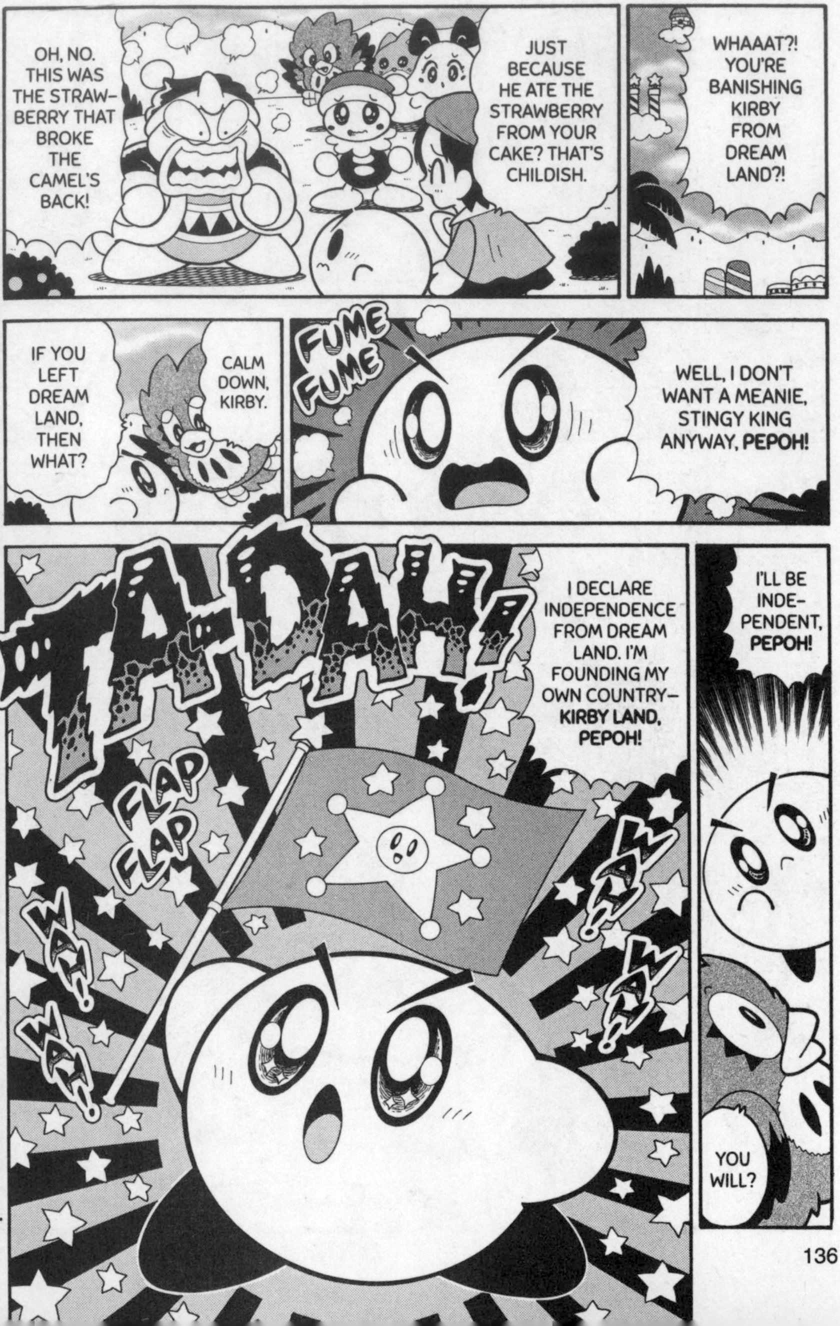
WHAAAT?! YOU'RE BANISHING KIRBY FROM DREAM LAND?!
JUST BECAUSE HE ATE THE STRAWBERRY FROM YOUR CAKE? THAT'S CHILDISH.
OH, NO. THIS WAS THE STRAW-BERRY THAT BROKE THE CAMEL'S BACK!
FUME FUME
WELL, I DON'T WANT A MEANIE, STINGY KING ANYWAY, **PEPOH!**
CALM DOWN, KIRBY.
IF YOU LEFT DREAM LAND, THEN WHAT?
I'LL BE INDE-PENDENT, **PEPOH!**
YOU WILL?
TA-DAH!
I DECLARE INDEPENDENCE FROM DREAM LAND. I'M FOUNDING MY OWN COUNTRY— **KIRBY LAND, PEPOH!**
FLAP FLAP

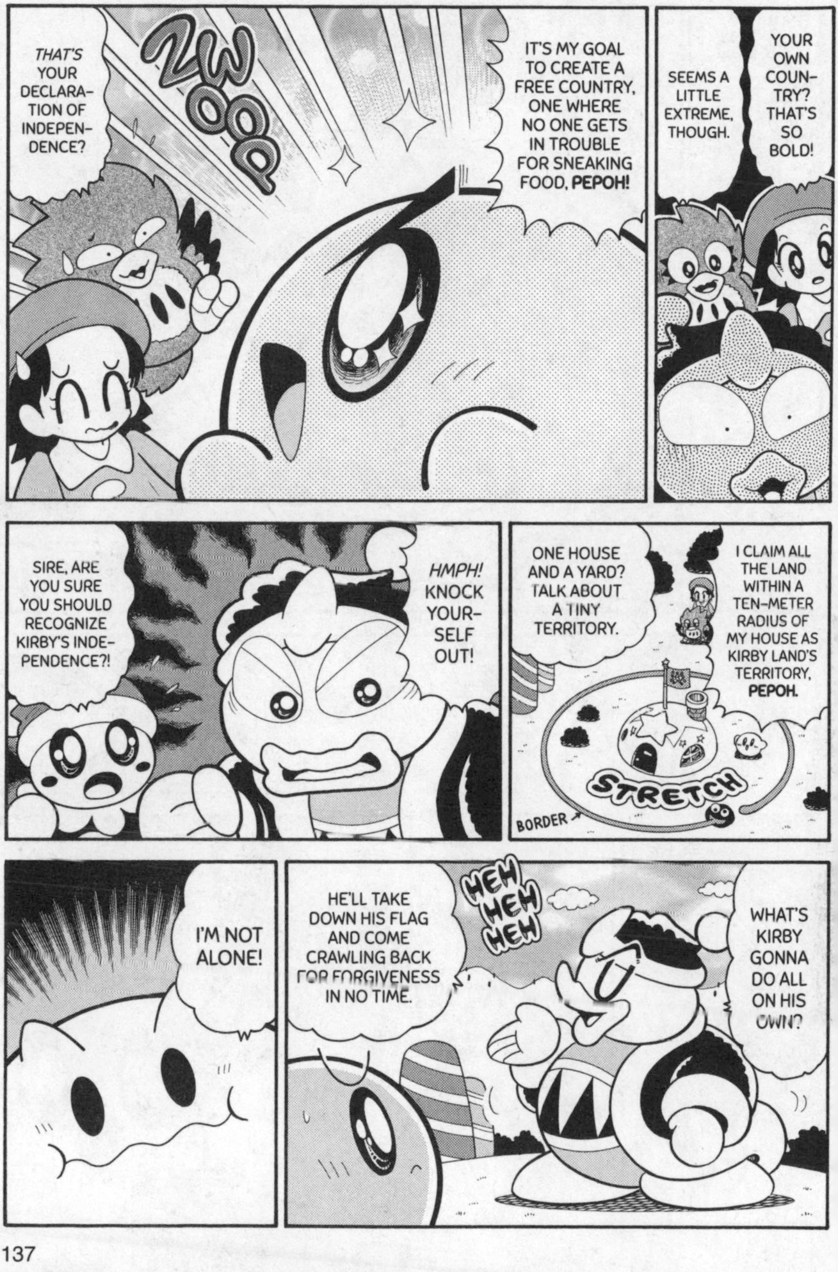
YOUR OWN COUN-TRY? THAT'S SO BOLD!
SEEMS A LITTLE EXTREME, THOUGH.
IT'S MY GOAL TO CREATE A FREE COUNTRY, ONE WHERE NO ONE GETS IN TROUBLE FOR SNEAKING FOOD, **PEPOH!**
ZWOOP
THAT'S YOUR DECLARA-TION OF INDEPEN-DENCE?
I CLAIM ALL THE LAND WITHIN A TEN-METER RADIUS OF MY HOUSE AS KIRBY LAND'S TERRITORY, **PEPOH.**
ONE HOUSE AND A YARD? TALK ABOUT A TINY TERRITORY.
STRETCH
BORDER
HMPH! KNOCK YOUR-SELF OUT!
SIRE, ARE YOU SURE YOU SHOULD RECOGNIZE KIRBY'S INDE-PENDENCE?!
WHAT'S KIRBY GONNA DO ALL ON HIS OWN?
HEH HEH HEH
HE'LL TAKE DOWN HIS FLAG AND COME CRAWLING BACK FOR FORGIVENESS IN NO TIME.
I'M NOT ALONE!

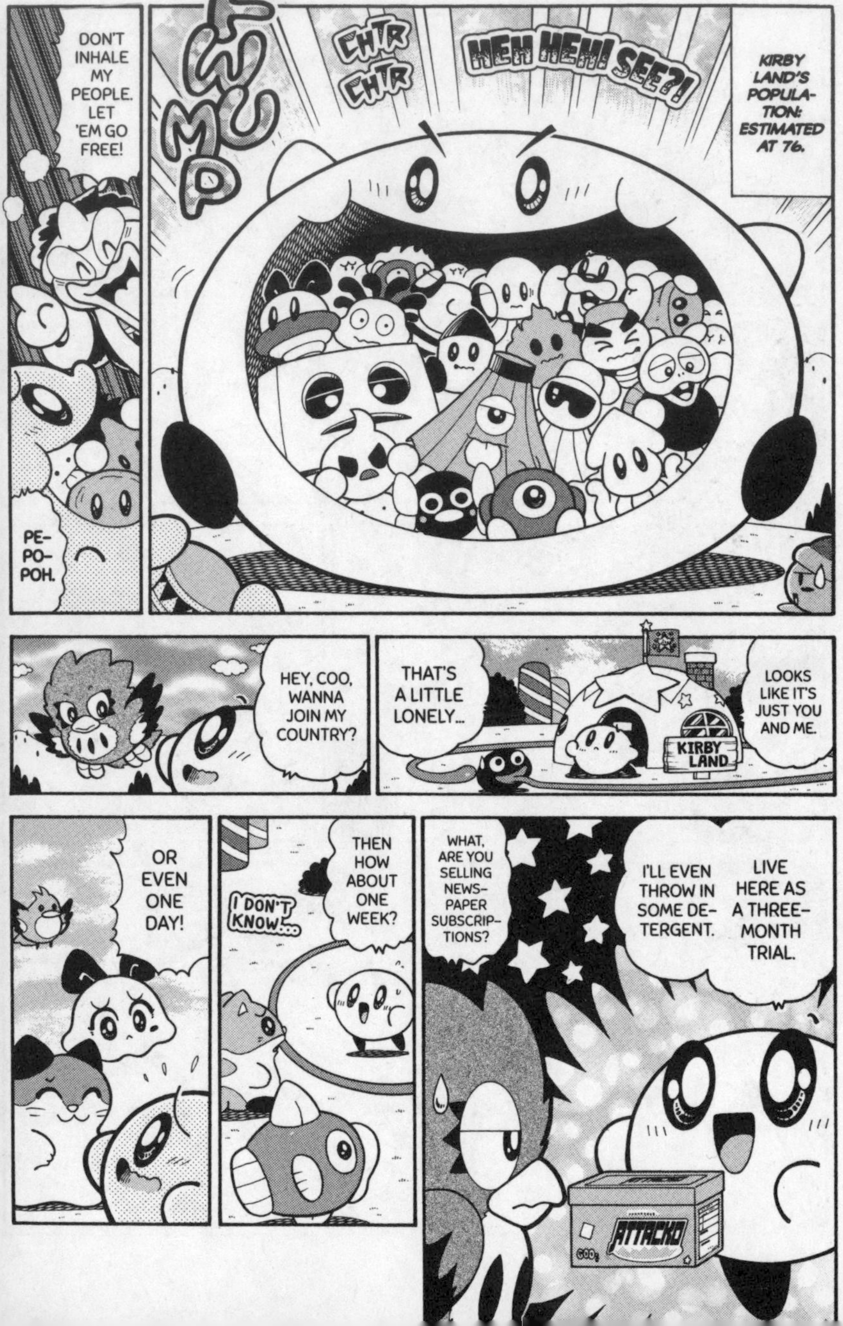
KIRBY LAND'S POPULATION: ESTIMATED AT 76.
HEH HEH! SEE?!
CHTR CHTR
FWUMP
DON'T INHALE MY PEOPLE. LET 'EM GO FREE!
PE-PO-POH.
LOOKS LIKE IT'S JUST YOU AND ME.
KIRBY LAND
THAT'S A LITTLE LONELY...
HEY, COO, WANNA JOIN MY COUNTRY?
LIVE HERE AS A THREE-MONTH TRIAL.
I'LL EVEN THROW IN SOME DE-TERGENT.
WHAT, ARE YOU SELLING NEWS-PAPER SUBSCRIP-TIONS?
ATTACKO
THEN HOW ABOUT ONE WEEK?
I DON'T KNOW...
OR EVEN ONE DAY!

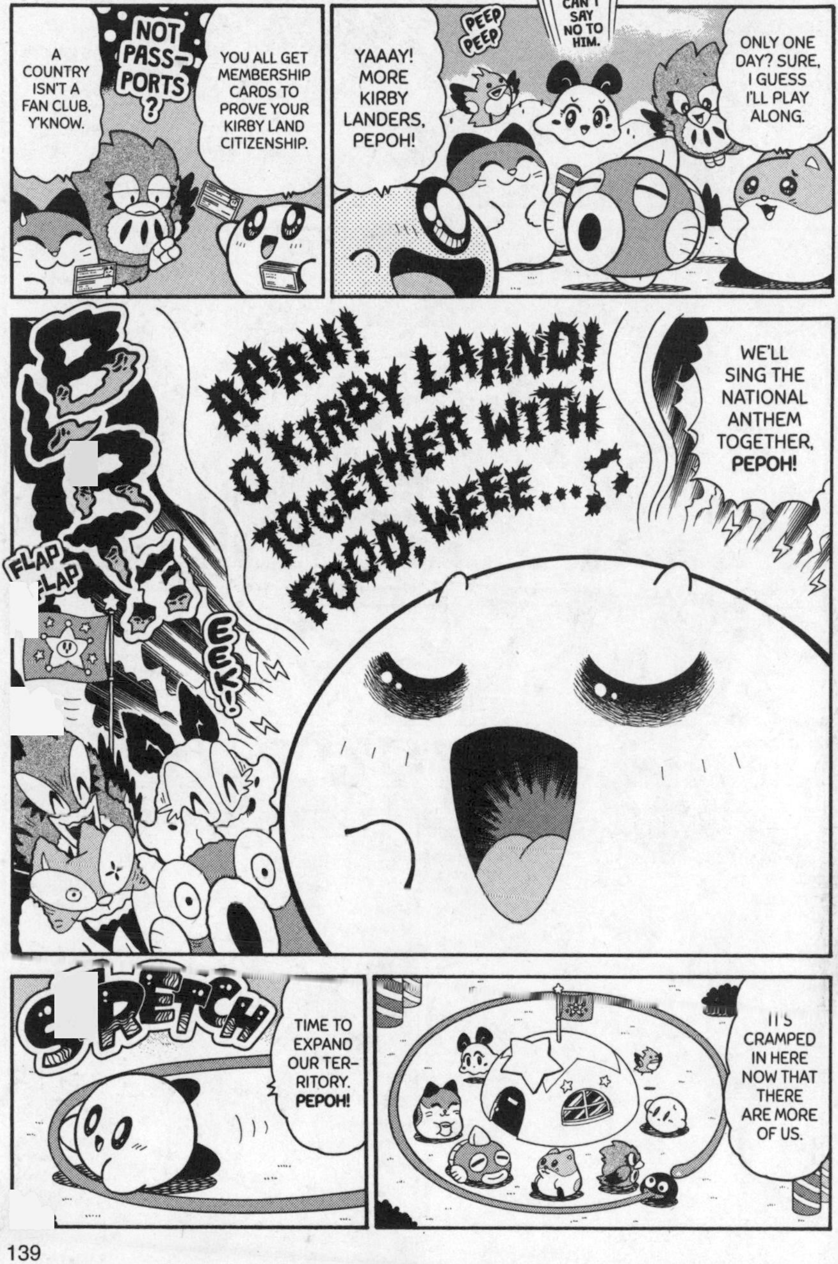
ONLY ONE DAY? SURE, I GUESS I'LL PLAY ALONG.
I CAN'T SAY NO TO HIM.
PEEP PEEP
YAAAY! MORE KIRBY LANDERS, PEPOH!
YOU ALL GET MEMBERSHIP CARDS TO PROVE YOUR KIRBY LAND CITIZENSHIP.
NOT PASSPORTS?
A COUNTRY ISN'T A FAN CLUB, Y'KNOW.
WE'LL SING THE NATIONAL ANTHEM TOGETHER, PEPOH!
AAAH! O'KIRBY LAAND! TOGETHER WITH FOOD, WEEE...
EEK!
FLAP FLAP
IT'S CRAMPED IN HERE NOW THAT THERE ARE MORE OF US.
TIME TO EXPAND OUR TERRITORY. PEPOH!

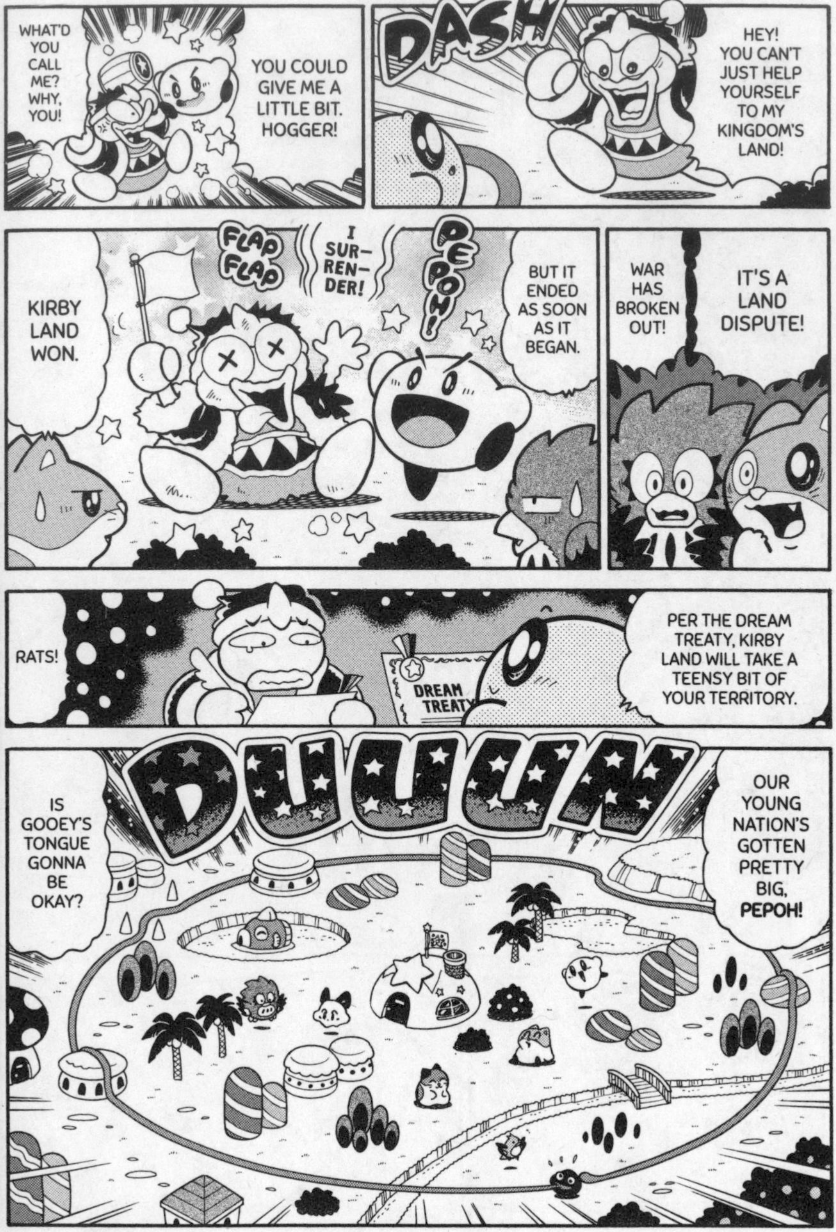
DASH
HEY! YOU CAN'T JUST HELP YOURSELF TO MY KINGDOM'S LAND!
YOU COULD GIVE ME A LITTLE BIT. HOGGER!
WHAT'D YOU CALL ME? WHY, YOU!
IT'S A LAND DISPUTE!
WAR HAS BROKEN OUT!
BUT IT ENDED AS SOON AS IT BEGAN.
PEPOH!
I SURRENDER!
FLAP FLAP
KIRBY LAND WON.
PER THE DREAM TREATY, KIRBY LAND WILL TAKE A TEENSY BIT OF YOUR TERRITORY.
DREAM TREATY
RATS!
OUR YOUNG NATION'S GOTTEN PRETTY BIG, **PEPOH!**
DUUUN
IS GOOEY'S TONGUE GONNA BE OKAY?

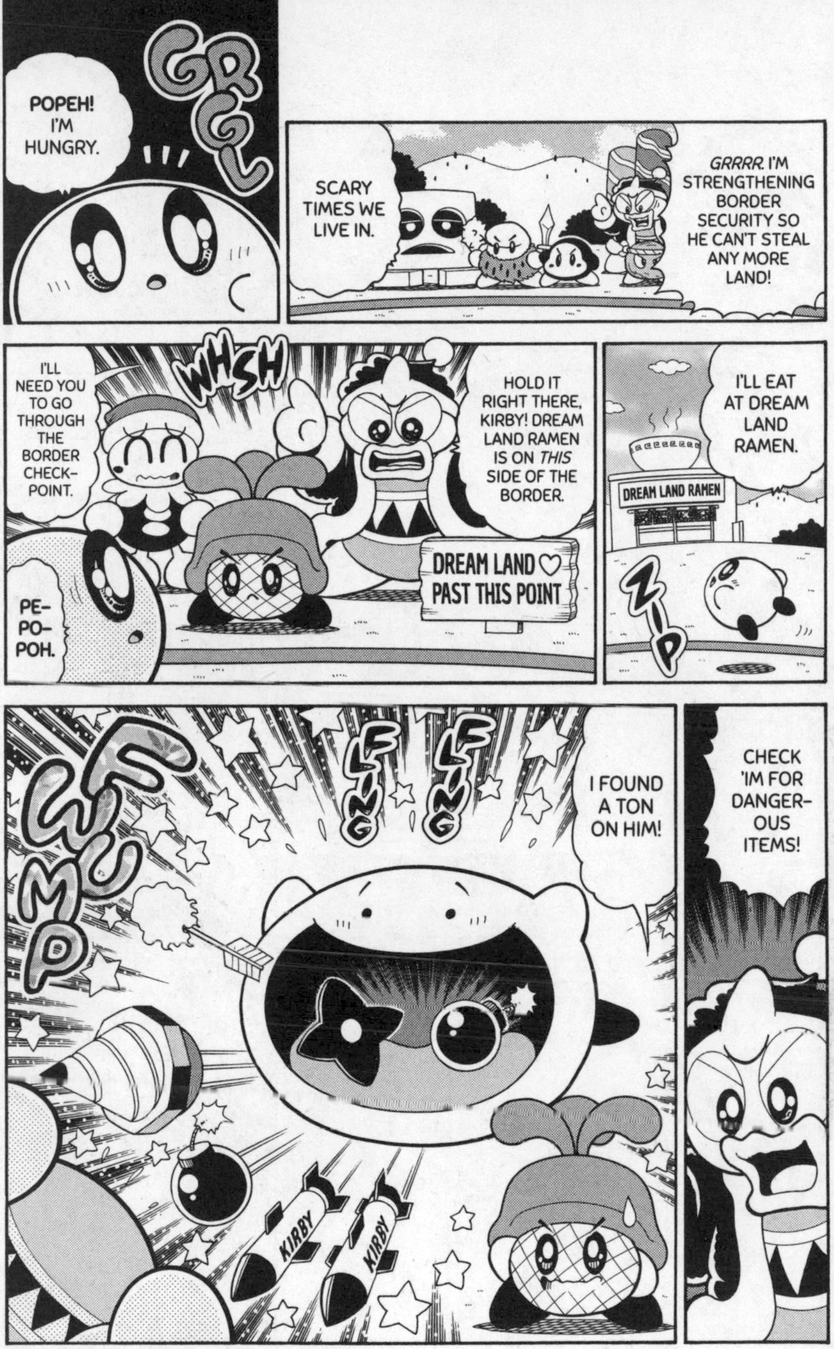
GRRRR. I'M STRENGTHENING BORDER SECURITY SO HE CAN'T STEAL ANY MORE LAND!
SCARY TIMES WE LIVE IN.
GRGL
POPEH! I'M HUNGRY.
I'LL EAT AT DREAM LAND RAMEN.
DREAM LAND RAMEN
ZIP
HOLD IT RIGHT THERE, KIRBY! DREAM LAND RAMEN IS ON THIS SIDE OF THE BORDER.
WHSH
I'LL NEED YOU TO GO THROUGH THE BORDER CHECK-POINT.
DREAM LAND ♡ PAST THIS POINT
PE-PO-POH.
CHECK 'IM FOR DANGER-OUS ITEMS!
I FOUND A TON ON HIM!
FLING
FLING
WUMP
KIRBY
KIRBY

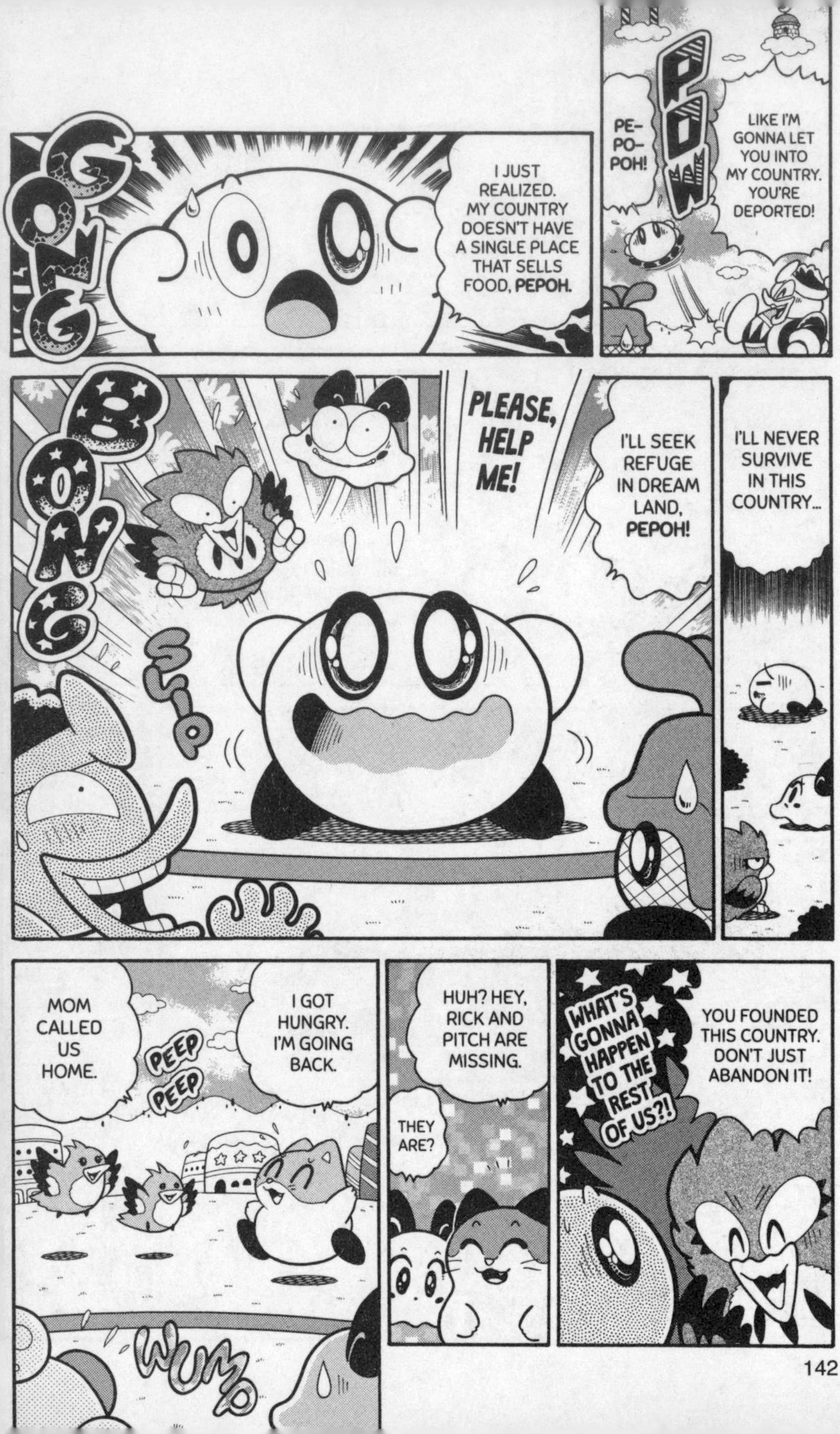
PE-PO-POH!
POW
LIKE I'M GONNA LET YOU INTO MY COUNTRY. YOU'RE DEPORTED!
I JUST REALIZED. MY COUNTRY DOESN'T HAVE A SINGLE PLACE THAT SELLS FOOD, **PEPOH**.
GONG
I'LL NEVER SURVIVE IN THIS COUNTRY...
I'LL SEEK REFUGE IN DREAM LAND, **PEPOH!**
PLEASE, HELP ME!
BOING
SLIP
YOU FOUNDED THIS COUNTRY. DON'T JUST ABANDON IT!
WHAT'S GONNA HAPPEN TO THE REST OF US?!
HUH? HEY, RICK AND PITCH ARE MISSING.
THEY ARE?
I GOT HUNGRY. I'M GOING BACK.
MOM CALLED US HOME.
PEEP PEEP
WUMP

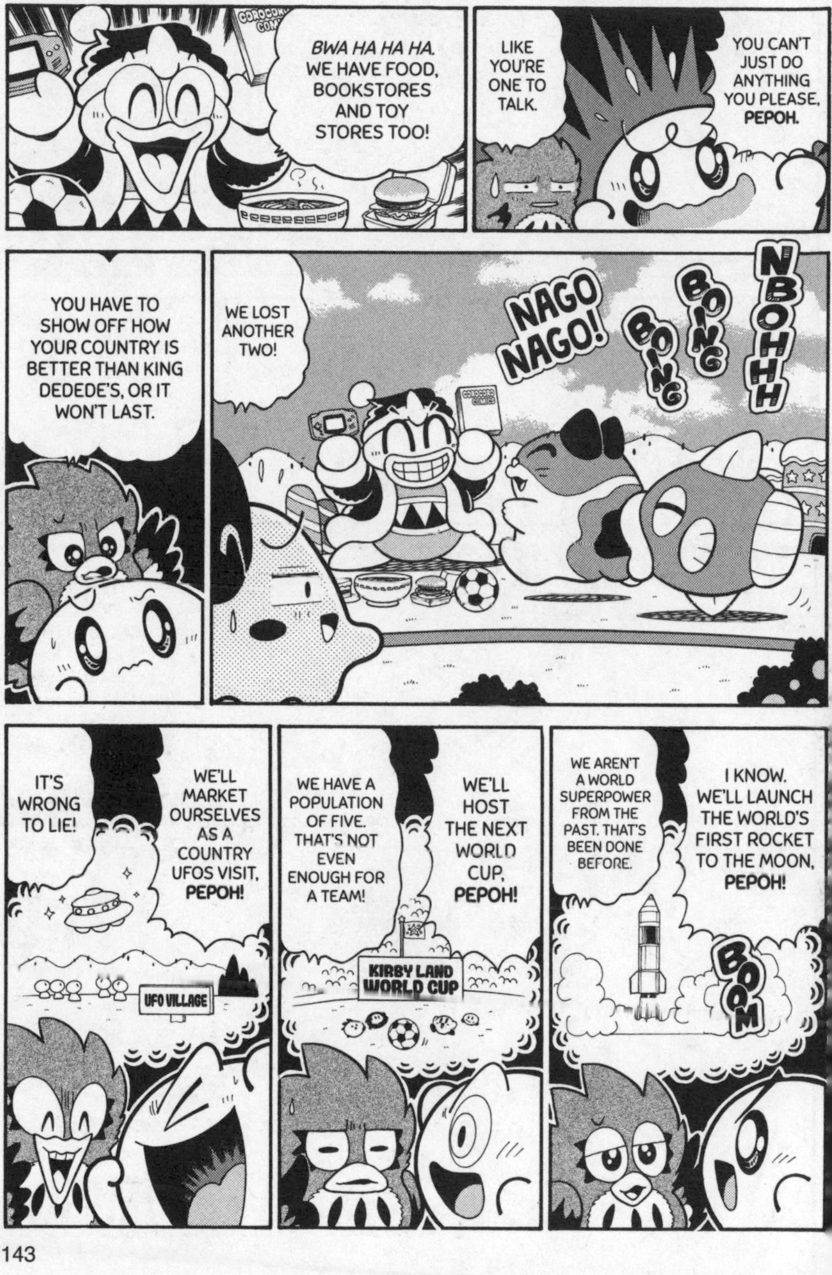
YOU CAN'T JUST DO ANYTHING YOU PLEASE, **PEPOH.**
LIKE YOU'RE ONE TO TALK.
BWA HA HA HA. WE HAVE FOOD, BOOKSTORES AND TOY STORES TOO!
NBOHHH
BOING
BOING
NAGO NAGO!
COROCORO COMICS
WE LOST ANOTHER TWO!
YOU HAVE TO SHOW OFF HOW YOUR COUNTRY IS BETTER THAN KING DEDEDE'S, OR IT WON'T LAST.
I KNOW. WE'LL LAUNCH THE WORLD'S FIRST ROCKET TO THE MOON, **PEPOH!**
WE AREN'T A WORLD SUPERPOWER FROM THE PAST. THAT'S BEEN DONE BEFORE.
BOOM
WE'LL HOST THE NEXT WORLD CUP, **PEPOH!**
WE HAVE A POPULATION OF FIVE. THAT'S NOT EVEN ENOUGH FOR A TEAM!
KIRBY LAND WORLD CUP
WE'LL MARKET OURSELVES AS A COUNTRY UFOS VISIT, **PEPOH!**
IT'S WRONG TO LIE!
UFO VILLAGE

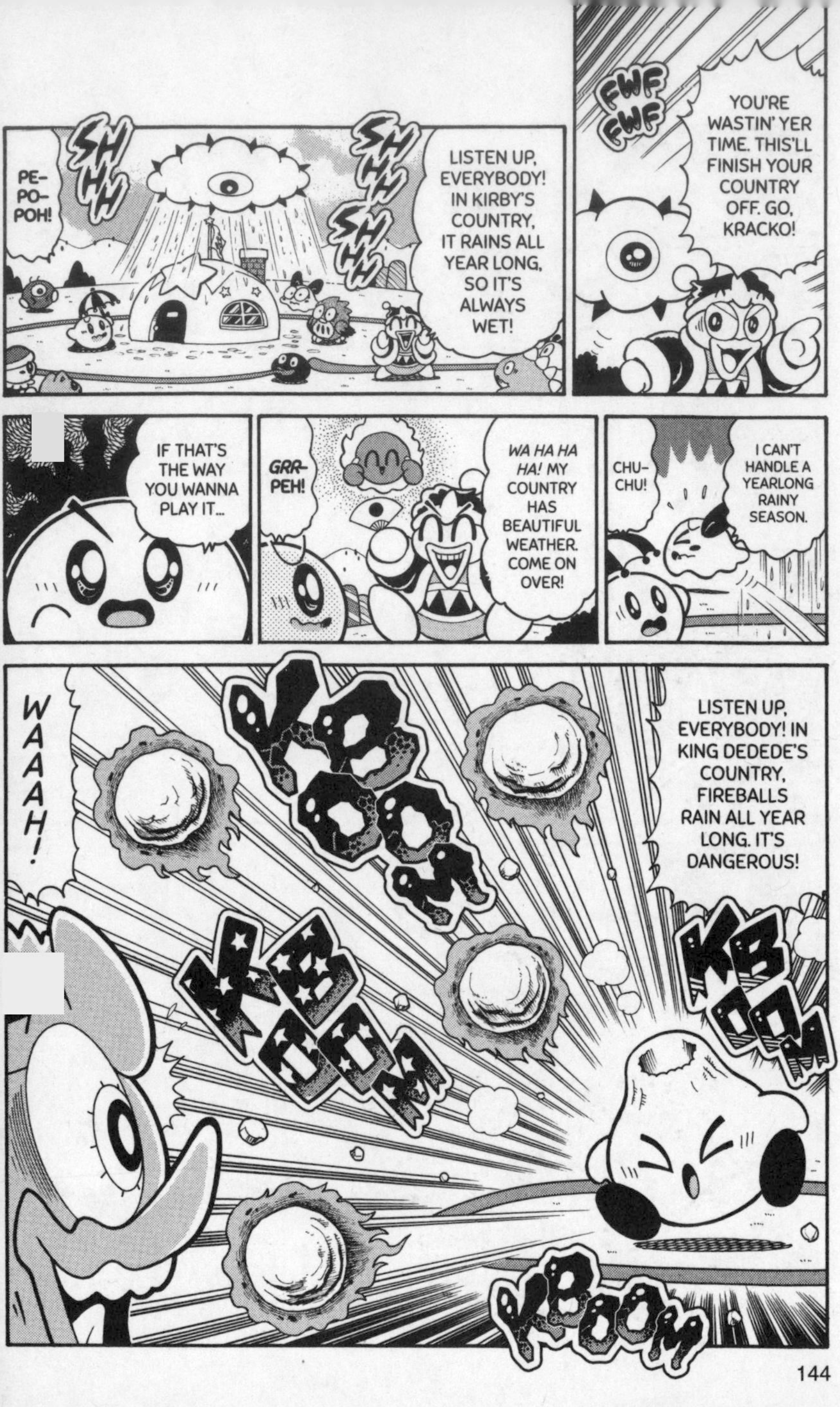
FWF FWF
YOU'RE WASTIN' YER TIME. THIS'LL FINISH YOUR COUNTRY OFF. GO, KRACKO!
LISTEN UP, EVERYBODY! IN KIRBY'S COUNTRY, IT RAINS ALL YEAR LONG, SO IT'S ALWAYS WET!
PE-PO-POH!
I CAN'T HANDLE A YEARLONG RAINY SEASON.
CHU-CHU!
WA HA HA HA! MY COUNTRY HAS BEAUTIFUL WEATHER. COME ON OVER!
GRR-PEH!
IF THAT'S THE WAY YOU WANNA PLAY IT...
LISTEN UP, EVERYBODY! IN KING DEDEDE'S COUNTRY, FIREBALLS RAIN ALL YEAR LONG. IT'S DANGEROUS!
KBOOM
KBOOM
WAAAAH!
KBOOM
KBOOM

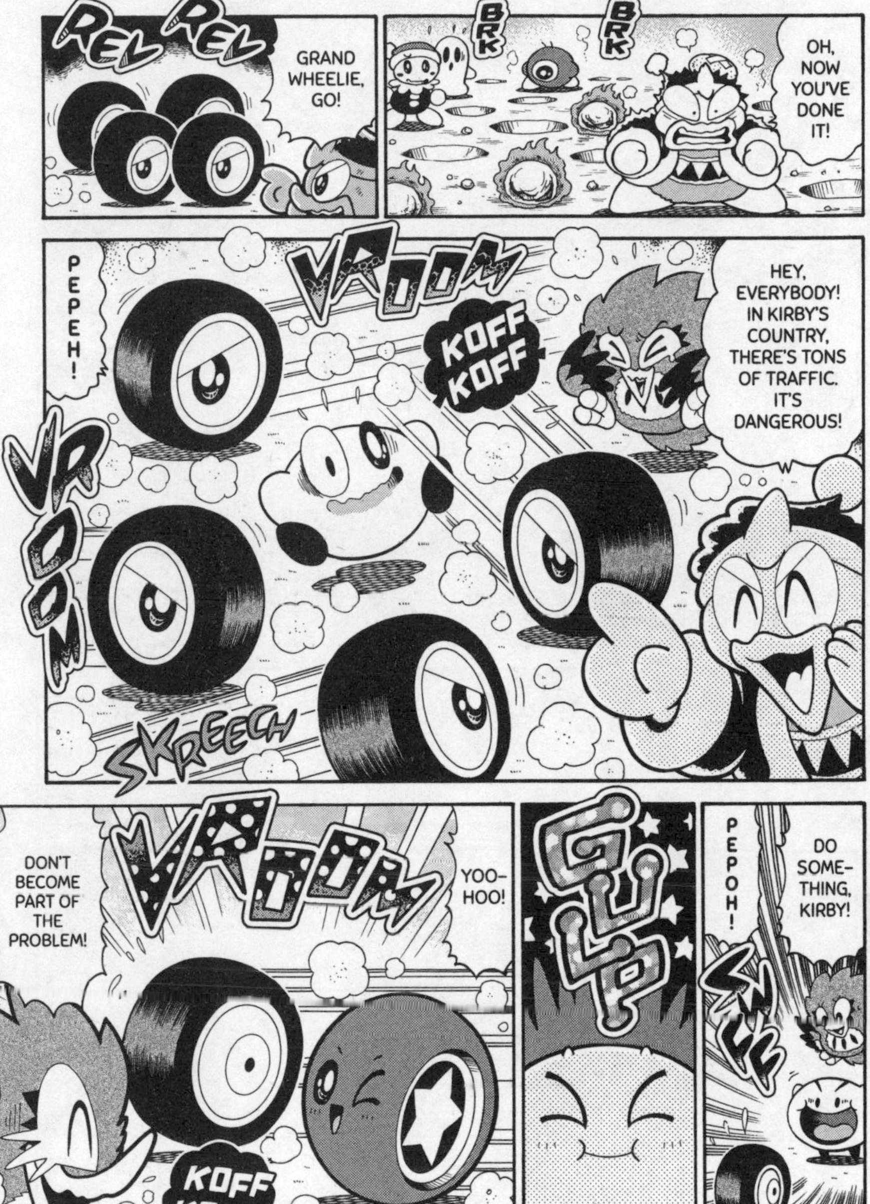
BRK
BRK
OH, NOW YOU'VE DONE IT!
REV REV
GRAND WHEELIE, GO!
HEY, EVERYBODY! IN KIRBY'S COUNTRY, THERE'S TONS OF TRAFFIC. IT'S DANGEROUS!
VROOM
KOFF KOFF
PEPEH!
VROOM
SKREECH
DO SOMETHING, KIRBY!
PEPOH!
GULP
YOO-HOO!
VROOM
DON'T BECOME PART OF THE PROBLEM!
KOFF KOFF

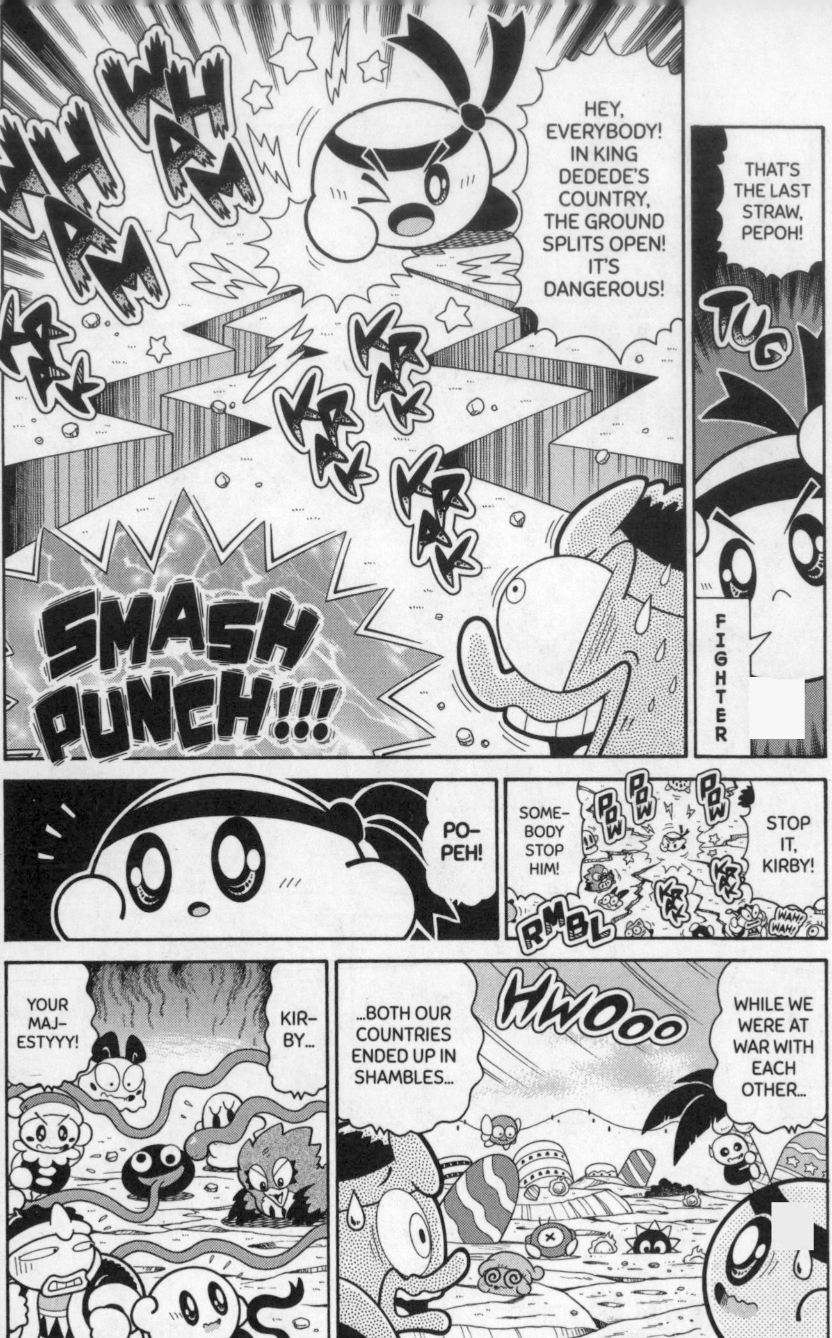
THAT'S THE LAST STRAW, PEPOH!
TUG
FIGHTER
WHAM
WHAM
HEY, EVERYBODY! IN KING DEDEDE'S COUNTRY, THE GROUND SPLITS OPEN! IT'S DANGEROUS!
KRAK
KRAK
KRAK
KRAK
SMASH PUNCH!!!
STOP IT, KIRBY!
POW
POW
POW
SOME-BODY STOP HIM!
KRAK
KRAK
RMBL
WAH! WAH!
PO-PEH!
HWOooo
WHILE WE WERE AT WAR WITH EACH OTHER...
...BOTH OUR COUNTRIES ENDED UP IN SHAMBLES...
KIR-BY...
YOUR MAJ-ESTYYY!

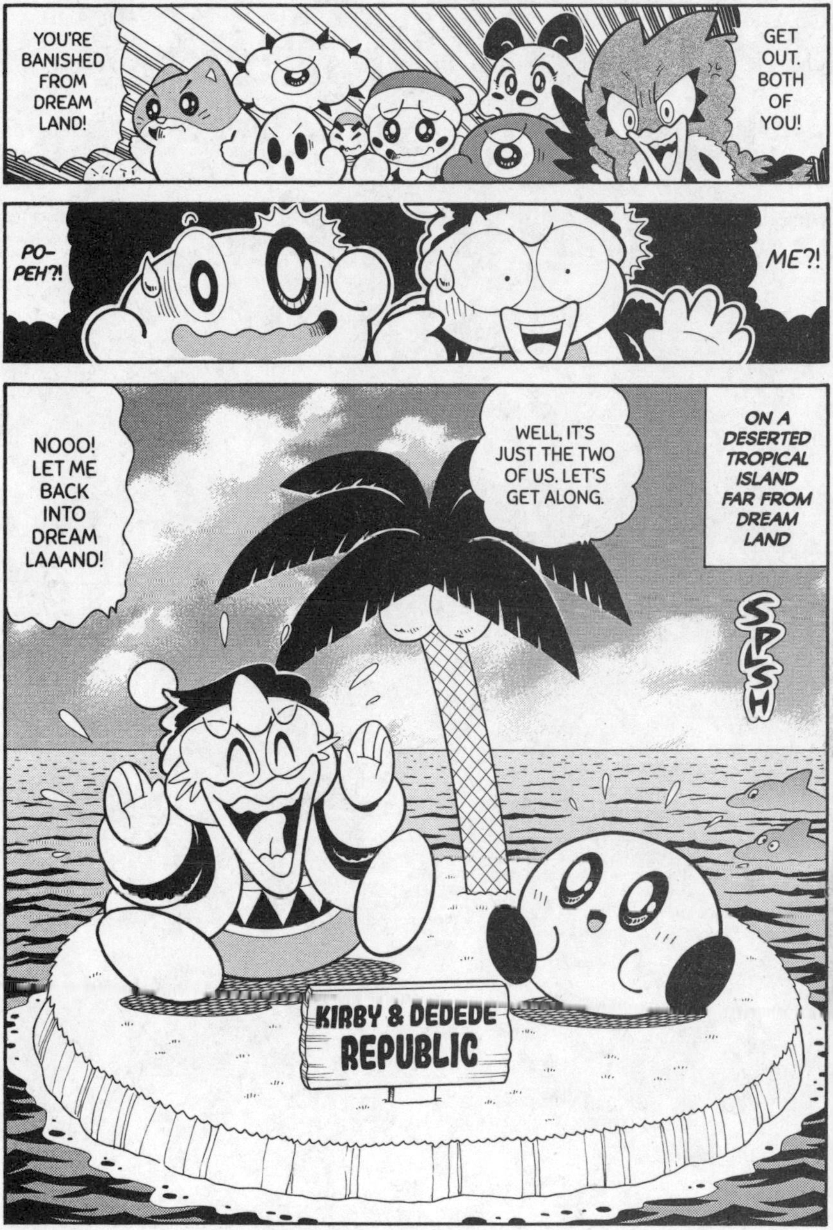
GET OUT. BOTH OF YOU!
YOU'RE BANISHED FROM DREAM LAND!
ME?!
PO-PEH?!
ON A DESERTED TROPICAL ISLAND FAR FROM DREAM LAND
SPLSH
WELL, IT'S JUST THE TWO OF US. LET'S GET ALONG.
NOOO! LET ME BACK INTO DREAM LAAAND!
KIRBY & DEDEDE REPUBLIC

CHAPTER 11: THE BIG COMEBACK! THINGS KIRBY ALWAYS WANTED TO TRY!

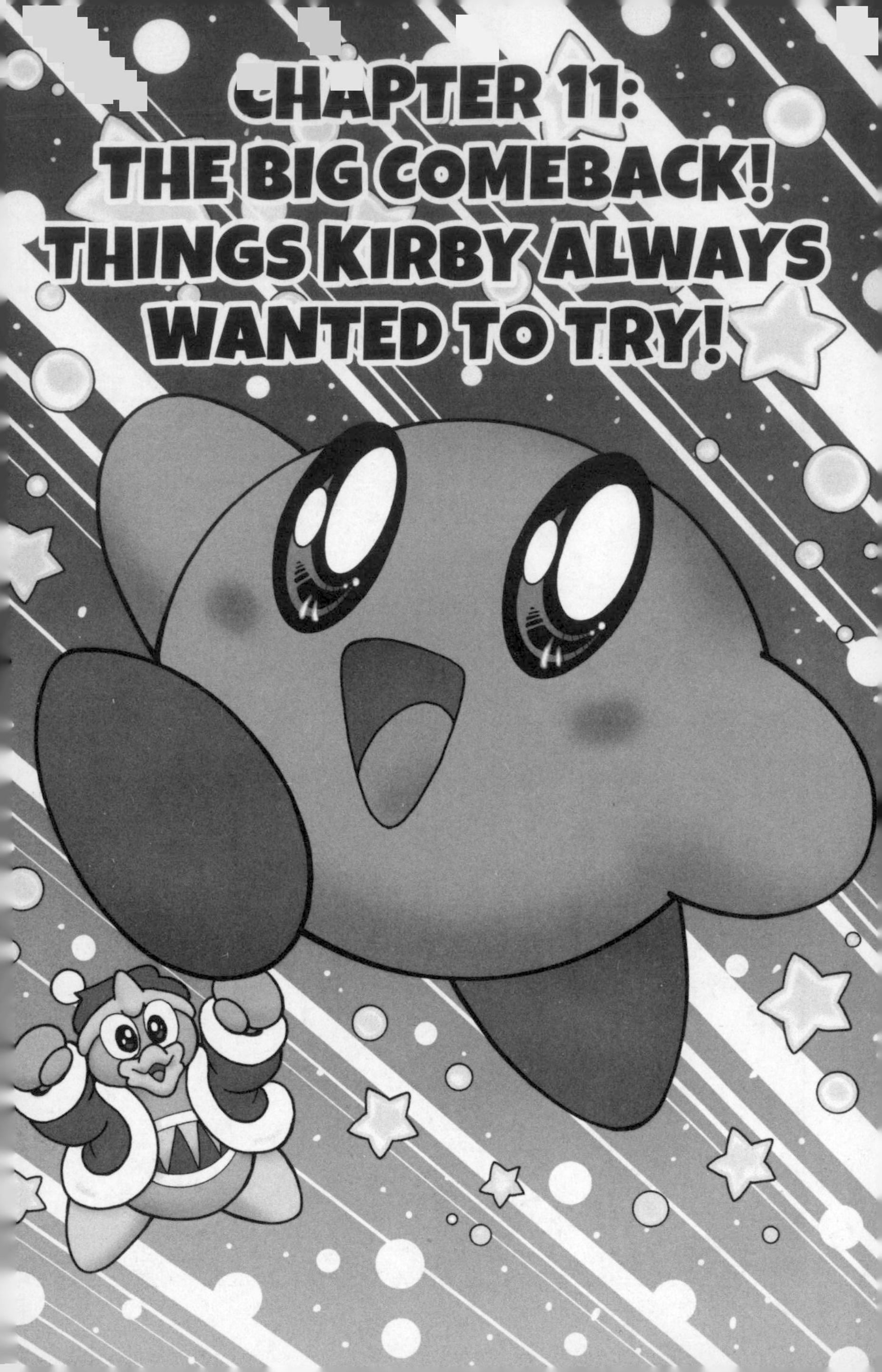

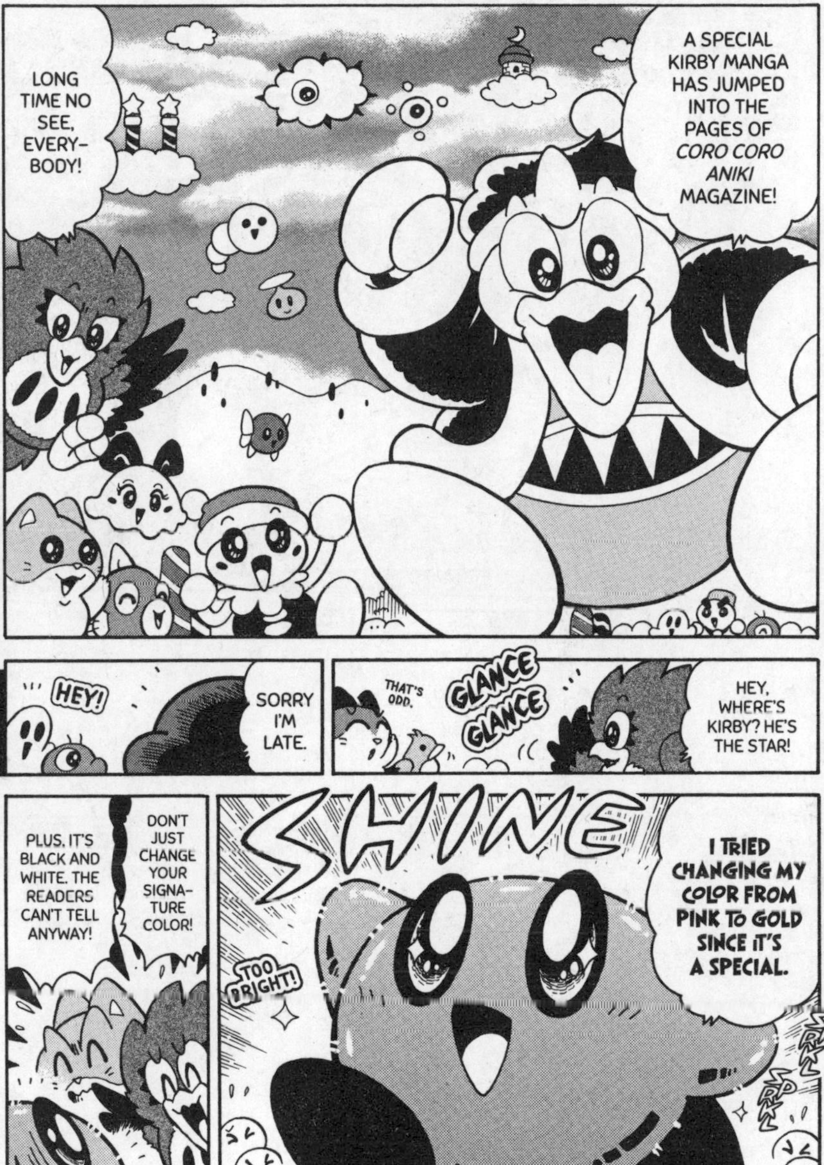
A SPECIAL KIRBY MANGA HAS JUMPED INTO THE PAGES OF *CORO CORO ANIKI* MAGAZINE!
LONG TIME NO SEE, EVERY-BODY!
HEY, WHERE'S KIRBY? HE'S THE STAR!
GLANCE GLANCE
THAT'S ODD.
SORRY I'M LATE.
HEY!
SHINE
I TRIED CHANGING MY COLOR FROM PINK TO GOLD SINCE IT'S A SPECIAL.
TOO BRIGHT!
DON'T JUST CHANGE YOUR SIGNA-TURE COLOR!
PLUS, IT'S BLACK AND WHITE. THE READERS CAN'T TELL ANYWAY!

AUTHOR'S COMMENT

THE FIRST CHAPTER IN TEN YEARS. I FORGOT HOW TO DRAW IT. ESPECIALLY THE PANELS—I STILL CAN'T REMEMBER HOW I USED TO LAY THEM OUT. I SHOULD HAVE SAVED MY OLD STORYBOARDS...

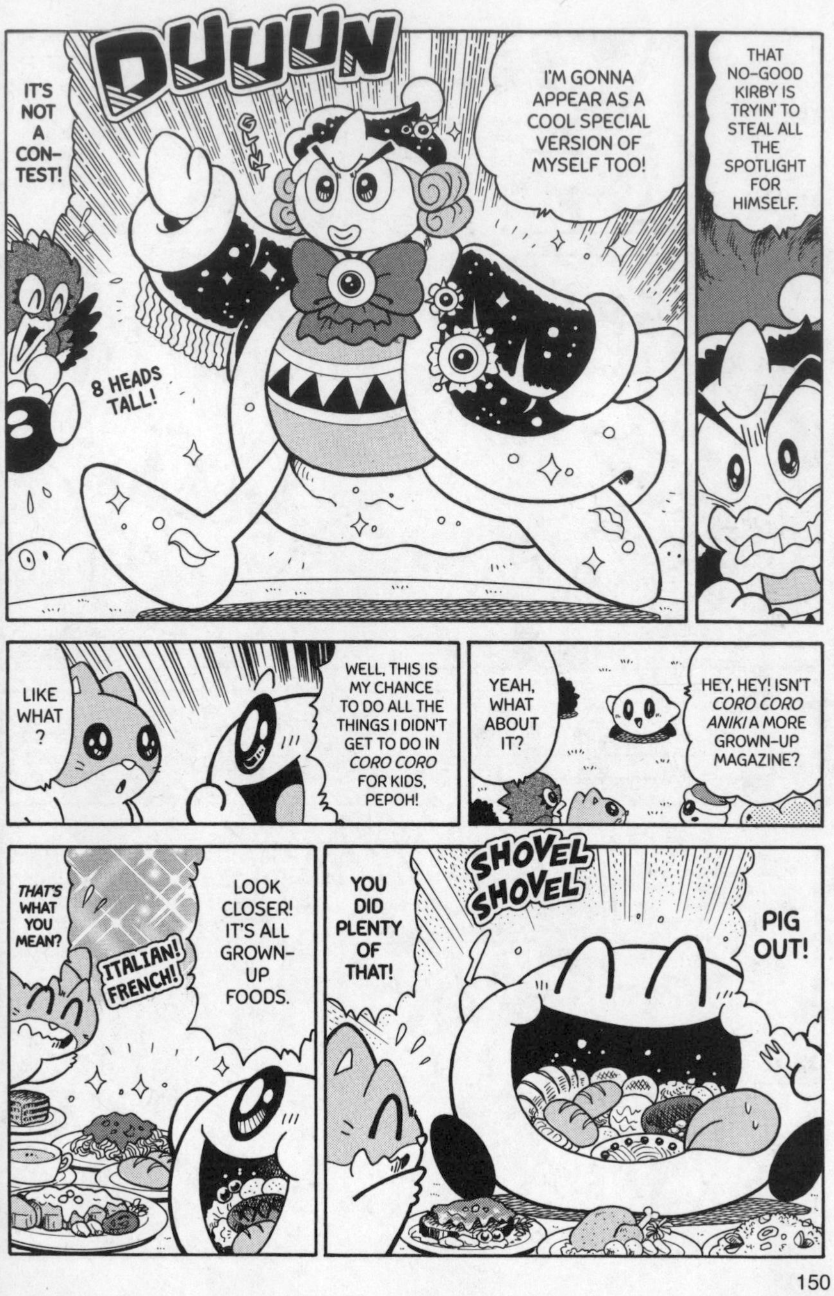
THAT NO-GOOD KIRBY IS TRYIN' TO STEAL ALL THE SPOTLIGHT FOR HIMSELF.
I'M GONNA APPEAR AS A COOL SPECIAL VERSION OF MYSELF TOO!
DUUUN
IT'S NOT A CONTEST!
8 HEADS TALL!
HEY, HEY! ISN'T *CORO CORO ANIKI* A MORE GROWN-UP MAGAZINE?
YEAH, WHAT ABOUT IT?
WELL, THIS IS MY CHANCE TO DO ALL THE THINGS I DIDN'T GET TO DO IN *CORO CORO* FOR KIDS, PEPOH!
LIKE WHAT?
PIG OUT!
SHOVEL SHOVEL
YOU DID PLENTY OF THAT!
LOOK CLOSER! IT'S ALL GROWN-UP FOODS.
ITALIAN! FRENCH!
THAT'S WHAT YOU MEAN?

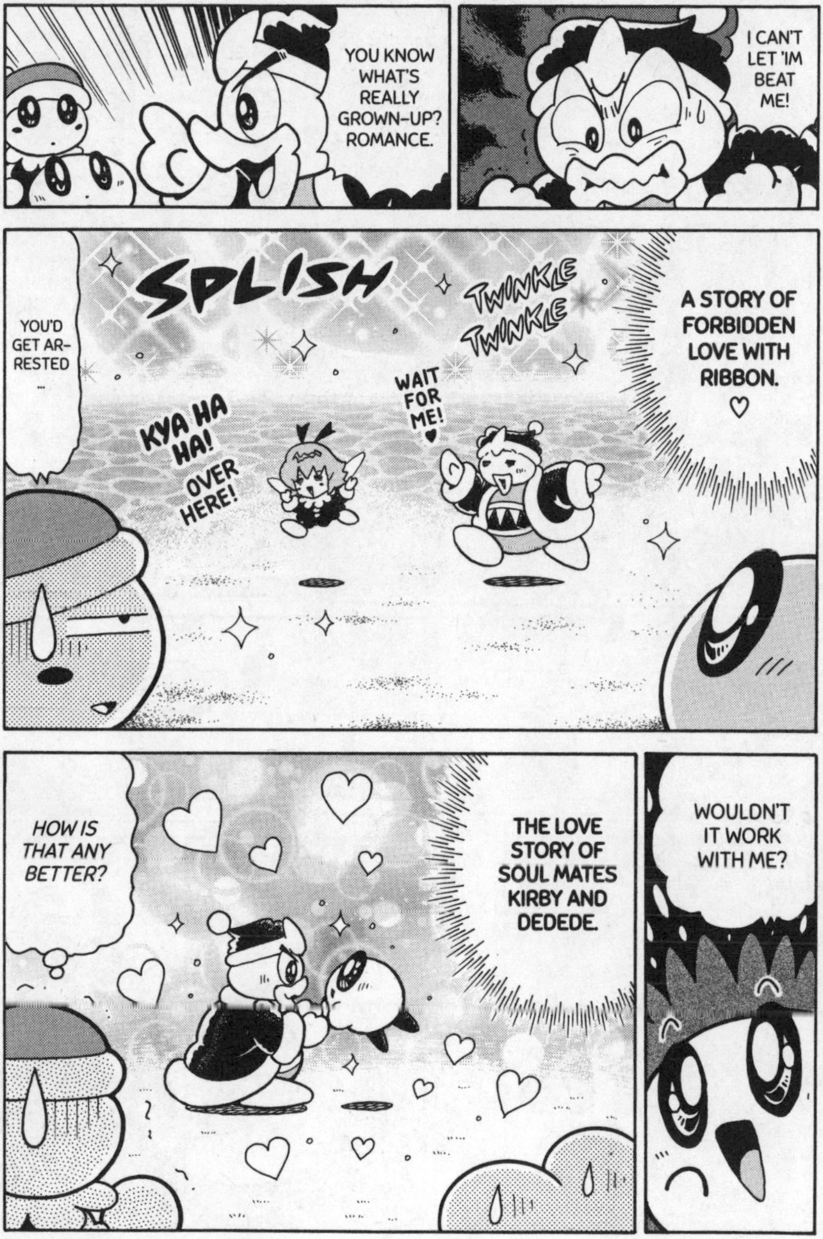
I CAN'T LET 'IM BEAT ME!
YOU KNOW WHAT'S REALLY GROWN-UP? ROMANCE.
A STORY OF FORBIDDEN LOVE WITH RIBBON. ♡
TWINKLE TWINKLE
WAIT FOR ME! ♥
SPLISH
KYA HA HA! OVER HERE!
YOU'D GET AR-RESTED ...
WOULDN'T IT WORK WITH ME?
THE LOVE STORY OF SOUL MATES KIRBY AND DEDEDE.
HOW IS THAT ANY BETTER?

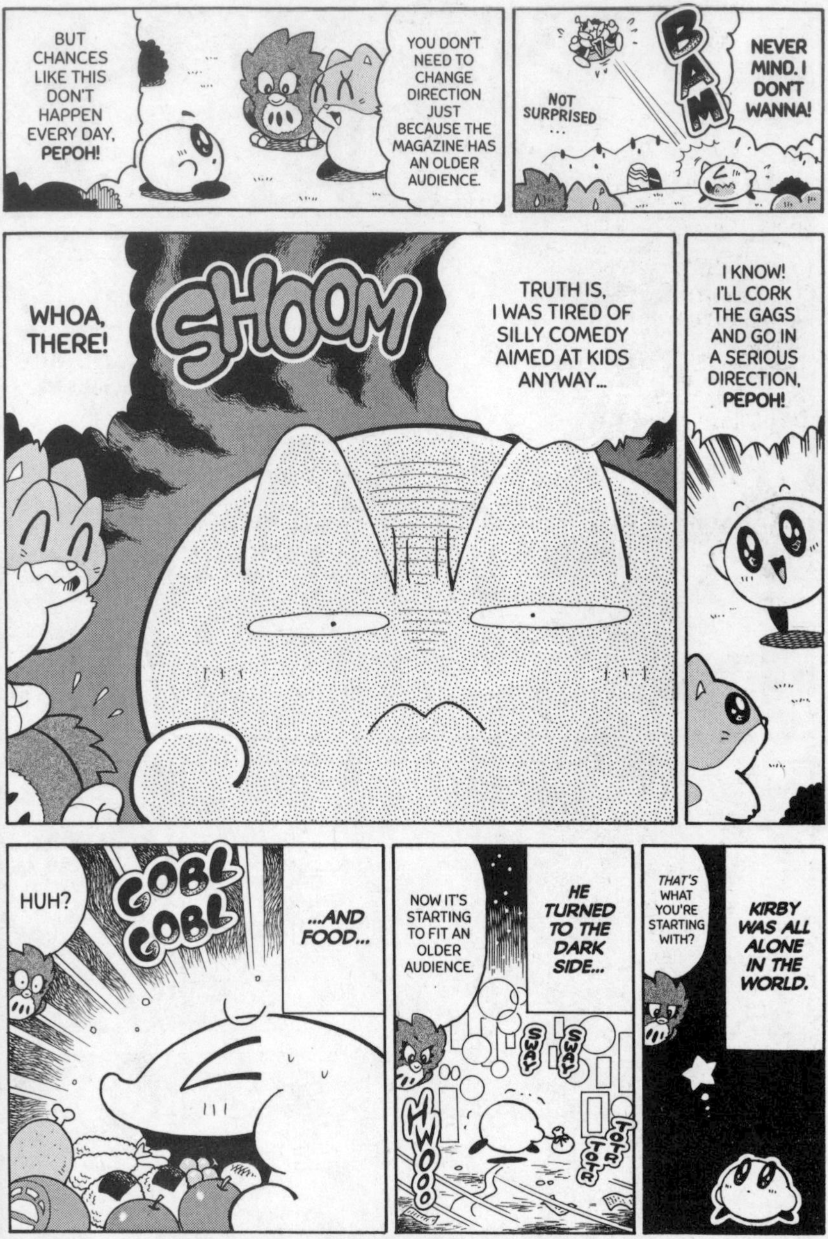
NEVER MIND. I DON'T WANNA!
BAM
NOT SURPRISED ...
YOU DON'T NEED TO CHANGE DIRECTION JUST BECAUSE THE MAGAZINE HAS AN OLDER AUDIENCE.
BUT CHANCES LIKE THIS DON'T HAPPEN EVERY DAY, **PEPOH!**
I KNOW! I'LL CORK THE GAGS AND GO IN A SERIOUS DIRECTION, **PEPOH!**
TRUTH IS, I WAS TIRED OF SILLY COMEDY AIMED AT KIDS ANYWAY...
SHOOM
WHOA, THERE!
KIRBY WAS ALL ALONE IN THE WORLD.
THAT'S WHAT YOU'RE STARTING WITH?
HE TURNED TO THE DARK SIDE...
NOW IT'S STARTING TO FIT AN OLDER AUDIENCE.
SWAY
SWAY
TOTR
TOTR
HWOOO
...AND FOOD...
GOBL GOBL
HUH?

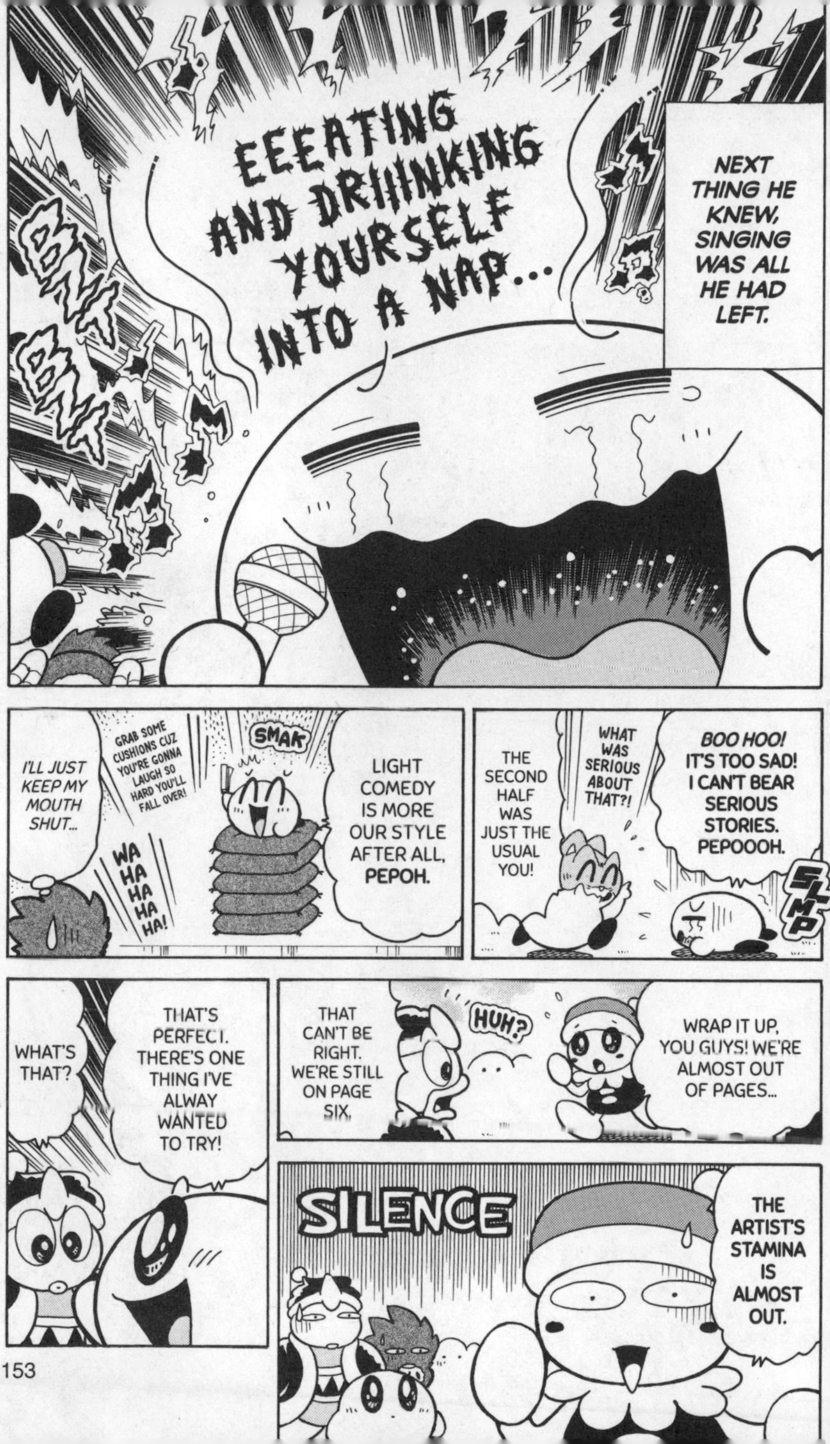
NEXT THING HE KNEW, SINGING WAS ALL HE HAD LEFT.
EEEATING AND DRIIINKING YOURSELF INTO A NAP...
BOO HOO! IT'S TOO SAD! I CAN'T BEAR SERIOUS STORIES. PEPOOOH.
WHAT WAS SERIOUS ABOUT THAT?!
THE SECOND HALF WAS JUST THE USUAL YOU!
SLMP
LIGHT COMEDY IS MORE OUR STYLE AFTER ALL, PEPOH.
SMAK
GRAB SOME CUSHIONS CUZ YOU'RE GONNA LAUGH SO HARD YOU'LL FALL OVER!
I'LL JUST KEEP MY MOUTH SHUT...
WA HA HA HA HA!
WRAP IT UP, YOU GUYS! WE'RE ALMOST OUT OF PAGES...
HUH?
THAT CAN'T BE RIGHT. WE'RE STILL ON PAGE SIX.
THE ARTIST'S STAMINA IS ALMOST OUT.
SILENCE
THAT'S PERFECT. THERE'S ONE THING I'VE ALWAY WANTED TO TRY!
WHAT'S THAT?

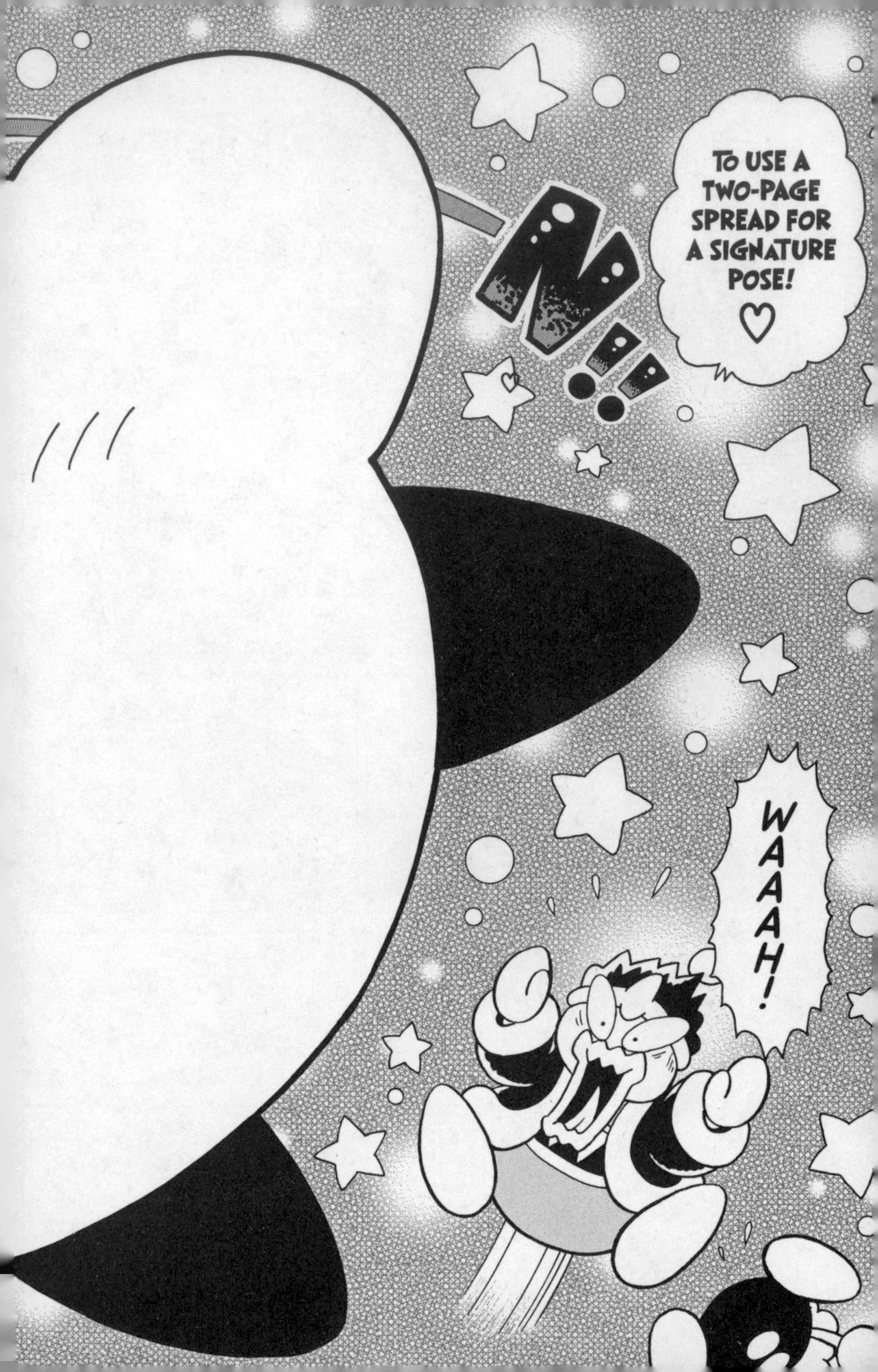
TO USE A TWO-PAGE SPREAD FOR A SIGNATURE POSE! ♡
N!!
WAAAH!

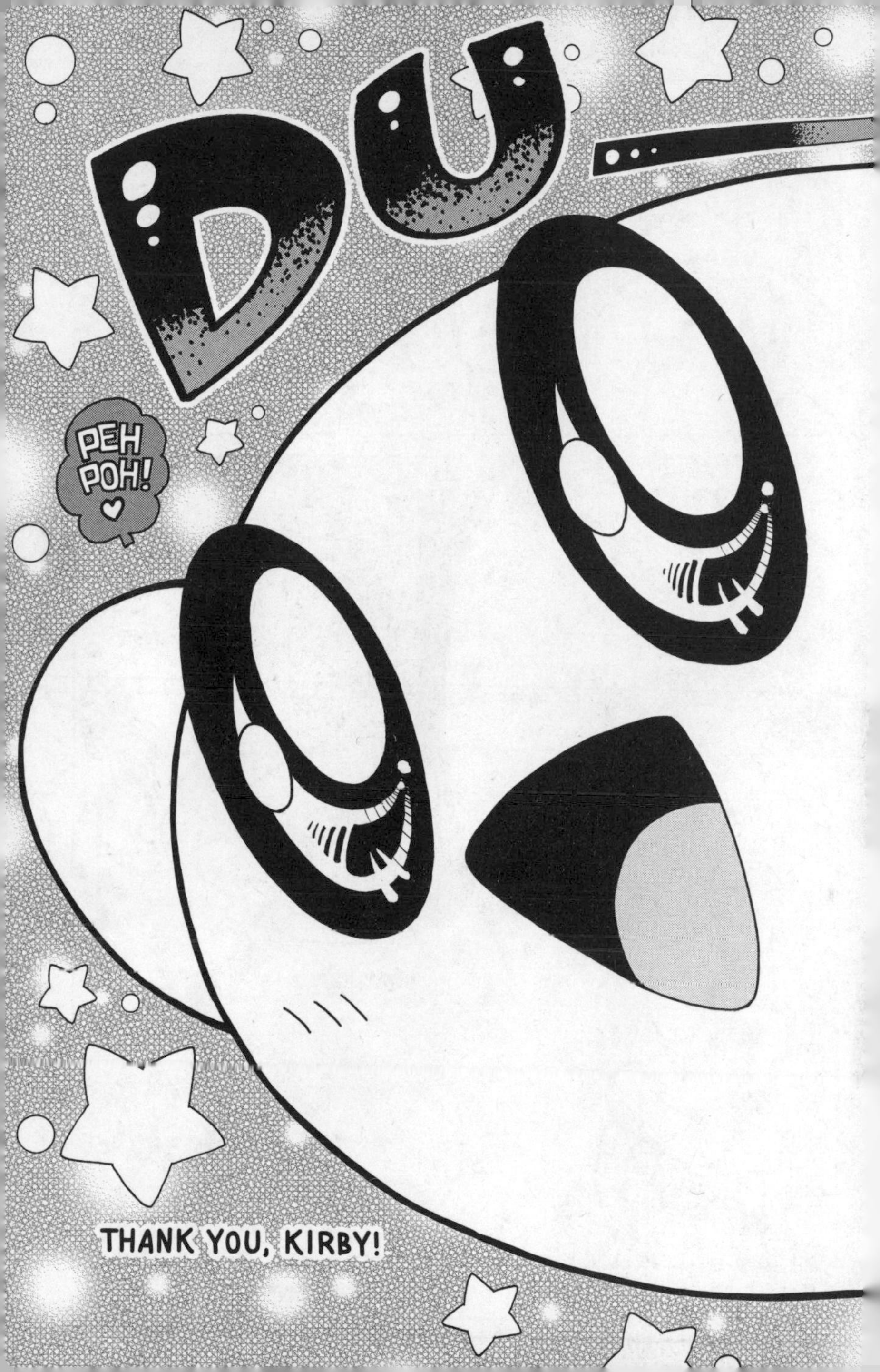
DU-
PEH POH! ♥
THANK YOU, KIRBY!

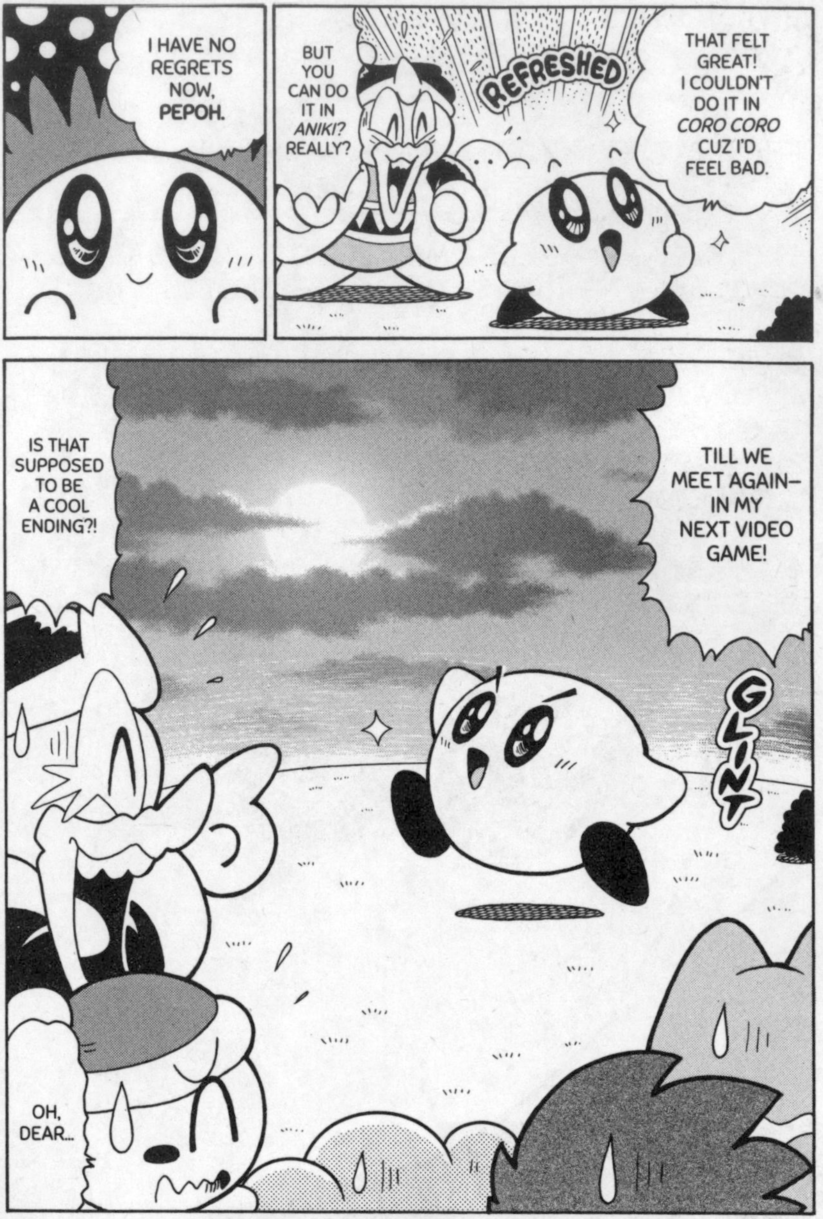
THAT FELT GREAT! I COULDN'T DO IT IN *CORO CORO* CUZ I'D FEEL BAD.
REFRESHED
BUT YOU CAN DO IT IN *ANIKI*? REALLY?
I HAVE NO REGRETS NOW, **PEPOH.**
TILL WE MEET AGAIN— IN MY NEXT VIDEO GAME!
GLINT
IS THAT SUPPOSED TO BE A COOL ENDING?!
OH, DEAR...

KIRBY MANGA MANIA 1: THE END!

AUTHOR NOTE

THANK YOU FOR READING *KIRBY MANGA MANIA* VOL. 1.

NOW, APOLOGIES FOR THE ABRUPTNESS, BUT THE ART BELOW IS A 15-PAGE GAG MANGA I DREW THAT WON AN HONORABLE MENTION IN THE 14TH FUJIKO FUJIO AWARD.

TO BE CLEAR, THOUGH, I'M LOUSY. I SPENT MY WHOLE CHILDHOOD WATCHING RERUNS OF THE COMEDY THEATER GROUP YOSHIMOTO SHINKIGEKI, THE COMEDY GROUP THE DRIFTERS AND THE CARTOON *TOM AND JERRY*. I LOVE COMEDY, BUT I'M HONESTLY A WEAK ARTIST.

SO HOW DID A TOTAL AMATEUR LIKE ME MANAGE TO BECOME A MANGA ARTIST? FIND OUT IN *KIRBY MANGA MANIA* VOL. 2.

HIROKAZU HIKAWA

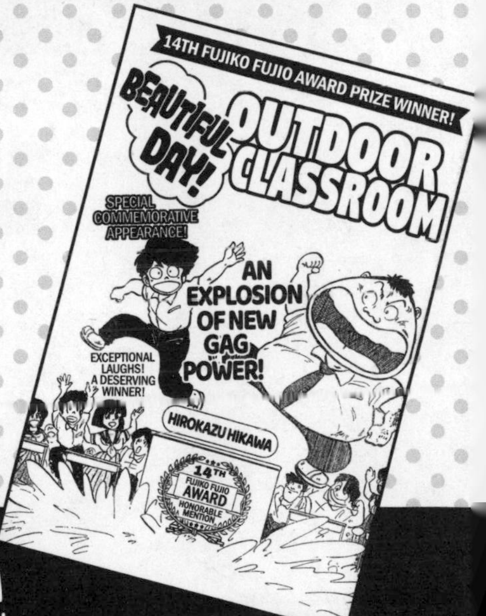
14TH FUJIKO FUJIO AWARD PRIZE WINNER!
BEAUTIFUL DAY!
OUTDOOR CLASSROOM
SPECIAL COMMEMORATIVE APPEARANCE!
AN EXPLOSION OF NEW GAG POWER!
EXCEPTIONAL LAUGHS! A DESERVING WINNER!
HIROKAZU HIKAWA
14TH FUJIKO FUJIO AWARD HONORABLE MENTION

KIRBY MANGA MANIA
VOL. 2 COMING SOON!

Just once, I'd like to be addressed as "King."

This is my first best-of collection. I selected the funniest stories out of the *Kirby* manga series' 25-volume run. I also drew the series' first brand-new chapter in 11 years, as well as some bonus comics. I hope you'll enjoy those too.

HIROKAZU HIKAWA

· ·

Hirokazu Hikawa was born July 4, 1967, in Aichi Prefecture. He is best known for his manga adaptations of *Bonk* and *Kirby*. In 1987, he won an honorable mention for *Kaisei!! Aozora Kyoushitsu* (Beautiful Day! Outdoor Classroom) at the 14th Fujiko Fujio Awards.